# GREY EYES

# GREY EYES

## FRANK CHRISTOPHER BUSCH

Roseway Publishing
an imprint of Fernwood Publishing
Halifax & Winnipeg

Editing: Sandra McIntyre
Design: John van der Woude
Printed and bound in Canada

Published by Roseway Publishing
an imprint of Fernwood Publishing
32 Oceanvista Lane, Black Point, Nova Scotia, B0J 1B0
and 748 Broadway Avenue, Winnipeg, Manitoba, R3G 0X3
www.fernwoodpublishing.ca/roseway

Fernwood Publishing Company Limited gratefully acknowledges the financial
support of the Government of Canada through the Canada Book Fund,
the Canada Council for the Arts, the Nova Scotia Department of Tourism and
Culture and the Province of Manitoba, through the Book Publishing Tax Credit,
for our publishing program.

Library and Archives Canada Cataloguing in Publication

Busch, Frank Christopher, °d1978-, author
Grey eyes / Frank Christopher Busch.

ISBN 978-1-55266-677-7 (pbk.)

I. Title.

PS8603.U815G74 2014      C813'.6      C2014-902928-4

*Dedicated to the lost children of Turtle Island—survivors of the Indian residential schools, Indian day schools, Indian and Métis mission schools, Inuit federal hostels, 60's and 70's Scoop, forced adoption, foster care, and group homes—and to all other victims of colonial assimilation policy.*

*May you find in these pages that which was wrongfully taken from you.*

# VILLAGE CHART

**BEAR CLAN**
*(Walking Moon Woman and Waving Willow Man are brother and sister. Painted Turtle Man is their 1st cousin)*

Walking Moon Woman *(Bear)* – Rising Hawk Man *(Crane)(deceased)*
Walking Cloud Man *(Bear)* – Red Feather Woman *(Turtle)*
Brown Bear Man *(Bear)* – Rolling Shield Woman *(Wolf)*
White Bear Man *(Bear)* – Circling Hawk Woman *(Marten)*
Singing Doe *(Bear)* – Brown Shield Man *(Wolf)*
    Flying Rabbit Boy *(Bear)*
White Willow Woman *(Bear)* – Blue Elk Man *(Marten)*
    Little Grey Bear Boy *(Bear)*
    Yellow Hawk Girl *(Bear)*
Waving Willow Man *(Bear)* – Standing Sun Woman *(Crane)*
Painted Turtle Man *(Bear)* – Nesting Doe Woman *(Deer)(deceased)*

**MARTEN CLAN**
*(Blue Cloud Man and Gliding Heron Woman are brother and sister)*

Blue Cloud Man *(Marten)* – Green Wing Woman *(Turtle)*
    Red Feather Woman *(Turtle)* – Walking Cloud Man *(Bear)*
    White Feather Woman *(Turtle)* – Blue Bird Man *(Crane)*
    Swimming Bear Man *(Turtle)* – Speaking Fox Woman *(Deer)*
Gliding Heron Woman *(Marten)* – Black Sturgeon Man *(Deer)(deceased)*
    Standing Elk Woman *(Marten)* – Black Buffalo Man *(Wolf)*
        White Elk Woman *(Marten)* – Shining Tail Man *(Sturgeon)*
            Blue Heron Girl *(Marten)*
            White Hawk Boy *(Marten)*
    Walking Sky Woman *(Marten)* – Speaking Thunder Man *(Wolf)*
        Green Star Woman *(Marten)* – Big Feather Man *(Turtle)*
            Little Star Girl *(Marten)*
            Yellow Bear Girl *(Marten)*
    Blue Elk Man *(Marten)* – White Willow Woman *(Bear)*
    Coming Thunder Man *(Marten)* – Red Dragonfly Woman *(Wolf)*
    Black Elk Man *(Marten)* – White Rain Woman *(Eagle)*

**EAGLE CLAN**
*(Soaring Star Woman was married twice, she outlived her two children from the second marriage)*

Soaring Star Woman *(Eagle)* – Grey Bear *(Bear)(deceased)*
    Dark Cloud Man *(Eagle)*
Soaring Star Woman *(Eagle)* – White Lightning Man *(Loon)(Deceased)*
    Spirit Dance Woman *(Eagle)(Deceased)* – Wading Elk Man *(Deer)* *(Deceased)*
        White Star Woman *(Eagle)* – Red Spear Man *(Wolf)*
            Diving Hawk Woman *(Eagle)*
            Bright Stone Boy *(Eagle)*
            Laughing Cloud Boy *(Eagle)*
        Shining Star Woman *(Eagle)* – Laughing Oak Man *(Crane)*
            Singing Loon Woman *(Eagle)*
            White Shield Girl *(Eagle)*
    Shimmering Sky Woman *(Eagle)(Deceased)* – Hunting Lynx Man *(Turtle)(Deceased)*
        Grey Lightning Woman *(Eagle)* – Swimming Duck Man *(Deer)*
            Rolling Hoop Girl
        White Rain Woman *(Eagle)* – Black Elk Man *(Marten)*
            Red Hawk Boy *(Eagle)*
        White Spear Man *(Eagle)*

**WOLF CLAN**

Blue Lightning Woman *(Wolf)* – Jumping Buffalo Man *(Sturgeon)(deceased)*
Black Buffalo Man *(Wolf)* – Standing Elk Woman *(Marten)*
Speaking Thunder Man *(Wolf)* – Walking Sky Woman *(Marten)*
Rolling Shield Woman *(Wolf)* – Brown Bear Man *(Bear)*
White Butterfly Woman *(Wolf)* – Standing Rainbow Man *(Crane)*
Tall Spear Boy *(Wolf)*
Standing Arrow Boy *(Wolf)*
Flying Turtle Man *(Wolf)* – Little Doe Woman *(Deer)*
Red Dragonfly Woman *(Wolf)* – Coming Thunder Man *(Marten)*
Waiting Rainbow Woman
Big Cloud Boy
Little Spear Boy
Red Spear Man *(Wolf)* – White Star Woman *(Eagle)*
Brown Shield Man *(Wolf)* – Singing Doe *(Bear)*

**DEER CLAN**

Talking Stone Woman *(Deer)* – Searching Fish Man *(Loon)(Deceased)*
Smiling Hawk Woman *(Deer)* – Tall Bear Man *(Crane)*
Little Doe Woman *(Deer)* – Flying Turtle Man *(Wolf)*
Soaring Spear Man *(Deer)*
Speaking Fox Woman *(Deer)* – Swimming Bear Man *(Turtle)*
Many Fish *(Deer)* – Drifting Butterfly Woman *(Crane)*
Swimming Duck Man *(Deer)* – Grey Lightning Woman *(Eagle)*
Little Rock Girl *(Deer)*
Blue Stone Man *(Deer)* – Shining Moon Woman *(Crane)*
Red Stone Man *(Deer)* – Little Wing Woman *(Turtle)*

**CRANE CLAN**

Standing Sun Woman *(Crane)* – Waving Willow Man *(Bear)*
Tall Bear Man *(Crane)* – Smiling Hawk Woman *(Deer)*
Yellow Cloud Woman *(Crane)* – Diving Eagle Man *(Eagle)*
Standing Rainbow Man *(Crane)* – White Butterfly Woman *(Wolf)*
Laughing Oak Man *(Crane)* – Shining Star Woman *(Eagle)*
Shining Moon Woman *(Crane)* – Blue Stone Man *(Deer)*
Brown Bird Boy *(Crane)*
Blue Moon Girl *(Crane)*
Drifting Butterfly Woman *(Crane)* – Many Fish *(Deer)*
White Arrow Boy
Red Willow Girl
Standing Bow Boy

**TURTLE CLAN**

(Yellow Moon
Woman and her
daughter Water
Lily Woman were
adopted from
anther tribe)

Green Wing Woman *(Turtle)* – Blue Cloud Man *(Marten)*
Swimming Bear Man *(Turtle)* – Speaking Fox Woman *(Deer)*
Red Feather Woman *(Turtle)* – Walking Cloud Man *(Bear)*
Blue Feather Woman *(Turtle)*
Green Seed Girl *(Turtle)*
Little Wing Woman *(Turtle)* – Red Stone Man *(Deer)*
Blue Tail Girl *(Turtle)*
White Hoop Girl *(Turtle)*
White Feather Woman *(Turtle)* – Blue Bird Man *(Crane)*
Red Tail Girl *(Turtle)*

Yellow Moon Woman *(Turtle) (Ojibway)*
Water Lily Woman *(Turtle) (Ojibway)*

*"My people will sleep for one hundred years,*
*but when they awake,*
*it will be the artists who give them their spirit back."*
Louis Riel, Jr. (1844-1885)

# PIYAK

The old man fought his way home through deep snow. Beneath a ragged buffalo skin robe, he wore a buckskin shirt and leggings. Once adorned with intricate flower and vine quillwork, the shirt was now bare, the leather scuffed and scratched. His long grey hair was half loose and half braided, to show he was still in mourning.

*"Kitchi Manitou,"* he called out in prayer. "It is your servant, the one they call Painted Turtle Man. Thank you for letting me be alive to see this day. You have given me so many days upon Mother Earth, for which I am grateful. I am ashamed to ask you for just one more, so I can live to see the miracle you have promised."

The wind howled. There were not enough hides to keep out the cold, not enough meat to stave off hunger. He had walked long and far to check his snares, which he had been forced to set farther and farther from the village. This was a job for a much younger warrior, but *Kitchi Manitou* had given the old man a task of the highest importance. He had to do it himself.

With his right hand he clung to the tattered robe, his only refuge from the icy grip of Old Man Winter. In his left hand he carried the body of a half-starved rabbit, the fruit of his labour. Last night, he'd had to dig a hole in the snow for shelter, so he was desperate to make it home tonight. He thought about crossing the frozen lake to save time, but the wisdom his years had earned him argued against it. The open wind of the lake would cut right through him and his shoddy robe. If his old joints locked up on him out there, he would surely die and his family would starve.

The edges of the lake were deep with drifting snow and the old man steadied himself from one tree to the next. It was hard to break the trail and he had to be mindful of the rocks beneath the snow. He had run these paths as a boy and knew every hill, rock, and root on them, but his body had begun to lose its willingness to undertake such journeys.

From the edge of the forest by the shores of the lake he could see the circle of hide-covered lodges—*Nisichawayasihk*, the place where three rivers meet. His people were the *Nehiyawak*, the two-legged ones. The land did not belong to them, but they to the land. The *Nehiyawak* were not the only two-legged ones, though one would have to travel for many moons to find another people.

As Painted Turtle Man approached, he heard something: a woman wailing and moaning against the beat of a drum. The heaviness in his body lifted. He was not too late.

"Thank you, *Kitchi Manitou*, for giving me my legs that have carried me home."

# NĪSO

A scream ripped through the cold winter night. The glowing lodges continued to flicker their fire light, as though not to notice or care. Wind whistling through pine trees was the only answer to the sound. The inhabitants of the other lodges remained quiet, both out of respect for *Kitchi Manitou's* coming blessing and out of fear for the danger to mother and child.

The labour cries came from a small and ragged lodge made of mismatched buffalo hides strewn together against the bitter cold. Bear lodge was the home of Walking Moon Woman, the grey-haired matriarch of the Bear clan. She shared her home with her two daughters and their husbands. Her three elder children, boys, were gone, married into other clans as was the way of the *Nehiyawak*. Her sons tried to help when they could, but their obligations were to their new clans.

The days of glory for the Bear lodge had passed, and its inhabitants struggled to prove their value to the village. For their hunters, fish were hard to catch, berries hard to find, and animals scarce. Times were hard for all of the *Nehiyawak*, but hardest for the Bear clan.

In the old days, when Painted Turtle Man and his wife still walked together, he helped her make the medicines for the people, evoking the spirits of the ancestors to take pity on the sick and suffering. Now that she was gone, he had been all but forgotten by those he had dedicated himself to helping. The emptiness in their bellies was mostly what the *Nehiyawak* thought about.

Of course a true medicine carrier gifted by *Kitchi Manitou* could call upon the ancestors for visions and heal wounds and ailments with a little magic and a wave of the hands. But Painted Turtle Man had not been born with such abilities. He had to make do with what he had been taught: the secrets of the plant world, how to guide a hunter to good hunting grounds, healing the sick with medicines, and the mysteries of the medicine wheel. He could pray and that he did, every day, asking *Kitchi Manitou* to take pity on the *Nehiyawak* and make life easier for everyone.

It mattered not that the other clans snickered at Painted Turtle Man's prophesy, whispering behind his back. It mattered not that the villagers would accept neither his teachings nor his medicine cures, and would not send their young to him to be guided in the healing ways. None of it mattered now, for Painted Turtle Man knew that *Kitchi Manitou*, the Great Spirit, was about to bestow a great blessing upon the Bear clan, a blessing that was sure to restore their former glory.

The wind had blown snow over the lodges, covering the door flaps. Painted Turtle Man put down the rabbit and dug the snow away so he could pull the flaps open. He picked the rabbit back up and brushed the snow from its fur. His own clan had begun listening to the talk of the other clans, and doubting him. This did hurt a little, but he pretended not to notice. It would be forgotten when the miracle occurred in this once-dignified lodge. But first, the mother-to-be would have to pass the test of all life-givers in bringing new life into the world.

"We have been blessed by the Grandmother Rabbit," the old man declared, proudly displaying his prize as he entered the lodge.

"Close the door!" snapped Walking Moon Woman. "You are letting the cold in." She continued about her midwife duties without another thought or consideration to Painted Turtle Man. The old man curled his lip and shuffled in. He had expected a warmer reception from the remaining Bear clan, none of whom had eaten for two days. He gave the skinny rabbit to Singing Doe, Walking Moon Woman's eldest daughter.

"Thank you, Uncle," she whispered and began skinning the rabbit with a dull stone knife.

Singing Doe had yet to be blessed with a child. Last summer she had tried, but the baby girl had been born without breath. The young woman's face and body still bore the strain of losing the new life. For the Bear clan, the loss signalled the moment their luck finally ran out. The people of *Nisichawayasihk* expressed their sympathies, but some whispered that it was the Bear clan's fault. That they had brought it upon themselves. That the child was better off…

The expectant mother pulled and stretched the braided leather ropes looped around the lodge poles above her. The leather moaned under the strain of her weight as she pulled herself into a squatting position during each contraction.

Two men tended the small fire and chanted their medicine songs in support. The man beating a buffalo hide drum was Brown Shield Man of the Wolf clan. He was husband of Singing Doe. Brown Shield Man always had a kind word or a joke to share. He ignored the rumours and gossip about the loss of his child and laughed it off when one of the younger men questioned his manhood, as though his seed had been too weak. Today his face was serious as he tried hard to ignore his fear that tragedy would strike the Bear clan again.

The other singer, the expectant father and husband of White Willow Woman, was a tall and muscular man called Blue Elk Man of the Marten clan. In contrast to his brother-in-law, he was stoic in nature, speaking only when words were completely necessary. A fierce warrior and hunter, Blue Elk Man now looked helpless. All his speed and strength were no help to his labouring wife. Adding to this was the fact that his left leg was bound below the knee where he had been injured by a sharp rock hidden by deep snow. He had not hunted in four days.

"Throw some more wood on the fire," commanded the old man casually, still trying to shake the cold out of his old bones.

"*Motch!*" replied the matriarch, who fired a quick frown at him. "We don't have much wood left."

"Wood," scoffed Painted Turtle Man. "Do you think we will need wood to stay warm when our clan's Grey-Eyed boy is born?"

Silence gouged the tattered lodge. Even the expectant mother was quieted at the prospect. The Bear clan had not produced a Grey-Eye in over three generations. The other clans of *Nisichawayasihk* had begun to murmur that there was no magic left amongst the Bears. To them, the notion that the child about to be born was a Grey-Eye was at best an old fool's fantasy, at worst a cruel joke.

Painted Turtle Man was the only one among them, besides Walking Moon Woman, who had seen the last Grey-Eye of the Bear clan and had felt his magic as a boy. He had been called Grey Bear and they said his magic had no limits. Grey Bear had raised the Bear clan to prominence in his time, using the Grey-Eye magic to help all of the *Nehiyawak*. Grey Bear's magic was a distant legend now as the cold bit the Bear clan and the hunger in their bellies robbed them of sleep. Of the people of *Nisichawayasihk*, only the Eagle clan possessed the Grey-Eye magic. They alone kept the *Nehiyawak* safe.

Blue Elk Man stood up with difficulty and took the old man's arm and sat him down next to the fire.

"I know you mean well, but this is not the time for such words. White Willow Woman must not have any distraction from her purpose." He spoke in a hushed voice.

The two other women frowned at the old man while White Willow Woman prepared herself for the next contraction.

"Do you doubt my dreams? Do you no longer believe I have the sacred sight?" Painted Turtle Man asked, locking his eyes on the warrior.

"*Motch*, Uncle, it's not that…" Blue Elk Man lowered his eyes out of respect.

"I am her mother's cousin!" Painted Turtle Man said, speaking of Walking Moon Woman. "I was best friend to her father. I made a vow the day he was killed by the Red-Eye that I would give his descendants the teachings. Who took you to the sweat lodge? Who sponsored you in the sundance? Who taught you the medicine wheel?"

Painted Turtle Man paused to compose himself. He regretted mentioning the Red-Eyes, from whom the *Nehiyawak* truly needed protection. Only the Grey-Eye magic used in the proper manner could keep the Red-Eye evil at bay. No one in *Nisichawayasihk* wanted to

6

acknowledge that the Eagle clan's Grey-Eye had grown old and that her time on Mother Earth was nearing its end. Painted Turtle Man's prophesy forced them to face this fact. Rather than face it, they chose to push him away. Some in the village even suggested his journey might end out on the frozen lake, on the Long Walk.

"*Tapwe!*" Blue Elk Man capitulated, bowing his head lower. "It was you, Uncle, and I am forever grateful. I just don't want any of us to get false hope if it is not the will of *Kitchi Manitou*."

A sudden scream from White Willow Woman silenced the men.

"Baby is coming!" Walking Moon Woman shouted.

# NISTO

"Is the water warm?" Walking Moon Woman asked as she tended to her daughter.

Singing Doe put down the skinned rabbit and hastily wiped her hands with snow. She grabbed the water skin that hung near the fire. It was barely warm.

"It's here," she said, moving to her sister's side.

Blue Elk Man took his place behind his wife, singing softly in her ear and supporting her body with his strong arms as she clutched the lodge poles. With a final forceful growl, White Willow Woman collapsed backwards into her husband's arms as the cries of a newborn baby filled the night. The sound of the new voice could be heard by all of the *Nehiyawak* of the village.

"Lu-lu-lu-lu-lu-lu-lu-lu-lu-lu!!" the women of *Nisichawayasihk* ululated as one, though not as enthusiastically as they may have for a wealthier clan.

"*Ekosi!*" old Walking Moon Woman said casually. "It is a boy."

The women were grateful for the new addition, and tried not to show their disappointment. The Bear clan would need a female heir if it were to survive in *Nisichawayasihk*.

"*Tapwe*! I knew it!" the old man said. "What colour are his eyes?" He pushed forward but Brown Shield Man stopped him.

"Let him breathe a bit." He held the old man back, but gently.

The baby continued to cry, eyes tightly shut as the old matriarch washed his body with the cool water and an icy wind slipped through the tattered hides.

"The spirit of our Grandmother Bear will need to be with us this winter if he is to have a chance," prayed Walking Moon Woman as she wrapped him in a fur. She handed the bundle to a weary White Willow Woman.

"I know you have given so much, my girl," said Walking Moon Woman, "but now you must give more."

She positioned the baby at his mother's breast. He latched on to her immediately, suckling hungrily.

At the sight of this most sacred moment between mother and child, the Bear clan forgot all of their troubles. A tear escaped from Blue Elk Man's eye as he stared in wonder at his newborn son. The baby seemed satisfied for a brief moment but began to shiver against the cold. The shiver seemed to touch the entire family, snapping them all back to the reality of their poverty. Again they were reminded of their misfortunes and the hunger in their bellies. In a panic, the three women looked at each other and knew what the other was thinking. Would her milk hold up?

Only one among them was not concerned about their situation. He craned his neck over Singing Doe and Brown Shield Man and tried desperately to see the baby up close.

"What colour are his eyes?" Painted Turtle Man's voice rose as he asked again, more forcefully this time.

Now that old Walking Moon Woman was no longer occupied with the birth, she was ready to unleash her anger at her old cousin. For months he had been telling everyone in *Nisichawayasihk* that White Willow Woman would give birth to a Grey-Eye who would have great magic. She spun at him with a look that could pierce the heart of even the bravest warrior.

"*Ekosi!*" she snapped. "I am terribly tired of your…" A change in the air stopped her. The lodge suddenly felt warm, as though something deflected the wind from the outer walls.

"What is happening?" asked Brown Shield Man to no one in particular. "I can hear the wind but it does not seem to reach us."

The fire grew in size without any more wood being added, burning bright and warm as if by its own choice. The dried roots, herbs, and other medicines hanging from the lodge poles came to life, blooming as though it were summer again. Blue Elk Man's bow and quiver of arrows and Brown Shield Man's hand drum floated in the open air of the lodge. The half-skinned rabbit Painted Turtle Man had snared grew large and plump.

Everyone turned toward the baby. No longer shivering, the boy was content, suckling at his mother's breast. The others looked at each other, puzzled.

"You remember what it felt like to be around Uncle Grey Bear, don't you?" Painted Turtle Man asked. Walking Moon Woman's eyes widened as she remembered.

The very air had changed, carrying on it a strange vibration which could be felt deep in the chest. They gathered around the child, whose skin was glowing with an ancient magic. His eyes began to open for the first time, revealing a sliver of grey. They gasped as the boy opened his bright grey eyes fully, resting them on the faces that met his. Painted Turtle Man's prophesy had come true. The miracle was unfolding before them.

The old man began to sing a medicine song with his moon rattle to honour *Kitchi Manitou* for this supreme blessing. The wisps of smoke from the small fire twirled about, dancing to the song. The stones within the rattle sparked in a rainbow of colours that seemed to flash all around the lodge. Every now and then the family could make out the silhouettes and shadows of the ancestor spirits who had gathered within the lodge to pay their respects.

All doubt was gone. Once again, the Bear clan would have the Grey-Eye magic. Once again, the *Nehiyawak* would have to give the Bears the respect they deserved.

# NIYO

The next morning was bitter cold and it took quite some time before anyone came to visit and discover the miracle. The news of the birth spread throughout *Nisichawayasihk* quickly, and the clan matriarchs began to gather. The village was made up of eleven lodges clustered together in seven groups representing the seven clans at *Nisichawayasihk*: Deer, Crane, Turtle, Wolf, Marten, Eagle, and Bear. Each clan was led by its matriarch, usually the eldest woman in the family, who was guided by the spirit of the clan's animal totem.

In their finest robes and adornments, the leaders of the six other clans brought forward their gifts to honour the miracle child of the Bear clan. Painted Turtle Man stood in front of the Bear lodge, nodding to each person, as the delegations lined up to enter the Bear lodge. It seemed everyone in the village—more than one hundred people—had come out, despite the cold.

Walking Moon Woman and Singing Doe had tidied the small lodge hastily. White Willow Woman and the baby sat opposite the doorway but close to the fire. The best buffalo robes the Bears owned were laid out on either side to accommodate visitors. Walking Moon Woman and Singing Doe placed their next-best buffalo robes behind mother and child, positioning them in such a way as to cover holes and scratches. Blue Elk Man stood behind his wife and child and Brown Shield Man stayed near the door to greet the guests.

The snow around the Bear lodge had melted, and though it was still mid-winter, grass had started to grow. Talking Stone Woman, matriarch of the Deer clan, was the first to come forward. The snow she shook from her *mukluks* melted quickly on the grass. A stout grandmother with a sharp mind, Talking Stone Woman liked to do what she could to keep the Deer clan strong in the eyes of the *Nehiyawak*. This occasion would be an opportunity to demonstrate the Deer clan's respect and generosity to the people of *Nisichawayasihk*. Painted Turtle Man guided Talking Stone Woman, with her two grandchildren, in. The Deer clan matriarch barely acknowledged the old man as she entered the lodge.

"*Tansi?* May the kindness of the Grandmother Deer guide the Bear clan," she began in the way of the Deer people.

"May the Grandmother Bear always bring her healing medicine to the Deer clan," responded Walking Moon Woman. This blessing might have seemed a little hollow yesterday, but things had changed. The Grey-Eye magic would benefit not only the Bear clan, but the entire village. Walking Moon Woman stood to embrace the Deer matriarch, inviting her to sit next to mother and child with a wave of her arm.

"We have come to honour the Bear clan and to show respect for the blessing *Kitchi Manitou* has given you. Please accept our humble gift to honour your lodge." Talking Stone Woman's grandchildren, a young woman wearing a white doe hide dress and a young warrior of seventeen summers, stepped forward. In their arms they held three carefully folded deer hides, which they set before White Willow Woman and her newborn child. Singing Doe took the hides, stroking them approvingly. Already she envisioned the new shirts and dresses she would make for the family.

"May the Grandmother Deer always bless this lodge with skins to clothe the body and good meat to fill the belly," said Talking Stone Woman. "*Ekosi*, there are others waiting to see the baby."

"*Ekosi*, my sister," said Walking Moon Woman, using the familial term even though they were not blood relations. They rose to their feet and bowed to one another, and the Deer clan representatives stepped out of the Bear lodge.

Standing Sun Woman, the bent and wrinkled matriarch of the Crane clan, was the next to enter. She was assisted by her husband, Walking Moon Woman's older brother. A young girl of four summers and her little brother followed them, dragging a sack as big as they were. Although the little boy was trying to help, his sister seemed to be dragging him along with the sack.

The little girl wore what appeared to be a new dress, likely brought out for the occasion. The girl strained against her labours, her carefully braided and beaded hair already unraveling. The old man moved to help but was quickly refused by the stubborn child. Singing Doe brought forward a rolled up buffalo robe for the Crane clan matriarch to sit on, but she refused.

"*Tansi?* My dear sister," Standing Sun Woman began proudly, acknowledging their relationship through marriage. "May the Grandmother Crane bless this lodge with the power of her voice." She wet her lips with a gnarled tongue. She struggled to breathe yet her voice carried. "Please accept this wild rice, which my children gathered last autumn." She took another deep breath. "May the blessing of our Mother Earth continue to sustain you and your new child. One day, your grandson will guide and protect our village with his magic. Perhaps one day, he will be chosen as a husband from among the Crane clan. We would be honoured to have him join our family." The mention of marriage was no accident, since the Cranes had an infant girl in their lodge, only two months old.

"*Tapwe*, the honour would be ours, my sister," replied Walking Moon Woman. "The Bear clan would be truly blessed to welcome a Crane into our family, as you have so honoured us." She nodded towards her older brother. "May the Grandmother Bear always bring her healing medicine to the families of the Crane clan, *ekosi*."

Brown Shield Man took the heavy sack from the Crane granddaughter. The rice was a great blessing to the Bear lodge—it would sustain the family for the rest of the winter.

The brazen little girl approached White Willow Woman and pulled back the fur covering to take a look at the baby. "Hmm," she huffed, against the muffled objections and embarrassment of her grandfather. Old Standing Sun Woman cackled a toothless laugh at her granddaughter's rudeness and the others in the Bear lodge laughed as well. Grandfather came forward and took the girl's hand, laughing with his tongue out. The Bears laughed again to ensure that no offense was taken. As the Cranes exited the lodge, the little boy squawked as he ran after his sister.

Next to enter was Green Wing Woman, matriarch of the Turtle clan. With the arrival of the Grey-Eyed baby and the gifts that were being passed, the standing of the Turtle clan would change: they would become the poorest family in *Nisichawayasihk*. The Turtles were capable of hunting and gathering, but with five young children in their lodge to feed and clothe they needed more than most. Green Wing Woman came forward, accompanied by her husband, who held a small bundle. The Turtle clan would not have much to spare, but they would do their best to honour the new child.

"*Tansi?* May the Grandmother Turtle guide the Bear clan in the ways of learning," Green Wing Woman began. "Please accept our humble gift to honour the Grey-Eyed baby bear." Her husband unraveled the small bundle, revealing a sacred ceremonial rattle. Made from the shell of a small turtle hollowed out and fastened to a wooden handle with rawhide, the rattle was the size of a man's fist. The handle was adorned with an intricate pattern of quillwork all the way around. The inside was filled with moon stones painstakingly collected from an anthill.

"Ooooooooohhhhh," said the Bear clan in unison.

"This is a great honour," acknowledged Walking Moon Woman. "One we did not expect. When the child has grown, this sacred gift will make his magic stronger. This honour will be repaid many times over and we will never forget this day. May the Grandmother Bear always bring her healing medicine to the families of the Turtle clan."

Brown Shield Man accepted the rattle and gave it a little shake for the new baby. A squeal escaped from the bundle and the rattle flew from Brown Shield Man's grasp, floated in the air and shook again, guided by the Grey-Eye magic. White Willow Woman plucked the Turtle rattle from the air and handed it back to Brown Shield Man, who was still beaming as he put it away.

"*Ekosi*," said Green Wing Woman. The Turtles took their leave with heads held high.

Outside the lodge there was trouble. The two warrior clans, the Wolfs and the Martens, had brought the same gift, new buffalo robes.

"You should keep your robes," the eldest daughter of the Wolf clan said. "You Martens may need them if the hunting is not good. It may be a long time until you are able to find the trail of another buffalo."

"The Martens will always find good hunting," the daughter of the Marten clan retorted. "It is the Wolfs who should put them to use. Your warriors would not have to spend so much time in your lodges when they should be outside watching for danger."

The matriarchs, Gliding Heron Woman of the Marten clan and Blue Lightning Woman of the Wolf clan, stood by, not saying anything. As matriarchs, they could not insult one another, but they did nothing to discourage their daughters from hurling insults.

"Perhaps you Martens should give meat if you are so confident."

"Perhaps you Wolfs should wash more often, it may be your smell that is keeping the animals so far from the village."

"Daughters," Painted Turtle Man said, intervening finally. "Just look at the Bear lodge." He waved his arm towards the patchwork hides barely covering the lodge. "You are both generous and kind. This is simply the will of *Kitchi Manitou* and perhaps that is who guided you. You were both given the same message to fulfill an urgent need." The *Nehiyawak* did not like disharmony and it was the responsibility of the Bear clan to keep the peace.

The younger women looked at one another, surprised by Painted Turtle Man's obtrusion, but with most of the village watching, neither could dispute they were following *Kitchi Manitou's* divine guidance in their choice of gifts.

"*Tansi?* My sister," Gliding Heron Woman said to Blue Lightning Woman. "*Kitchi Manitou* has guided us together to demonstrate the unity of the warrior clans for all the people of *Nisichawayasihk*. Let us enter the Bear lodge together and share our blessings with the new arrival."

"*Tapwe*, my sister," Blue Lightning Woman replied. "We will walk the same path for a time. It should be up to you to speak first."

The crowd murmured their approval at this resolution. Some of the men came over to shake hands with Painted Turtle Man.

The two matriarchs entered the Bear lodge together, followed by their daughters, who were still scowling at one another as they carried in the large, neatly folded buffalo robes.

"May the Grandmother Marten guide the Bear clan across Mother Earth to find all the gifts she provides," said Gliding Heron Woman in the way of the Marten clan.

"And may the Grandmother Wolf guide and protect the children and families of the Bear clan," added Blue Lightning Woman, in the way of the Wolf clan.

"The warrior clans would like to honour the new Grey-Eye with a double blessing," continued Gliding Heron Woman.

With sweet smiles, the daughters laid out the robes before the Bears with a flourish of their hands, each trying to outdo the other.

"May these gifts help to protect you from Old Man Winter," added Blue Lightning Woman.

Walking Moon Woman spoke: "My sisters, your generosity is overwhelming. My heart is filled with a good spirit. May the Grandmother Bear always bring her healing medicine to the families of the Marten clan and to the families of the Wolf clan. *Ekosi.*"

Satisfied, the matriarchs of the warrior clans left the Bear lodge together, arm-in-arm, smiling and laughing like girls. Their daughters followed closely behind, continuing to cast their ugliest faces upon each other.

With only one clan left to pay homage to the new arrival, all the people were now gathered in front of the Bear lodge. The crowd parted as Soaring Star Woman, the Grey-Eyed matriarch of the Eagle clan and leader of the Circle of Clan Mothers, came forth. She was accompanied by her twin granddaughters. All three women floated towards the Bear lodge, carried just off the ground by the Grey-Eye magic. The white-haired woman wore a white beaded headdress shaped like a crown. A woman of over eighty summers, her high cheekbones accented her oval face and the lines she had earned with her years drew attention to her bright grey eyes. Her white dress was beaded and adorned with feathers, trinkets, and charms. Long leather fringes flowed from her arms and shoulders right down to her feet. Soaring Star Woman's eyes seemed to meet each person's gaze as she glided by. The people all bowed slightly as she passed, murmuring their blessings to her.

The Eagle twins, as her granddaughters were called, were similarly adorned, with smaller beaded crowns and long fringed dresses. They had their noses up slightly, as though they had an equal hand in the magic that carried them. They were both tall, slender women who had inherited their grandmother's looks but none of her charm. Many in the village feared the Eagle twins, especially those sharp tongues that were always finding fault in others. The Eagle twins had benefited from the Grey-Eyed magic their whole lives. They were satisfied only with the finest things, and today each carried a round, birch bark box with elaborate quillwork and snowflake designs bitten into the birch bark.

Like pelicans landing on a pond, Soaring Star Woman and her two granddaughters landed softly on the ground in front of the Bear lodge. Painted Turtle Man stood at attention just to the left of the door flaps. He bowed his head and offered his arm to the Eagle clan matriarch. She took his arm with a nod and a smile and walked towards the door. Before he could pull the flaps back, they flew up, then fell behind them once they were through.

All but mother and child rose to their feet and bowed. Walking Moon Woman greeted Soaring Star Woman with a loving embrace. "*Tansi?* Welcome to the Bear lodge, my mother," she said.

"May the Grandmother Eagle bless you with her far-seeing eye," said Soaring Star Woman, in the way of the Eagle clan, her words stifled by Walking Moon Woman's tight embrace. Her piercing grey eyes met the gaze of everyone in the lodge. Walking Moon Woman took the clan mother's arm and guided her to the place of honour, next to White Willow Woman and her baby.

"He certainly seems healthy." Soaring Star Woman beamed as she was handed the bundle to hold. "He'll be handsome like his father."

Blue Elk Man blushed. Brown Shield Man elbowed his brother-in-law in the ribs.

"What happened to your husband's leg?" the clan mother asked White Willow Woman.

"He cut himself on a rock while hunting," the new mother answered. "It's just a scratch."

"You should have come to me," the clan mother replied. As she spoke, the bindings around Blue Elk Man's wound began to glow with a soft bluish light. The bindings unraveled themselves and flitted into the fire. The wound had been healed.

"Love us, loving spirit," the Bear clan murmured in unison. The Eagle clan matriarch continued to rock the baby as though nothing had happened.

The Eagle twins stood as close to the door as possible, looking like they'd tasted something sour. They scrunched their shoulders in close to their necks, not wanting to touch anything and not wanting anything to touch them, while the Eagle clan mother cooed and cradled the baby as though he were her own. She was completely content and appeared to be lost in her own joyful world. One of the Eagle twins cleared her throat.

"We have brought gifts to honour your new blessing," Soaring Star Woman said finally.

The Eagle twins exchanged flashes of the eyes and made small movements with their mouths—part of their secret language. Reluctantly, the younger twin went first.

"Please accept this gift of medicine to keep your family healthy," she mumbled as she opened the birch bark box to reveal four compartments filled with sacred medicines: sweetgrass, sage, cedar, and bitter root.

"Please accept this gift of pemmican to keep your family strong," the elder Eagle Twin added with the same lack of enthusiasm.

Singing Doe approached the younger Eagle Twin, brushing the young woman's hand in the course of accepting the box from her. The younger Eagle Twin pulled her hand back quickly, as though bitten. Singing Doe lowered her eyes apologetically while the younger twin looked at her sister, horrified. Singing Doe turned to accept the second box. The elder Eagle Twin held it out from her body and let it drop onto her sister's box, avoiding contact in a most obvious way.

Singing Doe was a strong and proud woman. Her treatment at the hands of the Eagle twins did not go unnoticed and she became flustered. As she put the gifts away, she moved more quickly than she should have and tripped over something on the floor of the lodge. As she started to fall forward, the pemmican burst out of its box.

There was a sudden flash of blue light and Singing Doe and the two birch boxes and their contents froze in the air. Singing Doe's body began to turn upright, and the spilled pemmican returned to the box. The Eagle clan mother had used the Grey-Eye magic without so much as looking up from the baby.

The Eagle twins snickered. They would have a good laugh at Singing Doe's expense, later.

"Girls…" said the Eagle clan mother, drawing the single word into a long growl that frightened them to attention. They straightened up at the sound, biting their lips to stop from giggling. Brown Shield Man's fist clenched and the corners of his usually upturned mouth straightened, but it was not his place to speak. His wife met his gaze and nodded to show she was fine.

"I would have words with you, my sister," Soaring Star Woman said to Walking Moon Woman. "You girls can wait for me outside."

Shocked at this exclusion, the Eagle twins turned and walked right into the door flaps, which had not flown up as they expected. They pushed the flaps aside as though they were covered in mud. Blue Elk Man and Brown Shield Man followed. Behind them was Singing Doe.

Painted Turtle Man turned to follow, but the Eagle clan mother stopped him. "Not you," she said. "We will need your help."

# 5
## NIYĀNAN

It was a rare honour for a man to be included in discussions among the clan leaders. Nervous, Painted Turtle Man took a seat next to the Eagle clan matriarch.

Soaring Star Woman returned the baby to White Willow Woman, her face aglow like the new mother's. As he watched her, Painted Turtle Man found himself wondering if the Eagle matriarch would ever re-marry. She turned her attention to him then, met his gaze, and smiled. In her magical presence, he may as well have said it out loud. He lowered his eyes respectfully.

"Thank you for healing my husband, *Nookum*," White Willow Woman said as she exposed her breast to feed her child.

"Me?" the old woman said, smiling. "I appreciate that you were taking care of it on your own. Too many people in *Nisichawayasihk* want me to solve their everyday problems. If I did that, what will they do when I am gone?"

Painted Turtle Man nodded in agreement—though no one looked his way.

"Your need was genuine," continued Soaring Star Woman. "With your new addition, your husband must be out hunting. It is okay to ask for help when you really need it."

Walking Moon Woman and White Willow Woman exchanged looks. It was not the first time the pride of the Bear clan had been noted.

"We will need to have a sweat lodge ceremony to find out your baby's name," said Soaring Star Woman, taking up the reason for the meeting.

"There would be much work to do," said Walking Moon Woman. "Old Man Winter will try to make things difficult."

"*Tapwe*, it would be difficult," agreed Soaring Star Woman, "but it is nothing compared to the blessing your lodge has brought us. I am old. Soon I will return to be with the ancestors. I will have peace in knowing the Grey-Eye magic will still protect the people of *Nisichawayasihk*."

"Eagle Mother, you are still healthy…" said Walking Moon Woman, not wishing to imagine life without this woman's guidance to the people of *Nisichawayasihk*. Walking Moon Woman and her descendants owed their very lives to the Eagle mother, to say nothing of her day-to-day leadership. "Besides, it will be many years before our boy will be able to protect the village from…" Walking Moon Woman lowered her eyes. She had not meant to bring up the Red-Eyes in front of the Eagle matriarch.

"You will have to become comfortable talking about such subjects, my sister," Soaring Star Woman replied. "When I go on to the next life, your boy will be the only hope for the people of *Nisichawayasihk*. Even now, the Red-Eye and his warriors are waiting for me to die before they return. They wish to enslave the *Nehiyawak* and will seek to end our way of life."

The Eagle matriarch paused, allowing the silence to punctuate her words. What she said was true and until now there had been nothing the Bear clan could do to help.

"It is important the boy learn to use his magic properly," she continued. "I will do what I can, but I may not have enough years left in me. The Red-Eye is powerful and has learned to wield his magic over others. He has gathered many followers and will return to *Nisichawayasihk* to finish what he started."

"We would stop him!" blurted Painted Turtle Man. He closed his mouth quickly. Although he had been invited to stay, he had not been invited to speak.

"Perhaps," said Soaring Star Woman. "It will not be easy. The boy will need help to learn his power but he must first learn who he is and who he is destined to become. We cannot do all that is needed right now. We will start by finding him a name."

Walking Moon Woman paused for a moment, then rose and went to the corner of the lodge where she kept her meagre possessions. She drew out a small dark leather pouch tied in the middle with a lighter brown strap. She set the pouch in front of the Eagle clan matriarch.

"Soaring Star Woman, matriarch of the Eagle clan and leader of the Circle of Clan Mothers," Walking Moon Woman said formally, "will you host a sweat lodge ceremony and find our baby's name?"

The Eagle clan mother whispered to herself. She reached out and picked up the pouch, which she knew to contain tobacco, and gave her answer. "I accept."

The baby in White Willow Woman's arms whined a little and she gave him her breast. It was hard to imagine that a great evil could threaten their way of life, but it was even harder to imagine that this tiny bundle in her arms might one day protect the *Nehiyawak* from such evil. She knew not what the future held for her son, but she knew she loved him with all her heart.

# NIKOTWĀSIK

t was after midday when Painted Turtle Man emerged from the Bear lodge to find many of the villagers still standing around. All eyes were upon him.

"What's happening?" one of them asked impatiently.

"Soaring Star Woman, leader of the Circle of Clan Mothers, will host a sweat lodge ceremony to find the child's name."

"*Hiy, hiy!*" said those nearby and the crowd dispersed, most running off to chatter about the news. Although a sweat lodge was expected, the news that Soaring Star Woman would bring the Grey-Eye magic to the ceremony was extraordinary. It was not uncommon for people to be given visions or to see things in a sweat lodge ceremony, but in a Grey-Eye sweat lodge, the physical apparitions would be shared: everyone would see the same thing.

The Crane clan matriarch, Standing Sun Woman, sent her eldest daughter to announce the news of the sweat lodge ceremony.

"People of *Nisichawayasihk!*" the woman bellowed. "Come and hear the wisdom of the Circle of Clan Mothers." She repeated the announcement once in each of the four cardinal directions so that no one could claim they had not heard.

The people gathered in front of their lodges, forming a great circle. Aside from a few who were unable to attend due to age or illness, the entire village was there. The small children, who did not care for such things, ran about playing as usual, chasing each other with sticks, throwing snow, and laughing. As rambunctious as the children were, they were careful not to enter the circle.

Walking Moon Woman spoke for the Bear clan. "*Tansi*, my people," she began in the way of the Bear clan. "May the Grandmother Bear guide you in the ways of healing. The Bear lodge has welcomed a great blessing from *Kitchi Manitou*. The people of *Nisichawayasihk* have honoured us with many generous gifts and we are truly grateful. Now we must ask more of the people in finding the name the ancestors will bestow upon our new addition."

The people murmured their approval—this was the appropriate and humble way to ask for help, the way of the *Nehiyawak*. There was no more festive occasion than to welcome a newborn into the village. During the ceremony, the ceremony director would interpret the name from the vision shared by those in attendance. All of the people of *Nisichawayasihk* had been named in this manner.

"I have passed tobacco to our clan mother to sponsor a sweat lodge in order to reveal the name. She has accepted the tobacco and will sponsor the sweat lodge, but she cannot do this by herself." Walking Moon Woman introduced the problem to the *Nehiyawak* to solve.

"What is needed of the *Nehiyawak*?" bellowed old Standing Sun Woman, matriarch of the Cranes.

"First," began Soaring Star Woman, taking over for Walking Moon Woman. "We will need to gather the grandfathers of the rock world to help us speak with the spirits."

The young men of the village stood proud and alert, shoulders back and chest puffed forward, flexing their muscles. They wished to show they were ready and able to take on any task assigned to them. Gliding Heron Woman stepped forward for the Marten clan.

"The sons of the Marten clan would use their scouting gifts to find the grandfathers, to honour the people of *Nisichawayasihk* and our newest member."

As the Marten clan matriarch spoke, the young men of her lodge stood at attention.

"*Tapwe*," answered Soaring Star Woman, "it should be so. Forty-five grandfathers will be needed to find the name."

No sooner had she accepted than did the young men of the Marten clan step backwards, bow to the people, and run off to begin their assigned task.

"Next," continued Soaring Star Woman, "much firewood will be needed to awaken the grandfathers of the rock world."

Talking Stone Woman stepped forward and spoke for the Deer clan. "The sons of the Deer clan would gather the wood in a kind and gentle way to awaken the grandfathers," she said.

"*Tapwe*," answered Soaring Star Woman, "it should be so, my sister."

The young men of the Deer clan stepped back and began their promised duty. The young men of the remaining clans fidgeted and continued to puff themselves up. They were ready to accept any challenge to honour their clan and assist the people of *Nisichawayasihk*.

"Firekeepers will be needed to tend the grandfathers and prepare the sweat lodge," said Soaring Star Woman.

Blue Lightning Woman stepped forward for the Wolf clan. "The sons of the Wolf clan would serve as firekeepers," she said proudly.

"*Tapwe*," answered Soaring Star Woman "this is a fine task for the Wolf sons. It should be so."

The young men of the Wolf clan stepped back, bowed, and ran to gather their tools. One of the boys let out a joyful whoop as they ran off but was hushed by the bigger boys. Some of the people of *Nisichawayasihk* chuckled at the young warrior's enthusiasm.

"Water will be needed to quench the thirst of the grandfather rocks when they have awakened," Soaring Star Woman said. This was a duty for women, as women are the keepers of the water.

Green Wing Woman stepped forward for the Turtle clan. "The daughters of the Turtle clan would gather the life blood of Mother Earth, to quench the grandfathers' thirst," she offered.

"*Tapwe*," answered Soaring Star Woman, "there are many daughters among the Turtle clan. It should be so."

The young women of the Turtle clan pumped their knees to acknowledge their readiness to the task. They did not leave immediately, since there were still important things to discuss.

"The medicine songs should be sung, but who will sing them?" asked Soaring Star Woman.

Standing Sun Woman stepped forward for the Crane clan. "The sons of the Crane clan would offer their voices to the spirits," she said in her surprisingly loud voice. The young men of the Crane clan were stunned. This would mean they would enter the sweat lodge, a very great honour.

"*Tapwe,*" answered Soaring Star Woman. "It is the Grandmother Crane that gives us our voices. It should be so."

The young men of the Crane clan looked as though they had just won a lacrosse game. They stepped back, bowed, and jogged off, still not believing their good fortune.

With the work assigned, the participants would need to be selected.

"Clan mother," said Standing Sun Woman, as was the duty of the Cranes, "who will present the child to the grandfathers?"

"I have discussed this with my sister and we think it would be best for Singing Doe to present the child," responded Soaring Star Woman.

The people of *Nisichawayasihk* murmured their approval. The child was White Willow Woman's first born and so it was understandable she would be too weary from her ordeal to enter the lodge. To have the child presented by his maternal aunt was considered good and fitting.

"Then, perhaps her husband should keep the doorway," suggested Soaring Star Woman, turning towards Walking Moon Woman.

The Eagle twins gasped at the suggestion. Keeping the doorway was a place of honour for a man and one they assumed would go to one of their own husbands, especially since it was their clan that hosted the ceremony.

Realizing they meant him, Brown Shield Man looked like he'd been hit by a branch in the face, but he recovered quickly, standing at attention to signify his willingness. He would sit in the main doorway and accept the red-hot grandfather rocks as they came in. He would then have to place them in the shallow pit dug in the centre of the round lodge.

"*Nookum,*" whispered the elder Eagle Twin. "Would it not be better if an Eagle was given this task?"

"Would it not have been better if you girls had remembered your manners in the Bear lodge?" came the reply. In one motion, Soaring

Star Woman reprimanded her granddaughters while making an apology for their behaviour.

The elder Eagle twin balked and stepped back.

"*Tapwe*," answered Walking Moon Woman on behalf of her son-in-law. "That would be a good thing. Brown Shield Man would be honoured to be of service."

The Eagle twins frowned at Singing Doe, but composed themselves quickly. They liked to appear pleasant when the people of *Nisichawayasihk* were gathered.

"Who should sit in the east?" Standing Sun Woman asked. It was quite cold and the Crane clan matriarch needed to keep the meeting moving.

"A young Eag                                    " answered Walking Moon Woman.

"My great-g
Soaring Star V
mured their ap
sun, where ne
and it is a pl
placated the
honour. A n
forward and
smiled and nodded, taking
nervous but he did his best to puff himself up like the

"Who will sit in the south?" continued Standing Sun Woman.

Blue Lightning Woman stepped forward, again representing the Wolf clan. "My daughter would sit in the south, if she were asked," she offered with her eyes towards the Turtle clan. Since the Wolf and the Turtle share the guardianship of the southern doorway, it was only polite to seek approval. The southern doorway is the woman's place of honour. The daughters of the Turtle clan had already been tasked with gathering the water, but it was still necessary to show respect. Green Wing Woman nodded her approval.

"*Tapwe*," answered Soaring Star Woman "it should be so."

"Who will sit in the west?" asked Standing Sun Woman.

"That is where Walking Moon Woman will sit," stated Soaring Star

Woman. "I will sit there with her."

The people of *Nisichawayasihk* murmured approval. The western doorway was guarded by the Bear and Sasquatch, the gentle giant. It is the place where the family as well as the warriors who protect the family are honoured.

"*Tapwe*, it should be so," confirmed Standing Sun Woman formally. "Who will sit in the north?"

"It should be you, my sister and perhaps your husband too?" said Soaring Star Woman.

This was also a good appointment, since Standing Sun Woman was the second oldest person in the village, next to Soaring Star Woman, and her husband was Walking Moon Woman's brother. The Beaver and the Buffalo guard the northern doorway, and it is the place where the elders are honoured.

"We would be honoured to serve the people of *Nisichawayasihk*," answered Standing Sun Woman.

"Will anything else be needed?" asked Walking Moon Woman to the leader of the Circle of Clan Mothers, Soaring Star Woman.

"*Tapwe*," she replied, "someone will be needed to offer the prayers and provide guidance and direction for the ceremony. This person would also have to make the medicine for the grandfathers. I would have Painted Turtle Man undertake this task."

All but the Eagle twins cheered the appointment, and those standing near him nodded their approval to the old man. Directing the ceremony and making the medicine for the grandfathers was a great honour, one reserved for the village medicine carrier. Old Painted Turtle Man tried to remain composed but a tear escaped his eye, hiding quickly in the creases of his wrinkled face.

Soaring Star Woman handed a small pouch to one of her grandchildren and directed the child to walk around the circle from east to south to west, in the direction of the sun, until she reached Painted Turtle Man. Rather than hand it to him directly, the child held out the small pouch of tobacco for the man to take, giving him the opportunity to refuse without insult.

"For the love of life," he said as he took the pouch. "I accept this great responsibility."

# TĪPAKOHP

Painted Turtle Man made his way back to the Bear Lodge to begin preparations for the sweat lodge, his first since his wife's return to the spirit world. So many things needed doing before the ceremony could happen, and everyone would be depending on him to remember it all. She used to make sure everything was ready, so all he had to do was conduct the ceremony. How would he manage this task without her?

Painted Turtle Man arrived at the Bear lodge. He could hear the Bear clan women fussing over the baby from outside. Now that he was home, he only wished to be alone.

He headed for the forest. As he walked, a gust of wind caught him off guard, causing a shiver to ripple through his old bones. He headed for the one place he knew she would be with him: the spot where they had spent many evenings, sitting on a rock, watching the sunset. They usually only went there in the summer months, but today he was desperate.

"The *Nehiyawak* need me now, but I don't know if I am ready." He spoke as he walked. "I wish you were here. I was ready to leave this life until *Kitchi Manitou* sent me a dream about a Grey-Eyed boy. Now I feel I must stay here a while longer. I don't know why this boy has been sent to us and I don't know what part I will have in his journey. I imagine you must have had something to do with it. Who else would give me such a task at my age?"

He arrived at their place to find the rock covered in snow. Except for the distant croak of a raven, all was quiet. In his youth, he had been badly wounded. She had nursed him back to health. Because of his injuries, he couldn't offer her much. At the time he did not know whether he would ever walk again, much less hunt. For a time, he was not sure he wanted to go on living. She never gave up on him though, when so many others had dismissed his usefulness.

He worked hard to heal and worked harder to walk again. All that mattered was for him to win her affection and for her to choose him as her husband. He carried his flute to her lodge and played beautiful music for her ears only. He helped her carry water, as best he could, anyway. When he began to learn the secrets of the plant world, he collected the medicines she needed to heal the *Nehiyawak*. Somehow, after he had forgotten why he had started helping her in the first place, she chose him. All he wanted to do after that was be with her. It didn't matter to him if people thought of him only as her helper. He knew they were partners in all things and that was all he cared about.

"The *Nehiyawak* are so happy the Grey-Eyed child has been born. I am, too, but what does it mean? Creator sends a blessing only when we are most in need. What does the future hold for *Nisichawayasihk*? Are we in danger from the Red-Eye?"

The wind whistled louder and the icy fingers of Old Man Winter reached for him. It would be best not to wander too far. He could not shut these thoughts out of his head or push away the dull ache in the pit of his chest. Of the *Nehiyawak* only the matriarchs and a few others had witnessed the devastation the Red-Eye had brought upon *Nisichawayasihk*. The horror was unforgettable. Of course, he thought, life must go on.

The Bear clan had been kind to him, taking him in after his wife passed. How many times had he considered taking the long walk in the dead of winter to relieve the burden they carried? He wasn't afraid of death, but his wife would not approve. She always said, "Creator gives us our life and only Creator can decide when to take it back." Maybe she was right. He certainly didn't want for her to be ashamed of him when next they met.

"I am trying to make you proud," he called. "Though I am afraid,

I try to serve the *Nehiyawak* as best as I can. I know you are watching me, but I just want to be with you again. I don't know what I am supposed to do here…"

"Uncle?" came a young man's voice. Painted Turtle Man turned to see a warrior of seventeen or eighteen summers.

"Huh?" responded the old man wiping his eyes.

"Who were you talking to?"

"My wife."

"*Tapwe*! I am sorry I disturbed you. I will find you later." The young man turned to leave.

"It's all right, I'll have plenty of time to talk to her when I see her next. What did you need?"

"Oh, yes, I wanted to…" the young man stuttered. "I mean, if you need someone like me…if you haven't chosen anyone yet. Have you chosen anyone?"

"I am not sure what you are saying," said Painted Turtle Man. "You want to ask me for something?"

The young man took a deep breath.

"Yes," he began. "The Circle of Clan Mothers passed tobacco for you to run the sweat."

"*Tapwe*."

"I want to be your helper and learn the secrets of the plant world."

"My helper?"

"I am a hard worker. I can collect wood, get water. I can do whatever is needed. I just want to learn."

"No one has ever asked to be my helper before…"

"Really?" said the young man, feigning surprise. "There were three other warriors at the Bear lodge who were going to ask you. When we were told you must have gone to begin the preparations, we went looking for you. I guess I found you first."

"There are others?"

"*Tapwe*, Uncle. But none of them is as hard working as I am. My mother would tell you that I have always helped out around the lodge, even when I was just a boy…"

"I am afraid you are mistaken, I have only been asked to conduct a naming sweat. I am sure there are others who would be able to teach

31

you what you want to know. I'm just an old man preparing to return to the Great Mystery."

"That is not what the people are saying. They say you knew the Grey-Eye was going to be born. They say you are touched by *Kitchi Manitou.*"

"The *Nehiyawak* say a great many things, but not all of it is true. Yesterday they laughed at me and today they think I am blessed. Who knows what they will say about me tomorrow."

The young man looked down at his feet. He was determined, but didn't know what to say to change the old man's mind.

"What is your name, my boy?" asked Painted Turtle Man.

"I am called Soaring Spear Man of the Deer clan. I earned my warrior name last spring."

"Well, Soaring Spear Man of the Deer clan," said Painted Turtle Man. "Why do you want to become my helper and learn the secrets of the plant world?"

"Hmm," he pondered. "I hadn't really thought about it."

"What is the first thing that comes to mind?"

"I guess I want to learn things that will make me more useful to the village."

"That is a good reason." Painted Turtle Man examined the young man for a time. "Is there anything else?"

"Well, Uncle," said Soaring Spear Man. "I am a little embarrassed to say."

"If you expect me to teach you my secrets, you will have to tell me some of yours."

"*Tapwe...*"

"And anything said between us," added Painted Turtle Man, "will stay between us."

"Well, I don't think any of the women are interested in me. I thought if I learned something that other warriors don't know, one of the women might want to choose me for a husband."

"That's nothing to be embarrassed about. After forty-four winters together, I still don't know why my wife chose me. But I am glad she did. You are wise to seek out opportunities to improve yourself. That in itself is a quality women admire."

"*Tapwe?*"

"*Tapwe.*"

"I would be grateful for any knowledge you could share with me in this matter."

"I am afraid that is the extent of my knowledge," laughed Painted Turtle Man. "But there are many other things I could teach you."

"So, I can be your helper?"

"*Tapwe*, for as long as you feel you are learning. When you have learned from me all you need, you will move on and learn new things. One day, you might be able to come teach me something about the plant world that I did not know. That is the way wisdom is gained, in first recognizing that it can come from anywhere."

"*Hiy, hiy!*"

"Now let's go find the others. There is much work to be done."

As they began their journey back to the village, Painted Turtle Man said a silent prayer of thanks. Having a young person to help and to teach would make his tasks much less difficult. Perhaps there was more for him to do in *Nisichawayasihk* after all.

# AYINĀNĪW

Four days passed and the people of *Nisichawayasihk* went about their preparations for the ceremony. The few young men of the Turtle clan offered to help the Deer clan collect wood, while the Wolf clan warriors prepared the site for the sweat lodge, clearing away the snow covering it. The Crane clan warriors came to assist, practicing their songs as they worked.

This is the way of the *Nehiyawak*: they saw what needed doing and they did it. To be thought of as lazy was a great dishonour, so everyone tried to keep busy in some way. As sponsors of the ceremony, the Eagle clan would prepare a feast for the people and present gifts to all who helped. In being sponsored by the wealthiest clan and with two Grey Eyes in attendance, the ceremony promised to be a good one.

On the third day of preparation, Blue Elk Man led a small group of Marten clan warriors out in search of grandfather rocks. He was not strictly required, but there was little for Blue Elk Man to do at the Bear lodge and he was eager to stretch his legs after being healed of his injury. The five men decided to head southwest along the river to a spot where round rocks had always been found.

"I had hoped to be an uncle," said Coming Thunder, Blue Elk Man's youngest brother. "I wasn't expecting my nephew to be a Grey-Eye."

"*Tapwe*," said one of the others, pulling his toboggan over a stump. "I didn't think you had it in you." The men laughed.

"It is a great blessing," said Blue Elk Man. "It is *Kitchi Manitou* who deserves the credit."

"Don't be so modest. You've done us proud," continued Coming Thunder. "Now my wife wants a Grey-Eye too. It's been a good thing for me."

"I hope you aren't going to get her hopes up," said Blue Elk Man.

"About the baby, or does he mean the other thing?" teased one warrior to another. They shot a look back at Coming Thunder, who was last in the group.

"Don't worry about that," said Coming Thunder. "I'm a Marten."

No one laughed. Blue Elk Man had stopped in his tracks, as did the others.

"Come on," said Coming Thunder, pulling up alongside his brother. "Where is the pride—"

Blue Elk Man put his arm out, stopping him.

The men followed Blue Elk Man's gaze. Up. In all of their combined experience as scouts, none had ever seen anything like it. Strung high across two trees and suspended by leather ropes was an owl. The bird's shell of a body wavered in the wind: the eyes and tail feathers had been removed. The owl looked alive, frozen in place mid-glide, and yet without its eyes it seemed hollow, soulless. Blue Elk Man tried to read the message but failed. All he knew was that a dark purpose was at work here. The Marten warriors scanned the area, but saw no tracks or smoke from a camp.

Satisfied there was no other human presence, Blue Elk Man spoke. "Go get Painted Turtle Man."

Coming Thunder took off for the village.

//// 

"What did you find?" asked Painted Turtle Man as he trudged through the snow, assisted by the young warrior.

"I don't know how to describe it. It is an owl…was an owl…but the eyes are missing and it is tied up in the air," answered Coming Thunder. "You must see it."

The waiting Marten clan warriors parted for Painted Turtle Man as he approached. At first, he noticed nothing unusual—only the panic in the warriors' eyes. The Marten clan had a reputation for being serious and calm, so Painted Turtle Man did not take their agitation lightly. He looked to Blue Elk Man, who indicated the trees above with his lips.

Painted Turtle Man looked up and the colour left his face. He felt a dull ache creep into his old war wounds as he absorbed the scene. A twinge of anger grew behind his eyes. He did not speak.

"Who would do such a thing to Grandmother Owl, Uncle?" asked Blue Elk Man. "Is this bad medicine?"

"There are few who would dare harm one of Creator's messengers…" mumbled Painted Turtle Man. What did it mean, he wondered. Would the naming ceremony have to be cancelled? Was the village in danger? Then clearly, he said: "This is the work of the Red-Eyes."

The Marten clan warriors drew knives, spears, and bows and quickly formed a circle around the old man. They scanned the forest again for any sign of the enemy, hands clenched tightly on their weapons, ready to fight to the death if necessary.

Painted Turtle Man closed his eyes and raised his face to the sky. Concentrating, he extended his senses far beyond what the eyes could see and the ears could hear. Coming Thunder began to sing a war song, welcoming death. Like them all, he was prepared to lay down his life for the *Nehiyawak*.

"They are no longer here," Painted Turtle Man said. "We will cut Grandmother Owl down and show the proper respect. When we return, you warriors are not to say anything. I will inform the clan mothers quietly. We do not want to start a panic or create fear."

"What of the grandfather rocks?" asked Blue Elk Man.

Painted Turtle Man paused. He had forgotten their purpose in coming to this place. The enemy had already intruded on what should have been a routine activity. Was this to be the extent of their disruption?

"*Motch*," he answered. "A child is getting his name and we will not allow the Red-Eyes to upset the harmony of the *Nehiyawak*."

The warriors lowered their guard and did as instructed. They buried the owl with tobacco and sage. Painted Turtle man spoke prayers and gave apologies on behalf of all *Nehiyawak*, the Red-Eyes especially.

# KĪKĀ-MITĀTAHT

The warriors of the Wolf clan woke up early the day of the ceremony and made their way to the sacred sweat lodge grounds. They set to work building the ceremonial fire, laying out logs in a bed, and stacking the forty-five grandfather rocks in a pyramid on top. They surrounded the rocks with twigs and small branches, then with larger logs. When the rocks were completely covered with wood so that none could be seen, they sprinkled tobacco on top of the pile while the senior Wolf warrior prayed. The younger warriors tended the fire, adding new logs when the old ones were consumed and the grandfather rocks became visible.

With the fire roaring, the people of *Nisichawayasihk* began to gather, walking around the fire so as not to be in the way of its keepers, but close enough to stay warm.

The sons of the Crane clan wore their finest shirts and charms around their necks and their hair braided with leather ties and bright white crane feathers. They warmed their hand drums around the fire, checking often that they were in tune. People prayed to the fire using a large wooden bowl placed on a small stone altar for that purpose. Some left gifts of tobacco, tea, or arrows at the foot of the altar for the firekeepers.

Painted Turtle Man arrived, by his side, four young men carrying his medicines and charms in various pouches, bags, and boxes. Those gathered greeted Painted Turtle Man warmly, presenting him with gifts of fur, polished stones, cut porcupine quills, and tobacco. The senior warriors shook his hand and called him *moosum*. Grandfather. Not so long ago they had looked at him as something of a nuisance, with scorn even, but not now.

A large warrior from the Deer clan called Many Fish approached Painted Turtle Man with a pouch of tobacco and asked to speak privately.

"*Moosum*," he said nervously. "I have a problem and I would like for you to pray for me in the ceremony today."

"What is the nature of this problem?"

"It is very serious."

"What is it?"

"I am having problems…with my wife." Many Fish swallowed and looked away.

"That is very serious," said Painted Turtle Man. "How can I help you?"

"I am afraid she is getting tired of me. Every time I come home I worry she will put my belongings outside the lodge. Sometimes, I don't even want to leave the lodge because of this."

"That is not good," said Painted Turtle Man shaking his head. "You live in the Crane lodge?"

"*Tapwe*."

"Your wife is Drifting Butterfly Woman?"

He nodded.

"Were those your children who came to the Bear lodge with a bag of wild rice?"

"*Tapwe*." Many Fish straightened up a little.

"Well, that explains it, nephew. When a woman becomes a mother, her thoughts become occupied with her children. This can make us men feel as though we are being ignored."

Many Fish looked down and nodded.

"I will pray for you today," said Painted Turtle Man, holding out his hand to receive the tobacco. "But I don't think you need to be worried. Drifting Butterfly Woman needs you now more than ever. While she may be occupied with her children, she is counting on you to find food. This is the reason she chose you for her husband: you are a good provider."

Many Fish shivered, though not from the cold. He handed Painted Turtle Man the pouch of tobacco, then hugged him quickly. "*Hiy, hiy,*" he said.

"*Ekosi,*" replied Painted Turtle Man, patting the big man's back.

Young warriors pulling the clan matriarchs on toboggans began to arrive. Normally, they would have travelled by dog sled, but dogs were not allowed on ceremony grounds, which had to be kept clean. The young women arrived next, some pulled on toboggan by warriors trying to make a good impression. The Turtle clan arrived, and young men rushed over to help the women carrying water for the ceremony. One of the boys from the Deer clan offered assistance and was rejected by a particularly beautiful, older girl. Though his friends teased him, he showed no shame. Perhaps he would to try again another day, if she had still not chosen a husband.

Soaring Star Woman, matriarch of the Eagle clan and leader of the Circle of Clan Mothers, arrived, accompanied by the Eagle twins and Walking Moon Woman, matriarch of the Bear clan. Elevated by the Grey-Eyed magic, the four women glided rather than walked, landing just before the Holy Ground. Walking Moon Woman was not accustomed to flying in this manner, though she laughed easily as she set down clumsily beside the more practiced twins.

When all assembled had offered their tobacco to the fire, Brown Shield Man approached the matriarchs. "The grandfathers are almost ready," he said.

"Give our thanks to the warriors of the Wolf clan," answered Walking Moon Woman. "Here comes my grandson now."

Blue Elk Man, his leg fully healed, pulled a toboggan carrying his wife and her sister, who held the baby in her arms. Brown Shield Man handed the large shoulder bone he had been using to tend the fire to one of his younger Wolf clan brothers and went to assist his wife and nephew. White Willow Woman, still moving slowly, was wearing a new dress and coat made from the gifted deer hides. The people of *Nisichawayasihk* cleared a narrow path for the Bear clan but tried to catch a glimpse of the new baby, who was sleeping peacefully.

The preparations had been made and all of the people of *Nisichawayasihk* had gathered. The sweat lodge ceremony to find the name of the newborn child was about to begin. As Painted Turtle Man took one last look around, the memory of the strung-up owl rushed to his mind. When he had informed Soaring Star Woman of what the Martens had found, she assured him the village would be safe. Not wanting his own doubts and fears to affect the proceedings, he forced the image away. The Red-Eye were not present in body. It would not be him who would invite them in, in spirit.

# MITĀTAHT

"The grandfathers are almost ready," announced Brown Shield Man.

Those who would be entering the lodge began to undress. The men stood around the fire wearing only a short wrap around their middles. They shivered now and then but would say nothing of the cold. The women wore plain doe hide dresses covering their bodies from just under their arms to just above their knees.

The small dome-shaped building was ready; the floor was covered with pine boughs for insulation and those were covered with soft, tanned hides. Inside, coloured strips of hide hung from the willow frame ribs, marking the four cardinal directions: red in the east, yellow in the south, black in the west, white in the north, and blue, the colour of spirit, in the centre. A shallow pit had been dug in the centre to hold the rocks.

"Have you filled the pipe?" Painted Turtle Man asked Soaring Spear Man.

"Not yet, *Moosum*," the helper replied. This task should have been done by now, but Painted Turtle Man knew his helpers were still learning.

"It is time," said Painted Turtle Man. After some frantic searching and fidgeting with the ropes, Soaring Spear Man dropped to his knees and assembled the pipe.

Painted Turtle Man joined him, placing a hand on his shoulder. "You are doing well. Don't be nervous."

"*Tapwe, Moosum.*"

"Pray as you fill the pipe," instructed Painted Turtle Man. "Offer thanks to the four directions as you place the tobacco. Try not to pack it too tight, or it will be hard to smoke."

Satisfied everything was in order, Painted Turtle Man nodded to Soaring Star Woman. As the ceremony sponsor, she crawled into the sweat lodge first. Her achy joints rebelled as she maneuvered herself into the sweat lodge on all fours. Walking Moon Woman entered next.

Singing Doe moved toward the sweat lodge door, but the Eagle twins made to enter first, creating an awkward moment. But Singing Doe would not submit to the twins' subtle bullying. "It's your turn, little one," she said to the babe in her arms. All of the *Nehiyawak* knew that children, especially infants, were first in all things. The clan matriarchs had entered before the baby only to prepare the way. Singing Doe and the baby entered, taking their place in the west side between the two matriarchs.

The Eagle twins entered next, taking a lot of time to get settled, moving hides around and fussing. The rest of the women who followed had to adjust themselves around them to take up their places. When all the women were seated and comfortable, Soaring Star Woman said, "Painted Turtle Man, we are ready for the men now."

Painted Turtle Man crawled all the way around the sweat lodge, passing between the women and the centre pit. The other men took their places as assigned or sat on the northern hemisphere, as was customary. Brown Shield Man was the last to enter, taking his place between the main entrance and the pit. He tried to put forward a brave face, managing only an awkward smile. His mind was aware of the responsibility before him.

When everyone was settled, the helpers began to distribute the sacred objects, handing them in so they could be passed from person to person until reaching their owner. First, the Eagle fan for Soaring Star Woman. Next, the Crane clan singers' four drums. Then a small pair of four-point deer antlers for Brown Shield Man. Finally, more rattles, some made of buffalo horn, some of rawhide with moonstone, as well as deer hoof chimes. Singing Doe used the turtle shell rattle on behalf of her infant nephew.

"Pipe!" said Soaring Spear Man, holding the red stone pipe carved with a bear cub hugging the bowl. As each person took the pipe, they touched it to each shoulder and whispered their prayers before passing it to the person on their left. When it finally reached Painted Turtle Man, he performed the same motion and set the pipe on a small hide laid out in front of him next to a braid of sweetgrass and an assortment of medicine pouches.

Painted Turtle Man looked up at Soaring Star Woman, who nodded her approval to him.

"Bring in the grandfathers!" Painted Turtle Man ordered and the firekeepers snapped to their duty, starting the sweat lodge ceremony. The Wolf clan warriors used long sticks to separate the wood from the rocks and roll the rocks out one by one. One of the older Wolf clan warriors began to pick up one of the red-hot rocks with deer antlers. As he held the grandfathers with the antlers, he looked to his younger brother holding a pine bough.

"You have to brush them quickly so the branch won't catch fire," the older warrior whispered.

The first grandfather rock was brought to the main doorway and set down in front of Brown Shield Man, who picked it up with his antlers and set it in the centre of the pit.

The participants greeted the red-hot rock as they would every grandfather brought in. "*Tansi, moosumis*! Welcome, grandfathers!"

Walking Moon Woman took a pinch of ground cedar from a pouch and sprinkled it on the rock. The red-hot rock sparkled, and the sweat lodge filled with the sweet smell of burning cedar.

"Place the next four grandfathers in the four directions," said Painted Turtle Man.

////

When Brown Shield Man placed the next four in position, Painted Turtle Man sprinkled tobacco over them and then touched the end of his braid of sweetgrass to one of the red-hot rocks. It began to smoke and the smell of burning sweetgrass mingled with the smell of cedar and tobacco.

"I will now light the pipe," announced Painted Turtle Man. As he touched the smouldering ember at the end of the sweetgrass braid to the bowl of his pipe, the Crane clan singers raised their drums and sang the pipe song. The others shook their rattles in time with the beat, while Walking Moon Woman continued to sprinkle bits of cedar on the new grandfather rocks as they were brought in. The bits of cedar crackled and danced into flame. As she acknowledged the grandfathers, a calm and comforting energy filled the sweat lodge.

Painted Turtle Man smoked the pipe, offering it to the four directions and then to Father Sky, Mother Earth, and the Spirit Within. When the last of the grandfather rocks was brought in, the helpers prepared the water vessel—a hollowed log tied with a hide drooped on the inside and tied off around the middle. The helpers poured water from the hide bags brought by the Turtle clan women into the vessel and placed a carved wooden ladle inside. When the song was complete and Painted Turtle Man finished smoking the peace pipe, he handed it back to Soaring Spear Man with an approving nod. The youth tried not to smile as he ran off to clean it.

"Bring the water!" said Painted Turtle Man. He set the prepared water vessel before the pit. "*Ekosi*," he said casually. "Close the door."

The helpers outside pulled down the hides to cover the lodge completely and then stomped around the edges to ensure no light could get in. The lodge was dark except for the red glow of the grandfather rocks.

"Love us, Loving Spirit," prayed Painted Turtle Man as he sprinkled a mixture of ground herbs over the rocks. They sparkled brightly as though in answer to the medicine carrier's words. The people inside the lodge could feel a vibration in the air as the Grey-Eye magic began to add its power to the ancient ceremony.

"I will offer water-medicine to the grandfathers four times," said Painted Turtle Man. He splashed the water on the rocks and a searing hiss came from the centre pit. The red glow of the rocks diminished as the water cooled them slightly. The steam rose suddenly and followed the dome-shaped lodge down over the participants.

"Love us, Loving Spirit!" they chanted every time the water was poured.

When Painted Turtle Man had finished, the sound of the water bubbling and hissing could be heard from the base of the pit.

"*Kitchi Manitou*," Painted Turtle Man began, "the name you have honoured me with is Painted Turtle Man and I am of the Bear clan."

As he spoke a horizontal disk of smoky blue light began to glow and hover above the grandfather rocks. A small painted turtle flew out of the light and circled the lodge. A bear's roar sounded and a large shadow passed around the back of the lodge. Everyone felt hot breath snuffling the air behind their necks.

"We, the people of *Nisichawayasihk*, seek your guidance," Painted Turtle Man added. There was a flash of white light and the small turtle disappeared.

"Calling-in song," he announced. The singers began the drum beat and sang the welcome song, inviting the ancestral spirits to join the ceremony. One by one the seven sacred animals appeared and made themselves known.

Buffalo.

Eagle.

Bear.

Wolf.

Sasquatch.

Turtle.

Beaver.

Painted Turtle Man poured water over the hot rocks, once for each animal as it entered, and the lodge filled with hot steam. The participants struggled to keep their eyes open against the searing hot steam. When the song ended, the sacred animals dissipated into the blue mist.

"The spirits are with us," said Painted Turtle Man and the others murmured their acknowledgement.

"Burn tobacco!" one of the young women yelled.

"*Hiy, hiy!*" came the acknowledgement from outside. The fire-keepers threw a pinch of tobacco into the fire to acknowledge special prayers, visions, or suffering occurring within the sweat lodge.

"*Nookumis* and *moosumis* of the eastern doorway," Painted Turtle Man prayed. "We seek your guidance and blessing. We give thanks and praise for the gifts you have given us. We acknowledge the blessing of new life you have bestowed upon the people of *Nisichawayasihk*."

"Burn tobacco!" a man's voice called.

"*Hiy, hiy!*" came a muffled voice from outside.

Painted Turtle Man invited someone from the eastern doorway to speak. Soaring Star Woman's great-grandson, Laughing Cloud Boy, thanked the *nookumis* and *moosumis* for giving him life as the blue haze flashed.

"Burn tobacco!" his mother shouted when he was finished.

Painted Turtle Man took over, thanking the young warrior and inviting the *nookumis* and *moosumis* of the *Nehiyawak* to acknowledge the young brave.

Something began to stir in the smoky blue disk in the centre of the lodge. A large bird's head began to protrude beak first and the disk became a swirling cloud that flashed with lightning. It looked like a very large eagle, but when it had fully emerged it turned out to be a small Thunderbird. It screeched with crackling thunder and erupted with brilliant flashes of white light.

"Thunderbird song!" yelled Painted Turtle Man, barely audible over the thunder.

The deep boom of an elk hide drum echoed as one of the older Crane clan singers took up the song. The Thunderbird jerked and twitched its head curiously at the sound of the song. It was a powerful omen and Painted Turtle Man splashed the grandfather rocks continuously in a steady and gentle rhythm in perfect time with the drums.

As the song neared its end, the little Thunderbird began to retract its head into the cloud and the thunder and lightning subsided. The cloud became a smoky blue disk again.

"All my relations! *Ekosi*, open the door!" yelled Painted Turtle Man.

The firekeepers pulled up the hides covering the main doorway and steam poured out of the lodge.

The participants' heads and bodies gave off wisps of steam as they chattered excitedly about the first round of the ceremony and what they thought the omen meant. Brown Shield Man moved the rocks around with his antlers, occasionally splashing hot water here and there. He gathered them into a round, flat bed as he had seen others do at previous ceremonies. When the pit was ready, fourteen more red-hot grandfather rocks were brought in.

"*Ekosi*, close the door," said Painted Turtle Man. Again, the fire-keepers lowered the hides and stomped them flat from the outside.

"Love us, Loving Spirit," prayed Painted Turtle Man as he sprinkled new medicine over the red-hot rocks. The smoky disk hovering above the grandfather rocks was now a sandy yellow colour. "In the southern doorway, we honour the life-givers, our mothers, grandmothers, aunties, sisters, cousins, daughters, and granddaughters."

The next round of the sweat lodge was ready to begin.

This time, a large green turtle flew out of the smoky disk and zoomed around the sweat lodge. Then, a white wolf emerged and walked about slowly and gracefully, staying close to the disk.

"I will offer medicine four times for each of these grandmothers," announced Painted Turtle Man. As the water was splashed over the red-hot rocks the steam roared more intensely than in the first round. The hot steam struck the faces and shoulders of the participants, scalding them mildly.

The baby in Singing Doe's arms was well covered and continued to sleep peacefully despite the drumming, singing, and heat. This time, Painted Turtle Man invited the southern doorway to speak.

"My name is Red Dragonfly Woman of the Wolf Clan," the young woman began. She paused as Painted Turtle Man splashed water on the grandfather rocks four more times. The yellow disk swirled and flashed white light.

"I am honoured and grateful to be here today," she continued. "And to represent the women of *Nisichawayasihk*. I give thanks and praise to the Creator, *Kitchi Manitou*, for blessing White Willow Woman with her new baby boy."

"Burn tobacco!" one of the older women called.

"I would ask the ancestors, in a humble way, to give us guidance in seeking a name for our new blessing. I renew the pledge of the Wolf clan to protect this child from any who would threaten his harmony."

The other Wolf clan participants began a long slow howl in

acknowledgement and were joined by the apparition of the white wolf in the centre of the lodge.

"All my relations, *ekosi*!" Red Dragonfly Woman concluded.

"The Wolf clan honours us, and we shall honour them. Wolf song!" ordered Painted Turtle Man.

The Crane clan singers took up the drum beat, loud, fast, and strong. The white wolf began to prowl, sniffing the ground and the air. It howled loud and long, shaking the lodge. Five more wolves emerged from the smoke and joined in the hunt. The wolves ran around the lodge as though chasing something, barking and howling as they went. As the song came to a close the wolves pounced into the smoky yellow disk one by one, as though finding their quarry at last. The original white wolf pounced last, disappearing at the moment of the last beat of the drum.

"All my relations! Open the door!" shouted Painted Turtle Man, ending the round. The helpers outside pealed back the hides covering the entrance and steam poured out in a deep fog. The helpers had to wait a moment for the fog to clear in order to retrieve the empty water vessel. A few of the younger participants, including Soaring Star Woman's great-grandson, removed themselves from the ceremony and were greeted by the helpers with dry deer hides to help with the dripping sweat and steam. They would face no shame in deciding they had had enough.

"All right, bring in fourteen more grandfathers," Painted Turtle Man said after a short time. The participants were deep in prayer, mumbling or humming to themselves, preparing for the ordeal yet to come.

In this round, Walking Moon Woman was invited to speak. "My name is Walking Moon Woman and I guide the Bear clan in a humble way," she began. A full white moon rose out of a red smoky disk above the fire and a large blue bear jumped out of it. The bear stood for a moment, looking around the sweat lodge, surveying the participants. It began prowling and foraging as though in a forest.

"Thanks and gratitude to the Great Spirit, *Kitchi Manitou*, for all the gifts bestowed upon *Nisichawayasihk* and all the creatures living there. I also give thanks to Mother Earth for her bounty. She has always provided for us as a mother provides for her children. The Bear clan has been blessed with a new arrival and we have come here today to ask the ancestors to reveal his name. It is our children who give us purpose and meaning in our lives."

The Bear perked up its ears when she said this, then went back to foraging.

"In the western doorway, we pay honour to the family and to the warriors who protect it. We ask the Gentle Giant and the Bear to continue to watch over us as they have since the people of *Nisichawayasihk* were put on Mother Earth by *Kitchi Manitou*. I pray we may continue to heed the will of Our Creator and live in harmony with all the plants and creatures whom we share this life with. We are not lesser or greater than any of *Kitchi Manitou*'s creations. All my relations, *ekosi*."

The moon and the blue bear dissipated into the smoky red disk.

"Burn tobacco," one of the older women shouted.

Painted Turtle Man splashed the grandfather rocks four more times and the steam blasted the participants again. Some groaned and some clenched their teeth in response to the searing pain. The baby continued to sleep, safe under a hide strewn over Singing Doe's shoulder.

Now it was Soaring Star Woman's turn to speak. As she began, a bright white streak of light shot up out of the smoky red disk and swirled high in the air in long, smooth circles. The sweat lodge rumbled and reverberated with the ancient magic as the clan mother uttered her first words: "I give thanks and gratitude to all manner of creation, those that fly, those that swim, and those that creep or crawl upon Mother Earth." Animals and insects of all manner burst out of the smoky disk as though it were the cauldron of life.

"I give thanks to the four winds and the teachings they whisper."

The wind blew from each of the four doorways causing the hot air to sear the backs of the participants.

"Hear, *nookumis* and *moosumis* of the *Nehiyawak*, those who have come before us and have prepared our way."

The creatures disappeared and the aurora began to shimmer and shine above the smoky red disk in silver, green, and blue. The ancestors were visible within the lights and appeared to be listening.

"I give great thanks," Soaring Star Woman continued, "for the blessing of the Grey-Eyed child born to the Bear clan."

The participants whooped and cheered as though celebrating a great victory. Painted Turtle Man splashed the grandfather rocks and the drum sounded four times in acknowledgement. Silence quickly returned as the participants listened eagerly and Soaring Star Woman continued.

"I have grown old," she said, her voice trembling. "My body has become tired. Soon I will join the ancestors in the Great Mystery beyond this life…"

The people inside the lodge balked, shouting out their disbelief and praying for Soaring Star Woman's health and long life.

"It brings my heart great joy," she said, silencing them, "to know the Grey-Eye magic will continue to bless the people of *Nisichawayasihk* after I am gone." The participants cheered at this wisdom and many called for tobacco to be burned.

"I place all of my faith in you, *Kitchi Manitou*, to guide our people as you always have. I ask only that you give us the ears to hear your message and the eyes to see your signs. I have foreseen that the people of *Nisichawayasihk* will need your blessings in the troubling times to come…All my relations, *ekosi*."

Soaring Star Woman concluded her prayer, leaving all to wonder in silence about what she meant. The ancestors blurred themselves back into the shimmering light of the aurora and began to dissipate. The white light that had been circling around the top of the lodge fell back into the smoky red disk.

"Bear song! *Hiy! Hiy!*" said Painted Turtle Man.

The lead singer cleared his throat and began the fast drumbeat of the Bear song. A large glowing black bear began to emerge from the smoky red disk. This was an elder bear with hunched shoulders and a white face covered with scars. It stood on its hind legs and issued a roar that shook the sweat lodge. Someone outside the lodge screamed.

The elder bear began to snuffle and root around inside the lodge, looking for sickness. The elder bear took notice of Painted Turtle Man and charged him. The bear pinned his chest to the floor of the sweat lodge, pawing and roaring at his back.

"Brown Shield Man!" the old man yelled. "Offer the medicine!"

Brown Shield Man fumbled for the wooden ladle and scooped water out of the vessel, never having been asked to do this before.

He held the wooden ladle with his right hand and poured the water slowly over the grandfather rocks. The steam rose from the hot rocks and burned his hand. He cried out in pain, cradling the injured hand.

"No!" shouted Painted Turtle Man, still pinned by the great bear. "Splash the medicine. Don't pour it."

Brown Shield Man took the ladle with his left hand and began splashing the water onto the rocks. The steam heated the lodge beyond tolerance and the people suffered. Some of the drummers stopped singing and drumming, unable to continue against the heat and steam. The lead drummer soldiered on, drumming and singing in spite of the searing heat.

The elder bear released Painted Turtle Man and looked at Brown Shield Man. It took one step towards him and bit his burned hand. Brown Shield Man screamed but continued to splash water onto the rocks with his free hand. When the elder bear released the hand from his powerful jaws, the hand was healed. The bear sauntered around the lodge, ensuring that all those in need of healing received it. When the elder bear was satisfied, it walked into the smoky red disk as though into a burrow or cave. The song ended.

Still lying on the floor of the sweat lodge, a gasping Painted Turtle Man called for the door to be opened. The flaps burst open as he spoke. The helpers outside knew the participants would not want any delay in ending the warrior round. Steam billowed out of the lodge in a torrent, as though a volcano had erupted from inside the lodge. One of the helpers was seared in the face. He spun around quickly, gritting his teeth.

"Open the back door," instructed Painted Turtle Man as he slowly returned to a seated position.

The helpers ran around to the other side of the lodge and lifted the hides opposite the main entrance. Steam now poured out of both sides of the sweat lodge.

"Bring us some medicine," requested Painted Turtle Man as he placed the empty water vessel in the doorway.

The helpers brought forth the water skins and filled the vessel. Painted Turtle Man scooped water with the ladle and handed it to Brown Shield Man.

"Pass it to Walking Moon Woman to speak for the water," he instructed. The ladle of precious water was passed from person to person. They eyed it hungrily but did not drink. Prayers and thanksgiving to *Kitchi Manitou* always come first.

Walking Moon Woman took the ladle and held it up high, offering prayers under her breath. She lowered it to the floor and continued to pray. She then poured a dribble on the earth next to the grandfather rocks. She whispered her thanks to the water, then took a long sip from the ladle. She handed it over to Soaring Star Woman, who repeated the process, then drank the remaining half of the water. When the ladle was empty it was passed to Painted Turtle Man, who refilled it and drank.

Each participant was given the ladle to drink and refresh themselves. Those who had endured the ravages of the third round were quiet and calm. They had earned the right to pray for themselves in the last and final round, which promised to be milder. When everyone had been refreshed and the steam had subsided, Painted Turtle Man instructed the helpers to close the back door and bring in the remaining grandfathers.

The fourth and final round was ready to begin.

"Love us, Loving Spirit," prayed Painted Turtle Man. He sprinkled new medicine herbs over the red-hot rocks and shards. The glowing rocks sparkled in answer to the new medicine.

Painted Turtle Man invited Standing Sun Woman of the northern doorway to speak. As she began, a yellow sun rose out of the smoky white disk and hovered solidly above. A large crane emerged and walked around the lodge slowly, choosing carefully where to step with its long legs.

"I give thanks and praise to Creator for the teachings of the northern doorway," Standing Sun Woman said. The yellow sun wavered and became a heap of mud and sticks that a beaver crawled over, while scratching and cleaning his face. The crane flew up and away and was replaced by a bull buffalo grazing upon the smoky white disk.

"We would ask the *nookumis* and *moosumis* of the Spiritual World to show us the way ahead and to reveal the name of our newest member," Standing Sun Woman prayed. "I would ask the singers to sing the tree song."

The beaver and the buffalo looked towards the northern doorway a moment and then nodded their heads in unison. The Crane clan singers took up the drum beat as their clan mother had requested. The smoky white disk began to swirl faster and expanded, enveloping the beaver and the buffalo. The participants of the sweat lodge were treated to a strange assortment of visions that could not immediately be interpreted.

A burst of light flashed and the ceiling of the sweat lodge became the night sky. A shooting star streaked across the sky in a downward arch, disappearing somewhere low on the horizon.

The white light flashed again and the scene became a marshland in the summer. There, a pair of white cranes walked together.

Another flash and the floor of the sweat lodge became an aerial view of a *Nehiyawak* village. It was as though the participants were sitting upon a cloud high in the sky looking down. Two eagles circled the village and then shrieked and dove at the people below. The people ducked for cover and fled into their lodges to hide.

Another white flash and they were in a thicket where a red fox was trotting along with a snake in its mouth. The snake's head writhed from side to side and its body grew larger and larger. It struck the back of the fox's neck with its venomous fangs. The fox took a few steps, fell down, and was swallowed by the snake.

The light flashed again and those in the sweat lodge now appeared to be under water in a pond. From the southern doorway two grey turtles swam overhead, the first turtle larger than the second.

Another flash and the participants appeared to be near a mountain where a large grizzly bear was limping towards the mountain with one of its front paws up off the ground.

Next, they were back in the forest where sad-faced people were walking, carrying sacks and pouches and looking backwards from time to time, their eyes streaming with tears.

Another brilliant flash of white light and they were back in the sweat lodge, the disk of smoky white light swirling above the grandfather rocks again as the song ended.

"Thank you my ancestors for this vision," said Standing Sun Woman. "All my relations."

"*Tapwe*!" everyone in the lodge yelled at once.

"We have honoured all of creation and all of the teachings of the four directions," prayed Painted Turtle Man. "We would now ask for this child's name to be revealed to us."

Painted Turtle Man splashed water over the rocks seven times, the steam hitting the participants gently in waves. The smoky white disk began to swirl again and grow dark. The lodge began to reverberate with an unseen energy as something began to emerge from the dark swirl. It appeared to be the head and the shoulders of a warrior with his eyes closed. Many of the men murmured their approval of what they thought was to be interpreted as a strong warrior name. The spectral warrior breathed deeply and all of the people inside the lodge were face to face with him, regardless of their position or perspective.

Slowly the warrior's eyelids began to rise, revealing in his irises the colour of blood. Some of the younger participants screamed in horror at the image of a cackling Red-Eye, sworn enemy of the people of *Nisichawayasihk* and servant of evil. This image of the enemy seemed to be a bad omen, an omen of death. Suddenly the baby in Singing Doe's arms began to cry fast and loud.

"Do not fear!" yelled Painted Turtle Man as the participants began to panic. "You are safe within the womb of our Mother Earth!"

Out of the cries of the newborn emerged a small grey bear cub which roared and scratched at the ground in mock combat. The Red-Eyed warrior recoiled. The grey bear cub rolled around, continuing to roar and paw, standing on its hind legs. It glowed with a grey light and a magical energy and the Red-Eyed warrior began to shrink, screaming and cursing. When the warrior had diminished and faded, the grey bear cub stood triumphant in the centre of the lodge, roaring and pawing the air. The participants cheered.

"Little Grey Bear Boy of the Bear clan!" Painted Turtle Man shouted.

The people cheered, whooping and howling their approval.

"Singers!" said Painted Turtle. "Sing the Creator song!"

The deep boom of the drum answered him as they took up the song honouring *Kitchi Manitou*. The participants had accomplished what they came to do and had suffered. Now, it was time to receive gifts and feast.

# MITĀTAHT PIYAKOSĀP

"Has anyone seen my knife?" Blue Elk Man had been searching the Bear lodge for his prized hunting knife all morning. If he found it soon, he might still make it to his preferred campsite before nightfall.

"When did you use it last?" asked White Willow Woman, bouncing Little Grey Bear Boy on her lap. A brisk chill this morning would take care of the mosquitos but would send the ducks and geese away as well. The sour red berries had appeared in the moss, providing Mother Earth's last gift before she began her long slumber. Now would be a good time for her husband to find a moose.

"I have a knife you could take," offered Brown Shield Man. He was ready to leave, though not as anxious as his brother-in-law.

"Do you need a meal before you go?" asked Singing Doe to her husband.

"*Awas!*" said Walking Moon Woman. "You are always feeding him. It's a wonder we have any food left." As she spoke, Blue Elk Man's knife floated out from under the hides carpeting the floor of the lodge where he and his wife slept. The now familiar vibration of the Grey-Eye magic was in the air.

"That's daddy's boy!" said Blue Elk Man as he snatched the floating knife and went over to kiss his son.

"How did he know what you were thinking?" wondered White

Willow Woman aloud.

"It isn't just him," Painted Turtle Man chimed in from his spot to the right of the doorway, where he was grinding herbs. "His gift is meant to be shared. Those around him also have some influence."

"What do you mean?" Singing Doe asked as she bent over to scoop some rice out of the bag. Before Painted Turtle Man could answer, Singing Doe flew through the air into the arms of her husband. The others laughed while Brown Shield Man blushed. It was not the first time this had happened.

"You've gone and spilled the rice with your fooling around!" shouted Walking Moon Woman. "Can't you keep your thoughts to yourself?"

"*Tapwe*!" laughed White Willow Woman.

"Don't tease," said Painted Turtle Man. "He loves his wife and that is nothing to be ashamed of." The others tried to stifle their laughter.

"Well if he loves his wife so much, maybe she should go with him," said Walking Moon Woman.

Singing Doe locked eyes with her husband and smiled.

"I'm not sure how much hunting would get done…" White Willow Woman teased as Little Grey Bear Boy pulled at her to loosen her dress straps so he could nurse.

"Anything would be better than having you two spilling my rice and eating all the food," said Walking Moon Woman. "This lodge was feeling crowded anyway. Go."

Singing Doe jumped up, kissed her husband, and began gathering some belongings.

"Have a good hunt," said Painted Turtle Man as the young couple ran out soon after.

"Why did you do that?" asked White Willow Woman to her mother.

"Why not?" she replied. "They need some time alone and our clan still needs a girl."

"Maybe I should go with my husband then," suggested White Willow Woman, pinching Blue Elk Man playfully.

"*Awas*!" said Walking Moon Woman. "I want my baby grandson near me."

"Then I better get going," said Blue Elk Man, eager to leave before Walking Moon Woman's teasing turned on him. He gave his son another kiss and nodded at Painted Turtle Man as he left.

"Hunt well, nephew," said the old man.

////

The winter months were much easier to bear this year than those recently past. Blue Elk Man took a bull moose, one of the largest that had ever given itself to him. Brown Shield Man and Singing Doe had not had any such luck on their hunt, though the trip turned out not to be a total loss: Singing Doe was pregnant. The Bear Clan was starting to grow and the addition of children inspired the family to do better and try harder in all of their endeavours. The hunting was usually good and Singing Doe's sewing and quillwork were attracting attention in the village.

"I really hope this one's a girl," said Singing Doe, examining her growing belly.

"I'll be happy with any child who chooses us," said Brown Shield Man.

"I'll pray for you at the ceremony tonight," said Painted Turtle Man. "I may not be back for some time. I'll try not to wake him when I return."

"Be careful what you wish for," said White Willow Woman, pacing the lodge with Little Grey Bear Boy in her arms. "Baby won't let me leave and I really need to pee! I can't wait any longer."

"I feel sorry for you my girl," laughed Painted Turtle Man. "I'm afraid no one remembers what it was like to have a Grey-Eyed baby."

"That's not entirely true," said Walking Moon Woman. Painted Turtle Man frowned and began to gather his things to leave.

"What do you mean?" asked White Willow Woman, still pacing the lodge with her too-big-to-carry boy. Painted Turtle Man cleared his throat and gave Walking Moon Woman a quick scowl as he left.

"I wish I could help," said Blue Elk Man.

"Yeah, me too," chuckled Brown Shield Man.

"Don't you two have some work to do?" shouted Walking Moon

Woman. "You men get out of here. Soaring Star Woman is coming to visit."

"I am going to go too," said Singing Doe, grabbing a pair of *mukluks* she had made as she left with the men.

"What did you mean, mother?" pressed White Willow Woman.

"Never mind," answered Walking Moon Woman. "Soaring Star will be here any moment."

"I hope she hurries," exclaimed White Willow Woman, now bouncing from foot to foot to the great amusement of Little Grey Bear Boy.

"*Tansi?*" came a familiar voice from outside. Walking Moon Woman met the Eagle matriarch at the doorway and welcomed her in. White Willow Woman could wait no longer: she ran up to Soaring Star Woman and quickly handed her the child.

"*Tansi, Nookum,*" she almost yelled. "May the Grandmother Bear bless you with her healing gifts!" The young mother ran off to answer the call of nature. Little Grey Bear Boy was about to start crying when his grey eyes met those of the Eagle matriarch. The air vibrated as the old woman's magic filled the lodge, calming him.

"*Tansi,* baby," she said as she lowered him to his feet and helped him toddle back into the lodge. "May the Grandmother Eagle bless this lodge with her far-seeing eye."

"I am very sorry for my daughter's rude behaviour," said Walking Moon Woman. "She hasn't been able to be without the boy."

"I understand," laughed Soaring Star Woman. "I couldn't go very far either. When I really had to, I would use the magic to make him sleep for a moment so I could at least get out to take care of those matters. I can see where this is more of a challenge for her."

"We are all very grateful for your visits."

"I will try to come more often." Soaring Star Woman raised her hand and the turtle shell rattle rose up in the air, travelled across the lodge, and set down into her palm. She gave it to Little Grey Bear Boy.

"Many in *Nisichawayasihk* need your attention, clan mother. We do not wish to be a burden."

"I am glad you understand," said Soaring Star Woman. "It so happens I need your help with a rather delicate matter."

"Oh?"

"One of my granddaughters is having something of a dispute with a woman from another clan. I think it would be inappropriate for me to interfere in the matter, but she won't give me a moment's peace until it is settled. I told her I would bring it to you, as matriarch of the Bear clan, to resolve the matter."

"I see…" said Walking Moon Woman. Arbitrating a dispute between two willing parties was one matter. Resolving a disagreement involving the Eagle twins was something else entirely.

"You have concerns?" asked Soaring Star Woman.

"Well…" she paused.

"I know my granddaughters can be difficult and I know I am asking a lot. However, I have made it very clear to them that this is a matter for the Bear clan."

"I will do what you ask," said Walking Moon Woman. "It has been quite some time since anyone has asked for our help in this way. I sometimes worry we no longer have the respect of the people."

"Things change, my girl. Your grandson's arrival has made many people rethink their opinions. It's true you are the smallest clan in *Nisichawayasihk* and you do not have any girls, but that does not diminish your clan's task."

"*Tapwe*, my mother."

"My granddaughters will come visit you. Show them the Bear clan's healing ways. Do not give them any special treatment or allow them to intimidate you in any way."

"*Tapwe*," nodded Walking Moon Woman. With all the help the Eagle matriarch had given the Bear clan since the birth of Little Grey Bear Boy, it was impossible to refuse her any request.

////

"Willow, he's doing it again!" yelled Brown Shield Man. Whenever Little Grey Bear Boy noticed the fire, he would make it come alive. Dancing ropes of flame swirled around the Bear lodge.

"Where is his rattle?" called White Willow Woman.

"My mint tea!" laughed Painted Turtle Man, as he jumped up to snuff the flames on a bundle of dried tea leaves hanging from the lodge poles. "We will need to search out larger rocks for the fire pit as soon as the snows melt."

"*Tapwe!*" agreed Blue Elk Man and Brown Shield Man together.

"When is Soaring Star Woman coming to visit?" asked Blue Elk Man. Only the Grey-Eyed matriarch seemed to be able to contain the child's magic.

"Not tonight," answered Walking Moon Woman. "I thought he would be tired from attending the ceremony today. What was it about this time?"

"It was an induction ceremony for a young warrior of the Deer clan," said Painted Turtle Man.

"Why did they want a baby at an induction ceremony?" asked Singing Doe.

"It seems no one can do anything these days without our baby being there," grumbled Blue Elk Man.

"You didn't seem to mind when the Marten clan gave you new snowshoes for attending their memorial," laughed Brown Shield Man.

"That was different," said Blue Elk Man. "I am Marten, I would have attended anyway. Besides, everyone knows the Marten clan is generous." The others laughed.

"The Deer clan was generous today as well husband," said White Willow Woman. "They gave us six arrows and a bag of pemmican."

"I could use some new arrows…" said Brown Shield Man, raising an eyebrow to Blue Elk Man.

"It seems our Grey-Eye is already a good provider," beamed Painted Turtle Man.

"*Tapwe!*" smiled Walking Moon Woman. "You have also done well, cousin. A new buffalo robe?"

"I could use some new arrows…" repeated Brown Shield Man. Blue Elk Man examined the wrappings on his hunting knife. They were, after all, finely crafted arrows.

"Oh, one of the Wolf warriors gave it to me," said Painted Turtle Man. "He passed tobacco for a dreaming. I dreamt he went south with the others. I explained the dream to his matriarch and she let him go. He had never been so far from the village, being a Wolf and all. A young buffalo gave itself up to him on the hunt and he was so happy he gave me the robe."

"That was very kind of him," said Walking Moon Woman. She smiled at her cousin and continued to stare a while. In the new robe and with his hair plaited in a single braid, Painted Turtle Man looked younger than he had in a long while.

"So what was it that Soaring Star Woman asked of you?" asked Singing Doe.

"She wants us to settle a dispute," answered Walking Moon Woman.

"Us?"

"*Tapwe*, my girl."

"Who do you mean?"

"Willow will take baby over to the Crane lodge and you will stay and help me," explained Walking Moon Woman.

"Who exactly is having this 'dispute,' mother?"

"We should probably get going," said White Willow Woman. "Are you going somewhere, Uncle?"

"*Tapwe*," said Painted Turtle Man. "I am giving a teaching for the young warriors tonight. I won't be back until very late."

"I am going to help him," added Brown Shield Man, kissing his wife's swollen belly as he got up.

Singing Doe was losing her patience. "Mother?"

"My girl," began Walking Moon Woman. "It doesn't matter what our personal feelings are towards someone who needs our help. It is our clan's duty to be impartial when administering the Bear's justice."

"*Motch*!" exclaimed Singing Doe getting to her feet. "You are bringing them here?"

"Don't get upset, my girl. Think about your baby. You must be nice to them."

"And who are they picking on this time?"

"My girl," said Walking Moon Woman, raising her voice. "That does not sound impartial. We will learn the details when they all arrive tonight. I need you to help with the ceremony and the food. You don't have to do anything else or talk to anyone."

"You could have told me." Singing Doe was not feeling inclined to hide her true feelings, yet she knew duty to her clan must come first.

"I know, my girl. I know."

# MITĀTAHT NĪSOSĀP

"*Tansī*? Come in, come in," smiled Singing Doe as she welcomed Red Dragonfly Woman of the Wolf clan and her young daughter into the Bear lodge. "Would you like some tea?"

"I'm sorry this visit could not be under better circumstances," answered Red Dragonfly Woman. "The sooner this is all resolved the better. You know what they are like…"

"May the Grandmother Bear bless you with her healing," interrupted Walking Moon Woman.

"May the Grandmother Wolf protect you and your family," answered Red Dragonfly Woman. "I am sorry you have been inconvenienced by this matter. I am sure you would rather be with your grandson than have to listen to this…"

"Ahem!" came a voice from outside.

"May the Grandmother Bear bless you with her healing," said Singing Doe as the women entered.

"May the Grandmother Eagle bless you with her far-seeing eye," the elder Eagle Twin answered curtly. It was unclear who she was talking to as she locked eyes with Red Dragonfly Woman.

"Can we get this over with? My sister and I are very busy," added the younger Eagle Twin.

"Please come in," answered Walking Moon Woman politely. "Doe, did you offer our guests some tea?"

"*Motch*," answered the elder Eagle twin. "My grandmother asked us to come to you and so we came." She looked about the Bear lodge as she spoke, taking note first of the new hides covering the lodge, then of the bundles of roots and dried plants hanging from the poles.

"You just couldn't wait to mention your grandmother," snapped Red Dragonfly Woman. "Well, she isn't here to wipe your little noses, is she?"

"Excuse me?" the younger Eagle twin shot back.

"Daughters!" said Walking Moon Woman. "Please, sit down. You will both be given plenty of time to speak. I have been passed tobacco to help restore your harmony. You will both respect the tobacco and this lodge. The Grandmother Bear will be invited to hear you and she will decide what is to be done."

"*Tapwe*, Auntie," said Red Dragonfly Woman. "I will respect the Bear clan justice."

The Eagle twins crossed their arms and exchanged a look. The elder Eagle twin said nothing but nodded at Walking Moon Woman.

"I will light the sage and invite the Grandmother Bear to come witness our circle," began Walking Moon Woman. "I will ask Singing Doe to sing the Bear song and then we will begin."

The abalone shell with the smouldering sage was first offered to Singing Doe, who wafted the smoke over her body and through her hair. She set the shell down in front of her and waved her hand drum and drum stick through the smoke as well. When she was finished, she passed the smoking shell to Red Dragonfly Woman on her right. Singing Doe began the Bear song as the shell was passed around and the others anointed themselves with the smoke. When the shell came to Walking Moon Woman, she set it in front of herself and let the smoke continue to float up and around the Bear lodge until Singing Doe concluded the song.

"I have been passed tobacco," began Walking Moon Woman as she brought out her brightly coloured talking stick, "to ask our Grandmother Bear to share her wisdom with us. Our harmony has been disrupted and two daughters of *Nisichawayasihk* who should be as sisters have been hurt by hard feelings and harsh words."

The two women looked up at one another and shared a frown.

"We ask in a humble way," continued Walking Moon Woman, "that you hear us, Grandmother Bear, and show us your healing power."

Silence filled the Bear lodge until someone coughed.

"White Star Woman of the Eagle clan, have you claimed offense to something Red Dragonfly Woman of the Wolf clan has said or done?"

"*Tapwe*," answered the elder Eagle twin.

"And Red Dragonfly Woman, do you acknowledge giving offence to your sister?"

"*Motch*," she answered. "I have given no offense." The younger Eagle twin scoffed but was frowned at by Walking Moon Woman.

"I will ask White Star Woman to tell Grandmother Bear what has happened. Everyone gathered will have a chance to speak, so I ask that no one interrupt when another is talking. Speak from your heart and share only what you yourself have said and done." Walking Moon Woman passed the talking stick to the elder Eagle twin.

"*Tansi*, Grandmother Bear," she began, speaking to the fire. "I am White Star Woman of the Eagle clan. I am seeking your guidance in correcting an injustice. I am the mother of Laughing Cloud Boy, who has only been upon Mother Earth for six summers." She swallowed hard and a single tear fell down her cheek.

"My son admires his father as all boys do. He says often he wishes to be just like him when he walks the warrior's path. I wish I could keep him a child forever, but I know this is not the way of the *Nehiyawak*. As a mother, I only wish to see him happy and so I planned to give him a present. I wished to give him a bow exactly like his father's. I knew this would make him very happy."

The younger Eagle twin let out a sympathetic sigh.

"I had been told," the elder Eagle twin gulped, as she continued, "that Red Dragonfly Woman's husband made my husband's bow and that he was considered one of the best bow makers in *Nisichawayasihk*. I approached Red Dragonfly Woman and asked her if she would have her husband make my son a bow to match his father's. She told me that to do so would take a lot of her husband's time and that he would not be able to hunt for many days. I agreed to give her four bags of pemmican as compensation."

"My sister and I pounded the pemmican for two days. We filled four bags and when Red Dragonfly Woman came, we traded as agreed. All seemed to be well except that when I gave the bow to my son, he could not pull it because it was strung too tight. It made me very angry to watch my son so embarrassed and he was sad when his father laughed at his efforts. I turned my anger on my husband and sent him away for a few days. When I tried to get Red Dragonfly Woman to have her husband fix it, she said he could not. I told her to return my pemmican and she said she would not. I ask Grandmother Bear to give me justice and return what is ours."

"*Hiy, hiy*," said Walking Moon Woman nodding. "I will now ask Shining Star Woman of the Eagle Clan to tell Grandmother Bear how this ordeal has affected her twin sister." The talking stick was passed to the younger Eagle twin.

"*Tansi*, Grandmother Bear," she said, addressing the fire. "I am Shining Star Woman of the Eagle clan and I have come here today to support my sister. I hope this issue can be resolved quickly and justly, as my sister has been unable to eat or sleep because of the hurt she has in her heart." The younger Eagle twin paused to compose herself. "All she wanted was to make her son happy. What kind of mother could wish to deprive her of that? Why would someone wish to put her through this?" She turned her glare at Red Dragonfly Woman. "We demand justice!"

"*Hiy, hiy*," said Walking Moon Woman quickly, surprising the younger Eagle twin. "Singing Doe, please give our sister some water. I know it is difficult to see one's loved one suffer in some way. We must not seek to place blame; we must open our hearts and seek an understanding."

The Bear matriarch paused for a moment so that Singing Doe could offer the birch bark cup to the younger Eagle twin. The woman sobbed as she drank the water.

"Our Grandmother Bear has heard from our Eagle sisters, and now wishes to hear from our sister of the Wolf clan. Red Dragonfly Woman, I invite you to share your words to the Grandmother Bear."

Red Dragonfly Woman was sitting with her arms crossed, bouncing her leg. She sucked her upper teeth, making a loud chirping sound, while maintaining eye contact with the younger Eagle twin. After a time, she shifted her gaze to the fire.

"*Tansi*, Grandmother Bear," she said curtly. "I don't know why I came here. No disrespect intended to the Bear clan. They have always been kind and fair."

Walking Moon Woman nodded and cocked her head slightly as though straining to hear.

"Those Eagle twins…" Red Dragonfly Woman paused, shifting her gaze back to the twins. "They think they can say whatever they want because of who their grandmother is."

"Ahem," interrupted Walking Moon Woman, indicating the fire with her gaze.

"She came to me," continued Red Dragonfly Woman, "asking for my husband to make a bow. I said he would do it for four bags of pemmican, which was less than I would normally agree to. I regret that now. She said she wanted the bow to be just like her husband's, but small enough for her boy. I told my husband to do it, and he told me it would be made from the ash tree and would be hard to pull. I didn't expect her to want him to kill a moose with it at only six summers, and she said she wanted it to look the same as her husband's. But if any other kind of wood were used, it would not look the same, so I had him make it the way she asked for it."

The Eagle twins frowned.

"*Hiy, hiy*," said Walking Moon Woman. "Would your daughter like to share?"

Red Dragonfly Woman nodded at her daughter.

The girl spoke. "*Tansi*, Grandmother Bear. I am here to support my mother. We were asked to do something and we did it. My mother doesn't deserve to be treated like this. The Eagle twins asked for a bow, my father made it, and my mother gave it to them. The next thing we know, everyone in the village is talking about how we somehow cheated the Eagles."

The elder Eagle twin cleared her throat loudly.

"And then," the girl added quickly, "she has the nerve to ask us for her pemmican back. Well, I don't care who her grandmother is, my father did what was asked and we already ate the pemmican, which wasn't very good anyway."

"How dare you!" screamed the younger Eagle twin.

"*Hiy, hiy,*" interrupted Walking Moon Woman. "Grandmother Bear has heard enough. Let us stop for a while and have something to eat. Let's all try to think about what has been shared and try to put ourselves in the other's place."

Singing Doe got up and began preparing food for the guests. Every scrape and clatter was heard through the silence in the lodge. Walking Moon Woman added wood to the small fire.

"You can help if you want to, my girl," said Red Dragonfly Woman to her daughter, giving the Eagle twins a start. The girl stood up and assisted Singing Doe with the preparations. As the food was served, no one spoke. When all the guests were served, Singing Doe sat down next to her mother with some effort.

"How long until you have your baby, Auntie?" asked the girl.

"At least three more moons," answered Singing Doe.

"I hope you have a girl. I'll come and play with her."

"You would be welcome any time," smiled Singing Doe.

"How many children did you have, Bear mother?" asked the younger Eagle twin sweetly.

Red Dragonfly Woman frowned.

"I had five," answered Walking Moon Woman. "Singing Doe is my eldest daughter and I had three boys before her." The others began to eat and drink as they tried to focus their attention on the Bear matriarch and not at each other.

"I remember the first time I was pregnant," reminisced the old woman. "I was so sure I would have a girl. I was the only girl my mother had and she was the only girl my grandmother had. It seems Bears usually have boys."

The others laughed knowingly. Walking Moon Woman looked deep into the fire.

"I remember I was so convinced I would have a daughter that I asked the Deer clan matriarch to make me a cradle board. She made the best quillwork designs in the village. I asked her to make butterflies, the rivers, and the moon, so everyone would know I had a daughter even if she was covered up. It seemed like I gave the Deer matriarch everything I possibly could, to trade, even some things I still needed. All I could think about was how proud I would be to have a daughter who would carry on the Bear clan."

"And then you had a boy?" asked the girl.

"*Tapwe*, my girl."

"What did you do?" asked Red Dragonfly Woman.

"I felt very embarrassed," recalled Walking Moon Woman. "But when I held my son in my arms for the first time, nothing else seemed to matter."

"What did you do with the cradleboard?" asked the younger Eagle twin.

"Well, I don't quite remember…"

"Did you explain to the Deer clan matriarch what happened?" asked Red Dragonfly Woman.

"What could you have said to her?" interrupted the elder Eagle twin, scraping at her bowl. "She gave you exactly what you asked for…"

No one spoke. The elder Eagle twin's face went red.

Walking Moon Woman reached in front of her, taking tobacco from a small pouch. She muttered prayers softly and offered the tobacco to the four directions before throwing it in the fire.

"I feel the presence of the Grandmother Bear," said Walking Moon Woman. The others looked about the lodge, hearts racing. "The Grandmother wishes for Red Dragonfly Woman to speak first and then she wants to hear from White Star Woman."

"My Eagle sister," began Red Dragonfly Woman. "I am sorry your son wasn't able to use the bow the way you wanted. When you asked us to make the bow, I was so proud to have my husband's skill recognized by the Eagle clan. I hoped if he did a really good job, your grandmother would think well of us. I told him to make it exactly like your husband's bow and I didn't think about whether or not the wood would be too strong for a boy. I only wanted to give you what you wanted. When you first saw it, you were so happy. I was happy too, and I thought it would bring us closer. When I found out later you were unhappy, my heart was broken. Just tell me what you want to happen now. Your respect and friendship mean so much more to me."

Singing Doe crawled over and hugged the sobbing Red Dragonfly Woman.

The Eagle twins looked at one another, exchanging facial ticks and twitches and mouthing words too quickly for anyone else to understand. The younger Eagle twin was not happy, but the elder twin knew what must be said.

"My sister," she began. "It is I who must apologize. It seems I built up an expectation that turned out to be unrealistic. I was blinded by love for my son. I hope that as a mother you can forgive me. Your husband's reputation is well deserved, and I am sure with time and practice, my son will one day hunt with his father and earn his warrior name."

Red Dragonfly Woman stood up and stepped quickly over to the elder Eagle twin and hugged her. "My sister..." she said.

"Thank you, Grandmother Bear," prayed Walking Moon Woman. "You have brought your healing gift to this lodge and restored our harmony. Red Dragonfly Woman will send her husband to help Laughing Cloud Boy to learn how to use the bow. White Star Woman will explain to the village that this misunderstanding has been resolved. Is everyone satisfied with this?"

Everyone nodded. The younger Eagle twin coughed into her hand.

"You should all return to your families. I am sure they are missing you. May the Bear bring her healing gift to the Wolf clan and the Eagle clan. *Ekosi.*"

Singing Doe saw the women out.

Red Dragonfly Woman was the last to leave. "I do hope you have a girl, my sister," she said, pressing a hand to Singing Doe's womb. "You and my baby brother deserve much happiness together."

Later, as they were tidying up the Bear lodge, Singing Doe turned to her mother, a nagging question on her lips. "So what did you do with that cradleboard, mother?"

Walking Moon Woman knelt by the fire. "What cradleboard," she said, smiling into the flames.

# MITĀTAHT NISTOSĀP

The snows had melted and the trees and shrubs began to awaken when Singing Doe gave birth to a brown-eyed boy.

"Another boy?" said Red Dragonfly Woman as she held the new baby in her arms.

"Another hunter for our lodge, sister," replied Brown Shield Man.

"Until he is married at least," said Walking Moon Woman.

"The Bear Clan still needs a daughter," said Red Dragonfly Woman. "*Tapwe.*"

"Thank you for sponsoring his naming," said Singing Doe.

"It was the least I could do. Not only is he my brother's son, but I am so grateful that you were able to assist in that unpleasant situation with the Eagle twins. The younger one still gives me dirty looks when I see her…"

"How was the naming sweat?" asked Singing Doe, changing the subject.

"It was good. Very hot. You should have seen that rabbit come out! You never saw anything move so fast. A sweat lodge with the Grey-Eye magic is always something to see. I'm glad Soaring Star Woman was feeling well enough to attend. She has not been out of her lodge much."

"Flying Rabbit Boy," said Singing Doe to the infant in Red Dragonfly Woman's arms.

"I think that name is appropriate," added Walking Moon Woman. "I have never seen a baby born so quickly. He was in such a rush to join our family that I almost missed him when he fell."

"Most of *Nisichiwayasihk* expected him to have Grey-Eyes like his cousin," said Red Dragonfly Woman. "Everyone was talking about it, the bigger you got. Where is Little Grey Bear Boy anyway?"

"He is visiting Soaring Star Woman with his mother," said Walking Moon Woman.

"Are you still having difficulty with him?"

"*Tapwe*," sighed Singing Doe. "He has developed quite a temper. A few nights ago he got so angry when it was his bed time, that when he screamed '*motch*' he blew the hides right off the lodge!"

"We were all so surprised no one moved," added Walking Moon Woman. "You could see the full face of the Grandmother moon through the poles. He just stood there and said 'I found the moon, mommy!' as if nothing happened."

The women laughed.

"Our husbands had to find the hides and cover the lodge in the dark," said Singing Doe.

"Will you try again for a girl?"

"*Tapwe*, we will have to," stated Walking Moon Woman. "The Bear clan must have an heir."

"That is a concern for another time," interrupted Painted Turtle Man. "Now is the time to honour *Kitchi Manitou's* blessing. Creator would not allow the Bear Clan to simply fade away."

The others were silenced by his words. Red Dragonfly Woman returned the baby to Singing Doe, who held her new infant to her breast and smiled.

"Well, I have never seen my little brother so happy," said Red Dragonfly Woman as she stood up to leave. "I am glad I could be a part of this blessing. Let me know if you require anything. The Wolf clan stands ready to give any assistance you may need."

"*Hiy, hiy*," said Walking Moon Woman. "May the Grandmother bear bless you with her healing."

"And may the Grandmother Wolf protect you and your family," replied Red Dragonfly Woman as she left the Bear lodge.

Walking Moon Woman got up to add wood to the fire. "I wonder when White Willow Woman will come home."

"I hope Little Grey Bear Boy is tired," said Singing Doe. "I worry for my baby when he is in a bad mood."

"I am worried for Soaring Star," said Walking Moon Woman. "She is not as strong as she once was."

"Don't be afraid," said Painted Turtle Man. "He is high spirited, but that is normal for a child his age. It is we who need to learn how to manage his magic."

"That's easy for you to say," said Walking Moon Woman. "He only listens to you."

"*Tapwe*," added Singing Doe.

"Perhaps I am the only one who listens to him," grumbled Painted Turtle Man. "We must not fear his gifts; we must learn to live with them. In time, the Grey-Eye magic will benefit all of *Nisichawayasihk*."

"Can it help us have a girl?" asked Walking Moon Woman.

Painted Turtle Man did not answer; he knew his cousin's wit far too well.

////

"Wake up!" yelled White Willow Woman.

"What is it?" a weary Blue Elk Man yawned.

"Where is your son?"

"He was with you."

"What is going on?" asked Walking Moon Woman. "Go back to sleep."

"Where is Little Grey Bear Boy?" asked a frantic White Willow Woman.

"Get some bark on the fire," suggested Painted Turtle Man. Blue Elk Man fumbled about and tore birch bark into strips, throwing them onto the faintly glowing coals. The Grandfather Sun had not yet begun his journey and it was still very dark in the lodge. As the strips of birch bark caught flame, the lodge became illuminated.

"He's over there," said Brown Shield Man, indicating a corner by Painted Turtle Man's bedside.

"My boy!" yelled White Willow Woman as she jumped up to retrieve her son. "What have you got on yourself?"

"*Tansi?*" said Little Grey Bear Boy, who was covered in a greasy liquid that he had been scooping out of a leather pouch.

"Not my red clover medicine," said Painted Turtle Man with a sigh. "It took me days to make that much of it."

"It's even up his nose," said White Willow Woman, trying to wipe the medicine off with a deer hide rag. "Will it hurt him?"

"*Motch*, my girl," said Painted Turtle Man. "It's for burns and sickness of the skin."

Painted Turtle Man assisted White Willow Woman, but mostly in an effort to recover as much of the greasy liquid as he could.

"*Moosum!*" said Little Grey Bear Boy.

"You have to stay out of my medicines, my boy," said Painted Turtle Man. "When you get bigger I will begin teaching you about these things."

"I was hoping for a good sleep," said White Willow Woman with a yawn.

"We might as well get the fire going," said Painted Turtle Man, "it will not be easy to get this medicine off of him."

"I'll take care of it," said Blue Elk Man. "He's my son after all. I'm very sorry that he disturbed your medicines."

"He's just curious," said Painted Turtle Man. "There is nothing wrong with that."

//// 

It was springtime and the Bear clan was gathered in their lodge enjoying their evening meal.

"You should have told me you were going fishing," said Blue Elk Man. "I would have come with you. It must have been difficult with the water still so cold."

"I didn't know I would be fishing," chuckled Brown Shield Man. "You have your son to thank for the fish."

"My son?"

"*Tapwe?*"

"What happened now?"

"I was trying to bathe him in the river," explained White Willow Woman. "He didn't want to bathe and as soon as his foot touched the water he used his magic to blast the water away."

"The entire river?"

"*Motch*, just the water within a tree length of him."

"It was something to see," added Brown Shield Man. "The fish were surprised and flopped around on the bottom. I ran in and grabbed them where they fell."

"The other women were not very happy," said Singing Doe, sitting Flying Rabbit Boy in her lap. "They think he is a danger to the other children."

"He isn't dangerous," said Painted Turtle Man. "He has provided us with a fine meal this evening. The others just don't understand that his gifts are a blessing."

"Of course you always say that," said Walking Moon Woman. "What if someone was hurt? What then?"

"No one got hurt."

"Not this time, but what about the next."

"We cannot live our lives fearing what might happen. We must look to the future."

"What do you mean, Uncle?" asked Singing Doe. "Have you seen something?"

Painted Turtle Man finished his meal and wiped his bowl. The others kept their eyes on him in silence. When he was sure that he had everyone's attention he cleared his throat.

"I have had a dream."

"What happened?" asked Singing Doe.

"I saw a woman."

"What kind of woman?" asked White Willow Woman.

"A young woman," he explained. "Beautiful as her mother. She stood in front of the Bear Lodge wearing the black and red shawl of the Bear clan. All around her there were children. Many children. There must have been a dozen or more of them, all wearing the colours of the Bear."

"How can this be?" interrupted Walking Moon Woman. "How can a young woman have so many children?"

"What does it mean, Uncle?" asked Brown Shield Man.

"I have offered prayers and smoked the pipe," answered Painted Turtle Man. "I believe that White Willow Woman will give birth to a girl who will be the heir to the Bear Clan. She will be the mother of many children and the Grandmother Bear's teachings will be known throughout the lands of the *Nehiyawak*."

Everyone looked at White Willow Woman. She looked down at Little Grey Bear Boy who had fallen asleep in her lap.

"I have something to share," she said with a tear. "My moon time has not come. I think I am with child again."

"*Tapwe?*" asked Blue Elk Man.

"Love us, Loving Spirit!" exclaimed Walking Moon Woman. "This is a glorious day!"

////

The land began to change and the first hint of Old Man Winter was in the air at *Nisichawayasihk*. The men were back from the hunt and the women were busy drying meat and pounding pemmican for the hard months ahead. The labours of the Bear Clan were interrupted by the sudden disappearance of Little Grey Bear Boy.

"Where did you last see him?" yelled White Willow Woman, searching as frantically as her swollen belly would allow her.

"He was right here," explained Brown Shield Man as he searched the lodge.

"Did he get out somehow?" asked Blue Elk Man joining the search.

"What has happened?" yelled Walking Moon Woman.

"We can't find Little Grey Bear Boy."

"Where did you last see him?"

"I was just playing with him," explained Brown Shield Man. "He would hide under a buffalo robe and I would pretend to search for him. He was laughing and playing and then he just disappeared."

"Spread out," ordered Walking Moon Woman. "Ask the Wolf warriors if they have seen him."

Blue Elk Man and Brown Shield Man left the lodge and started hollering. Soon the neighbouring lodges were out searching for the missing child. Before long, all of *Nisichawayasihk* was in an uproar.

"What is going on?" asked Painted Turtle Man as he entered the Bear lodge.

"My son is missing!" cried White Willow Woman.

"He is near," said Painted Turtle Man. "Can't you feel it?"

The family had become so accustomed to the vibration of the Grey-Eye magic that they were beginning to forget when it was present.

"It's time to come out now, my boy!" called Painted Turtle Man.

"*Musoom*!" yelled Little Grey Bear Boy as he suddenly appeared.

"Where was he?" said White Willow Woman, grabbing the child.

"He was invisible."

"They can do that?"

"*Tapwe*," said Painted Turtle Man. "Grey Bear used to do it when he was hunting or scouting. I didn't think Little Grey Bear Boy would learn this so soon."

"Why didn't you tell me about this?"

"I'm sorry, my girl. It was a very long time ago, I can't always remember everything."

"We found him!" yelled Walking Moon Woman. The call was repeated throughout the village. Two Wolf warriors entered the lodge.

"The child is safe?" asked the elder of the two warriors.

"*Tapwe*," said Painted Turtle Man. "He was just invisible. We are sorry to have caused such a disturbance."

"He was here all along?" asked the younger warrior in disbelief.

"You don't know what it is like to have a Grey-Eyed child!" shouted White Willow Woman.

"We meant no offense," said the elder warrior. "We are just glad the child is safe now, we will go."

"Thank you my brothers," said Painted Turtle Man as they left. "Don't be upset, my girl. No one thinks less of you. We are all still learning."

////

Winter came upon *Nisichawayasihk* and Grandfather Sun was spending less and less time in the sky. Flying Rabbit Boy crawled about the Bear Lodge exploring his surroundings when he came across the Turtle Shell Rattle given to Little Grey Bear Boy by the Turtle Clan on the day he was born.

"*MOTCH!*" screamed Little Grey Bear Boy. "MINE!"

As he yelled, Flying Rabbit Boy was sent flying through the air by a blast of energy produced by his angry cousin. Painted Turtle Man happened to be in the right place to catch Flying Rabbit Boy before he was hurt.

"You must be careful not to hurt your cousin!" said Painted Turtle Man with a stern look.

"Sorry, *Moosum*," was Little Grey Bear Boy's answer.

"Give him to me" shouted Singing Doe, taking her baby. "You need to control him!"

"Oh!" gasped White Willow Woman. Singing Doe gathered some hides and bundled up her infant son.

"Where are you going?" asked Walking Moon Woman.

"To the Wolf lodge!" answered Singing Doe as she stormed out of the Bear lodge.

"Oh!" White Willow Woman said holding her swollen belly.

"What is it, my girl?"

"I think it's time!" she answered.

"It's time?"

"*Tapwe!*"

"Right now?"

White Willow Woman's water broke alleviating all doubt.

"Can you take Little Grey Bear Boy to the Eagle lodge?" shouted Walking Moon Woman. "I'm sure Soaring Star Woman will understand."

"Come with *Moosum*, little one," said Painted Turtle Man as he took the boy's hand.

"What's wrong with mommy?" the boy asked.

"Nothing is wrong, she is going to give you a sister!"

////

A new day dawned and the Bear clan finally had an heir. Painted Turtle Man brought Little Grey Bear Boy back to the lodge to meet his new sister.

"My sister?" asked Little Grey Bear Boy, admiring the little bundle.

"Yes, my boy," answered White Willow Woman, "she is very important to our Clan. You must be very careful not to hurt her..."

"*Tapwe...*" answered the little boy in awe.

"You are a big brother now," added Painted Turtle Man. "It is now your job to keep her safe."

"I wonder what her name will be," said White Willow Woman.

"We may have to wait a while to find out," said Walking Moon Woman. "The snow is very deep, it will be difficult to have a naming."

"I can wait," said White Willow Woman.

"I don't think there is any need to wait," said Painted Turtle Man. "I already have a good idea of what her name is."

"*Tapwe?*"

"Yes. When I dreamed about her the first time, I saw a hawk soaring out from the sun."

"And what name would you interpret from this?" asked Walking Moon Woman.

"I believe Yellow Hawk Girl would be appropriate, but I could smoke my pipe to be sure."

"Yellow Hawk Girl," said White Willow Woman. "I like it, it suits her."

"Then Yellow Hawk Girl it will be," confirmed Walking Moon Woman.

"So be it," said Painted Turtle Man. "I will let the others know."

////

The presence of his new little sister seemed to have a profound calming effect on Little Grey Bear Boy. He wanted to be near her at all times and became very helpful to his mother. The Grey-Eye magic seemed to subside and Soaring Star Woman was required to assist less and less often, a blessing to the aging clan mother.

As Little Grey Bear Boy approached his fourth summer he became more and more self-aware. His accidental use of the Grey-Eye magic occurred less frequently and the Bear lodge became peaceful again and harmony was enjoyed throughout *Nisichiwayasihk*. Having an heir to the Bear clan was a great relief to the whole family.

"Should we try for another girl?" asked Brown Shield Man one evening.

"*Motch*," replied Singing Doe. "The three of us talked about it and decided we need to be careful of having more children than we can feed. We are going to put our faith in Painted Turtle Man's vision and prepare the way for Yellow Hawk Girl."

"Are you sure, my love?" he stroked her arm as he spoke.

"Yes, I'm sure," she smiled. "If the hunting isn't good, we could have difficulty, especially if we had more boys before being chosen by another girl."

"Well it takes the pressure off of Blue Elk Man and me to find game."

"*Tapwe*, it also means you can spend more time with Flying Rabbit Boy and me."

"Nothing would make me happier."

# MITĀTAHT NIYOSĀP

"Again, Uncle, again!" squealed Little Grey Bear Boy as Brown Shield Man tossed him up into the air and caught him easily.

"You are getting them too excited before bedtime," scolded Singing Doe through a smile.

"It's my turn, Dada!" said Flying Rabbit Boy.

"Okay, just one more turn for each of you," laughed Brown Shield Man.

The children cheered and pushed each other playfully.

"Eh, he-hem." The sound of someone clearing his throat came from outside the Bear lodge.

Blue Elk Man went to the door flaps to welcome the visitor. Brown Shield Man continued throwing the children into the air in turn, while Singing Doe worked on a pair of moccasins, a commission for the Deer clan. Dried meat and fish hung from thin logs tied across the lodge poles and stretched hides dried near the fire. Bags of wild rice, dried berries, and cooking herbs hung in sacks around the edges of the lodge.

"Painted Turtle Man needs Little Grey Bear Boy to help with the storytelling," said Soaring Spear Man at the door.

With the birth of Yellow Hawk Girl, the Bear lodge had become crowded, so Painted Turtle Man had erected his own lodge, Bear medicine lodge. There, he shared the teachings and provided the people of *Nisichawayasihk* with the guidance, prayers, and healing medicine they sought.

"Yaay! Storytime!" yelled Flying Rabbit Boy as his father set him down. Little Grey Bear Boy took Yellow Hawk Girl by the hand and the children ran out and into the lodge next door.

In the Bear medicine lodge, Painted Turtle Man's young disciples tried—mostly in vain—to get the children seated and settled. Though young and full of wild energy, the children understood the importance of not disturbing the roots and dried herbs that hung from the poles of the lodge.

Painted Turtle Man was seated at the opposite end of the lodge, explaining the nine circles of law to a group of eager young listeners. He concluded his lecture when Little Grey Bear Boy entered. "Over here, my boy!" he called.

Little Grey Bear Boy walked in an arc along the outer edge until he reached his adopted grandfather. He took a seat, followed by his cousins.

"Drum!" said Painted Turtle Man.

The large fire in the centre cast a soft light on the faces of the gathered children. Soaring Spear Man held up a large elk-hide hand drum and boomed it four times. A few more children scurried into the lodge and took their seats. Outside, Grandfather Sun was setting. Darkness slowly settled over the village and the sound of many voices quieted to none.

Painted Turtle Man took Little Grey Bear Boy's hand and approached the fire. Whispering a soft prayer, the medicine carrier sprinkled medicine herbs on the fire, making it burn with blue smoke. The air began to vibrate with an ancient power and the flames of the centre fire burned low and blue. The smoke above the fire began to form shapes of animals. Rabbits and foxes, deer and raccoon appeared to be chatting and laughing together in a great forest. The figure of a sullen man entered from the south as the storytelling began.

# MITĀTAHT NIYĀNOSĀP

In the time before our ancestors, the world was a very different place. All the animals of the forest lived together in harmony. Wolves, bears, and coyotes did not eat the deer, mice, and rabbits and all the animals played together.

The only man at the time was called Wisageechak, the Trickster. Wisageechak thought the harmony of the creatures boring, so he caused trouble for entertainment. He would convince the animals to fight by telling them that another was saying bad things about them to the rest. The bear fought the wolf, the fox fought the marten, and even the birds in the sky would fight one another while Wisageechak laughed.

Blood started to cover the ground and the earth became dirty from the animals fighting. *Kitchi Manitou*, the Creator, did not like the blood all over Mother Earth and began to form the clouds in the sky. The clouds floated high above the earth and Creator breathed life into the first Thunderbird who flew high above them, its wings flapping thunder. Every now and then the Thunderbird's feathers would fall to the ground as lightning.

The clouds poured the first rains to cover the earth, washing away the blood. The rivers and lakes rose and soon the whole of Mother Earth was submerged. Wisageechak was about to drown when a large turtle swam by.

"My brother, let me climb on your back so I do not drown," pleaded Wisageechak.

"I should let you drown! It's your fault I have nowhere to climb up and warm myself by Grandfather Sun," answered the great turtle.

Wisageechak knew this was true and that he would have to use his magic to fix the problem. His magic was strong, but he did not have the ability to recreate the earth, only Creator had this power. He was soon joined by three animals also seeking refuge from the waters: a beaver, an otter, and a little muskrat. Wisageechak and the three animals huddled on Turtle's back.

"If one of you could dive into the water and find me a piece of the old earth, I could remake the world with it," Wisageechak told them. "Brother Beaver, you are the biggest and strongest of the three swimmers. Dive down and get me a piece of the old earth and I will form a large pond for you to build your home and find a wife."

"*Tapwe*!" exclaimed Beaver.

Beaver dove down into the water but came up some time later empty handed. He tried diving even deeper but again came up without a piece of the old earth. He tried a third time, and when he came up empty again he was completely exhausted and could not go back down.

"Brother Otter, you are much faster than fat old Beaver. If you can get me a piece of the old earth, I will build you a wide, slow river for you to float on eating tasty clams and shells," offered Wisageechak.

"*Tapwe*!" answered Otter.

Otter dove down into the deep waters, staying down longer than Beaver had. He came up without a piece of the old earth, gasping for air. Wisageechak convinced him to try again, and again he came up empty handed. He went a third time and came up gasping and coughing, still without a piece of the old earth.

"Lazy Otter, now we will all surely drown," lamented Wisageechak.

"Let me try," said Muskrat.

"You?" replied Wisageechak, bewildered. "You are too small. Beaver and Otter both tried and failed, and they are both much bigger and stronger than you."

"I may be small, but I swim fast and can hold my breath for a very long time," argued Muskrat. "At least let me try."

"Why not," said Wisageechak. "We are all going to die anyway."

Muskrat dove down into the dark water and was down for a very long time.

"He must have drowned," said Wisageechak to Beaver and Otter.

Muskrat burst out of the water, gasping for air.

"You didn't drown!" said Wisageechak.

"I just need a rest, and then I will try again," said Muskrat.

He rested for a time and when he was ready he said, "Let me climb up on your shoulders, Wisageechak, and jump off of you."

"Very well, jump high and swim hard!"

Muskrat scurried up Wisageechak's shoulders and dove off his head. He disappeared into the dark waters and was down even longer than the first time. Finally, he emerged from the waters, choking, coughing, and half-drowned. There was something on his whiskers and paws—bits of mud from the old earth.

"My brother!" exclaimed Wisageechak. "You made it down to the old earth. You must go back and get me a piece so I can remake the land. Will you try again?"

"I must rest," gasped Muskrat.

Wisageechak pushed Beaver and Otter off Turtle's back so Muskrat could lie down and rest. He slept for quite some time but Wisageechak grew impatient and woke him.

"That's enough sleeping," he chided. "Wake up and get me some earth!"

"I am ready," said Muskrat. "You promised Beaver a pond and Otter a river if they could get you some of the old earth. What will I receive as a reward if I succeed where my brothers have failed?"

"Don't be greedy," said Wisageechak. "Isn't it enough not to drown?"

"*Motch*, that's not fair," said Beaver.

"*Tapwe*, you need to give him something if he succeeds," added Otter. "It's only fair!"

"Fine, fine," conceded Wisageechak, rolling his eyes. "If you can bring me a piece of the old earth, I will make for you a great marshland where you can have all the fish and roots your greedy little heart desires."

"I accept," agreed Muskrat. "This time, toss me high up into the air."

Wisageechak picked up the little muskrat and threw him high into the air. He plunged into the water, swimming hard and fast, deeper and deeper into the dark. Wisageechak and the others waited and waited but he did not come up.

"He has been down there too long," said Beaver.

No one replied. They knew Beaver was right. After a long time had passed they heard a small *blurp* and saw fur sticking out of the water a short distance from Turtle. Otter jumped into the water and retrieved the limp body of little Muskrat.

"Stupid Muskrat," Wisageechak cursed. "Now we will all drown!"

"There is something in his paws!" exclaimed Beaver as they pulled Muskrat's body onto Turtle's back.

Wisageechak turned Muskrat onto his back and found he was clutching a chunk of mud in his little paws. It was a piece of the old earth, just big enough for Wisageechak to rebuild the land. Wisageechak rolled the mud in his fingers and sang a prayer song. The mud got bigger and bigger.

"Brother Turtle," said Wisageechak. "I will need to build the land on your back. You will have to grow larger for me to rebuild the whole of the earth."

"How will I do this?" asked Turtle.

"Beaver! Otter! Make yourselves useful and go catch him some fish so he can grow big enough to accommodate the land," commanded Wisageechak.

"You are very rude," chastised Beaver. "But we will do what must be done."

When there was enough room to walk around on the new land, Wisageechak breathed life back into Muskrat.

"What happened?" asked a groggy Muskrat.

"You did it!" explained Wisageechak. "But now I will need your help to fulfill my promise. Help Brother Beaver and Brother Otter catch fish to feed Brother Turtle so I can remake the earth."

Beaver, Otter, and Muskrat swam around catching fish and feeding them to Turtle, who ate and ate until his belly ached and his shell grew larger and larger.

"More fish! More fish!" Wisageechak shouted as he continued rebuilding the land.

Turtle kept growing bigger and bigger until he could gulp down entire schools of fish. Birds and animals flocked to the new land and grass and trees began to grow.

"My feet are touching the old earth!" exclaimed Turtle, who was now large beyond imagining. "But now my shell is so big, I can't move!"

"You have done enough," said Wisageechak. "Maybe you should have a rest."

Wisageechak began to sing a magic lullaby that lulled Turtle into a deep sleep, one he has not awoken from to this day. The rains fell regularly to keep the new earth clean, and drained out in rivers and creeks to the great water so it would not be submerged.

Creator then made the *Nehiyawak* to keep the harmony of the new earth and to keep Wisageechak and his mischief in check.

# MITĀTAHT NIKOTWĀSOSĀP

As the smoke figures began to dissipate, the children cheered and the fire returned to its normal light. "Now go back to your lodge and say your prayers of thanks to Creator, Mother Earth, and even little Muskrat," instructed Painted Turtle Man.

The children all groaned and mumbled about wanting to hear another story, but they left the Bear medicine lodge as instructed and returned to their homes.

As always, Little Grey Bear Boy, Flying Rabbit Boy, and Yellow Hawk Girl were the last to leave.

"Thank you for the story, *Moosum*," said Little Grey Bear Boy.

"It is I who should thank you for your magic," answered Painted Turtle Man, smiling.

"But *Moosum*, I did not do anything."

"You have done more than you know, my boy. Having the Grey-Eye magic added to the story is just as enjoyable for the teller as it is for the listener. Seeing the words come to life in the smoke reminds me of when your ancestor Grey Bear told me the same story when I was a boy."

"Tomorrow, I want to tell the story!" said Yellow Hawk Girl.

"One day, perhaps you will, my girl. Now go home to your parents and grandmother. They will be missing you. Little Grey Bear Boy, I will need you early to help with the sunrise ceremony, as usual."

"All right, *Moosum*," answered Little Grey Bear Boy. "I'll try to wake up on time."

Each of the three children gave Painted Turtle Man a hug and a kiss on the cheek and returned to their lodge.

Outside, in the centre of the circle of lodges, all the matriarchs but Soaring Star Woman stood around the village fire, talking. Around them, young people walked about in the shadows. The men carried their cedar flutes, hiding them from view to avoid being teased but keeping them ready to play should they see the girl they liked best.

Laughing Cloud Boy of the Eagle clan stood outside the Turtle lodge playing his love song. His efforts were rewarded when she opened her buffalo robe for him to share. The two stood face to face, whispering to one another while children pointed and laughed. The young lovers ignored them, aware only of one another.

"That's going to be you one day," said Little Grey Bear Boy as they passed Turtle lodge.

"*Awas*," laughed Flying Rabbit Boy.

"Rabbit loves the Turtle girls!" sang Yellow Hawk Girl.

The children entered the Bear lodge and found hides strewn across the poles, obscuring the sleeping areas from view.

"We are back!" announced Yellow Hawk Girl.

"So soon?" said White Willow Woman, pulling back the hide curtain.

"I'll have to ask Painted Turtle Man to tell longer stories," said Blue Elk Man and all the grownups laughed.

The children removed their moccasins and hung them by the fire. Yellow Hawk Girl yawned and the children made their way to their sleeping areas. They sat up and said their prayers before snuggling into their buffalo hides.

A little later, Walking Moon Woman returned to the Bear lodge, tidying up after the children and adding a little more wood to the fire to keep the lodge warm for the night.

"Any news about Soaring Star Woman?" Singing Doe asked.

"It's not good," answered Walking Moon Woman. "I'm afraid she will leave us any day now."

"She has to get better," said White Willow Woman. "What about Little Grey Bear Boy? Who will teach him the Grey-Eye magic?"

"We must prepare ourselves for whatever happens," the old woman sighed. "It is up to *Kitchi Manitou* to decide."

////

Early the next morning, Painted Turtle Man entered the Bear lodge quietly and roused Little Grey Bear Boy. "It's time," he whispered.

"Umnn...Do I have to?" Little Grey Bear Boy yawned and opened his droopy grey eyes.

"*Motch*, you don't have to, but it would not be the same without you."

Painted Turtle Man put some wood on the smouldering embers while Little Grey Bear Boy found his moccasins and wrapped a soft deer hide around his shoulders. His little sister and his cousin snuggled deeper into their buffalo robes and slept peacefully beside their parents.

Four of Painted Turtle Man's helpers were waiting for them outside in the cool morning air. The group followed the path out of the village and up the hill. When they came to the edge of a precipice, they stopped. The sunrise ceremony had been performed here every morning for many generations, ever since the *Nehiyawak* had returned to the old ways.

Painted Turtle Man's helpers rolled out a large elk hide and unpacked the sacred objects. They readied the pipe, built a small fire, and said the necessary prayers. When everything was ready, the six of them formed a semi-circle, facing east to greet the sun.

"Grandfather Sun!" began Painted Turtle. "We thank you for bringing your warmth and light to the earth. Life as we know it would not be possible without your blessing and we are truly grateful. We, the pitiful people of *Nisichawayasihk*, will try hard to make the very best of your blessing so as to honour you. We will smoke the peace pipe in the way of our ancestors and teach our children to hold true to the sacred ways. I will now light the pipe."

One of the helpers lit a twig in the small fire and offered it to

Painted Turtle Man. The medicine carrier began to puff white smoke, then offered the stem of the pipe to each of the seven sacred directions. When he had given thanks to all of creation, he offered the pipe to Little Grey Bear Boy. The young boy touched it to both of his shoulders and handed it to the older boy on his left. The older boys puffed on the pipe, trying unsuccessfully not to cough, and offered prayers. Painted Turtle Man took up his moonstone rattle and sang an ancient song, one the others had never heard before.

"I will ask my grandson to offer his prayers," said Painted Turtle Man.

"*Kitchi Manitou*!" prayed Little Grey Bear Boy. "Thank you for my mother and father. Thank you for my cousin and my sister. Thank you for my *nookum* and for Painted Turtle Man too. Help me to learn the ways of the *Nehiyawak* so I can take care of my family when I am big."

Painted Turtle Man nodded. "We thank you, *Kitchi Manitou*, for giving the people of *Nisichawayasihk* all of the gifts of Mother Earth. We give thanks for the joy we will experience and the hardships that will make us strong. The waters that will refresh us. The plants and animals that will feed and clothe us. If today should be the day you call us back to the Spirit World, we will come along willingly, as children returning to the arms of a loving parent. We will know no fear in this life, for all things are your will. We ask only for the wisdom to know how best to serve you, Creator. All my relations, *ekosani*."

"All my relations!" repeated Little Grey Bear Boy with the others.

The participants shook hands and went about repacking the sacred objects. They passed a water skin around and let the fire burn down. They covered the smouldering embers with sand. As they walked back to the village, Painted Turtle Man reminded his followers of the work to be done this day. He had just begun explaining the ingredients that would be needed to make a tea to break a fever when a Crane clan warrior came running up the path.

"*Moosum*!" said the young man to Painted Turtle Man. "You must hurry! Soaring Star Woman is leaving this world and she is calling for him." The man did not look at Little Grey Bear Boy, who was the only one not to understand that it was him she was calling for.

Painted Turtle Man grabbed Little Grey Bear Boy by the arm and started to run, leaving the younger men behind. "We must be as swift as the deer," he said.

"But I don't...." The sound of running hooves cut the boy's words short as, one after another, large blue deer jumped over his head.

Painted Turtle Man leaped into the air, becoming a great blue stag with large antlers.

"You did it my boy, climb onto my back!" the stag commanded. Little Grey Bear Boy, confused as to what part he played in the transformation, did as instructed and the herd galloped all the way back to *Nisichawayasihk*, heading straight for the Eagle lodge. They slowed on approach, returning to human form as they arrived. Painted Turtle Man let Little Grey Bear Boy down off his back and escorted him in. Atop the lodge, a large black crow cawed loudly.

# MITĀTAHT TĪPAKOHPOSĀP

All of Soaring Star Woman's children, grandchildren, and great-grandchildren had gathered in the Eagle lodge. The old woman lay on the opposite side of the lodge, coughing now and then. The twins sat on either side of their grandmother, holding her small, soft hands, a steady stream of tears running down their faces.

"Bring him to me," said Soaring Star Woman weakly. "I need to speak to him."

Little Grey Bear Boy approached the clan mother, holding tightly to Painted Turtle Man. His eyes met the sullen faces of those gathered and he wondered if he had done something wrong. This was the first time he could not feel her magic.

"My boy," she began. "There is so much I meant to teach you. I am afraid my old body has given up too early. I wanted to wait until you were older to teach you the Grey-Eye magic. It will be difficult for you to learn all by yourself. I must tell you about my life before I go…" The old woman coughed several times, her chest rattling loudly.

"You don't have to do this, *Nookum*…"

The old woman composed herself and waved the twin away.

"I was once married to your ancestor, Grey Bear. I was a young girl, only sixteen summers, and I loved him dearly. He was a gentle and caring man. We were both Grey-Eyes and the people of *Nisichawayasihk* rejoiced at our union. We had a son, and he had the Grey-Eye magic too."

"Please, *Nookum*. Don't speak of him," implored the younger twin, but again Soaring Star Woman waved a hand to silence her.

"For a time, I was happier than I have ever been in this life, but it wasn't long before I realized there was something not right about my new child. He wasn't caring like his father. He was mischievous and cruel, even as a boy. He thought himself better than the other children and was quick to anger. But these feelings I buried. The people began to lose their harmony, but they were scared to speak out against the Grey-Eyed magic. I was blinded by a mother's love and did not see what he had become. The people began to call him Dark Cloud Man, since it seemed the sky would darken whenever he was near. When he began to walk the warrior's road he fell in love with your grandmother, Walking Moon Woman."

"My *nookum*?"

"*Tapwe*," Soaring Star Woman answered with a cough. "She was his cousin and they would not have been able to wed even if she had returned his affections, which she did not. Who could love someone with a cruel heart? She married Rising Hawk Man, and my son became jealous. Sought to destroy him. He began to use the Grey-Eyed magic against him, trying to make his death seem like an accident."

"I was a boy then," said Painted Turtle Man. "But I still remember."

"*Tapwe*." Soaring Star Woman nodded at the old man. "One day, during the buffalo hunt in the south, he tried to make the herd trample Rising Hawk Man. That was when Grey Bear…my husband… used his magic to save the young warrior and was himself killed in the stampede. That was the day I saw my son for what he truly was, a Red-Eye."

The old woman put her hand to heart and swallowed hard.

"His eyes burned like fire and he was blinded. The clan mothers decided to punish him for his misdeeds. Some called for his life to be taken in return for Grey Bear's. Since it was my son and husband affected, I was given the final say. He had already lost his sight, so I chose banishment. I thought it justice then, but now I realize I just couldn't bear to lose them both.

"Some years later he came back. My son. His eyesight had returned and he had followers. He was strong with the Red-Eye magic. He had come for revenge. Fiery stones rained down from the night sky, striking the earth with great force. I tried to use my magic to protect the village, but he was so strong. Your grandfather, Rising Hawk Man, and many others were killed. I managed to overpower him and his warriors, but I still could not bring myself to kill him. He alone escaped, vowing to come back one day and finish what he started. This has been my everlasting shame and regret. I could not take this with me to the next life."

"*Ekosi, Nookum*," said the elder twin. "Speak no more of this."

"You must try to help the people of *Nisichawayasihk*," Soaring Star Woman said, shaking through a cold sweat yet ignoring her grand-daughter. "You must help them to see the best in themselves. Most of all, you must protect them from the Red-Eyes, especially Dark Cloud Man. They will seek to unbalance our harmony and divide the *Nehiyawak*. You have the ability to stop them. Like I should have. I am sorry I must leave you with this burden. Listen to Painted Turtle Man. He can help you discover what is inside…"

With that confession and final instruction, Soaring Star Woman, matriarch of the Eagle clan and leader of the Circle of Clan Mothers, drew her last breath on Mother Earth. The crow atop the lodge cawed loudly and flew off. The matriarch's granddaughters took up the mourning wail, the sound of their pain rising on the air. Painted Turtle Man took Little Grey Bear Boy by the arm and led him out.

"What is happening, *Moosum*?" Little Grey Bear Boy asked, the tears turning his eyes a softer grey.

Painted Turtle Man's gaze was solemn. "Our grandmother has gone home to the Spirit World. You must not speak her name until this time next summer. That is the way of the *Nehiyawak*. We must all go back when we are called by *Kitchi Manitou*."

"But why, *Moosum*? Why would *Kitchi Manitou* want us to be sad?"

"Some mysteries cannot be explained by us," answered Painted Turtle Man. "Know we will see her again in the next life. For now, we must take care of the ones who are still here and will be suffering."

Painted Turtle Man led Little Grey Bear Boy back to the Bear lodge, trying to hide his own fear and sadness. Without the Eagle clan matriarch, the road ahead was going to be long and difficult. Painted Turtle Man knew that he too was growing old. Would there be time enough to teach the boy?

The death of Soaring Star Woman, the leader of the Circle of Clan Mothers, was hard for the people of *Nisichawayasihk*. They prepared for the funeral, mourning her passing for four days. She had been a great listener and a considerate leader, and while no one could replace her, the clan mothers had to appoint someone to lead the circle. The Eagle twins had been appointed to lead the Eagle clan, and when it came time for the election, they expected the other clan matriarchs to appoint them in their grandmother's place. But the people elected Standing Sun Woman of the Crane clan as clan mother to all of *Nisichawayasihk*. The Eagle twins had to be satisfied with the responsibility of leading the Eagle clan as its new joint matriarchs.

"How could they be so stupid?" said the younger Eagle twin on returning to their lodge.

"Standing Sun Woman's time is not long. Another election of the Circle of Clan Mothers is not far off," replied the elder Eagle twin.

"That old crow could live forever."

"We just need to make sure that when she does go, we are ready."

"The Turtles and the Bears will never support us…"

"Oh yes they will," said the elder twin with no trace of doubt.

# MITĀTAHT AYINĀNĪWOSĀP

For the most part, life returned to the way it had been for generations. In his ninth summer, Little Grey Bear Boy devoted himself to Painted Turtle Man. Instead of playing with other children he was often busy learning the sacred teachings of the medicine wheel and the secrets of the plant world. He still had responsibilities to his family and would often pick berries, catch fish, snare rabbits, and shoot birds to contribute. Much of what he foraged he gave to the struggling Turtle clan. Blue Elk Man always smiled at this, proud of his son's generous nature.

Little Grey Bear Boy tried to learn the Grey-Eye magic, but he did not yet understand how it worked. Often, the magic manifested itself in those around him as he sat daydreaming. On more than one occasion, Little Grey Bear Boy turned his cousin into an otter or a duck as they swam, and once he burned Painted Turtle Man's hand with blue flame when making a fire for a ceremony. At no time did they feel the loss of Soaring Star Woman more than when Little Grey Bear Boy struggled to understand the magic in him.

"The Grey-Eye magic will be with you when you most need it," Painted Turtle Man would say. "Creator's gifts are not to be used for day-to-day nonsense. Learn the ways of your ancestors and they will give you guidance."

"*Tapwe*, I know you are right," Little Grey Bear Boy would respond.

"I am glad you are here to teach me."

During these times, Painted Turtle Man reminded himself of the winters after his wife's passing, when he seemed so alone in this world. He had despaired, feeling like his life would never again have meaning. The old man was always humbled by these memories. He would never have thought the Creator would save the best days of his journey for the end.

"*Moosum*," Little Grey Bear Boy asked one day while they dug for wild ginseng in the forest, "tell me how the Seven Teachings came to the *Nehiyawak*."

"Again, my boy?"

"It is one of my favourite stories." Painted Turtle Man leaned back and looked up into the sky. It was not quite midday and they already had enough roots for the winter. They were near the river and could hear the gentle voice of the water running across the rocky shore through the trees. A cool breeze was blowing and the large pine trees swayed and creaked in rhythm with the wind. It was as good a time as any for a teaching.

"Many generations ago," Painted Turtle Man began, "a great sickness fell over the land. All of the *Nehiyawak* were living in fear and despair. There was no harmony or unity amongst them, no clans and no villages. The strong preyed upon the weak, the smart took advantage of the simple, and the elders were left to starve when they could not find their own food."

Little Grey Bear Boy's bright grey eyes went wide at the thought.

"Two brothers walked along a path together, discussing the state of affairs in the world. They were hungry and had nowhere to call home. They wished something could be done to end the suffering and bring harmony to the land. As they walked along the path a white buffalo calf crossed in front of them. The brothers knew immediately that the animal was a sacred being. The white buffalo calf turned and began to walk towards them. As it did so it transformed into a beautiful woman in a dress of white."

"The White Buffalo Calf Woman!" said Little Grey Bear Boy.

"The elder brother looked upon her body and thought he would like to have this woman for himself. As their eyes met, the elder brother burst into flames and was immediately destroyed for his bad-hearted thoughts."

Little Grey Bear Boy gasped.

"The younger brother averted his eyes from the woman out of respect. Her beauty belonged to her and it was up to her alone to decide whom to share it with. The White Buffalo Calf Woman presented the young man with the White Buffalo Calf peace pipe and gave to him the Seven Teachings."

"I can name them all, *Moosum*!" exclaimed Little Grey Bear Boy.

"Well go ahead then," laughed Painted Turtle Man.

"Respect, courage, love," began Little Grey Bear Boy confidently, "humility...honesty...truth and..."

"And? The last one?"

"Umm..." Little Grey Bear Boy thought hard. "Wisdom!"

"That's right, my boy." Painted Turtle Man patted his shoulder. "She gave him the Seven Teachings and explained to him the seven sacred animals that could teach him best."

"But Grandfather, if he was told the Seven Teachings why did he still have to learn the seven sacred animals?"

"Ohhh," said Painted Turtle Man, "do you think because you can name the Seven Teachings you know the Seven Teachings?"

"Well, what's the difference?"

"If someone asks you what my name is and you tell them, does that mean they know everything there is to know about me?"

"*Motch.*"

"Definitely not," confirmed Painted Turtle Man. "It takes a lifetime to truly know another person, and even after fifty years together, they could still surprise you. To learn the Seven Teachings takes a lifetime of living them."

Painted Turtle Man pulled a large ginseng root out of the ground and showed it to Little Grey Bear Boy. Not to be outdone, the boy pulled on the root he had been digging and it snapped. They both laughed.

"I think I understand, *Moosum*. The Bear teaches courage—my mother taught me that one."

"Yes. And the Wolf teaches humility."

"What does that mean, 'humility'?"

"It means understanding you are not greater than any of Creator's children. This includes the plants, animals, bugs, other people, and even the rocks."

"Oh," wondered Little Grey Bear Boy. "Not even Yellow Hawk Girl?"

"Especially not your sister!" laughed Painted Turtle Man. "With the seven sacred teachings of the peace pipe, the young man returned to the *Nehiyawak* and shared this new knowledge with them. Soon, the *Nehiyawak* began to share with one another and to look after their families. The clans were formed and many people could live in villages together and work towards the greater good. Harmony came to the land and the *Nehiyawak* became happy, living the way *Kitchi Manitou* intended for us."

"That is my favourite story," said Little Grey Bear Boy dreamily.

"But the story does not end there, my boy," added Painted Turtle Man as he covered the hole he had dug and offered a pinch of tobacco.

"There's more?"

"There will be," explained Painted Turtle Man. "In my dreams I have foreseen a time when the *Nehiyawak* will turn away from the seven sacred teachings and from all of the teachings of the medicine wheel. They will not give thanks and praise to *Kitchi Manitou*, or practice the sacred ceremonies of their ancestors. In that time, the White Buffalo Calf Woman will return and another young person will have to take the peace pipe back to the *Nehiyawak*."

"When will this happen, *Moosum*?" asked the boy.

"That, I have not seen."

The two finished up their medicine-picking in a contemplative silence. Little Grey Bear Boy trusted the old man's dreams and had faith that when Painted Turtle Man said something would happen, it would. After all, the old man had foreseen his own birth. This new prophesy, however, Little Grey Bear Boy hoped would never come to pass. Perhaps this time Painted Turtle Man would be wrong.

# MITĀTAHT KĪKĀ-MITĀHTOSĀP

Upon returning to the village, Painted Turtle Man and Little Grey Bear Boy came upon a long-anticipated sight. Visitors had arrived in *Nisichawayasihk,* carrying with them exotic goods from their homelands. Known to the *Nehiyawak,* their leader was a man they called simply 'the Trader.' Large, loud, and jovial, the Trader swept in with his wares—trinkets and tools, rare medicines and jewels—but also, and more importantly, news.

The Trader's company was a group of people from far away corners of Turtle Island. A young woman with blue lines and dots running from her lips to her chin smiled at Little Grey Bear Boy. He looked away immediately, not wanting to burst into flames like the elder brother in the White Buffalo Calf story.

"Let's go and gather our things from the medicine lodge while the caravan sets up the big lodge," suggested Painted Turtle Man. "I hope they have desert sage this time. Maybe you can get some abalone shells to make something for your mother."

The people of *Nisichawayasihk* milled about the big lodge, looking at the items up for trade. There were all manner of beads, shells, furs, stone, jade, turquoise, obsidian, tobacco, herbs for cooking and for medicine, and all manner of toys and trinkets from across Turtle Island. The traders spent their year travelling and trading with the villages as well as other caravans instead of hunting and fishing. Most would live this way for only a time, in order to experience life outside of their own villages, coming and going as it suited them. Others, like the Trader, chose to live their whole lives this way. The villagers brought forward dried meats and pemmican as well as crafts made during the winter months. Half the fun was deciding what to trade and for how much. The *Nehiyawak* loved to get a good bargain, then brag about it to their family and friends.

The matriarchs of the village were mostly interested in trading for information that would help them determine when and where to send the hunters for buffalo. They stood in front of the Trader's big lodge, speaking to him as he waved people in. They shared their own news, namely, that Soaring Star Woman had passed into the Spirit World.

"I am very sorry for your loss," said the Trader sincerely. "I am sure she will continue to bless us from the Great Mystery. There seem to be fewer and fewer Grey-Eyes these days. You are not the only village without one."

"Thank you for your kindness," said Walking Moon Woman. "But we are not without the Grey-Eye magic."

As she said this, Little Grey Bear Boy ran up. "*Nookum. Nookum.* Look what I got for you." Little Grey Bear Boy held up a small vessel that seemed to shine light on its own. "You can make your tea with it. The man I traded with said it is made of 'copper' and comes from his people in the west. They are called the *Git Hayetsk*, the people of the copper shield, and they live beside the great water and travel in canoes bigger than a lodge! And they have trees that reach up all the way to the clouds. I want to go there someday, *Nookum.*"

"This is my grandson, Little Grey Bear Boy," said Walking Moon Woman as she accepted the copper pot. "Thank you my boy, this is just what I needed. *Hiy, hiy!*"

"I see," said the Trader, turning to the boy. "*Tansi*, young warrior. Did you get a good deal?"

Little Grey Bear Boy turned his bright grey eyes on the Trader. Despite towering over the small boy, the man at once felt powerless under the boy's upward gaze. "I sure did! I traded some of the medicines I picked with my *moosum.*"

"He means my cousin, Painted Turtle Man," said Walking Moon Woman.

"Excellent," said the Trader, recovering. "Painted Turtle Man's medicines will be needed when we go east. There has been some sickness amongst the villages out that way."

"Did you get something for your mother?" Walking Moon Woman asked.

"Not yet. I better go back before all the good stuff is gone." With that, the excited child ran off.

"You are blessed, Walking Moon Woman," said the Trader. He turned to the other matriarchs: "You are all truly blessed."

"*Tapwe*," the Bear matriarch responded, watching her grandson until he disappeared into the big lodge. "Has there been any word of the Red-Eyes?"

"Unfortunately, there has. Perhaps we should discuss this away from the others. I don't want to spread fear and disrupt the harmony of the village."

"I agree," said Walking Moon Woman. Looking at the other matriarchs, she said, "We will hold council this evening after the feast."

Back at the Trader's big lodge, Little Grey Bear Boy and friends were admiring the boy's latest acquisition, a turquoise necklace for his mother.

"Let me see, let me see!" demanded Yellow Hawk Girl.

"Careful, I don't want you to break it," answered Little Grey Bear Boy, handing his sister the necklace.

"What did you trade?" asked one of the other boys.

"All of my toothache medicine," answered Little Grey Bear Boy proudly.

"That's it?" asked the boy. "He probably gave you a deal because of your grey eyes."

"*Motch*. That medicine is hard to make and you need different roots and herbs. You have to put in the right amount of each."

"So what? Anyone could dig up that stuff."

"We'll see if you are still saying that," interjected Flying Rabbit Boy, "when you get a toothache and come crawling to the Bear medicine lodge." Flying Rabbit Boy limped around, holding his jaw and moaning. The children laughed while they waited their turn to examine the necklace.

"I wish *I* could get something nice for our mother," said Yellow Hawk Girl.

"It will be from both of us," said Little Grey Bear Boy. "You can be the one to give it to her."

"*Tapwe*? Best brother!"

"How would you know," teased Flying Rabbit Boy. "You only have one."

The children's laughter was drowned out by the sound of a large drum.

"People of *Nisichawayasihk*!" announced a Crane clan warrior. "Take notice! The Dog Soldier Society is taking in a new warrior."

All the people nearby stood up to show their respect. The senior warrior of the Dog Soldiers stood before a large hide covered by furs. The warriors of the Dog Soldier Society had assembled, dressed in their finest regalia, faces painted as though they were going to battle. A young man entered the circle, flanked by two warriors, one of whom was Blue Elk Man, himself a Dog Soldier.

"Show your respect!" boomed the Crane clan warrior. "A new warrior walks among you. He was called Laughing Cloud Boy, but now he needs a man's name."

The senior warrior of the Dog Soldiers spoke next. "This boy has proven himself a man in the eyes of the *Nehiyawak*. He has gone on the hunt alone and returned with meat to feed his family. Any man who is capable of this is strong enough to start his own family. Before he can be considered by any woman who would have him, he must put away childish things."

As the senior warrior said this, one of the others removed the furs to reveal the young man's childhood possessions scattered across the hide.

"A man is not a man who cannot make his way by the sweat of his efforts and by the skill of his own two hands. Therefore, he will begin to walk man's road with nothing, just as he was born and the same as when he dies. Let any who is in need come forward and receive these things for which this man no longer has use."

There was an awkward silence as no one stepped forward to claim the possessions. The fierce pride on the young man's face was starting to drain away. Little Grey Bear Boy saw this and began to feel bad for the young warrior, as did his sister beside him. No sooner had they each had the thought to go up, than was Flying Rabbit Boy thrown forward. As he walked out, he looked back at his cousin with a red-faced scowl.

"Come forward Flying Rabbit Boy of the Bear clan!" announced the senior warrior of the Dog Soldiers.

"You are brave to come first," said Laughing Cloud Boy. "For that, I will give you my most prized possession."

The young warrior reached down to his assortment of childhood items and picked up a short bow made of ash. The assembled crowd murmured in approval at this gift, fitting for a youth like Flying Rabbit Boy.

"With this bow, I killed the moose that proved me capable of walking man's road. May it serve the same purpose for you when the time is right."

The crowd cheered at this example of continuity and the promise of a strong future for the people of *Nisichawayasihk*. The other children, having seen Flying Rabbit Boy's good luck, ran forward to claim an item from the young warrior. When all of Laughing Cloud Boy's childhood possessions were gone, the senior warrior continued the ceremony.

"Who sponsors this young warrior to join the ranks of the Dog Soldier Society?"

"I, Blue Elk Man of the Marten clan, warrior of the Dog Soldier Society, present this warrior."

"Blue Elk Man, will you hold him to the oath of our sworn brotherhood?"

"I will," answered Blue Elk Man solemnly.

"We would hear him take the oath," said the senior warrior.

"I hereby pledge," began Laughing Cloud Boy, "to defend the weak, to feed the hungry, and to hold my ground no matter what the cost. I will give my life so others may live and I will never take a life, even in battle. This I swear in Creator's light, and before all the

*Nehiyawak* gathered here today, and before you my brothers of the Dog Soldier Society, until *Kitchi Manitou* calls me home."

The warriors of the village and visitors from the Trader's caravan whooped and the women ululated in acknowledgement of the vow.

"We have all heard the pledge," said the senior warrior, "and have accepted the promise of this young man, that he will serve the *Nehiyawak* until his dying day. He was called Laughing Cloud Boy of the Eagle clan, but he will be called this no longer. From this day forward he has earned the name Sharp Stone Man of the Eagle clan, warrior of the Dog Soldier Society!" The men whooped and cheered and sounded the drum loudly. His face beaming with pride, the newly minted warrior's father came forward and put a new deer hide shirt over his son's head. Blue Elk Man came forward and tied a long rope with a wooden stake around the warrior's waist, the symbol of the Dog Soldier Society.

"Receive the rope of the Dog Soldiers," continued the senior warrior. "Let all of our enemies know that when a Dog Soldier plants his stake into the earth, he will hold his ground even if it costs him his life."

The men who held the drum took up a beat and sang an honour song as the people of *Nisichawayasihk* lined up to pay tribute to the new warrior with a hug or handshake. Little Grey Bear Boy and his cousin Flying Rabbit Boy paid close attention to the proceedings, imagining the day when they would be called to walk man's road. They fell in line with the crowd to shake hands with the newly appointed Dog Soldier.

"You two will make fine warriors one day," said a voice from behind them.

Little Grey Bear Boy turned to see a man with a hooked nose like the desert people far to the south and a scar on the left side of his mouth. He seemed young but had small crow's feet wrinkles behind his eyes, so of his age Little Grey Bear Boy could not be sure. Painted Turtle Man had once explained that in the deserts far to the south the sun is much hotter and it is always summer, never winter. Perhaps the climate of this man's homeland accounted for his looks.

Little Grey Bear Boy had received more than his fair share of attention, but there was something strange about the way the young man looked at him. Maybe he had never seen a Grey Eye before.

"You really think so?" asked Flying Rabbit Boy.

"*Tapwe*," said the strange man. "If you have the right arrows, you will be killing your own moose, elk, or even buffalo. I just so happen to have some fine arrows that would go well with your new bow."

"My *moosum* says a hunter should make his own arrows," explained Little Grey Bear Boy, "so that if he should miss, he can blame no one but himself."

"Your *moosum* sounds like a wise man. I do have other things that may interest you. I was a young boy myself once and I know how hard it can be to prove yourself. If you come and see my wares I might find a small gift for you."

Little Grey Bear Boy was uneasy. Painted Turtle Man had taught him that if something seemed too good to be true, it probably was. On the other hand, he did not want to seem rude to one of the Trader's men.

"That is very kind of you," said Little Grey Bear Boy, "but we must help our mothers with the feast. Perhaps we can come and see you later. I am sure our fathers will want to trade."

Flying Rabbit Boy shot his cousin a glare but was subdued by the bright flash of grey that shot back.

The boys reached the front of the line. They shook hands with the new warrior, and Flying Rabbit Boy thanked him for the bow. The boys found their mothers and set to work. Until they earned their warrior names, they served the elders at a feast. When everyone was fed, the fire was built up. The drum sounded and the people began to sing and dance. The celebrations continued into the night, with the Trader's caravan performing some new dances. The hurt brought by the loss of Soaring Star Woman was starting to heal.

The Trader and his caravan remained in *Nisichawayasihk* for three more days, conducting business with the willing. Before they left, Little Grey Bear Boy took his father out to find the stranger with the scar on his mouth, but no one seemed to know the man, the Trader least of all.

# NĪSTANAW

Little Grey Bear Boy returned to his daily chores and work, collecting fire wood and setting rabbit snares. Flying Rabbit Boy was anxious to learn to hunt with his new bow, but it was made of ash and required a lot of strength to draw—strength the boy didn't yet have. Brown Shield Man told his son to keep trying, explaining that in trying he would gain the muscles needed to use it properly. Little Grey Bear Boy was always happy to go out into the forest with his cousin. He often stopped to collect a plant or herb that Painted Turtle Man had taught him was good for medicine. Little Grey Bear Boy's meandering gave Flying Rabbit Boy plenty of time to practice with the bow.

Life had improved greatly for the people of *Nisichawayasihk* since the winter of Little Grey Bear Boy's birth. The boy himself did not believe he had anything to do with the good fortune of the village, but this did not stop the *Nehiyawak* from feeling they benefitted from the presence of the Grey-Eyed boy. They gave him thanks or gifts for what they perceived as his influence. The boy would pass the gifts on to those in need and try to remember what Painted Turtle Man had taught him: thanks is due to *Kitchi Manitou* for all things and to Mother Earth for her bounty. In truth, Little Grey Bear Boy was happiest away from the village, out in the forest, where he would speak to the plants, rocks, and animals, even if they rarely spoke to him.

"Look, I've got it!" said Flying Rabbit Boy, his drawstring arm shaking hard from side to side as he pulled.

"You've barely pulled it halfway back," observed Little Grey Bear Boy with a smile. The two continued on with their hunt, managing to track down a rabbit, but Flying Rabbit Boy's clumsiness with the bow gave the rabbit ample time to get away.

It was midsummer and food was plentiful, so the boys were able to laugh at their poor results. When Grandfather Sun was high in the sky, they stopped by a small lake to cool off with a swim. They laughed and played and splashed in the water, children still.

As the day continued into late afternoon, the boys made their way home. They were free to roam the village and surrounding forest when the sun was up, but they had to return home before dark. The boys arrived at the Bear lodge to find their mothers and grandmother cooking the evening meal. White Willow Woman wore the turquoise necklace her children had acquired from the Trader's caravan. Painted Turtle Man was there helping Yellow Hawk Girl work on a corn husk doll.

The grey-haired matriarch of the Bear clan was enjoying this quiet time with her family after the excitement of the Trader's visit, but could not push away some troubling news. The Trader had reported that Red-Eye warriors had attacked some villages to the west, killing the men, children, and elders and taking the young women as prisoners. Walking Moon Woman prayed to *Kitchi Manitou* for protection and for the young women, who had been captured for some unknown purpose. She raised the point with the Circle of Clan Mothers that the village was vulnerable without the presence of their former leader, but the Trader had reassured the matriarchs that these troubles were very far away—near the Holy Mountains.

When the evening meal was ready, the Bear clan gathered together in a circle. Walking Moon Woman offered the prayers.

"Oh, *Kitchi Manitou*," she prayed. "Thank you for your blessings and your bounty. Thank you for keeping us together as a family. Give us the guidance to remain united with one another. Please share your blessings and guidance with families less fortunate. You have been very generous to the Bear clan and we give you thanks and praise. All my relations, *ekosani*."

"All my relations!" repeated the family.

The Bears began to enjoy their meal of fresh moose meat, wild rice, and berries. The meat had been cut into small pieces and spiced with cooking herbs that Singing Doe had acquired from the caravan.

"*Moosum,* is there going to be a story tonight?" Yellow Hawk Girl asked.

"Not tonight, my girl," smiled Painted Turtle Man. "The *Nehiyawak* have had plenty of late nights these last few days. I want to give the families some time together to give thanks for the blessings we have received. Tomorrow we will begin preparations for a sweat lodge, for the *Nehiyawak* to cleanse themselves of want and desire so life can return to normal. We will have to work hard to make the necessary preparations for the coming winter. As always, the people of *Nisichawayasihk* must store enough dried meat and fish to last the hard-faced moons of Old Man Winter."

"*Tapwe,*" said Walking Moon Woman. "Especially the Turtle clan. They have so many small children to feed right now and too few hunters."

"We will remember them in our prayers," agreed Painted Turtle Man. "We will remember them also when we are able to share. They have always been kind to our clan."

"Once I get my new bow working," said Flying Rabbit Boy, "I'll go and shoot an elk and give it to the Turtle clan. Then maybe one of the Turtle girls will choose me for a husband."

"*Awas,*" exclaimed Singing Doe. "I am the only woman you have to impress!"

"I thought that was my job," laughed Brown Shield Man. The whole family laughed too.

"When did you prove yourself a warrior, father?" Little Grey Bear Boy asked.

Blue Elk Man looked up from his meal and contemplated the question. "A warrior must prove himself every day of his life," he answered.

"Can you tell us about the first time?"

"Yes, I remember the day. It was an elk. I went out hunting with my father. We had been tracking the elk for two days and we came upon a small creek. The tracks led into the water and we could not tell on which side of the bank the elk had come out. My father made me cross the creek to search for tracks on the other side. We walked along the creek together and it began to widen and deepen. We were beginning to worry we had followed the creek in the wrong direction but then I found fresh tracks on my side and signalled my father."

Blue Elk Man paused to take a sip of water.

"He indicated for me to have a look around while he back-tracked to find a better place to cross. I followed the tracks and came upon the elk suddenly. It was grazing in a small patch of grass and wildflowers. I was clumsy and it noticed me immediately. I froze and the elk froze and stared at me, waiting for me to do something. My father was not close enough and I knew any sudden movement would cause the elk to flee. So very quietly and carefully I drew an arrow, moving slowly, with my heart pounding in my chest. I raised my bow, trying to control my breath. I shot the elk through the heart. It didn't happen the way I expected. I remember it kept looking at me and then just…fell over. I was still frozen when my father came upon me and clapped me on the back. We went to retrieve the arrow together and found the elk lying in a patch of blue flowers. We began to make our prayers for our brother elk. Then we prepared the carcass for the long journey back to the village.

"We returned to the village and shared the meat with the *Nehiyawak*. I was inducted into the Dog Soldier Society by my uncle. It happened much the same way as you saw the young warrior the other day. They called me 'Blue Elk Man' because of the place where the elk had lain."

"*Tapwe?*" said Little Grey Bear Boy. "That is a very good story."

"Actually," said Blue Elk Man, "it saddens my heart to think of that day. I have since taken the lives of many of our brother animals, but I always remember that first time. When I met the gaze of the elk, I always wondered if there would have been something else if I had not killed it. Perhaps it would have spoken to me and we would have become friends. I was thinking of my family when I made the kill, but I still felt guilty afterwards. My father helped to guide me through those feelings and reminded me that we must live in harmony with all of creation."

"*Tapwe*, well said," remarked Painted Turtle Man. "A man does not kill so he can brag to his fellow man. When one of our animal brothers presents itself to a hunter it is sacrificing itself for the good of the *Nehiyawak*. We must always honour our brother animals. We need them for food and furs. That is why we make every effort to see that the entire animal finds a purpose and that nothing is ever wasted. That would dishonour the sacrifice made by our brother animals."

"I feel sorry for the elk," said Yellow Hawk Girl. "Maybe he just wanted to play with you."

"You can't play with an elk," said Flying Rabbit Boy, rolling his eyes. "Their antlers are too big."

"Yes I can," argued Yellow Hawk Girl. "You'll see when I'm bigger."

"Don't argue with your cousin," Singing Doe said to her son.

"I remember when you and your father came home that day," White Willow Woman said, smiling. "That was the day I started to admire you."

Blue Elk Man blushed and looked down at his food.

"In any event," continued Painted Turtle Man, hoping to save Blue Elk Man from further embarrassment, "we are honoured to have you in the Bear clan."

"*Hiy, hiy*," agreed Walking Moon Woman.

"What about you, father?" asked Flying Rabbit Boy.

"Well," said Brown Shield Man, "I am not sure my story is quite as exciting as your uncle's."

"Please?" pleaded Yellow Hawk Girl, always hungry for a story.

"There isn't much to tell," Brown Shield Man began. "When I was about fifteen summers, the warriors were being sent south for the buffalo hunt. I wasn't especially fast and my tracking skills were not so good. I was always heavier than the other boys. I was not allowed to hunt yet, since I had not proven myself. My uncle said I could come along and help carry his things. I was so grateful to him for not leaving me behind with the women and children."

Brown Shield Man paused, a little choked up by the memory of his late uncle.

"Our hunting party was soon joined by hunters from other villages. There were many families to feed and the buffalo had come late that year. The warrior societies held a council and decided we would attempt to run a herd into a buffalo pound in a ravine. I was allowed to help build the buffalo pound, and because I was heavy, they said I could wave one of the hides to scare the herd into the pound."

"That can be a very dangerous job," said Painted Turtle Man.

"Everything was going very well," recalled Brown Shield Man. "But then the herd turned on us. The thundering hooves were coming towards me and some of the younger warriors. The earth shook beneath our feet. I raised my hide, waving it hard and yelling, but still the herd thundered towards us. I knew I would not be fast enough to get away from them and my only chance was to keep waving. The others were already getting set to run for it. I took a step toward the herd, still waving my hide high and yelling as loud as I could. My throat burned. Just as I was about to be trampled, the herd turned. We sealed the pound and trapped the herd.

"Some of the senior warriors saw what I had done and came over to tease me. They said I looked like I had a big brown shield. And that is how I got my name."

The adults smiled and Brown Shield Man laughed, but Flying Rabbit Boy looked concerned. "I think that was very brave, father," he said.

"*Motch*, I don't know," shrugged Brown Shield Man.

"*Tapwe*, you probably saved the lives of some of those young warriors," said Blue Elk Man. "And you stood your ground. You should have been invited into the Dog Soldier Society."

Brown Shield Man nodded at the honour bestowed on him by the comment and said, "Well, my uncle sponsored me into the White Wolf Warrior Society."

"You are a hero, uncle!" said Yellow Hawk Girl excitedly.

"*Motch*..." blushed Brown Shield Man.

"You will always be a hero in my eyes," said Singing Doe, arching one eyebrow. Brown Shield Man smiled and laughed politely.

"What can I do to prove myself?" asked Flying Rabbit Boy.

"Boys are always in such a hurry to become men," said Walking Moon Woman.

"*Tapwe*," said Painted Turtle Man. "A man's time always comes too soon. When you have the duties and responsibilities of a man, you will wish you could be a carefree boy again."

"Is that how you felt?" asked Little Grey Bear Boy.

"I still feel that way sometimes." Few people remained who would remember the day the old man earned his name. Painted Turtle Man's eyes wandered from the circle and his thoughts drifted deep into distant memory.

"I think it is time we got ready for sleep," said Walking Moon Woman.

The family did not question the matriarch and went about the clean-up and prepared for the journey to the dream world.

Little Grey Bear Boy curled up, a dull ache in his chest. The manner in which he proved himself would largely influence the name he was given. Could he earn a hunter's name like his father? Would he perform a heroic deed like his uncle? Most of the time, Little Grey Bear Boy wandered the forest picking medicines with his *moosum*. Perhaps it would be Digging Root Man or Scraping Bark Man. Little Grey Bear Boy snickered at these silly thoughts. When he had mastered his magic, the *Nehiyawak* would be forced to give him a strong warrior name. Shining Thunderbird Man. Burning Eagle Man. Grey Bear, like his legendary ancestor.

As the fire died down, Little Grey Bear Boy looked up at the flickering shadows dancing off the lodge poles. They slowed their movements and lulled him to sleep.

# NĪSTANAW PIYAKOSĀP

The sun went down and the moon grew bright while Walking Moon Woman enjoyed a cup of tea made with her new copper pot. Everyone else slept. The night was warm so she did not add any wood to the cooking fire, and slowly the embers burned down. A cool breeze was blowing but it did not look like rain. Finally, Walking Moon Woman shuffled off to bed, falling asleep easily, like one wanting for nothing.

Near her, Little Grey Bear Boy dreamed. A fox searched along a rocky cliff face, sniffing at openings in the wall. It stopped at one opening marked with scratches and examined it carefully. The fox crept along the side of the rock wall and entered the cave. It made its way inside the den and sneaked around the large sleeping bears. Spying a sleeping bear cub, its ears perked up. The fox suddenly crouched down and began inching toward the cub, as though about to pounce and make a kill.

Little Grey Bear Boy awoke to the sound of Flying Rabbit Boy screaming. In the half-light he could see an upright figure. The tiny embers of the cooking fire exploded with a bright blue light. Others were screaming now as the dark figure held up his cousin. Blue Elk Man and Brown Shield Man jumped out of the dark, yelling and heading for the figure.

Little Grey Bear Boy went dead with fear. He wanted to do

something but didn't know how or what. Then he saw it: a stone knife coming down toward his cousin's chest. A flash and the knife struck the hard shell of a turtle's underbelly and broke with a loud snap. The figure dropped the turtle as the two Bear men grabbed him. The turtle rolled and landed on its belly, head and legs tucked into its shell. It peeked its head out as the men struggled on the floor of the lodge. The women were still screaming, angry now instead of scared. The turtle's arms and legs popped out and it limped under the hides and out of the lodge.

"Get me a rope!" yelled Blue Elk Man.

Little Grey Bear Boy snapped out of his shock. He found some strips of rawhide and handed them to his father. Blue Elk Man's eyes were cold and he was breathing hard. He picked the man up by the hair, forcing him into a kneeling position.

The warriors of the Wolf clan burst into the Bear lodge.

"Go and find the turtle!" yelled Brown Shield Man to one of the young Wolf warriors. "He is my son!"

The intruder's chest was heaving and gasped for air as he raised his head. He looked directly at Little Grey Bear Boy. The scar on his mouth stayed a neutral line while his lips formed a sneer. His eyelids were painted red. He was one of the Red-Eye's followers, a servant of evil.

The warriors of the village gathered around the Bear lodge. The entire village was awake and alarmed. The men were yelling as they dragged the intruder out into the centre of the circle of lodges. Some of the women stood by Walking Moon Woman, Singing Doe, and White Willow Woman, who cried and held her children close. A young Wolf warrior entered the circle, carrying a large turtle, which had again tucked itself into its shell. As the warrior approached Walking Moon Woman and the Bear clan, the turtle transformed into Flying Rabbit Boy.

In the torch light, they could see he was bleeding from his arm and shoulder and had a long white scratch across his chest. Painted Turtle Man grabbed Flying Rabbit Boy and carried him into the Bear medicine lodge. Singing Doe went too.

The women of the village, including the clan matriarchs, were having a difficult time controlling the men, who were coming forward to kick and strike the offender. Torture is not in the nature of the *Nehiyawak*, but attacking a child was a grave offence. The villagers were in chaos: some were crying, some were yelling and arguing. Trying to stay calm, the Circle of Clan Mothers gathered and conferred. Grandfather Sun was starting to come up. They would act quickly to restore harmony to *Nisichawayasihk*.

# NĪSTANAW NĪSOSĀP

To determine the right course of action, the Circle of Clan Mothers called for a sentencing circle. Since it was the Bear clan that had been offended, it was up to Walking Moon Woman to speak first.

"*Tansi*, people of *Nisichawayasihk*," she began, her voice dull with sorrow. "May the Grandmother Bear guide you in the ways of healing. Tonight, an intruder attacked my grandchild and my heart is heavy. This person has broken the harmony of the village and has taken away the safety I would normally feel in my home. I feel weak, as though I am no longer able to keep my family from harm. It is a bad feeling in my heart."

"As you all know," she continued, crying now, "it is the responsibility of the Bear clan to administer justice, but the hurt I feel inside would cloud my judgment in this matter. As such, I would leave the decision-making to my sisters, whom I trust to determine the right course."

She waved her arm to indicate the other clan matriarchs. The people of *Nisichawayasihk* murmured their approval at this wise decision.

The Eagle twins read each other's minds with a quick glance. The elder twin spoke on behalf of the Eagle clan. "*Tansi*, people of *Nisichawayasihk*. May the Grandmother Eagle bless you with her far-seeing eye. It is the judgment of the Eagle clan that to attack a child in this village is to attack all the children of the *Nehiyawak*. Therefore, the only option is to punish this intruder most severely."

There was a long period of silence while the *Nehiyawak* digested the gravity of the Eagle twin's statement. Some of the warriors began shouting their approval. Gliding Heron Woman of the Marten clan stepped forward.

"*Tansi*, people of *Nisichawayasihk*," she said. "May the Grandmother Marten guide you across Mother Earth to find all the gifts she gives. The Marten clan agrees with the judgment of the Eagle clan. Only in this way can our harmony be restored."

The Marten clan had always been strict in the application of laws. The Marten warriors whooped and stomped their approval, all except Blue Elk Man.

Green Wing Woman of the Turtle clan spoke next. "*Tansi*, people of *Nisichawayasihk*," she said. "May the Grandmother Turtle guide you in the ways of learning. It is the judgment of the Turtle clan that the intruder would not have the opportunity to learn anything by the most severe punishment. It would be better if he were instead marked, and lived out the rest of his life in banishment. Perhaps then he could have the chance to learn the error of his ways."

Under the Turtles' plan, the Red-Eye intruder would have his nose cut off, so that anyone he met would know he had committed a grave offense. He would not be welcome in any village of the *Nehiyawak* and would live the rest of his life in exile.

Talking Stone Woman of the Deer clan stepped forward to speak.

"*Tansi*, people of *Nisichawayasihk*," she began. "May the Grandmother Deer guide you in the ways of kindness. We agree with the judgment of the Turtle clan, that banishment in this case would be an act of kindness. The Grandmother Deer teaches that offensive actions should be dealt with in a kind and gentle manner when possible."

The Eagle twins were becoming noticeably annoyed by the judgments of the last two clans. They folded their arms and frowned.

The matriarch of the Wolf clan stepped forward to announce her judgment. "*Tansi*, people of *Nisichawayasihk*," she began, her tone apologetic. "May the Grandmother Wolf always protect your families.

As you are all aware, it is the duty of the Wolf clan to watch over the village and its children in the night. Last night, we failed in our responsibility and we sincerely ask for forgiveness of the *Nehiyawak*."

The warriors of the Wolf clan hung their heads.

"In order to restore the harmony," she continued, "not only do we support the Eagles and the Martens in punishing the intruder in the most severe manner, we also volunteer to undertake the task of exercising final judgment."

The people of *Nisichawayasihk* were astonished by the apology. No one who had supported the death penalty had considered who would carry out the sentence. To take the life of another human for any reason they believed to be a great offense against *Kitchi Manitou*. By taking on the responsibility, the Wolf clan was removing the other clans from this sin.

The matriarch of the Crane clan stood up, but it was her eldest daughter, Drifting Butterfly Woman, who stepped forward.

"*Tansi*, people of *Nisichawayasihk*," Drifting Butterfly Woman began on her mother's behalf. The matriarch of the clan in charge of internal communication had lost her voice in her old age. "May the Grandmother Crane bless you with the power of her voice. We can see that the council is divided in this matter, and therefore we must reserve our judgment. The Crane clan would hear an explanation from the intruder before making our decision."

The men of the village grumbled at this request but were quickly silenced by their matriarchs. Even an outsider who had committed a grave offense and had been caught in the act was entitled to speak for him or herself. Though the Cranes had not judged against the Eagles, the Eagle twins were offended.

"Perhaps our niece should ask the questions she wishes to have answered," said the elder twin, using the word 'niece' even though the two women were fairly close in age.

The people of *Nisichawayasihk* nodded in agreement and all eyes fell on Drifting Butterfly Woman. She raised her chin and marched over to where the intruder was guarded by Brown Shield Man and the other Wolf warriors. Mustering her courage, Drifting Butterfly Woman cleared her throat and said, "Speak your name."

The servant of the Red-Eye did not respond.

"Whom do you serve?" she continued.

Again, silence. The Eagle twins were basking in what seemed an apparent failure and an embarrassing moment for Drifting Butterfly Woman. The people of *Nisichawayasihk* were beginning to grumble. Drifting Butterfly Woman stepped toward the Red-Eye and grabbed him under the chin, forcing him to meet her gaze.

"Why did you attack the child?" she demanded, her booming voice calling to mind the voice of her mother long ago, reminding the others she was worthy to be called 'Crane clan.'

"I didn't mean to attack *that* child," he said clearly. "I meant to kill the other one."

The people of *Nisichawayasihk* roared with anger. One of the Wolf clan warriors kicked the Red-Eye intruder in the ribs and he collapsed, coughing and sputtering. Drifting Butterfly Woman raised her open hand, stopping the warriors from beating the man any further.

As he returned to kneeling, the servant of the Red-Eye began chuckling. He spit bright red blood in the direction of the warrior who had kicked him. Squaring himself up, he announced in a loud voice, "I serve the Red-Eye. I have vowed to bring death to any of the Grey-Eyed pretenders. I do not answer to women like you pathetic dogs. I serve the only true power in this life, and I will continue to serve him in the next. Dark Cloud Man alone can command me. And he will give me vengeance!"

Women and men screamed, children cried, and voices demanding justice rose up into the sky. Drifting Butterfly Woman stared hard into the eyes of the Red-Eye warrior, her face full of rage. The man was defiant at first, but finally he turned away. She looked towards her mother. The aged matriarch of the Cranes nodded solemnly. Drifting Butterfly Woman addressed the village.

"It is the judgment of the Crane clan," her voice boomed, quieting the villagers, "that this sworn enemy of the *Nehiyawak* face our most severe justice."

The matriarch of the Deer clan stepped forward again.

"We the Deer clan must thank the Cranes for their wisdom. We can see there is no kindness in this man's heart and therefore we change our judgment."

The warriors of the village whooped and stomped their approval. The matriarch of the Turtle clan stepped forward once more.

"We the Turtle clan see there is no room in this man's heart for learning a better way. Knowing he chooses not to learn from his mistakes, we too change our judgment in favour of our Eagle sisters."

With consensus, there was nothing left to do but administer the final justice.

On behalf of her mother, Drifting Butterfly Woman said: "Now that the Circle of Clan Mothers has made its decision, we ask all of the children to return to their lodges. The clan mothers do not want for their harmony to be upset any further by witnessing the punishment."

The Red-Eye warrior cackled as the women took the children home to their lodges. The Wolf clan warriors lined up shoulder to shoulder behind their matriarch, at the ready. One of the guards struck the prisoner hard in the stomach to silence him. Some of the younger boys who had not yet earned their warrior names but had seen at least fourteen summers were held back by their fathers, to bear witness. They were old enough to see what becomes of those who gravely offend the *Nehiyawak*.

The Eagle twins looked at each other, realizing their attempt to embarrass and discredit Drifting Butterfly Woman had backfired. They acted quickly to regain control. "*Tansi*, people of *Nisichawayasihk*," said the elder Eagle Twin. "Although our sister of the Wolf clan has offered the services of her warriors, the Eagle clan would offer our warriors to perform the deed that must be done."

It was in poor taste for the Eagles to introduce a new problem for the Circle of Clan Mothers at this particular time.

The matriarch of the Wolf clan stepped forward again. "I thank you, my sisters, but I would have a Wolf undertake the task in order to atone for our previous failure. Surely my sisters would allow the Wolf clan this opportunity to redeem itself in the eyes of the *Nehiyawak?*"

The elder twin looked thoughtful. "Perhaps there is a way to best serve this purpose. There is, after all, a Wolf in the Bear lodge. If he were to undertake the task, justice would best be satisfied." The younger Eagle twin smiled at her sister.

The remaining people were silent. Although he had been born of the Wolf clan, Brown Shield Man was known by one and all to be of a kind and gentle disposition—the last of the Wolf warriors who might be considered for such a task.

Brown Shield Man was taken aback by the request but he composed himself quickly and stood at attention. The other warriors looked at him, unable to hide their astonishment. All of the remaining people of *Nisichawayasihk* looked to Walking Moon Woman, his matriarch. Her eyes contained a mixture of sadness and anger. She had chosen to remove herself from the decision-making in order to uphold the sanctity of the sentencing circle. The Eagle twins had taken advantage of her decision and it was too late to take back her words. Without looking up, she nodded her head reluctantly.

Blue Elk Man approached his brother-in-law and drew out his hunting knife. He took Brown Shield Man's right hand and placed the knife in it, clasping it with both hands. Brown Shield Man looked at his brother-in-law, taking in the fierce resolve he saw there. Only he himself knew the pounding in his heart and the weakness in his legs as he walked toward the prisoner.

The Red-Eye warrior looked up at Brown Shield Man, his would-be executioner. Noting a hint of weakness there, he cackled, even as Brown Shield Man took his position and placed the blade of Blue Elk Man's knife under his chin.

"Do you have anything to say before you go?" asked the elder Eagle twin.

The Red-Eye warrior's chest rose and fell at an unnatural pace. The women began the death chant to begin preparing the way for his journey. All eyes of the remaining villagers were on the man with his eyelids painted red.

The man shouted in a loud voice, "LONG LIVE THE RED-EYE," as Brown Shield Man cut his throat in one swift swipe.

# NĪSTANAW NISTOSĀP

The warriors of the Marten clan began to prepare the body of the Red-Eye intruder for burial. The marten is an animal equally comfortable on land and water; so too were the Marten clan comfortable in both the Physical World and the Spirit World. Therefore, the duty of preparing the funeral rites often fell to them.

Although the intruder had been an enemy of the *Nehiyawak* and had been executed by the sentencing circle, the ancestors demanded they treat his body with the same respect and kindness they would show one of their own. Regardless of this person's mistakes in life, at one point in time he was some woman's baby. The Red-Eye warrior would be prepared for the next life as though he were as innocent as a child.

First, the Martens washed the filthy red paint from the intruder's eyes. They sewed up the wound across his neck and washed the dirt and blood from his body. They brushed and braided his hair and put fine clothes upon him. They covered him and conducted the mourning rituals for four days to purify him for his journey.

During this time, one of the warriors of the Eagle clan had been dispatched to alert the Trader that one of his men had betrayed them. On the fourth day of the funeral rites, the Trader arrived, alone. He came wishing to see the body of the strange man with the scar on his mouth.

"This was not one of my men," he explained. "He must have come to the village under the guise of being a member of my caravan. I am very sorry to the people of *Nisichawayasihk* that I had any involvement in the terrible tragedy."

"The clan mothers understand this was not your doing," said Walking Moon Woman. The other matriarchs nodded in agreement, all but the Eagle twins.

"Nevertheless, I must take some of the responsibility. Is there anything I can do to help restore your harmony?"

"There is something you could do for us," suggested Walking Moon Woman. "Perhaps it would be best to keep my grandson a secret in order to protect him from further danger."

"*Tapwe*! I will do my best. But there are many in my caravan I cannot speak for. Many of them saw the Grey-Eyed boy and some of them spoke and traded with him. I am sure they would all understand the need to keep our children safe. I can only promise to speak to each one and try to explain the importance of this decision."

"That is as much as anyone can ask," replied Walking Moon Woman. The other clan matriarchs were pacified. The Trader apologized sincerely to all the people of *Nisichawayasihk* and asked *Kitchi Manitou* to bless and protect them. He left, heading southeast, to return to his caravan.

Dark clouds were rolling in from the south and the air felt thick. The light breeze the people had enjoyed these last few days began to pick up, becoming a sharp wind. The people of *Nisichawayasihk* began preparing their lodges for the coming rain.

# NĪSTANAW NIYOSĀP

P ainted Turtle Man administered his healing to Flying Rabbit Boy. The shallow scratch across the boy's chest had formed a wide, white scar—a forever reminder that the Grey-Eyed magic saved his life. The worst damage was to his left arm and shoulder, where he had been cut by the knife. Painted Turtle sewed the wounds shut with sinew and applied a salve to speed the healing. He bound the arm and shoulder tightly.

"You will have to keep your arm tied up like this in order for the wounds to heal," he informed the boy. "And don't get it wet. I will have to change your wrappings every two days."

"How am I supposed to use my bow with only one arm?"

"I am afraid your bow will have to wait until your arm has healed. Don't worry. You are young and strong, I am sure it will be as good as new by the time of the next Grandmother Moon."

"But that will be forever. Now I will never impress the Turtle girls."

"You must learn patience, my boy," Painted Turtle Man said, trying not to laugh. "Maybe they will be impressed by the fact that you turned into a turtle."

This placated Flying Rabbit Boy only a little. He knew from the other children that the attack had not been meant for him. He was comforted by this fact, until he realized how vulnerable his best friend and cousin was. For a boy of only eight summers, it was a heavy burden to carry.

Walking Moon Woman, too, was dealing with the effects of the attack on her family. The Bear Lodge now seemed less of a home than before. There was a long gash in the hide covering the back of the lodge where the intruder had evidently cut his way in. Although she had the damaged hide removed, burned, and replaced with a new one, somehow the safety of her home had been broken. The grey-haired matriarch found it difficult to sleep at night so she would sit up, watching over her family.

The sleeplessness began to take a toll on Walking Moon Woman's health. Her grey hair began to show streaks of pure white and she moved about the lodge restlessly, doing and redoing chores or fidgeting with the centre fire. She wrung her hands constantly, producing a sound like a rope being stretched. The children had also been affected. Now they slept very close to their parents, waking often from troubled dreams.

Brown Shield Man was a warrior broken. Although a successful hunter who had killed many of his brother animals, he had never taken the life of a human being. The people of *Nisichawayasihk* began to avoid him, and the village children ran away whenever they saw him. Being a person who instilled feelings of fear in those around him weighed heavily on Brown Shield Man's heart.

The situation was hard for Singing Doe as well. She could not bear to see her husband in pain, but whenever she tried to console him with a hug or a simple touch, his body tensed and he pulled away. Try as she might to understand what he was going through, she could not accept that her once loving and affectionate husband was now distant and stony.

Under her mother's guidance, Drifting Butterfly Woman looked after the day-to-day needs of the *Nehiyawak*. She made daily rounds to make sure all the people of *Nisichawayasihk*, especially the children, had hides for warmth and food to eat. The hunters were staying close to the village for fear of leaving their families unprotected from the Red-Eye and his followers. The people now ate mostly small game such as rabbits, birds, and berries as the men would not go on long hunts after bigger game.

The Crane clan matriarch and Drifting Butterfly Woman expressed their concern to the Circle of Clan Mothers that the food supplies around the village would soon be exhausted. The Eagle twins could not be bothered with such mundane issues. These were the concerns of the poor and did not affect their clan.

It didn't help that the Eagle twins also made rounds every night at sunset, going from lodge to lodge asking each family if proper security protocols had been observed. Were it not for these nightly reminders of the attack, on some days Brown Shield Man and the people of *Nisichawayasihk* might have forgotten the incident for one evening and slept soundly. Fear was becoming a way of life for the *Nehiyawak*.

# NĪSTANAW NIYĀNOSĀP

The changing colours of the forest told the warriors it was time to go south and join the great buffalo hunt. But with no way of knowing if the Red Eye, Dark Cloud Man, knew of Little Grey Bear Boy's existence or if the intruder had acted alone, Blue Elk Man and Brown Shield Man felt it was not a good time to leave the village. The Bear lodge would be vulnerable without them. They decided not to join the hunt, though it would be a hard winter without the meat and hides from it. Warriors of the Wolf and Marten clans offered to share their spoils with their brothers, provided the hunting was good. Painted Turtle Man made charms and offered prayers for the blessing of Grandmother Buffalo.

The women were filling the soft, soaked water skins down at the river. They always came to the same rocky spot where they could sit on the round rocks at the river's edge without getting their feet too wet. The water was calm here, but not so still as to become stagnant.

"Mother," said Singing Doe as they dipped their skins. "We can't rely on the generosity of others. We need our own meat and hide for winter."

"What do you expect me to do?" Walking Moon Woman said, sloshing water as she dipped her water skin into the river, not hiding her agitation.

"We have to do something. Our husbands are not the only ones who did not go south. Those who return will have to share with many more than just us."

White Willow Woman lifted up her water skin and bobbed it up and down. It was about half full. "We are worried about you, mother. You haven't been sleeping."

"There will be plenty of time to sleep when I'm dead."

"That's what we are worried about," snapped Singing Doe, splashing water as she worked.

Walking Moon Woman did not respond. White Willow Woman tied off her water skin and reached for one of her mother's.

"Mother, you aren't comfortable in the Bear lodge right now," she said as she submerged the dried out water skin. "That's understandable. Why don't we leave *Nisichawayasihk* for a while? Maybe our husbands will find a moose."

"And what about Flying Rabbit Boy? He can't go anywhere while he is hurt. Should we leave him behind?"

"You know I wouldn't go anywhere without my son," said Singing Doe, her eyes wide.

White Willow Woman touched her shoulder to calm her, then said: "Flying Rabbit Boy will heal faster if he is able to sleep. So will all the children. None of us feels safe right now. We need a change."

"Where would we go?" barked the matriarch.

"We can go to *Otowhowin*," said Singing Doe.

Walking Moon Woman paused. "We only have two canoes," she said after a moment.

"We can borrow two more from the Cranes," said White Willow Woman. "I can talk to Drifting Butterfly Woman. I'm sure she will understand."

The matriarch scoured her daughters' faces. "I see the two of you have thought a lot about this. Is this how decisions will be made in the Bear lodge?"

"We are only thinking of your health and harmony," said White Willow Woman. "And that of our families."

"I need this, mother. For my son and my husband." Singing Doe lifted her water skin and tied it off tightly. The wet rawhide strap she was using snapped and she discarded the broken piece.

"We all need this," added White Willow Woman. "We will have food for winter and will be able to restore our harmony."

When the women had returned to the bear lodge, Walking Moon Woman put down her water skins and picked up her old elk hide satchel. She dusted it off and walked around the lodge, looking at their meager belongings. When her eyes settled on her daughters, she frowned. "Well...pack then."

White Willow Woman smiled and Singing Doe heaved a sigh of relief.

After two days of careful preparation, the four canoes were ready. To balance the canoes and ensure the best use of rowing power, Singing Doe, Brown Shield Man, and their injured son took the lead canoe, followed by Walking Moon Woman and Little Grey Bear Boy in the next, then White Willow Woman and Blue Elk Man and most of the supplies in the third. Painted Turtle Man paddled the fourth, with Yellow Hawk Girl as his passenger.

As the autumn wind could often be treacherous, the Bear clan decided to paddle north along the shore, rather than straight across the large lake. It would be a longer journey, but a safer one. The canoes travelled at different speeds, ensuring the hunters would be spread out should a moose or elk come to the shore for a drink. The canoes paddled along at a slow but steady pace—they were in no rush to get to their destination. As Grandfather Sun climbed the sky, the wind was calm and the lakeshore still. The rhythmic dip and splash of the paddles lulled them. Flying Rabbit Boy fell into a deep sleep, the kind that had eluded him since the attack.

"This is nice," said Singing Doe.

"*Tapwe*," answered Brown Shield Man curtly.

"It will be good to return to *Otowhowin*," she continued. "Do you remember the last time you took me there?"

Brown Shield Man cleared his throat.

Singing Doe smiled as she raised the paddle over to the other side of the canoe and dipped it back into the water with a deep, smooth stroke. "It was before our son was born. My mother was annoyed every time I was thrown into your arms by the Grey-Eye magic."

"I'd rather not talk right now. I am hoping we will find a moose."
He scanned the shore line, squinting deeply.

"We didn't find any moose that time," she reminded him. "Of
course, that wasn't why we went, was it?"

Brown Shield Man only grunted.

////

In the second canoe, Little Grey Bear Boy was doing most of the
paddling from the front. Walking Moon Woman seemed to paddle
only when the canoe veered too far to one side. He was trying in his
mind to find the words to ask the only question on his mind since the
attack. He finally gave up thinking about it and decided to ask plainly.

"*Nookum*, why did that man want to hurt me?"

Walking Moon Woman's heart tightened. She did not want to
have this conversation, but as the matriarch of the Bear clan, she
knew it was her duty. She would have to explain the danger to her
young grandson. "Well my boy," she began, taking a wobbly stoke
of the paddle and banging the shaft against the side of the canoe.
"Not every person on Turtle Island walks a path of gentle kindness.
There are those who wish to see fear spread throughout our villages.
There are those who want to control the lives of all the people around
them."

"Why would someone want to control other people?" asked Little
Grey Bear Boy, pulling his paddle out of the water and turning to
look back at his grandmother. "Wouldn't that go against the Seven
Teachings of the Peace Pipe?"

"Not everyone follows the Seven Teachings, my boy."

"But…why wouldn't they? Isn't it the best way to live one's life?"

"Keep paddling." She tilted her chin towards the front of the
canoe. "It is the best way the *Nehiyawak* know. It is the way our ancestors have lived for many generations. We believe each person has the
inherent right to choose their own destiny. There are those who wish
to take away our birthright and decide our fates for us."

"So that is what Soaring Star Woman was trying to tell me the day
she went back to the Spirit World."

"*Tapwe*, that is exactly what she was trying to explain. I wish she were still with us, but it was not *Kitchi Manitou's* will."

"But this man could not have been her son, he was too young," Little Grey Bear Boy pointed out.

"*Motch.* He was not himself a Red-Eye, he was one of his followers. We have heard rumours that there are others, but I know only of Dark Cloud Man. The one who attacked us had chosen to follow the Red-Eye teachings."

"He chose to follow the Red-Eye?" exclaimed Little Grey Bear Boy. "But isn't the Red-Eye evil?"

"We perceive the Red-Eye and his followers to be evil, because their way of life is opposite to our own," she explained as she raised the paddle over her head to the other side. "Some are drawn to the power of the Red-Eye magic. The magic they use is beyond imagining, they have a terrible ability to destroy. Some misguided people see this as power and the Red-Eye feeds off their selfish desires. The Red-Eye tells his followers that they too can harness the magic if they devote their lives to his teachings."

"Is it true?" asked Little Grey Bear Boy.

"*Motch*, I don't believe it to be so," answered Walking Moon Woman. "I have seen firsthand the destruction the Red-Eye and his followers can bring. They have only the ability to destroy, not to build, and to deceive, not enlighten. Dark Cloud Man killed your grandfather."

"I know this," said Little Grey Bear Boy, switching his paddle to the other side. "I asked Painted Turtle Man about it after our Eagle mother passed. He told me not to ask you about it because it would make you sad."

"I am very grateful my cousin Painted Turtle Man has grown so wise," she said through teary eyes. "It is not something I like to talk about."

"I am sorry, *Nookum*. I didn't mean to make you sad."

"No, no," laughed Walking Moon Woman wiping the tears from her eyes with the back of her hand. "It is time you knew the truth."

She took a deep breath and searched for the right words.

"Dark Cloud Man was once a Grey-Eye just like you. For some

reason that I still do not understand, he thought he was better than all those around him. When I was a young woman, he admired me. I was considered beautiful back in those days."

"You are still beautiful, *Nookum*."

"Thank you, my child," she said. "Dark Cloud Man wanted me to choose him to be my husband, even though we were cousins. I knew he only admired me for what I looked like on the outside and was not interested in knowing who I am on the inside."

"Like the elder brother in the White Buffalo Calf story?"

"I guess that part would be similar," said Walking Moon Woman, taken aback by the comparison. "So when I chose Rising Hawk Man, he became very jealous and angry. He began using his magic to try and kill my husband so I would have to choose again. Your grandfather was too quick and too smart for Dark Cloud Man's tricks and traps. Eventually, one of the traps at the buffalo hunt was going to work, but your namesake, Grey Bear, used his magic to trade places with my husband. Dark Cloud Man had unwittingly killed his own father. After that he was banished from the village by his mother."

////

"Paddle faster. They are too far ahead," ordered White Willow Woman, accidentally splashing water back at her husband.

"They are okay," said Blue Elk Man, trying to shield himself from the cool water with his paddle. "We must also stay near Painted Turtle Man. He's not a young man anymore. We need to go at his pace."

"We should have taken them both with us."

"Little Grey Bear Boy is too big to sit in the middle. Your mother needs him paddling. She's not young either."

"Maybe we should have stayed home."

"My love, don't let your harmony be disturbed. We will all be together at *Otowhowin*. The hunting is always good there and we will have lots of things to occupy our time. It's better than hanging around the village listening to everyone talk like scared children."

"Can you blame them?" said White Willow Woman. "The Red-Eyes could come back. It was our son they were after. What if they come to *Otowhowin*? What will we do without the protection of the village?"

"They will never find us," Blue Elk Man assured his wife. "Most of the village wouldn't be able to find us if they came looking. This place has been my family's hunting grounds for generations. I know this area better than my father did. We will have nothing to fear."

"I knew it was going to be hard having a Grey-Eyed child, but I never thought anyone would try to hurt him." She was crying now.

"It wasn't our son who was hurt."

"*Motch*, it was our nephew. He was hurt because of our son. What if my sister and mother think we are putting them all in danger?"

"That is not how they feel. We are a family. We face whatever comes together."

"How can you be sure?"

"Easy," said Blue Elk Man digging the paddle deep into the water. "We don't have any other choice."

////

Singing Doe could stand her husband's silence no longer. "Why don't you talk? I am your wife. Has something changed?"

"You know what has changed," Brown Shield Man said.

Flying Rabbit Boy snorted and muttered in his sleep, rocking the canoe slightly as he shifted.

"Have your feelings changed?"

"*Motch*," he said. "You know they haven't."

"Then why do you push me away?"

"I don't feel right. You wouldn't understand."

"I want to understand," said Singing Doe. "How can I…"

"Please," he pleaded. "Let's not wake our son. He needs his sleep after what he has been through."

"He's not the only one who is hurting," Singing Doe said, resigning herself to her husband's sorrow.

////

Walking Moon Woman lifted her paddle out of the water and placed it across the two sides of the canoe with a thump. She reached into her satchel for a birch bark bowl and dipped it in the water. She took a few deep gulps. "When I lost my husband, it was my love for my five children that pushed me to get through those dark days. Soaring Star Woman lost her husband as well as her child. She was the strongest-hearted woman I have ever known."

"But how did Dark Cloud Man kill my grandfather if he had already been banished?" asked Little Grey Bear Boy, straining against the water as he navigated the canoe on his own.

"Dark Cloud Man knew he was not strong enough with the magic to take on his mother, so he started acquiring followers from the surrounding villages. He promised them the power to control their destinies and fulfill all of their selfish desires. He had his followers paint their eyelids red to show their devotion to him and his teachings. Years later, when he had a large following, he returned to the village to take his revenge."

"And grandfather died defending the village?"

"You could say that," said Walking Moon Woman. "The Red-Eye and his followers did not defeat him in battle, but he was defending the village when he died. He was fighting off the Red-Eye warriors, empowered by Soaring Star Woman's magic. When Dark Cloud Man knew his followers were being defeated, he used his magic to call down fiery rocks from the sky. I watched helplessly as my husband was destroyed by one of these fiery rocks. There was nothing left of him for us to bury, which made saying goodbye much harder. This is why I have never chosen another husband."

"You must have been so lonesome."

"*Tapwe*," she said. "Until you came along. You remind me of him."

Little Grey Bear Boy's muscles pulled with the effort of the paddle.

"Mother Earth provides enough for all of creation, even for the Red-Eye and his followers. Somehow, nothing is ever good enough for someone who has only anger in their heart. They will always want that which others have worked hard to earn. They always think others live life so much easier or better than they do. There is just no way to make any sense of their motivations. We are not able to think the way they think, or feel the way they feel. So, in order to live in harmony we try to make it clear that they are not welcome among us as kindly and as gently as possible."

Little Grey Bear Boy paused both to take a break and to think about his grandmother's words. A mother loon swam in front of the canoe with a chick on its back. Startled by the canoe, the chick jumped off and swam quickly for the shore. The mother called loudly, feigning injury in an attempt to lure the canoe away from its offspring. As the canoe passed, the mother quickly retrieved her chick.

////

Yellow Hawk Girl sat at the front of Painted Turtle man's canoe with her corn husk doll.

"When I am in charge of the Bear clan," she said to the doll, "I'm going to make sure everyone is nice to each other. I won't let anyone say mean things about anyone else."

# NĪSTANAW NIKOTWĀSOSĀP

The canoes pulled up at the hidden beach of *Otowhowin* and the Bear clan unloaded the supplies. The shore was lined with long grey willows that obscured the view of the sandy shore from either side. The pine trees grew tall and thick here and the ground was covered in a soft moss. Brown Shield Man insisted they pull the canoes deep into the forest and cover them with pine boughs. The women got to work on a makeshift lodge as the men unpacked the supplies. Blue Elk Man scouted the area.

"I have seen some moose sign," he reported. "Judging by the tracks it is a big one."

"Can I see?" asked Flying Rabbit Boy, struggling to stand up.

"*Motch*," said Brown Shield Man. "You need to rest."

"How am I supposed to learn to track if I never get to go?"

"You can help me pick out spots to set snares," said Little Grey Bear Boy. "You are good at that."

"I'd rather get a moose than a rabbit…"

"We can get started on that in the morning," said Painted Turtle Man. "Right now, we need to get some firewood for tonight. It is already starting to get cold."

"*Tapwe*," said Brown Shield Man. "I'll stay here with my son."

"He's perfectly safe with the others," said Blue Elk Man. "We will need to carry as much wood as possible."

"I'm a Wolf," snapped Brown Shield Man. "It's my job to protect the camp."

"*Tapwe*," said Painted Turtle Man, intervening. "We'll manage with just the three of us."

Blue Elk Man stared disapprovingly at his brother-in-law. Painted Turtle Man kept smiling and led him away by the arm.

The women were taking a long time to put up the lodge, though it was a task they had done many times before.

"Pull the rope up higher," said Walking Moon Woman.

"This is as high as it can go," said White Willow Woman. "Do you expect me to fly?"

"I expect you to do it right."

"Would you rather do it yourself?"

"Don't speak to me that way. I'm still your mother."

"I know how to tie a lodge."

"Is that what you think?"

"Stop arguing," said Singing Doe. "We are all tired. Let's just get the lodge up so we will have somewhere to sleep tonight."

The next morning, the Bear clan rose with barely a word to one another.

"It is going to be a fine day today," said Painted Turtle Man, smiling. "Why don't we all greet the sun as a family?"

No one responded.

"I need to go find that moose," said Blue Elk Man, getting up to leave. "The tracks I found were only a day or two old. If it is moving slow and feeding often I should be able to find it."

"Then the rest of us can pray for your success."

"I need to keep lookout around our camp," said Brown Shield Man, collecting rawhide straps from his pack. "I'll collect more wood as I do so."

"We have enough wood now to last a few days," countered Painted Turtle Man.

"My girl and I are going berry picking," said White Willow Woman, taking her daughter by the hand. "If we don't find cranberries along the shore, we will pick moss berries instead."

"I am going to haul water," added Singing Doe, quickly untying her pack while looking in her husband's direction. "All the water skins we brought are empty and we aren't very close to the shore. If anyone is looking for us, we may get spotted if we are constantly at the water's edge."

"Will you join me, cousin?" said Painted Turtle Man to the matriarch.

"*Motch*," said Walking Moon Woman. "I have work to do."

"Oh?"

"*Tapwe*."

"Well boys," said the old man with glassy eyes. "I guess it's just us."

"Do we have to?" whined Flying Rabbit Boy. "My shoulder hurts."

"We would be happy to, *Moosum*," said Little Grey Bear Boy, casting his cousin a frown. "Where will we go?"

"East of course."

Painted Turtle Man was distracted. Little Grey Bear Boy felt it even as they greeted Grandfather Sun. He changed Flying Rabbit Boy's bandages quickly and without his usual gentle touch,

"That's too tight," said Flying Rabbit Boy, gritting his teeth.

"I don't want it to get dirty," said Painted Turtle Man. "You boys go set your snares and don't forget where you put them. It would be ungrateful to Grandmother Rabbit for us to leave one behind."

"*Tapwe, Moosum*," agreed Little Grey Bear Boy. "We will be careful to remember."

"Where are you going?" asked Flying Rabbit Boy.

"I need to find some medicines."

"Don't we have everything we need?" asked Little Grey Bear Boy.

"*Motch*," answered Painted Turtle Man. "Not everything…" The old man walked into the forest with purpose.

"I think he's getting stranger," said Flying Rabbit Boy.

"*Awas*," said Little Grey Bear Boy. "Let's go snare some rabbits."

When Grandfather Sun began to set, Little Grey Bear Boy and his injured cousin came home to find the camp empty. There was smoke spiraling up from the makeshift lodge, so they figured someone must be there. As they got closer, they noticed a sweet, unfamiliar scent emanating from the smoke.

As they entered the lodge, they found the sleeping hides had been unrolled and arranged in a circle. Painted Turtle Man sat opposite the doorway, dressed in his finest ceremonial clothing. The deer hide shirt and leggings that Singing Doe had made for him after Little Grey Bear Boy's birth still looked new. Fine quillwork and tufted moose hair designs had been added in a mesmerizing display of flowers and vines across the chest and back, and down the arms.

Painted Turtle Man cradled his peace pipe in his right arm. His ceremonial objects he had laid out in front of him. A shiny red stone, an eagle wing fan, a rawhide moon rattle, an old black spear head, an abalone shell, and several small medicine pouches. His head was raised slightly and his eyes were closed as though he were deep in prayer.

"*Moosum?*" asked Little Grey Bear Boy. Without a word, Painted Turtle Man extended his left arm, palm up towards his left hand side.

"*Tapwe…*" said Little Grey Bear Boy, taking a seat next to the old man. He motioned for Flying Rabbit Boy to do the same. Little Grey Bear Boy closed his eyes, like Painted Turtle Man, and allowed his mind to clear.

Flying Rabbit Boy looked around the lodge, unsure of what to do. He adjusted his seating position and tugged on the strap of his sling. He glanced over at Little Grey Bear Boy and saw that beneath his closed eyes a grey light was starting to glow. Flying Rabbit Boy felt a tingle in his spine, then a vibration in his back teeth. His neck turned his head on its own as his eyes were compelled towards the fire. He could feel the power of the Grey-Eye magic and could see the faint silhouettes of people in the smoke.

Outside the lodge came the sounds of the happy chatter and footsteps of Yellow Hawk Girl. As the girl and her mother entered the lodge, the chatter stopped. White Willow Woman let out a small gasp and dropped her basket of cranberries. Little Grey Bear Boy's eyes glowed as his left arm slowly rose and indicated, palm up, the spot to the left of Flying Rabbit Boy. Mother and daughter sat down. The dropped basket floated in the air and the spilled cranberries returned to it. The basket drifted gently over to White Willow Woman and set down softly behind her. Mother and daughter now looked to the vague figures in the smoke above the fire.

Singing Doe entered the lodge quietly and set down her water skins. She had felt the Grey-Eye magic before she entered. Little Grey Bear Boy's arm rose and indicated a spot to the right of Painted Turtle Man. She took her place and peered into the smoke.

Blue Elk Man and Brown Shield Man came running to the lodge, bursting in with their knives drawn.

"What happened?" shouted Brown Shield Man as he was stopped by an unseen force. The two men were directed by Little Grey Bear Boy to take seats next to their wives.

Not far from the lodge, Walking Moon Woman was mindlessly scrubbing Little Hawk Girl's other dress. She was startled by the echoed sound of a woman's scream in the distance. She looked around and listened but didn't hear anything. The birds chirping around her had not been disturbed. Was it her imagination? She returned to her task, scrubbing harder than before. A feeling crept up her spine and caused her to scrunch her shoulders together as she heard the scream again. She had the feeling that something wasn't right. There was something oddly familiar about the scream and she was worried for her family. She shook out the dress and gathered the other clothes she had been washing and made her way back to camp.

As she got closer and closer a strange panic made her heart pound and her legs move faster than they had in years. The scream seemed to come from all around her as the makeshift lodge came into view. She felt the vibration of Grey-Eye magic in the air and she threw the children's clothing aside and burst into the lodge to see the Bear clan gathered in a circle with only one seat remaining.

"What is going on?" asked a bewildered Walking Moon Woman. "What is the meaning of this?"

Little Grey Bear Boy's right arm rose and indicated the seat to the right of Painted Turtle Man.

"I am the matriarch," she said. "I did not pass tobacco for a sharing circle." As she looked over at the fire she heard the same scream coming from one of the figures. She recognized the voice of the person screaming. It was her own.

Walking Moon Woman took a seat to the right of Painted Turtle Man and looked deep into the smoke. Now that the circle was complete, the images became clearer. They were seeing *Nisichawayasihk*; the Bear lodge was ablaze with bright red flame.

The Red-Eye intruder was attacking the Bear lodge, but this time he was not alone. He overpowered Brown Shield Man and threw him to the ground. Two more Red-Eye warriors pulled Blue Elk Man off the intruder and pinned him to the ground. White Willow Woman ran to help her husband but was stabbed in the belly. Yellow Hawk Girl tried to run but was caught at the door and dragged out by the hair. Little Grey Bear Boy charged the intruder and knocked him down. He tried to knock over the men holding his father down but was struck across the head.

The two men who were holding Blue Elk Man stabbed him repeatedly in the chest as more Red-Eye warriors entered the burning lodge. Walking Moon Woman was still screaming when she was silenced by an arrow in the throat. Two of the men jumped on Singing Doe and tore at her dress. Painted Turtle Man dove over her body to protect her and was stabbed through the back with a spear. Singing Doe coughed bright red blood as the spear pierced her chest through the old man's body. One of the Red-Eye warriors found a turtle and threw it into the fire pit, laughing. The remaining men gathered around Brown Shield Man, holding his arms behind his back. The intruder approached him and painted his eyelids red with his family's blood.

Blue Elk Man's stern façade broke as a tear rolled down his cheek. Brown Shield Man ground his teeth and breathed loudly through his nose. Yellow Hawk Girl nestled into her mother's embrace with wide eyes and Flying Rabbit Boy stared glumly at the floor of the lodge.

"What we are seeing," said Painted Turtle Man, "is the fear that has entered our hearts. We may think we are out of danger now, but the wound has not been closed. It will continue to bleed and become infected. It will fester and eventually destroy our clan."

The family hung their heads low. White Willow Woman sobbed.

"I am an old man now," continued Painted Turtle Man. "I may not be able to fight off our enemies like a young warrior, but that doesn't mean I am useless. I have gathered you all to share your thoughts and feelings with one another so we can begin to heal. We must restore our harmony in order to move forward."

Painted Turtle Man reached down and picked up his abalone shell and placed it before him. He placed a thin stick into the coals on the edge of the fire and left it to ignite. He took some sage from one of his medicine pouches and rolled it into a ball in his hand. He placed the little ball of sage in the abalone shell and lit it with the small stick from the fire. When the smoke rose from the shell he rubbed his hands together, then waved the smoke over his eyes, ears, nose, and mouth. He waved the smoke over his head and through his hair. He wafted it over his arms, chest, and legs. After using the smoke to cleanse all of his sacred objects, he passed the shell to Walking Moon Woman.

The matriarch paused for a moment and looked into Painted Turtle Man's eyes. She cleared her throat and took the shell and began to smudge herself with the smoke. She passed the shell on and the rest of the Bear clan repeated the action. When Little Grey Bear Boy was finished, he placed the shell in front of Painted Turtle Man.

The old man picked up his eagle wing fan and touched it to his chest four times. He paused for a moment but did not speak. He then passed the fan to Walking Moon Woman to begin the ceremony.

"*Tansi?*" she said. "I am Walking Moon Woman, matriarch of the Bear clan." She paused for a moment and held the fan to her heart. "I say those words but I feel no power. I am supposed to lead my clan but I feel so helpless. I can't even protect the children in my home from danger. I don't deserve to lead the Bear clan. If my mother had any other daughter, I don't think I would be matriarch right now."

Walking Moon Woman started to cry, letting the tears and sobs come freely.

"Let it go," whispered Singing Doe as she embraced her mother. After a time, the matriarch composed herself and continued.

"The last time I saw a Red-Eye warrior was the day my husband was killed." She stroked the feathers on the eagle wing fan. "They took him from me."

Painted Turtle Man threw some cedar into the fire to protect the deceased from being drawn back from the Spirit World. The cedar flared and crackled quickly and Walking Moon Woman swallowed hard.

"I won't allow them to tear my family apart again. I want to apologize to everyone for being so hard on all of you lately. I think I was trying to take my power back but I should not have done it in that way. I draw my strength from my family, I don't wish to take your strength from you. All of my relations, *ekosi.*"

Walking Moon Woman passed the eagle wing fan to Singing Doe as Painted Turtle Man sprinkled tobacco into the fire. The family remained silent as she gathered her thoughts.

"*Tansi?*" she said when she was ready. "I am Singing Doe of the Bear Clan. I want to acknowledge what my mother has said. I, too, want to apologize to everyone for being so angry all the time."

She took a deep breath and looked at Flying Rabbit Boy.

"It isn't my family I am angry with. I am angry with the Red-Eyes for trying to take my son away from me. It wasn't easy for my husband and me to be given a child. I lost my first."

Painted Turtle Man threw more cedar into the fire.

"I feel like I am losing my husband now," she said looking over at Brown Shield Man. "He's not the same man."

Brown Shield Man kept his gaze down, to the fire.

"I haven't heard him laugh since that night. We used to laugh together so much. I want to feel that way again." Singing Doe brushed falling ashes off the eagle wing fan with her free hand. "That is all I want to share for now. All my relations, *ekosi*."

Painted Turtle Man threw tobacco into the fire as Singing Doe passed the fan to Brown Shield Man. Brown Shield Man looked at the fan and looked around at the others. He nodded and held the fan out for Blue Elk Man to take. Blue Elk Man shook his head, refusing.

"If you don't have anything to say, then just say your name," said Painted Turtle Man.

Brown Shield Man frowned at Blue Elk Man and touched the fan to his heart four times. He looked around at the others as he spoke.

"*Tansi*, I am Brown Shield Man of the Wolf clan." He held the fan for a moment and was about to pass it on when he noticed Flying Rabbit Boy. Tears were streaming down the boy's face, his eyes pleading for his father to speak. Brown Shield Man pulled back the eagle wing fan and set it in his lap.

"I want to apologize for the way I have been acting," he said. "I have never been like other men."

Brown Shield Man looked at Painted Turtle Man, who nodded.

"I never thought of myself as a fearsome warrior," he continued. "I never wanted people to be afraid around me. I wanted people to like me and to smile when I approached. They don't do that anymore. Ever since I…did my duty…" His voice started to shake.

"Children run away when they see me. Women won't look me in the eye. The men…" He paused. "The men either puff themselves up trying to look threatening or they cower. That is not the way I want people to react to my presence, but I just don't feel joy in my heart anymore. What's worse," he said, coughing as a sob bubbled in his throat, "I failed to protect my own son."

"Let it out," said Painted Turtle Man. "You have held onto this pain for too long."

"How can I call myself a Wolf if I can't even protect my own son? What place do I have now?" Brown Shield Man was crying now. He took several deep breaths and held the fan out to Blue Elk Man. "All my relations, *ekosi*."

Painted Turtle Man sprinkled tobacco over the flames slowly, allowing a little time to pass. After Brown Shield Man's breathing slowed, the old man nodded for the ceremony to continue.

"*Tansi*, my name is Blue Elk Man of the Marten clan. I want to thank my brother here for sharing." He looked around the circle, meeting each person's gaze before lowering his eyes to the fire. "I am feeling better after hearing what you all have said. I don't always show how I am feeling, but this has been hard on me as well."

Blue Elk Man paused to examine the eagle wing fan in his hands. He cleared his throat before continuing. "We have underestimated the Red-Eyes."

Walking Moon Woman nodded.

"We were very lucky that only one of us was injured," he said. "The Red-Eye came meaning to kill. He meant to kill my son..."

Yellow Hawk Girl burst into tears and her mother pulled her close.

"We will not underestimate them again," Blue Elk Man went on. "Even now that they have gone, the damage to our family continues. We have to stand together if we are to hold our ground. I am willing to do my part, and I know everyone else will do theirs. All my relations, *ekosi*."

The medicine carrier threw a pinch of tobacco into the fire to acknowledge Blue Elk Man's words. The eagle wing fan was passed on to White Willow Woman. Little Grey Bear Boy reached behind him and put more wood in the fire. Sparks flew up into the night sky as the new wood stoked the fire. Grandfather Sun had set without their notice.

"One last thing," said Blue Elk Man, taking the fan back. "Before I was overcome with the urge to run back, I found the moose I was tracking and it gave itself up. It will be too dark to get it tonight, so we will have to get it at first light. I hope a bear or a pack of wolves don't find it before morning."

He gave the fan back to his wife as the others nodded in approval of his success.

"*Tansi*? My name is White Willow Woman of the Bear Clan," she began. "I am very grateful to Creator that we are all here together." A loud pop from the new wood in the fire startled her, but she recovered and carried on. "There are some who would not have it so. I know that now. When my son was born," she said while looking into Little Grey Bear Boy's eyes, "I felt so blessed. I felt like I had been chosen to receive a miracle. I was so happy and so proud. I thought about how my child would grow up to protect the village with his magic. It never occurred to me that it would be dangerous. I never thought for a moment that he could die…"

Blue Elk Man put one hand on his wife's shoulder and rubbed her back with the other.

"I feel like I have brought this upon us. Now we are all in danger. I feel responsible for Flying Rabbit Boy getting hurt by the intruder. It makes me feel terrible to admit to myself that for a moment I was comforted that it wasn't one of my babies who was injured. It makes me feel like a terrible person for thinking such a thing. The child of my sister is as much my child as any who came from my womb."

Her eyes met Flying Rabbit Boy's and she smiled at him as best as she could.

"You are just like another son to me," she continued. "I want you to know that. I want all the children to know I love them. You are the reason we do what we do every day. We want to give you all a good life, a happy life. Even though it will be hard after what has happened. All my relations, *ekosi*."

Painted Turtle Man threw tobacco into the fire for White Willow Woman's words. Now that it was time to hear from the children, it dawned on the adults that they hadn't taken any time to explain to them what had happened, much less try to find out how they were feeling. The fire crackled as Painted Turtle Man nodded to White Willow Woman and closed his eyes. The time had come. The time was now.

# NĪSTANAW KĪKĀ-MITĀTAHTOSĀP

White Willow Woman handed the eagle wing fan to Yellow Hawk Girl and whispered in her ear to be careful with it.

Yellow Hawk Girl sat up straight and cleared her throat as she had seen others do.

"All right, *tansi*, my name is Yellow Hawk Girl of the Bear Clan. I have walked Mother Earth for seven summers. I talked with *Moosum* about the bad man who came into our lodge. I still don't understand why he did that. Why didn't he just come talk to us? I think we would have been nice to him if he would have been nice to us. Anyway, he should have been more careful because he hurt Flying Rabbit Boy's arm and he should come back and say he's sorry."

Painted Turtle Man threw some cedar on the fire.

"Anyway, I am glad we are finally talking about this. No one ever tells me anything and I don't like that. *Nookum*, Auntie, and my mother are always telling me how I am going to lead the Bear clan when I am older, but how am I supposed to do that if I never know what's going on?" She frowned at each of the women. "Anyway, that is all I wanted to say. All my relations, *ekosi*."

"*Hiy, hiy*," said the adults.

Painted Turtle Man offered tobacco to the fire.

"*Tansi*," Flying Rabbit Boy said with a slight giggle as he accepted the fan from Yellow Hawk Girl. "I am Flying Rabbit Boy of the Bear

Clan. Thank you all for what you have shared, especially my little cousin."

Yellow Hawk Girl nodded seriously.

"I am sorry this happened." The boy's smile faded. "All I ever wanted was to prove myself. I thought I could become a great hunter and warrior, but now I am not so sure. I used to think I was brave, but ever since I got hurt, I have felt so afraid all the time. It wasn't the pain that hurt the most, it was the fact that someone would want to hurt me. I never did anything wrong, so why did this happen?"

Flying Rabbit Boy stroked the eagle wing fan, turning it over in his hands.

"You know..." he continued. "I've always been a little jealous that I don't have grey eyes. I used to think things would be so much easier if I had the Grey-Eye magic. I don't feel that way now. It bothers me that someone would want to hurt someone just because of the colour of their eyes."

He looked at Little Grey Bear Boy. Their eyes met and they held each other's gaze for a time.

"I won't be jealous anymore. I want us to be best friends forever. When I get big and my shoulder is healed, I'll protect you. I won't let anyone come between us. Together, we will take care of the people of *Nisichawayasihk*. All my relations, *ekosi.*"

All of the grown-ups nodded and Painted Turtle Man offered tobacco. Flying Rabbit Boy passed the fan to his cousin, who stared at him still through glassy eyes.

"Thank you, cousin," said Little Grey Bear Boy before clearing his throat. "I am Little Grey Bear Boy of the Bear Clan. I don't really know what to say. I think everything has been said."

Little Grey Bear Boy adjusted himself to lean on his opposite side. He looked around at the family. Everyone was staring at him. He thought it strange that they were all looking now when before their heads were down. He felt nervous and looked down himself.

"I just want things to be the way they were before." He glanced up, they were still staring. "I know what you all expect of me..." He cleared his throat again.

"I'm not ready. I don't know how to use the magic. It just happens,

I don't know how else to explain it. I never asked for this. I only wanted to be a normal boy. I want to help my family. I want to learn the ways of the *Nehiyawak* but I feel like I am expected to do much more. I don't think I am capable. I feel like I am going to disappoint everyone."

A lump had formed in his throat and a bad taste soured his mouth. There was something else he had to say.

"I need to apologize to my cousin," he said with a gulp. "The intruder didn't come for you, he came for me. I feel really bad that you got hurt in my place. If the Red-Eye warrior had grabbed me, I know I couldn't have turned myself into a turtle. I don't even feel like I did it for you, it just happened. My point is…" Little Grey Bear Boy paused and took a deep breath. "…you saved my life."

Flying Rabbit Boy held his breath as a tear dropped down his cheek. The adults were stunned, not having thought the situation through to such an end.

"That is all I have to say. All my relations, *ekosi*."

Painted Turtle Man paused as he accepted the eagle wing fan from Little Grey Bear Boy. He sprinkled tobacco into the fire.

"We will have difficult days ahead of us," he said. "We can make things a little easier for all of us if we stand together as a family. Perhaps we have become a little too comfortable. That is not to say we don't deserve some comfort, but we need to find a new balance between comfort and safety."

Brown Shield Man and Blue Elk Man met the other's gaze and nodded. Walking Moon Woman's sat with her eyes closed, deep in thought. The fire cracked and hissed.

"Now that everything is out in the open, we can begin to move forward as a family. Even though we are all one, we must be considerate of the fact that it is up to each of us to do our part to the best of our ability. We will not expect too much of any one person…" He looked over at Little Grey Bear Boy.

"And we understand that some will be expected to do more than others…" He looked over at Walking Moon Woman, who opened her eyes to meet his gaze.

"We will love one another." He added, glancing over at Singing

Doe and Brown Shield Man. "And we will be respectful of everyone's contribution, no matter how small." He smiled at Yellow Hawk Girl.

Painted Turtle Man reached down and picked up his moon stone rattle. "I will sing a song to give thanks to *Kitchi Manitou* for giving us the ability to get through this difficult time. Then we will eat and drink. In the morning, we will rise early and go find Blue Elk Man's moose."

He shook the rattle and sang his song. It seemed to the others that there was something deeper and stronger in the old man's song and his voice warbled. The family took the time to contemplate their place and purpose as individuals and as a family. This is the way their ancestors must have intended for them to live as they passed this ceremony and this song down to them for generations. When he was finished the song Painted Turtle Man offered prayers and more tobacco. He carefully wrapped and stowed his ceremonial objects into his medicine bundle. As he did so, the rest of the family began to shift and stretch.

"Can I have some water?" asked Yellow Hawk Girl.

"Of course, my girl," said White Willow Woman. She picked up one of the water skins and helped her daughter to drink. She passed the water skin on to Flying Rabbit Boy and picked up her basket of cranberries.

"Does anyone want some berries?" she asked. "They are very juicy but sour."

"I'll have some," said Brown Shield Man, taking some from the basket. As he bit into one he made a face, and the others laughed, relieved and happy.

# NISTOMITANAW

In the morning, the family retraced Blue Elk Man's steps together and found the moose. A pair of crows had pecked at one of its eyes, but the birds were scared off when the family approached. The women got to work skinning and butchering the moose. The men helped by lifting the large animal, while Little Grey Bear Boy and Flying Rabbit Boy gathered wood and built a fire.

Walking Moon Woman removed the stomach of the moose and tied off the bottom. She put small scraps of meat into the stomach and placed three round rocks in the fire. Painted Turtle Man found some logs and tied them off to make a four-point stand over the fire. He then gathered some thin willow and peeled off the bark, tying them to the stand in rows for hanging the meat. When the fire was ready, the women began to cut the meat into long strips. Blue Elk Man and Brown Shield Man stretched the hide, using sharpened sticks to stake it to the ground.

The smell of roasting meat filled the air as the family worked, talked, and laughed together. At midday, Walking Moon Woman poured water into the moose's stomach, then she had the boys fish the three round stones out of the fire with sticks and drop them into the stomach. The rocks made the water hiss and steam. Walking Moon Woman tied off the open end of the stomach pouch. When the hot rocks had heated the water and cooked the meat, the family gathered around and enjoyed the rare delicacy together.

"Can we go check our snares after?" asked Flying Rabbit Boy.

"I guess you could," said Walking Moon Woman, looking over at her daughters. "Get some more wood first, so we won't run out while you are gone."

"Can I go too?" asked Yellow Hawk Girl.

"*Tapwe*," said White Willow Woman. "But stay close to your brother."

"Bring your snares with you," said Painted Turtle Man. "We should have enough meat to take back to *Nisichawayasihk*. Remember what I said about not forgetting any."

"*Tapwe, Moosum*," said Little Grey Bear Boy. "That would be disrespectful of Grandmother Rabbit."

The children did as instructed, piling up more wood from the forest before collecting their snares. They caught four rabbits and returned to the family. The butchering was nearly complete. Singing Doe and White Willow Woman removed the rows of dried meat from the rack and headed for the camp. Painted Turtle Man had prepared more peeled willow poles. Walking Moon Woman began filling the rack with new strips of meat.

"This has gone a lot faster than I would have thought," observed Painted Turtle Man.

"*Tapwe*," said Walking Moon Woman. "We should be done drying the meat by sunset, but the hide will need another day."

"As will the rabbit furs," he added. "When do you wish to return to *Nisichawayasihk*?"

Walking Moon Woman sighed.

"We don't have to go back too soon if you don't want to," said the old man.

"*Motch*," she said. "The village will worry if we are gone too long."

"I think most people would understand."

"Most, but not all…"

It was dark by the time all the Bear clan returned to their camp. The four rabbit furs, which Painted Turtle Man had helped the children stretch and scrape on willow hoops, hung on the lodge facing south to get the most of the autumn sun. The family crawled into their buffalo robes, cheerful but exhausted from the day's labours.

A chill in the air and a dusting of frost on the ground greeted them in the morning. No one spoke of it, but everyone knew it was time to return to *Nisichawaysihk*. The dried meat could not be pounded into pemmican at camp, as that would take days. Blue Elk Man and Brown Shield Man left to retrieve the moose hide and the others began packing their belongings into the canoes.

When the men finally returned with the moose hide, the family began to break camp.

"Can't we just stay a few more days?" asked Yellow Hawk Girl.

"*Motch*, my girl," answered White Willow Woman. "We need to go home now. If it starts getting cold, it will be too dangerous to travel by canoe."

"Why don't we just stay here for the winter?" asked Flying Rabbit Boy.

"Once the lake freezes, anyone could come here," said Walking Moon Woman. "We would be better protected being with the others in the village."

Brown Shield Man took much of the meat and supplies in his canoe and took Yellow Hawk Girl with him, to balance the weight. Singing Doe didn't care for this idea, but Walking Moon Woman asked her to come in her canoe. White Willow Woman offered to take Flying Rabbit Boy so that Little Grey Bear Boy could help Painted Turtle Man paddle his. Before they cast off, Painted Turtle Man offered prayers and tobacco in gratitude to *Otowhowin* and its bounty.

The four canoes cast off with Painted Turtle Man and Little Grey Bear Boy in the lead.

"Let's not get too far ahead of the others, my boy," said Painted Turtle Man, slowing his stroke.

"*Moosum*," said Little Grey Bear Boy, "why do I call you '*moosum*'?"

"What?" laughed Painted Turtle Man. "You always ask the strangest questions. Any other boy your age would be asking about how to get their name or which warrior society will take them in. What made you think of such a thing?"

"Well, Walking Moon Woman is my *nookum* because she is my mother's mother," Little Grey Bear Boy explained, "but you are not my mother's or father's father."

"So you no longer wish to call me '*moosum*'?" smiled Painted Turtle Man.

"*Motch, Moosum*, it's not that. I just mean, why do I call you my 'grandfather'?"

"I am your grandmother's cousin," the old man explained. "Therefore we are related. Also, I am almost old enough to be your grandfather. Since I am giving you the teachings, it is out of love and respect that you call me '*moosum*' even though I am not."

"*Tapwe*," said Little Grey Bear Boy. "I can understand that."

Little Grey Bear Boy continued to paddle in long deep strokes.

"I wonder, why you are asking this?"

"On the way to *Otowhowin*, I was talking to *Nookum* about Rising Hawk Man."

"Oh?" said the old man. "What did she tell you? That is, if it is not a private matter..."

"She told me that he had been killed defending the village from Dark Cloud Man and his followers."

"I remember that day." Painted Turtle Man took a long stroke with his paddle and then rested it across his lap.

"You were there?"

"Well of course. That was the day I earned my name."

"You never told me how you got your name."

"You never asked me about it," chuckled Painted Turtle Man.

"Would you tell me the story now?"

"I guess this is as good a time as any," he considered, plunging his paddle back into the water. "Where do I begin? I was not much older than you are now when Dark Cloud Man came back to the village seeking revenge. When the Red-Eye and his followers attacked I took my sister and hid inside a lodge. Some of his warriors who had their eyelids painted red found us and wanted to take my sister away. I could not allow them to do so, but I was too small to fight them. I threw myself over top of my sister so they could not drag her away."

"That was brave!" said Little Grey Bear Boy.

"The Red-Eye warriors started beating me with their war hammers and with the shafts of their spears. They kept hitting me over and over and over until my back was black, blue, purple, and red with blood.

The beating hurt horribly but I would not let them take my sister away. Some of the warriors of *Nisichawayasihk* heard the commotion and came into the lodge. They fought and eventually killed the Red-Eye warriors who had beaten me and tried to kidnap my sister. When it was over, I was still covering my sister with my body and they said I had looked like a painted turtle.

"That must have hurt."

"After the battle was over, I was inducted into the Black Bear Warrior Society and named 'Painted Turtle Man.' Unfortunately, my back has troubled me since that day, especially when it is cold or raining."

"Wow," exclaimed Little Grey Bear Boy. "That story is even better than my father's!"

"Well I don't think it is better," laughed Painted Turtle Man. "It's just different. Your story will be different and just as good I'm sure."

"But you were so brave to protect your sister."

"I didn't feel brave at the time," Painted Turtle Man explained. "I just did the first thing that came to my mind. You would do the same for Yellow Hawk Girl."

"I would?"

"Yes, my boy," said the old man. "It is in your blood."

Painted Turtle Man looked up into the sky thinking of Grey Bear, the last Grey-Eye of the Bear clan. He was a kind uncle who did not deserve to have the Red-Eye for a son. It dawned on the old man that he was much older now than his uncle had been when he died. It still seemed as though Grey Bear would have been so much wiser, even though he was a younger man. They would have to rely on what wisdom could be inherited through blood now that there were no Grey-Eyes left to teach Little Grey Bear Boy,

# NISTOMITANAW PIYAKOSĀP

Three winters passed with no sign of the Red-Eye or his followers. Blue Elk Man and Brown Shield Man were still reluctant to leave the village for more than two days at a time. With no big game coming in, the Bear clan had descended back into poverty.

Luckily, Painted Turtle Man had become a good provider. More and more, the warriors of *Nisichawayasihk* relied on his visions, charms, and prayers for success on the hunt. It seemed that Painted Turtle Man's dreaming eyes always led a warrior to good hunting. Unfortunately for the Bear clan, this ability could not be used to the full benefit of the family as the best hunting was many days' away.

The Eagle twins continued to expand their influence in *Nisichawayasihk*. When Sharp Stone Man, the son of the elder Eagle twin, came of age, one of the Turtle daughters presented herself at the Eagle lodge. The people of *Nisichawayasihk* saw this as a good match, since the Eagles had many sons and the Turtles had many daughters (and too few hunters). But the Eagle twins did not think this was the right match for their son and turned her away. They would not allow an Eagle son to marry a Turtle—or a Bear, for that matter. This upset the harmony of the village. No one was more disappointed than Sharp Stone Man, who had admired the Turtle daughter for many years.

The Eagle twins somehow exerted some influence over every

aspect of village life. Some Eagle clan warriors even assisted the Wolf clan in standing watch over *Nisichawayasihk*. Whenever the Wolf clan matriarch tried to protest—arguing that protecting the village was not the responsibility of the Eagles—the twins would gently remind her of the incident with the Red-Eye intruder. "Think of the children," they would plead, and the Wolf clan matriarch would of course capitulate.

To make matters more difficult, not long after the snow had melted, Talking Stone Woman, matriarch of the Crane clan and leader of the Circle of Clan Mothers, passed on into the Spirit World. As expected, the Crane clan appointed Drifting Butterfly Woman to lead them.

The time the Eagle twins had been waiting for had come: there would have to be an election to select a new leader of the Circle of Clan Mothers. Out of a mixture of fear of the twins' sweeping influence and, in some cases, gratitude for recent gifts, the clan matriarchs appointed the Eagle twins to lead the people of *Nisichawayasihk*.

Walking Moon Woman opposed the appointment, but with most of the other clan mothers supporting the Eagle twins, she felt to oppose them would disrupt the harmony the village was slowly gaining back.

"It should have been you, my mother!" Singing Doe could not keep the disgust from her voice.

"*Tapwe*," agreed White Willow Woman. "Who knows what troubles they will lead us to."

"*Motch*! Put those thoughts out of your hearts," Walking Moon Woman commanded. "The Circle of Clan Mothers has spoken and we must support our new clan mothers. *Kitchi Manitou* alone will decide the fate of the *Nehiyawak*."

Walking Moon Woman's wisdom could not be argued with. The structure of the clan system and the need for consensus would always overcome the ambitions of the few people like the Eagle twins. The new Crane clan mother, Drifting Butterfly Woman, busied herself with keeping all the people informed of any news, while taking it upon herself to discourage gossip. She was quick to call people out for starting rumours. Although this was effective, those on the receiving end of her chastisements would sometimes hold a grudge. Their complaints never got far, as the gossip always seemed to originate with the same few individuals.

The Eagle twins had finally achieved what they wanted, but somehow it wasn't enough. They eyed Drifting Butterfly Woman with suspicion, jealous of how the people respected her.

Little Grey Bear Boy continued his education under Painted Turtle Man's wisdom and guidance. He had grown strong in his knowledge of the medicine wheel teachings and the secrets of the plant world. The Grey-Eye magic and its uses, however, continued to elude him. He sometimes despaired that he would never truly be able to control the magic.

"How many times will I have to remind you?" Painted Turtle Man would say. "The Grey-Eye magic will be with you when you most need it."

They were sitting in the Bear medicine lodge with mortar and pestles grinding herbs. The Trader's caravan would return at the end of the next season and medicines always traded well. With Blue Elk Man and Brown Shield Man unlikely to go south to hunt buffalo, trading for buffalo robes where possible was a good option for the Bear Clan. The preparations were giving Little Grey Bear Boy the opportunity to learn how to mix a variety of medicines, knowledge it would have otherwise taken him years to acquire.

"Don't you remember how you saved your cousin's life by turning him into a turtle?"

"I didn't do anything," insisted Little Grey Bear Boy, pounding dried bitter root.

"Well then how do you explain what happened? You were the only Grey-Eye in the village. Who else could have turned Flying Rabbit Boy into a turtle?"

"Well I do not know how I did it. It just sort of happened…"

"Perhaps that is the way it works," said Painted Turtle Man.

"But what about Soaring Star Woman?" He stopped pounding the roots. "Remember how she was able to float above Mother Earth? Not only that, she could make others around her float above the ground too. She could heal people with blue light and make things move by themselves without touching them."

"I remember she used to float everywhere she went," the old man said, pausing to examine the contents of his mortar. "Do you remember when we went to see her in the Eagle lodge the day she passed on? Do you remember seeing her knees?"

Little Grey Bear Boy blushed. "Her knees? What are you saying?" It was taboo to speak of a woman's body parts much less look at them.

"Do not be alarmed," Painted Turtle Man reassured his protégé. "I noticed that her knees were large and swollen. Sometimes, when a person gets older, their joints get bigger and cause them pain. See how it is happening to my hands?" Painted Turtle Man showed Little Grey Bear Boy the enlarged joints of his fingers.

"I believe Soaring Star Woman suffered from this infliction," Painted Turtle Man explained. "It must have been very painful for her to walk or even stand for that matter."

"She never spoke of this affliction," said Little Grey Bear Boy.

"Of course not, my boy," said Painted Turtle Man. "One should never burden others with their private troubles. You see, every person walking Mother Earth has their own challenges to overcome. To whine and complain about ours is to burden those who already carry their own concerns. It does our neighbours a great disservice, as it distracts them from their own journey and its challenges."

"I never thought of it like that."

"*Tapwe*. We must always try to help those around us, not cause them more suffering. That is the way of the medicine wheel."

"*Tapwe*," said Little Grey Bear Boy "But then, who will help us when we have troubles?"

"We must always try to help ourselves first," said Painted Turtle Man. "We can only hope and pray that those around us would help us if we were in need. And so we must always treat others the way we would wish to be treated in the same situation."

"That is a very powerful teaching," observed Little Grey Bear Boy.

"*Tapwe*, it is the most powerful teaching we have been given by *Kitchi Manitou*."

"What is the teaching called?"

"It does not have a name. I would simply refer to it as 'The Way' if I had to."

"The Way?" Little Grey Bear Boy paused for a moment, then said: "Let us give thanks to *Kitchi Manitou* for teaching us The Way."

"A very good idea." Painted Turtle Man smiled proudly, putting down his mortar and pestle and dusting the powder off his hands. "Prepare my pipe and we will smoke and pray and give thanks."

Little Grey Bear Boy unpacked the medicine bundle and prepared the pipe as he had many times before. As they gave their thanks to the Great Spirit, they heard an eagle screech overhead, an acknowledgement that their prayers had been heard. When they had completed their ceremony, Little Grey Bear Boy dutifully cleaned the pipe and repacked the medicine bundle.

They rolled up the medicines they were making in soft deer hide and went to the Bear lodge to help prepare the evening meal. They entered the lodge to find everyone standing and smiling. Many Fish, husband of Drifting Butterfly Woman, stood between Blue Elk Man and Walking Moon Woman, holding something in his hands.

"*Tansi*, Uncle," said Little Grey Bear Boy politely.

No one spoke. Everyone kept looking at him and smiling.

"What is going on?" he asked.

Many Fish stepped towards the Grey-Eyed boy. "Little Grey Bear Boy of the Bear clan," he said formally, "will you accept this whistle?"

Many Fish held out an eagle bone whistle with a leather strap tied around the middle. Little Grey Bear Boy bit his lip. The gift of an eagle bone whistle meant only one thing to the *Nehiyawak*: Many Fish was offering to sponsor him into the sundance, the holiest of ceremonies. Little Grey Bear Boy did nothing until Painted Turtle Man gave him a nudge.

"*Tapwe*, I accept, Uncle!" he said, louder than he meant to.

Many Fish handed him the whistle.

"There will be much to prepare," said his sponsor.

"I will do whatever you ask of me," promised the boy.

"Good, then I will see you in the morning, *ekosi*."

Many Fish shook hands with Blue Elk Man, Brown Shield Man, and Painted Turtle Man. He gave Walking Moon Woman a hug and a kiss on the cheek and nodded at the other women. He wished them well as he left the Bear lodge.

Everyone congratulated Little Grey Bear Boy. Everyone except his mother. White Willow Woman was busying herself about the evening meal, trying to conceal her tears.

"It will be okay, my girl," said Walking Moon Woman, giving her daughter a hug.

"*Tapwe*," said White Willow Woman. "I just didn't think it would be so hard."

"It is always hard for a mother to see her child take the first steps on man's road. I had three sons. I know. But it is his time."

# NISTOMITANAW NĪSOSĀP

Summer. It was a special time for the people of *Nisichawayasihk*, as it was their turn to host the sacred sundance ceremony. There was much work to be done as pilgrims from the surrounding villages would be coming to participate. The people of *Nisichawayasihk* would feed them and care for them for seven days. Little Grey Bear Boy had twice the responsibility of any boy his age. Not only did he have to make his own preparations for the sundance ceremony under the guidance of Many Fish, but he also had to assist Painted Turtle Man prepare the medicines. The old man would serve as the host sundance chief, though he would be assisted by sundance chiefs from other villages.

White Willow Woman was accorded the honour of choosing the centre pole for the sundance. The pole, also known as the Tree of Life, would serve as the focal point of the ceremonies and all prayers and intentions would be made to the tree. She paid no heed to the rumour that she had only been chosen for the honour because of her Grey-Eyed son, a rumour perpetuated, she had no doubt, by the meddling Eagle twins. Whatever the reason she was selected, she was honoured, and set about selecting a white poplar tree in a manner befitting a mother of the *Nehiyawak*.

She walked the forest for four days, one day in each of the four cardinal directions. On the fifth day, she made a selection after careful thought, prayer, and consideration. The warriors set about the task of relocating the great white poplar to the sundance grounds. Every effort was made to save the tree from too much damage, but they had to cut many roots.

"I hope you picked the right tree," said Singing Doe to her sister when the work was done. "We don't need to give the Eagle twins any reason to find fault with us right now."

"It is *Kitchi Manitou* who selects the tree," said Painted Turtle Man. "Long before any of us were born. White Willow Woman's job was only to determine which tree Creator intended for us to use."

"*Tapwe*, Uncle," said Brown Shield Man. "Besides, the Eagle twins have never needed a reason to find fault with someone."

Singing Doe and White Willow Woman laughed, but Painted Turtle Man cleared his throat and continued with his work.

"I don't like the idea of people from other villages finding out about our son," said Blue Elk Man. "Too much attention will be brought on him. We already know the danger this might pose."

"I never thought of that," said White Willow Woman. "Perhaps we should wait until next year."

"That is, of course, up to you," said Painted Turtle Man. "Though he would then be the oldest boy in the village to not have sundanced. He is after all, twelve summers."

"He is a good boy," said Singing Doe. "He will understand."

"And what will we do when it is time for him to earn a name?" asked Painted Turtle Man. "How long will we put it off?"

"He can't remain a child forever," said Brown Shield Man. "It's been three years since the Red-Eye warrior came. I believe he acted alone and we are safe."

"*Tapwe*," said Blue Elk Man. "It would not be right to allow our own fears to intrude on his life's path."

"*Tapwe*…" said White Willow Woman, not attempting to hide the reluctance in her voice.

Pilgrims and their sponsors began to arrive at *Nisichawayasihk* and for a time there were many more lodges than usual. The participants did not sleep in the village but in a special campsite at the holy grounds. The sundancers who lived in *Nisichawayasihk* slept at the sundance campsite as well.

The night before the sundance ceremony the *Nehiyawak* served a great feast—the sundancers' last meal for four days. Little Grey Bear Boy had completed all of his preparations, thanks to his sponsor Many Fish. Singing Doe made the boy's ceremonial garb, a grey shirt trimmed with black and red lines and a matching apron with a yellow sun painted on the front. She had painted a small grey bear cub across the back of the shirt. Around his neck hung the eagle bone whistle on the leather strap. Tied around his head like a laurel he wore bundled white sage wrapped with red leather lacing. Wrist and ankle bands of the same kind adorned his hands and feet. When it was time to leave the village and walk to the ceremony grounds, Many Fish was waiting to take Little Grey Bear Boy to present him as his sponsor.

"I think you are ready," said Many Fish when it was time. All of the preparations and teaching came down to this moment. Many fish was carrying a rolled up hide with 4 poles under his arm.

"Thank you for everything, Uncle," said Little Grey Bear Boy as they began to walk. Others were leaving the village as well, some accompanied for the first time by their sponsors.

"Remember, the sundance ceremony is the time when the *Nehiyawak* give back to *Kitchi Manitou* for all blessings. We believe the only way to know Creator's bounty is to go without it for a short time. That is why sundancers must suffer themselves by dancing in the hot sun for four days without food and water."

"I'm ready. I will make you proud."

"Are you nervous?"

"I am prepared to dance, but I…"

"You are worried about piercing?"

"*Tapwe.*" Little Grey Bear Boy lowered his eyes as he walked.

"You are not obligated to pierce," said Many Fish. "It is only for those who have special intentions. They give of their flesh and blood in honour of *Kitchi Manitou*'s intervention in their lives. You will see people piercing themselves through the chest or back and by offering small pieces of their own flesh to the sacred fire."

"But won't people think I am scared if I don't pierce?"

"Piercing is not about other people or what they think. It is about you and *Kitchi Manitou*. Everyone knows you are afraid, so don't worry about that. I was afraid at my first Sundance too, it's natural. Your father was with me and he was scared too."

"My father was afraid?"

"*Tapwe.*"

"I didn't think he ever got scared."

"Like I said," smiled Many Fish, "it's natural."

They continued their walk in silence. Little Grey Bear Boy thought of how strange it would be to sleep somewhere besides in a lodge with his family. For the four days and nights of the Sundance ceremony, he would sleep in a simple tent that Many Fish provided. It wasn't much more than a moose hide to be laid across elevated set of four poles. When they arrived at the Sundance grounds, Many Fish gave him the rolled up hide and poles.

"This is it," said Many Fish when they arrived at the ceremony grounds. From this point onwards it was sundancers and helpers only. The villagers would not be allowed to enter until the third day.

"I want to thank you for everything," said Little Grey Bear Boy.

"Don't worry about it; I am glad to be able to do it. To tell the truth, it is I who should be grateful to you."

"What do you mean?"

"You are letting me repay a kindness that Painted Turtle Man showed me a long time ago. All you need to do for me, is to do a kindness for someone else when the time is right."

"*Hiy, hiy.*" Acknowledged Little Grey Bear Boy.

"*Ekosi,*" said Many Fish as he turned and went back to the village.

////

Early on the morning of the first day, a Crane clan warrior woke the participants by announcing in each of the four directions: "*Tansi,* sundancers! Get Ready!"

Day one represented the years of a person's childhood experience. Having only just begun their fasting, the sundancers were quick to emerge from their tents and begin the day. They laughed and talked as they made themselves ready for the special sweat lodge ceremony.

There were four sweat lodges, each hosted by one of the four sundance chiefs, including Painted Turtle Man. After two rounds of the sweat lodge, the four groups quickly donned their garb and lined up, senior dancers at the front and junior dancers, such as Little Grey Bear Boy, at the rear.

They marched into the sundance circle to the shake beat of the drum, a series of short, quick taps, where they would be presented to the Tree of Life. When they reached the tree, they gave their offering: an arm's length of light hide encasing a handful of tobacco tied in the middle with rawhide. Each sundancer hugged the Tree of Life and spoke his intention into the tobacco. The tobacco he then handed to one of the ceremony helpers, who tied it to the tree. By the time it was Little Grey Bear Boy's turn, he could hardly see the bark of the tree as nearly one hundred offerings had been tied to it. At the base of the tree, a great buffalo robe had been laid on the ground. Here, the sundance chiefs would do their work.

"Oh *Kitchi Manitou*, I am your servant Little Grey Bear Boy of the Bear clan," he whispered into the tobacco through the deer hide. "I give thanks and praise for all of creation. I have come to this sundance ceremony, having reached the proper age under your guidance, prepared to repay my debt to you for saving the life of my cousin, Flying Rabbit Boy. May your will be done. All my relations, *ekosani*."

He handed the offering to the helper who tied it along with the others to the Tree of Life. Little Grey Bear Boy was then ushered by another helper to his place in the sundance circle. The lead drummer hit the drum four times bringing to life the steady, heartbeat rhythm as they sang a sacred sundance song. The dancers placed their eagle bone whistles in their mouths and tweeted in response to each beat of the drum. They picked up one foot on one beat and placed it down on the next. This was as much dancing as they were required to do, a relatively easy task on the first day.

Daylight was divided into four segments between which the dancers would take a break by sitting down for a short time. The dancers who had earned a peace pipe were required to smoke during the break and offer prayers.

During the third round of the first day, one of the senior dancers had chosen to 'walk with the buffalo,' as it is called by the *Nehiyawak*.

He would have a small section of the flesh of his back pierced below the shoulder on both sides. A wooden peg, about the size of a child's finger, would be placed through the flesh and a rawhide thong strung over the flesh and under the peg in a loop. Sinew would be tied around the flesh of the pierced area to keep it in place during the ordeal. The thongs were then attached to a harness, which was tied to seven brightly painted buffalo skulls with jawbones removed. Walking with the buffalo entailed dragging these skulls around the circle. The senior warrior pledged to do this in repayment to *Kitchi Manitou* for healing his wife of sickness.

The *Nehiyawak* believe one must suffer to show gratitude to the Creator. The sundancers whooped and cheered as the man struggled to drag the seven buffalo skulls around the circle while the upper teeth clawed at the ground. The skin of his back was pulled back tightly, stretching far from his body. A trickle of blood ran from the wounds. When the man had dragged the ceremonial skulls all the way around the sundance circle, one of the sundance chiefs from another village stopped him.

The man embraced the sundance chief, weeping not from the pain, but because he had fulfilled his oath and proven his gratitude to *Kitchi Manitou*. His tears were tears of joy and he wept loudly and unashamed, but his ordeal was not quite over. Seven of his friends and family held down each buffalo skull, still attached to his back. Some even sat on the brightly painted buffalo skulls as the man was backed up towards them, with one of the helpers guiding the rope. When he was ready, the sundance chief shouted and the man ran at full pace away from the skulls. When he got to the end of the length of rope, the skin stretched and broke and the wooden pegs went flying.

Some of the other dancers caught the man as he fell forward. They whooped and cheered in honour of his sacrifice. The wooden pegs were found and returned to the man as a token of the day he walked with the buffalo.

After a short rest, the drum sounded and the dancers got up again and danced, picking up one foot and then the other. They started to feel the effects of physical fatigue combined with thirst and hunger from fasting. When the sun began to set, the drum beat stopped and the dancers lined up to be marched back down to the sundance campsite. The sundancers changed out of their ceremonial garb and re-entered one of the four sweat lodges for another two rounds, completing the ceremony and the first day.

Although tired from the day's ordeal, the sundancers took some time to catch up with old friends and distant relations from other villages. Many were connected through blood or marriage. They reminisced about old times and learned about who had gotten married and who had been blessed with children. The conversation was kept positive. They avoided speaking of those who had passed away as well as any reference to the Red-Eyed demons. As Father Sky darkened, the sundancers made their way back to their tents and settled in to sleep.

# NISTOMITANAW NISTOSĀP

The second day dawned and the hunger and thirst began to gnaw at the sundancers.

"*Tansi*, sundancers!" called the Crane clan warrior, "Wake up and get ready!"

They entered the four sweat lodges for two rounds, still in good spirits but moving a little more slowly. The second day of the sundance ceremony represented the years of a person's youth. The sundancers donned their ceremonial garb, gathered their sacred items and medicine bundles, and formed a line. The drum sounded the shake beat as the sundancers marched up the hill to the sundance circle. Today there would be piercings, buffalo-skull dragging, and flesh offering. When the dancers were ready, Painted Turtle Man signalled the drummers to begin. The sundancers responded to the steady beat with their whistles and their feet. Grandfather Sun rose and began to radiate his heat upon their faces and bodies.

A helper brought the first four sundancers who had pledged to 'go to the tree' to the buffalo hide. This time, pegs pierced the chest. Long ropes attached to the top of the tree were secured to the harness, which in turn was attached to the chest pegs. One by one and to the beat of the drum, the sundancers were taken back and forth to the tree four times. Each time, the sundancer was walked backwards away from the tree. When the sundancer reached the end of the rope, they would be encouraged by the sundance chief to lean back and stretch the skin. On the fourth time the piercer was taken to the tree, they would run backwards as fast as they were able and at the end of the rope would jump back in an attempt to break free.

Once in a while, the piercer would be unable to break free. If they were willing and able, they would try again. Although it was not a contest, it was believed by some that if a sundancer could not break free, it meant they did not truly believe in their purpose. It was a foolish superstition, but most of the sundancers worried about it nonetheless. On this day, the four who went to the tree were able to break free. When the drum stopped and the round ended, the dancers gathered to acknowledge them and their suffering.

During the break, anyone who wished to make a flesh offering could approach one of the sundance chiefs and offer tobacco to be cut. If the sundance chief accepted the tobacco, the sundancer would present their arm and the sundance chief would use a needle to poke the sundancer's outer arm just below the shoulder to draw out a very small section of skin and cut it off. This would usually be done four times. The sundancer making such an offering would be left with four small holes, barely the size of a drop of water, on their outer arm. The tiny pieces of flesh would be put into a small section of hide or fur and given back to the sundancer to offer to the ceremonial fire.

Little Grey Bear Boy and his age mates would not be required to make such an offering until the third day of the sundance ceremony. Three more sundancers walked with the buffalo on the second day and about forty fulfilled their oaths of going to the tree.

During the last round of the second day, one of the sundancers pledged to 'fly with the eagles.' This was the most difficult and severe form of self-sacrifice and was a rare occurrence. Only a senior warrior could make this particular pledge as it required the sundancer to have earned two eagle wing fans in his lifetime, a difficult task for anyone. The fact that this warrior pledged to fly with the eagles on the second day was remarkable as it would make it more difficult for him to complete the ceremony.

To fly with the eagles, one of the sundance chiefs (Painted Turtle Man in this case) again pierced the chest, this time gathering more flesh, piercing deeper and with a larger peg. Instead of being attached to the Tree of Life and running back and forth to break free, to fly with the eagles the sundancer would hang from it. When the sundancer was in the air, he would have to flap the eagle wing fans, which were tied to his wrists. The senior warrior was in the air for what seemed an eternity and his flapping had begun to slow. Painted Turtle Man signalled the warriors to let him down, feeling his pledge had been fulfilled by his suffering.

Little Grey Bear Boy watched as the dancer was lowered. From where he was standing, it appeared that one of the sundance chiefs was questioning Painted Turtle Man. Little Grey Bear Boy knew this was unlikely—it would have been completely out of order for a visiting sundance chief to question his host—but there seemed to be some sort of disagreement among the Sundance chiefs.

As Grandfather Sun became merciful, beginning his descent for the night, the sundancers were marched back down to the sundance campsite and cleansed in one of the four sweat lodges. Many of the sundancers went directly to their tents this time, especially those who had been pierced. Only a handful stayed out to socialize and even those went to their beds much earlier than the night before. The hunger of two days' fasting was now more intense and the sundancers found it harder to sleep. Eventually, the physical exhaustion won out.

# NISTOMITANAW NIYOSĀP

Grandfather Sun began his journey much earlier than usual on the third day, or so it seemed to the sundancers when the Crane clan warrior woke them up.

"*Tansi*, sundancers!" he called reluctantly. "It is time to get ready!"

This would be the most difficult day of the ceremony as it represented the years of a person's adult life. Hunger became an afterthought compared to the dryness in the sundancers' mouths and throats. The same dryness could also be felt in their joints and muscles. While they were waiting to go into their sweat lodges for the usual two rounds, one of the young sundancers began to vomit a bright yellow liquid, and the sundance chiefs decided his sundance was finished. It seemed by the smaller crowd a few others had also completed their sundance early. There was no shame in leaving early. When sundancers had given all they could give, their oath to *Kitchi Manitou* was considered fulfilled.

The senior warrior who had flown with the eagles was still there, though his eyes were droopy and he looked pale. When anyone went over to check on him, he would straighten up and nod that he was fine. As soon as they walked away, his smile faded and he found something to lean on.

After the sweat lodge, the dancers donned their ceremonial garb for the third time. The strain of the previous days showed in their faces. This day, they would be tested.

The drummers began the shake beat and the sundancers lined up and began the long walk up the hill to the sundance circle, the slope steeper than they remembered. Each sundancer was taken to the Tree of Life to reiterate prayers and oaths. By now their tiny spot on Mother Earth felt like a second home. Their feet had worn ruts in the ground. When every sundancer was in place, Painted Turtle Man signalled the drummers to start singing the sacred sundance songs.

Grandfather Sun threatened to be relentless on this third day of the ceremony. Little Grey Bear Boy was especially nervous as this would be the day he and his age mates would be expected to 'go to the tree' or make a flesh offering. Most of the boys his age had pledged the latter but he was one of four boys who had received serious interventions by *Kitchi Manitou*. As far as Little Grey Bear Boy was concerned, *Kitchi Manitou* had spared his cousin's life the day the Red-Eye warrior came and he was determined to repay the debt. In his heart he knew a flesh offering would be insufficient. He would have to go to the tree.

As the drum sounded, the sundancers picked up one foot and then the other while tweeting their eagle bone whistles with dry mouths. Most of the sundancers were falling behind the beat of the drum, but most of the sundance chiefs overlooked this. One Sundance chief, the same one who had appeared to be arguing with Painted Turtle Man, was not as kind. He pointed at a sundancer's feet and gesticulated with his hand or eagle wing fan to dance harder or faster.

After the first break, Grandfather Sun was merciless, and some of the dancers started to fall. Whenever one of the sundancers collapsed or fainted from the heat, the helpers ran over and dragged them down the hill, ending their sundance ceremony. The *Nehiyawak* had gathered from all around and had been brought up the hill to the sundance circle in order to seek healing. Those who were sick or suffering would be brought to the large buffalo robe at the base of the Tree of Life. One of the sundance chiefs would administer healing with their rattle, whistle or by laying of hands.

There seemed to be a delay with the first batch and people were looking and pointing at Little Grey Bear Boy. After talking to Painted Turtle Man and the other sundance chiefs, a helper went to the spot where Little Grey bear Boy was dancing.

"You are needed at the tree," said the helper, reaching for Little Grey Bear Boy's white sage wrist band. The boy held out his arm and the helper grabbed onto the wristband and guided him to the tree. Little Grey Bear Boy thought it must be time for him to go to the tree and fulfill his pledge. He was nervous and his heart was pounding, but he had made an oath to *Kitchi Manitou* and he was determined to fulfill it.

Painted Turtle Man approached his adopted grandson. "The *Nehiyawak*...want you to dance for them as they receive their healing." Little Grey Bear Boy removed the eagle bone whistle from his mouth with some effort, it stuck to his lip and he had to pull hard to release it.

"I am not brought here to pierce?"

"No, my boy that will have to wait."

Little Grey Bear Boy was puzzled.

"Will you do this for the *Nehiyawak*?"

"*Tapwe, Moosum*," answered Little Grey Bear Boy. "I will perform any task the *Nehiyawak* require of me."

Painted Turtle Man smiled with pride at his adopted grandson and pointed at a spot near the great buffalo hide. The strict sundance chief folded his arms across his chest in disapproval at this irregular occurrence. The *Nehiyawak* who had come seemed happy with this—they clamoured about for a place in line. Clearly, word that a Grey-Eye was participating in the sundance ceremony had spread.

A woman carried a large child whose body was strangely twisted and whose eyes seemed to see things no one else could. The child was placed upon the buffalo robe and the woman wiped the foaming saliva from his mouth and chin.

"What do you need?" asked Painted Turtle Man.

"My son was born this way," whispered the woman. "He was touched by the spirits. It is not that I am ungrateful to Creator, it is just that he is too big for me to carry anymore."

"You wish the spirits to leave him?"

"*Tapwe*," answered the woman, placing her tobacco pouch down with tears in her eyes. "No one has ever accepted my tobacco…"

Painted Turtle Man placed his hands on the crippled boy's chest and closed his eyes. The boy continued to look about with his leg twitching and his breathing laboured. Someone in line for healing cleared their throat impatiently. Painted Turtle Man removed his hand slowly and sat back on his knees, eyes still closed. The woman reached for her tobacco pouch but the old man opened his eyes quickly and stopped her with his gaze. He reached down and picked up the small pouch.

"For the love of life," said Painted Turtle Man, holding the woman's teary gaze.

Painted Turtle Man lit a ball of white sage and placed it in his abalone shell. He used the smoke and his moonstone rattle to work his healing medicine. Little Grey Bear Boy danced hard and his grey eyes began to glow. The ground started to vibrate and the air around him seemed to buzz. The old medicine man's hands glowed with a blue light and the stones inside his hide rattle flickered green, red, blue, and gold. He placed his glowing hands on the child and his body jerked. The boy cried out, moaning loudly as three spectral figures emerged from his screams. The figures flew about wildly but were bound to the Tree of Life. The sickness was drawn into the tree and absorbed into the earth.

The child lie still upon the buffalo robe and his body relaxed. The woman went to him weeping loudly and fearing the worst. The child reached out his arm and pushed himself into a side sitting position. His body was shaky and weak as he looked around. His eyes met the woman's and he reached his other hand out to her.

"Mother?" he said as he took her hand.

The woman burst into tears and hugged her son. The people nearby stepped back and murmured to each other.

The tree itself was glowing with an ancient magic and its light was connected like a rope to each of the remaining sundancers. The sundancers danced hard for the *Nehiyawak*. For many of them it was the first time they had felt the Grey-Eye magic. Soon the entire Sundance ceremony had been imbued with the ancient power of the ancestors.

More of those who came before Painted Turtle Man would receive miraculous healing as their sickness would be drawn out of them right before the very eyes of all who had gathered. Sometimes the sickness would manifest itself as a smoky black worm or insect while more serious ailments poured out as dark smoke or demonic figures. The sickness would be drawn to the Tree of Life as though it was a great magnet, absorbing the spectral figure, whatever its manifestation.

The sky began to cloud over and the Grey-Eye magic began to subside. Everyone who had come to find healing had been miraculously healed of all that ailed them. To Painted Turtle Man's knowledge, this was the first time in which the helpers had to drag some of the spectators down the hill. The power of what they had witnessed was overwhelming to some. The sky began to darken and the drum stopped its rhythmic beat, signalling the end of the third day. The weary sundancers whooped and cheered, they had passed the test, thanks in part to the Grey-Eye magic.

Although they were all exhausted, many of the sundancers clamoured around Little Grey Bear Boy wanting to hug him, shake his hand, and thank him for using his magic on them. He did not know what to say or do. He wasn't even sure he had done anything. His fellow sundancers admired his humility in performing such wondrous miracles. Eventually, the helpers had to shoo away the sundancers so the exhausted Little Grey Bear Boy could sleep.

# NISTOMITANAW NIYĀNOSĀP

"*Tansi*? Sundancers! You have done it!" cheered the Crane clan warrior. "Come and celebrate your final day!"

The exhausted sundancers, including Little Grey Bear Boy, emerged from their tents slowly but enthusiastically. They had been reborn of spirit in the night and felt as though they had awoken to a fresh new world. They could sense the spirit within everything around them and felt a connection to all of creation. Every rock, tree, and insect felt like an old friend being met after a long separation. The senior warrior who had flown with the eagles was no longer among them, but the remaining sundancers were not discouraged by this. Once again the sundancers clamoured around Little Grey Bear Boy and flocked to Painted Turtle Man's sweat lodge until he was forced to turn most away for want of space.

From his nearly empty sweat lodge, the strict sundance chief scowled, barking at his helpers to close the door. When the sundancers had completed two mild rounds in the sweat lodge they donned their ceremonial garb one last time. As they lined up, they were given a medicine tea that Painted Turtle Man had prepared to help ease the breaking of their fast at the end of the day. After three full days with no food or water, this bitter medicine seemed to be the best thing they had ever tasted.

The drummers began the shake beat and the sundancers lined up.

"We did it!" shouted one of the sundancers and all the rest whooped and cheered. They were led back up the hill to the Tree of Life.

When the drum started, Painted Turtle Man walked over to Little Grey Bear Boy and said, "You and three of your age mates will go to the tree, but not until after the contraire dance." He spoke loudly, so as to be heard over the drummers.

Little Grey Bear Boy nodded at his *moosum*, the whites of his eyes the whiter against the dark circles under them.

They danced through the first round and Grandfather Sun was gentle on them by hiding behind the occasional cloud. During the break, Little Grey Bear Boy felt dizzy and tried hard not to faint. He had come so far in the ceremony—he wanted to see it through.

When the drum sounded on the second round, the singers began the *windigo-con* song. Unknown to Little Grey Bear Boy in his weary state, some of his fellow sundancers had snuck off down the hill to don the ceremonial garb of the contraires. From all directions, they emerged from the forest, yelling and waving branches, descending on the sundance circle in disorder and folly. The contraire dancers harassed the singers at the drum, painted the other sundancers with mud, and even mimicked the strict sundance chief, who seemed less amused than most. Little Grey Bear Boy could not help but laugh at their antics. His laughter refreshed him in his mind and spirit, though his body was still weary. As the round ended, the sacred clowns disappeared back into the forest to the sound of cheers and whoops from all.

Little Grey Bear Boy's heart began to beat faster. It would soon be time for him to fulfill his oath to *Kitchi Manitou* by going to the tree. It reassured him to know he would not be going alone and he could tell by the expressions on the faces of three of his age mates which of them were going too. In addition to the sundancers, hundreds of *Nehiyawak* had gathered to bear witness to what was about to occur. Spectators were allowed to observe from outside the sundance arbour, though they were required to stand while the singers were drumming.

The drum sounded four times and felt like a knock of dread inside Little Grey Bear Boy's chest. Father Sky had begun to cloud over, threatening rain. Little Grey Bear Boy could feel the familiar vibrations of the magic in the air and he tried to clear his mind of doubt. He sincerely hoped it was not his anxiety that was causing the sky to cloud; this was after all a 'sun' dance ceremony.

Little Grey Bear Boy and his age mates were not dancing for very long before the helpers came to get them one by one. For a fleeting moment, when the three others had been taken ahead of him, a thought crept into Little Grey Bear Boy's head: perhaps he would be forgotten. His heart dropped when one of the helpers came back, walking towards him. The helper reached his hand out towards Little Grey Bear Boy and grasped his white sage wrist band, which had raised itself without his knowing. With a gentle tug, the helper led Little Grey Bear Boy to the great buffalo hide next to the Tree of Life.

The first of the four young boys was about to be pierced, as he had pledged himself to do. As the thin, sharp bone tool pierced the boy's chest, the boy stiffened, then scowled. The chief inserted the wooden peg, tied it off with sinew, and looped the rawhide thong over it. The boy was brought up to his feet and the harness was attached to the rawhide thongs. The boy seemed in good spirits.

The second boy was different. He shook from head to toe. The sundance chief who was piercing put down the piercing tool and rubbed white sage on the boy's chest, chanting an ancient medicine prayer. This calmed the boy down. He winced for a moment when the chief pierced him but remained calm while the chief pegged and harnessed him and led him to the tree.

Painted Turtle Man pierced the flesh of the third boy. Little Grey Bear Boy felt it should have been his adopted grandfather who pierced him, but then changed his mind. It would be strange to have the old man cause him pain. Little Grey Bear Boy shook these thoughts from his head and tried to remain focused on his pledge.

Now it was Little Grey Bear Boy's turn. The strict sundance chief would do the piercing—perhaps not Little Grey Bear Boy's first choice, but such things did not matter. The sundance chief rubbed white sage on Little Grey Bear Boy's chest as he prepared for the piercing. Little Grey Bear Boy felt some anxiety but was determined to face his pledge with courage. He reminded himself of the night his cousin Flying Rabbit Boy had been hurt and the miracle that had saved him.

He wanted to repay *Kitchi Manitou* for his many blessings and this was the best way he knew how.

Little Grey Bear Boy looked up into the sky, which had begun to grow quite dark indeed. He tried to think of happier thoughts so as not to ruin the ceremony. He felt the strict sundance chief's hard and calloused hands upon him and a hard pinch as the hand gathered skin between the finger and thumb. There was a hard pull which lifted him slightly off his back, then a stab that was stronger and more painful than he had anticipated. The pain intensified when the chief shoved into his flesh the hard wooden peg. Little Grey Bear Boy gasped and his eyes burst open as the sundance chief pinched the other side of his chest to repeat the process.

"Oh settle down, young warrior," growled the man.

Little Grey Bear Boy took a deep breath as he was again stabbed hard in the chest and another wooded peg rammed in.

"*Ekosi*. That was not so bad, was it?"

"I am fine," lied Little Grey Bear Boy. "I can do this."

Little Grey Bear Boy was helped to his feet. His legs shook. The sundance chief attached the harness to the rawhide thongs with as much care and grace as a grizzly bear might have used. The sound of a Thunderbird flapping its wings echoed in the distance. Little Grey Bear Boy's harness was attached to the rope and he lined up beside the third boy, who dropped his eagle bone whistle from his mouth when he saw Little Grey Bear Boy's chest. He fumbled with his whistle, getting it back into his mouth, before gluing his eyes to the Tree of Life as he had been taught.

One by one each of the boys was taken back and forth to the tree four times. Little Grey Bear Boy felt every vibration of the ropes and it seemed like his entire chest was on fire. He knew he must endure. He knew he was suffering himself for the good of the *Nehiyawak*. He never thought it would be this hard or that the pain would be quite so intense. The first two boys broke free of the ropes in their turn amid the cheers of the sundancers and the assembled crowd. The third boy again looked at Little Grey Bear Boy's chest with wide eyes before being taken back and forth to the tree.

Painted Turtle Man was there to make sure the third boy did not trip over his rope or lose his balance when going backwards. On the fourth time going to the Tree of Life, Painted Turtle Man shouted for him to go fast. He was smiling as the boy ran back and broke free. It was then he turned to Little Grey Bear Boy. His smile faded and for a moment Little Grey Bear Boy thought he had done something wrong.

"What have you done?" shouted Painted Turtle Man, turning to the strict sundance chief.

"What?" asked the sundance chief.

"You have used the wrong pegs. Those are for flying with the eagles!"

Little Grey Bear Boy looked down at the pegs. Blood streamed freely down his chest and torso.

"Oh no," said the strict sundance chief casually. "I must have grabbed the wrong ones…My eyes are not what they used to be."

The strict sundance chief chuckled and shrugged his shoulders at Painted Turtle Man. The old man was not amused. The singers were no longer singing and some were craning their necks to try and see what was going on.

"Should we just pull them out?" suggested the strict sundance chief.

"And have all the *Nehiyawak* think he was too weak to fulfill his oath? *Awas*! You have done enough."

The chief grumbled something and walked away, leaving Painted Turtle Man to tend to his adopted grandson.

"I am sorry this happened, my boy. This is not how it is supposed to be. I must pull out the pegs. Even a grown man could not break free of these. You saw the warrior who flew with the eagles. He did not even break free while hanging with all his weight."

"Everything happens for a reason, *Moosum*," said Little Grey Bear Boy. "I must at least try to fulfill my oath."

"I do not understand why this has happened at our holiest ceremony. But I know in my heart that it was not the will of *Kitchi Manitou*. I will pull out the pegs and we will tell all the *Nehiyawak* about what that fool has done."

"*Motch, Moosum*." Little Grey Bear Boy was close to tears now. "I will not bring dishonour to our clan."

"There is no dishonour, my boy. I cannot bear to see you suffering."

"I suffer for good of the *Nehiyawak*."

The old man prayed. "Oh, Great Spirit, hear my plea. Forgive me for what I am about to do."

Painted Turtle Man raised his eagle wing fan and led Little Grey Bear Boy to the Tree of Life. Every step felt like knives twisting from the inside of the boy's chest. He hugged the Tree of Life and concentrated hard on his pledge.

"You must run back quickly and pull hard at the end of the rope," Painted Turtle Man told him. "You will need to try to break free all four times in order to loosen the flesh up enough to break."

Little Grey Bear Boy heeded the old man's advice and ran back quickly and got to the end of the rope. The roped jerked him forward and he nearly lost his balance. Painted Turtle Man caught him and tried to act as though nothing had happened. The old man's eyes were glassy. He looked over at the strict sundance chief, who appeared to be smirking. Painted Turtle Man led his adopted grandson back to the Tree of Life for another try.

"That was a good attempt, my boy," he whispered. "But you will have to try much harder than that."

Little Grey Bear Boy gritted his teeth and launched himself backwards, running as fast as he could and jumping as he had seen the other boys do on their fourth attempt. The *Nehiyawak* were cheering. They must have thought he was confused. Again, when he had reached the end, he was stopped abruptly by the snap of the rope. It felt as though he had hit a rock wall.

"Ohhhhh!" yelled the *Nehiyawak*. Little Grey Bear Boy could feel the hot blood running down his stomach. It soaked into his apron.

"That was very good," said Painted Turtle Man. "This time pull hard when you get to the end of the rope and let the skin stretch. It is going to hurt, but do it for as long as you can stand it. If you start to see dark spots, stop pulling."

Little Grey Bear Boy nodded and took a deep breath. He again launched himself backwards and ran as fast as his will would allow. He jumped back before he reached the end of the rope and landed just at the end of its reach. He leaned back hard on the heels of his feet.

The skin of his chest stretched farther than any other sundancer, even those who were heavy. The *Nehiyawak* were cheering loudly, but Little Grey Bear Boy could not hear them. All he could hear was ringing in his ears and screaming in his flesh as the searing pain threatened to engulf him. The outer edges of his vision began to cloud and grow dark. He meant to heed Painted Turtle Man's instructions, but now he could not control his legs or arms. A firm slap on the back from the old man's eagle wing fan snapped him out of it.

He was taken back to the Tree of Life for the last time. Had his efforts been enough? He felt the ground shaking as all of the sundancers gathered behind him. They were dancing with their arms raised in the air, filling Little Grey Bear Boy with a feeling of brotherhood and unity.

"This is it," said Painted Turtle Man. "No matter what happens, know that I love you and will stand by you. You are like the son I never had and you have given my life purpose and meaning. If ever there was a day when you discover the power of the Grey-Eye magic, I hope and pray that it is this day. If it is not the will of *Kitchi Manitou*, so be it. This will not end here!"

Little Grey Bear Boy squeezed the tree hard and gritted his teeth, pouring all of his mind, body, and soul into this one purpose as he launched himself backwards. Time seemed to move slower and he felt the vibrations of the earth on every step. Fat raindrops fell from the sky and the water splashed beneath his feet as he ran. When he got near the end of the length of rope he bent his knees deeply and jumped back high into the air, and hit the wall.

He did not crash to the ground as he had expected but remained hovering in the air just above Painted Turtle Man. The rope was pulled taunt and the tree of Life was bending towards him. He pulled hard with a force unknown, yet could not break free.

"I am Little Grey Bear Boy of the Bear clan!" he shouted in a voice so loud it shook both Mother Earth and Father Sky. Lighting flashed across the sky and the Thunderbirds roared.

"I will walk without fear upon the Earth. I serve *Kitchi Manitou* in all things. Make me worthy of You, *Kitchi Manitou*. I suffer myself for the good of the *Nehiyawak*. Hear my plea!"

The loudest eagle cry sounded. Two blue eagles burst forth from the rain clouds and dove at Little Grey Bear Boy. The sundancers on the ground below him ducked as the massive spectral eagles grabbed Little Grey Bear Boy's arms and pulled him backwards. The flap of the blue eagles' wings created such a force of wind that the people below were knocked over. Little Grey Bear Boy screamed so loud that the earth shook as the skin on his chest stretched and tore. The large pegs flew up as he broke free and the blue eagles disappeared in an instant.

The boy fell and his fellow sundancers reached up into the sky and caught him. The rain stopped and the wind died.

Painted Turtle Man picked the unconscious boy up in his arms and hurried down the hill, past the sundance campsite.

# NISTOMITANAW NIKOTWĀSOSĀP

The skin on Little Grey Bear Boy's chest had been torn wide open and bright red blood covered both the boy and the old man.

"Damn that old fool!" growled Painted Turtle Man as he and his helper tended to the wounds. Little Grey Bear Boy was unconscious but breathing.

"The skin is shredded," said Painted Turtle Man. "There are no pieces large enough to sew together!"

"What will we do, Uncle?" the worried young helper asked.

"All we can do is clean the wounds and seal them with the red clover medicine. This is going to leave quite a scar."

Blue Elk Man burst through the door flaps of the medicine lodge, wearing the same look he wore when the Red Eyed intruder had invaded the Bear lodge.

"He is going to be all right," Painted Turtle Man said before Blue Elk Man could speak. "I am tending to him."

Again the door flaps flew open. It was White Willow Woman and Singing Doe. Blue Elk Man tried to stop her before she saw the state of her son, but he was not fast enough. The sight was too much and she fainted. Blue Elk Man caught her and took her up in his arms just as Brown Shield Man burst in.

"Get them out!" barked Painted Turtle Man. "No one else is to enter the Bear medicine lodge!"

"*Hiy, hiy!*" said Brown Shield Man as the injured boy's family left the lodge.

A crowd had gathered in the centre of the village and was making its way closer and closer to the medicine lodge. Brown Shield Man stood staunch in front of the door flaps, his folded arms a challenge to those who would come closer. Still the crowd nudged forward, some trying to peer around or over Brown Shield Man. One man, not of *Nisichawayasihk,* got too close.

Brown Shield Man cleared his throat aggressively. "Ra-hem!"

"We wish to see the child!" said the man. Brown Shield Man stood firm, ignoring the statement.

"Did you not hear what I said?" pressed the man.

"Do not challenge him," another visitor warned. "That is Brown Shield Man of the Wolf clan. He once killed a man in cold blood. He might kill again."

The assembled crowd murmured and those nearby moved back a little. Still, Brown Shield Man did not acknowledge the crowd. It appeared the remaining sundance chiefs had ended the ceremony, since more people joined the crowd. Wearied sundancers, still in their ceremonial garb, began to arrive.

"Please, my brother," said one of the sundancers falling to his knees before Brown Shield Man. "I must pay my respects to the Grey-Eyed one who is blessed by *Kitchi Manitou.*"

The crowd was murmuring and growing restless. They all wished to see the boy who had produced the miracle. Just as those near the Bear medicine lodge surged forward, several men armed with war spears and wearing white wolf skins over their head and shoulders quick-marched in and assembled behind the lone warrior. These were his brothers of the White Wolf Warrior Society.

"You will all respect the wishes of the keeper of the Bear medicine lodge, Painted Turtle Man of the Bear clan. Press your luck and you will come to know the true meaning of pain!" No one would challenge the senior warrior and the dozen fully armed and hard-faced warriors that stood with him. The crowd began to disperse and find their way back to their lodges or tents. The sundancers and the truly faithful remained, kneeling and quietly muttering chants or prayers.

Little Grey Bear Boy did not wake until the sun had begun to set. His chest had gone numb, thanks in part to Painted Turtle Man's medicine, but he could still feel a dull throbbing deep beneath the skin.

"*Moosum…*" he mumbled. "I am thirsty…"

"I thought you might be." For the first time since he noticed the pegs in the boy's chest, Painted Turtle Man smiled.

The young helper held a birch bark bowl with clear water to Little Grey Bear Boy's lips. He drank a bit, but coughed and sputtered as he tried.

"Drink slow," instructed Painted Turtle Man. "You are still recovering. Just let your mouth have the water, but do not swallow it yet."

Little Grey Bear Boy knew it was best to listen to Painted Turtle Man. He wet his lips and tongue with the water and felt his dry mouth absorb it without having to swallow. He wanted more but he started to feel dizzy.

"Rest now, my boy."

Little Grey Bear Boy slipped back into unconsciousness as Blue Elk Man and White Willow Woman entered the medicine lodge and knelt by their son.

"He is going to be all right, my girl," said Painted Turtle Man to a teary-eyed White Willow Woman.

"You had better go," said Blue Elk Man. "The man who pierced Little Grey Bear Boy is addressing the Circle of Clan Mothers."

"What?" exclaimed Painted Turtle Man. "You mean he is still in the village?"

"*Tapwe…*" Blue Elk Man nodded as Painted Turtle Man stood up.

"Let the boy rest. If he wakes up give him some water. Do not make him talk about anything. He is still too exhausted from his ordeal."

Painted Turtle Man walked out of the Bear medicine lodge and the White Wolf Warriors stood at attention. There was a large bonfire burning at the centre of the village and the *Nehiyawak* were gathered.

The Circle of Clan Mothers had apparently granted the sundance chief a special audience. Painted Turtle Man marched to Walking Moon Woman's side, followed closely on either side by two White Wolf Warriors.

"I am called Red Sky Man," the sundance chief was saying. "I have travelled a very long way from the southeast, *Bonibonibee*, the place where the water rises and dips. I have long practiced the ways of our ancestors and have learned the secrets of the plant world. I would offer my services to the people of *Nisichawayasihk* to help the young Grey-eyed boy find his magic."

"And how is it that you are knowledgeable in the ways of the Grey Eye magic?" inquired Walking Moon Woman.

"Amongst the people of *Bonibonibee* there was a young man who was gifted with the Grey-Eye magic," Red Sky Man explained. "He was the only Grey-Eye among us and I helped him find the way. Under my humble guidance, he was able to find his magic and was then chosen by a woman of another village. Since my wife went on to the Spirit World and the Grey Eye found his way, there has been little use for me amongst my own people."

Green Wing Woman of the Turtle clan stepped forward to speak. "My sisters," she said. "The Grandmother Turtle would be well served if Little Grey Bear Boy was tutored by one who has experience in such matters."

"My sister," countered old Walking Moon Woman, "Little Grey Bear Boy is already well attended by my cousin, Painted Turtle Man."

The assembled crowd looked over at Painted Turtle Man, who stood weary but firm.

"Mothers of the *Nehiyawak*," interjected Red Sky Man, "I do not mean to intrude on the responsibilities of any of the people of *Nisichawayasihk*. I would, of course, merely add my knowledge to that of your own teachers."

Painted Turtle Man cleared his throat.

"I would hear what Painted Turtle Man has to say on the matter," said Walking Moon Woman.

"Mothers," he began. "My Grey-Eye grandson lays upon his back, deeply wounded from the actions of the man who would be his teacher. This man used the wrong pegs and cut too deep into the boy's flesh."

The crowd reeled at this revelation, talking and whispering for some time.

"*Tapwe*, people of *Nisichawayasihk*," said Red Sky Man. "What he says is true, I do not deny it."

The crowd was silent for a moment.

"But consider this," he added. "Had it not been for my error, the *Nehiyawak* would not have been blessed with the miracle. I do not assume to know the will of *Kitchi Manitou*, I am just honoured Creator chose to act through me."

Painted Turtle Man's eyes could not contain his fury at this convenient interpretation of Creator's will. The *Nehiyawak* considered Red Sky Man's words. Some were intrigued and some were offended. The people and the Circle of Clan Mothers were divided.

Drifting Butterfly Woman stepped forward for the Crane clan.

"My sisters," she began. "It would seem there are many ways in which the miracle could be interpreted. How are we to proceed in the best interest of *Nisichawayasihk*?"

"Perhaps," interjected Talking Stone Woman, matriarch of the Deer clan. "We should hear the thoughts of our leaders on this matter."

All eyes turned to the Eagle twins. They had so wanted the honour of leading the Circle of Clan Mothers. Now they would have to prove they were prepared for the responsibility. The twins were having one of their silent debates through eye and head movements. With the people of *Nisichawayasihk* so obviously divided on the issue, taking a stance one way or the other was dangerous.

"My sisters," began the elder Eagle twin, "we have given much thought and consideration to this situation..."

"Forgive my ignorance," Red Sky Man said.

A string of gasps from the crowd. For a man to interrupt a matriarch, much less the leader of the Circle of Clan Mothers, was unheard of.

"Am I right in understanding that the people of *Nisichawayasihk* are led by two Eagle mothers?"

"What of it?" said the elder Eagle twin.

"Please forgive me," begged Red Sky Man lowering his eyes. "Creator's message just became apparent to me."

"And what message would that be?" asked Drifting Butterfly Woman.

"The miracle at the sundance," said Red Sky Man matter-of-factly. "Do you not see? Twin eagles flew out of the sky to help the Grey-Eye child. Creator was choosing the Eagle clan to guide the boy. I was born of the Eagle in my homeland, but here, in *Nisichawayasihk*, the Eagle lodge must be very strong with the Grey-Eye magic."

Painted Turtle Man was becoming tired of this man's readings of Creator's will. "That would seem a very convenient interpretation—one that would most benefit the Eagle clan."

The Eagle warriors were in an uproar, shouting out and flipping their hands in the air towards the old man. Not only had Painted Turtle Man spoken without the permission of the clan mothers, he had also insulted the Eagle lodge. The Eagle twins looked to Drifting Butterfly Woman with raised eyebrows.

"My sister," Drifting Butterfly Woman began, addressing Walking Moon Woman. "Please announce to the circle if you wish someone to speak on your behalf."

"*Tapwe*, my sister," replied Walking Moon Woman, maintaining eye contact with Painted Turtle Man as she spoke. "I will remember to do that."

By this time, the crowd had considered Red Sky Man's interpretation of the day's events. They could not deny that the appearance of two eagles seemed to be a strong omen in favour of the Eagle lodge.

"My sisters. Since this man is new to *Nisichawayasihk*, it is reasonable to assume that he is not aware of my late grandmother, Soaring Star Woman. The power of her Grey-Eye magic blessed the Eagle lodge and all the people of *Nisichawayasihk* for many, many years. It would seem that my grandmother continues to bless and guide the *Nehiyawak* from the Spirit World." The elder Eagle twin spoke with a new-found confidence.

"*Hiy, hiy!*" yelled the crowd in agreement.

"As Red Sky Man was born of the Eagle," continued the elder twin, "we would welcome him into the Eagle lodge to serve the people of *Nisichawayasihk*."

"That is of course, your prerogative," said Walking Moon Woman. "Just as the teaching of my grandson, Little Grey Bear Boy, is mine."

The people of *Nisichawayasihk* went silent and the sky rumbled in acknowledgement. No one who heard the Bear matriarch speak or who saw the look on her face dared to challenge her. To come between a mother bear and her cub was dangerous.

"*Tapwe*, my sister. It could not be any other way."

"People of *Nisichawayasihk*!" boomed Drifting Butterfly Woman. "We welcome Red Sky Man of the Eagle clan. Come forward and acknowledge the newest member of our village."

The *Nehiyawak* cheered and lined up to shake hands with Red Sky Man. The Bear clan, Painted Turtle Man especially, was reluctant, but they lined up with the others as expected. When Painted Turtle Man's turn came, he put out his hand and looked Red Sky Man in the eye. The two men shook hands slowly while the *Nehiyawak* pretended not to watch.

Painted Turtle Man went to move on but Red Sky Man clutched his hand, squeezing it painfully. "You would be wise," he whispered through a tight smile, "to stay out of my way."

Painted Turtle Man jerked his hand away. He felt as though he had met this person long ago, but when and where he could not remember. It could not have been that long ago—the man was easily thirty years his junior.

# NISTOMITANAW TĪPAKOHPOSĀP

"How did you make those eagles appear?" asked Flying Rabbit Boy.

"How come they were blue?" added Yellow Hawk Girl.

"Honestly," answered Little Grey Bear Boy. "I don't know how I did it. I can barely remember what happened myself." The Bear clan had crowded into the medicine lodge—all but Brown Shield Man, who maintained his position on the door.

"You mean you don't remember the giant blue eagles coming out of the sky?" Yellow Hawk Girl asked, amazed.

"Yeah," added Flying Rabbit Boy. "You screamed like someone very awake to what was going on when the pegs tore out of your chest" He re-enacted the miracle, with some exaggeration.

"*Ekosi*!" said White Willow Woman, "*Awas*!"

"*Tapwe*!" said Painted Turtle Man. "You need your rest, my boy."

"What happened at the circle?" Blue Elk Man stood to the side, arms crossed, trying to contain his anger.

"I still cannot believe it," said Painted Turtle Man shaking his head. "The fool who did this has been adopted by the Eagle clan. He also said it should be him to teach Little Grey Bear Boy about the Grey-Eye magic."

White Willow Woman turned. "*What*? What did my mother say?"

"Don't worry. Your mother made herself heard."

"She always does," said Blue Elk Man, who was rewarded for his wit with a slap across the shoulder from his wife.

"*Moosum*," said Little Grey Bear Boy. "I want you to continue to teach me. That man was so strict at the sundance, even to the young ones."

"Rest, my boy. Do not worry yourself with such matters. Your family will take care of you as we always have."

"And always will," added Blue Elk Man.

"*Tapwe*," said Little Grey Bear Boy, "you have never given me any reason to doubt that."

"Hard times are ahead," Painted Turtle Man said. "It is very important that whatever happens, no matter what is said, we stick together as a family. There are those who would seek to keep the Bear clan small and weak. We must do our duty and stay strong in the ways of the Grandmother Bear. Not for us, but for all the people of *Nisichawayasihk*."

"*Tapwe!*" said the others in unison.

"You must recover your strength," said Painted Turtle Man once the others had gone off to the Bear lodge for the night. "I doubt the *Nehiyawak* will give you much time to heal before they load you up with burdens."

"What will I do, *Moosum*?"

"What will *we* do," corrected Painted Turtle Man, "I will be with you through whatever challenge the future holds."

Little Grey Bear Boy slept for the next two days. Whenever he woke, Painted Turtle Man gave him water or medicinal tea. His mother was usually there, feeding him a mixture of berries and pemmican. The wounds on his chest were starting to scab over.

"*Moosum*! He's scratching again!" called Yellow Hawk Girl.

"I can't help it. It is so itchy!"

"And to think I was jealous you got to go to the sundance!" teased Flying Rabbit Boy. "Now I am glad I didn't."

"*Motch*! This was not supposed to happen," stated Painted Turtle Man. "You will have to go next year when it is your time."

"Maybe I should wait until I am a bit older."

"Well that is the first time I have ever heard you say something like that," chuckled Painted Turtle Man.

Little Grey Bear Boy sat up, trying to hear the voices coming in from outside. The others were acting as though they did not notice.

"Would you like some more of the red clover medicine?" Painted Turtle Man asked.

But the boy would not be distracted. "What is going on outside?"

"It is nothing. Your uncle, Brown Shield Man, is taking care of it."

Blue Elk Man entered the medicine lodge. When he saw Little Grey Bear Boy's face, he tried to compose himself. "You are awake."

"Who was it?" asked Painted Turtle Man.

"The Soaring Eagles," he answered. "That makes all of them."

"All except the Dog Soldiers."

"*Motch*, they were the first," explained Blue Elk Man. "They came to me and I refused them."

"Would someone please tell me what is going on?" pleaded Little Grey Bear Boy.

The others looked at him in silence. Blue Elk Man did not like the idea of keeping secrets from his son. Painted Turtle Man gave him a nod.

"All of the warrior societies in the village, as well as some from other villages, have asked to induct you."

"Me?" exclaimed Little Grey Bear Boy.

"Him?" parroted Flying Rabbit Boy, earning him a frown from his grandfather.

"I have only seen twelve summers," said Little Grey Bear Boy. "Can I join a warrior society?"

"*Motch*," said Painted Turtle Man. "All they want is the prestige of having a Grey-Eye in their ranks. Especially after what happened at the sundance."

"You must earn that honour," said Blue Elk Man. "You have not killed an elk or a moose, nor have you saved a life…"

"Then why are the warrior societies asking to induct me? They must not agree with what you are saying."

"If he gets inducted, will he be able to be chosen as a husband?" asked Flying Rabbit Boy. Painted Turtle Man frowned again.

"I hope you understand these things," said Blue Elk Man. "Most boys your age would think they are somehow special. They would feel they deserve that which they have not earned. It would show that you are growing into a very fine warrior indeed, if you were to wait until it is time. I had sixteen summers before I became a warrior and twenty-two before your mother chose me."

Singing Doe entered the medicine lodge. "I don't think they are going to leave," she said.

"Who will not leave?" asked Little Grey Bear Boy. "The warrior societies?"

Singing Doe looked at Blue Elk Man and Painted Turtle Man, realizing she may have spoken out of turn. The men simply nodded at her. He might as well know this too.

"Some of the sundancers have been sitting outside the Bear medicine lodge, wanting to see you again," Singing Doe explained. "They haven't broken their fast…"

"I don't understand," said Little Grey Bear Boy.

"They think the miracle was part of the ceremony," explained Painted Turtle Man. "Even after the sundance chiefs told them it was finished, they did not listen. They think it will not be over until you say it is finished."

"I am not a sundance chief!"

At this, Blue Elk Man's chest puffed. "Though, it would seem your fellow sundancers want to think of you as something much greater. Most of them have never seen the Grey-eye magic before."

Little Grey Bear Boy thought to himself for a moment and offered a quiet prayer to *Kitchi Manitou*. When he had made his decision, he threw the soft deer hide blanket off his legs and got up.

"What are you doing? You are not supposed to move."

"I am sorry, mother," he said, "but I cannot allow my fellow sundancers to suffer any more."

Painted Turtle Man stood up and began to speak. Instead he rushed to Little Grey Bear Boy's side and helped him onto his feet. The boy's legs were weak and shaky as he dragged himself towards the door. He looked up at his father, who held open the door flaps. If his father did not believe him ready to become a warrior, Little Grey Bear Boy would have to prove himself.

Little Grey Bear Boy had not seen the light of day since the miracle happened. It took him a moment to open his eyes, but as he did he saw the surprised faces of several White Wolf Warriors and a group of dusty sundancers.

"Ah-ho!" said Brown Shield Man as he stepped aside.

The sunburned warriors jumped to attention and looked at the boy.

"It is him!" croaked one of the sundancers. The others cheered weakly. They muttered prayers of thanks with dry, cracked lips.

Little Grey Bear Boy mustered his strength and drew himself up as straight as he was able. The scabs on his chest had opened slightly with his movement and a slow trickle of blood dropped down his torso.

"Sundancers," Little Grey Bear Boy said, "it is time for you to break your fast. I am just another sundancer, the same as you. I do not know how what you saw happened. I was just as surprised as you were. Please, I beg of you, do not continue to suffer yourselves because of me."

"But I saw you call to *Kitchi Manitou* and were answered! You could help me. My mother is very sick…"

"*Motch*, I prayed to *Kitchi Manitou* the same as you did. Creator did not obey me, Creator took pity upon me! I do not know how or why this has happened. I will pray for your mother and for all of your families. Only *Kitchi Manitou* can know what will happen in the days ahead. Please, my brothers, drink some water, eat some food, and when you have recovered your strength, return to your villages to serve your clans. You will see me again next year at the sacred sundance."

"We wish to stay here and serve you!" pledged one of the younger sundancers.

"I am just a boy who has not yet earned a warrior name," said Little Grey Bear Boy, looking back at his father. "I must serve my mother and my clan. Our village is large and although Mother Earth has been generous with us, it would be asking too much to expect her to feed so many. Your own villages need strong warriors to hunt food and gather wood for the hard faced-moons of Old Man Winter. Return home and serve your clan, the same as I will. We have danced the Dance of Life together and now we are bound in spirit."

The sundancers looked at one another.

"We will always be connected in the way it matters to our Creator, *Kitchi Manitou,*" the boy added. "You are my sundance family and you will remain so until the day *Kitchi Manitou* calls us back to the Spirit World. Go now, and may the Grandmother Bear guide you in the ways of healing."

"All my relations!" the sundancers holding vigil croaked in unison. They began muttering prayers of thanks to Creator and the ancestor spirits. Little Grey Bear Boy's legs were shaking and Blue Elk Man and Painted Turtle Man came up behind him, catching him just as he fainted. The two men helped him back into the medicine lodge and put him back onto his bed roll.

The senior warrior of the White Wolf Warrior Society stepped in front of the medicine lodge.

"All right, my people," he said. "You have seen the boy and you have heard his words. Now I would ask you humbly to do as he wishes. You will see him again next year. Go now and serve *Kitchi Manitou* in all things!"

White Willow Woman and Singing Doe went about the sundancers with water skins. Some were reluctant at first, but when the two women explained who they were, the parched sundancers took the water.

# NISTOMITANAW AYINĀNĪWOSĀP

As the sundancers broke their fast and recovered their strength, they began to leave *Nisichawayasihk* and return to their home villages, though throughout the villages what happened at the sundance ceremony was being talked about.

Little Grey Bear Boy's healing was difficult, but after a few days he was able to walk around the village. Everyone was hard at work trying to replenish their stores of food for the winter. Hosting the sacred sundance ceremony had taxed their resources—none of the clans had any dried meat, wild rice, or berries. The village had given all it could to be good hosts to the pilgrims. That is the way of the *Nehiyawak*; they welcome visitors as though they are family and would have them want for nothing while under their care.

The Marten, Wolf, and especially the Eagle clans sent their many hunters out often and recovered quickly. The Bears and Turtles were not faring so well and getting discouraged. But not Flying Rabbit Boy—he would awake early to complete his chores, collecting wood and cleaning out the ashes from the centre fire, then go off hunting with his bow. Although he was not able to travel far from the village, he could go as far as the lakeshore in search of ducks and geese, hoping to take some before they migrated south. Time was running out—the leaves of the forest were already changing.

Painted Turtle Man decided it would be good for Little Grey Bear

Boy to walk the forest with his cousin. The two boys scoured the marshlands in search of waterfowl. Coming upon a pair of ducks, Flying Rabbit Boy drew back an arrow and released it.

"Not again," he whined as the arrow flew off wildly and the startled ducks flew away.

"You are getting closer."

"*Motch*, it's my arm. I'll never be able to aim the bow properly." He pushed the heel of his palm into the deep scars where the Red-Eye warrior had cut him. It had been three years since the attack.

"I can pull the bow back," he explained, "but my bow arm shakes when I aim it. Before you turned me into a turtle, he cut me deep into the meat. It does not work as well as it did before."

"At least Painted Turtle Man was able to save your arm," joked Little Grey Bear Boy. "You would have a hard time aiming the bow with your teeth!"

The two boys laughed at the thought.

"You are just trying to make me feel better," said Flying Rabbit Boy. "All the other boys my age are bringing home ducks and geese. How will I prove myself a warrior if I can't do the tasks everyone else my age can do? Can't you use the Grey-Eye magic to make me a better hunter?"

"*Motch*, I can't even use the Grey-Eye magic to make myself a better hunter. We will keep trying. There are more ducks around here somewhere."

"*Tapwe*," sighed Flying Rabbit Boy, "I am bound to get lucky eventually."

"*Tansi?* Young warriors." The startled boys looked up to see Red Sky Man of the Eagle clan approaching through the bush. Little Grey Bear Boy's heart started pounding. He felt a lump in the back of his throat as he looked upon the man who had wounded him.

"I couldn't help overhearing your conversation as I was picking medicines."

"We did not mean to disturb you, Uncle," said Flying Rabbit Boy respectfully.

"I explained to your family," Red Sky Man continued, ignoring Flying Rabbit Boy, "that I had worked with a young Grey-Eyed boy years ago. When I met him, he was in the same situation you are in.

He had no idea how to use the magic. I might be able to help you…"

"How could you teach him, Uncle, when you do not have grey eyes yourself?"

Red Sky Man scowled at Flying Rabbit Boy. The boy lowered his eyes to apologize for his impudence.

"Maybe I could show you," suggested Red Sky Man. "We can find some more ducks."

"*Motch*, we would not want to keep you from your work, Uncle," said Little Grey Bear Boy. "Besides, it's starting to look like it might rain…"

"Nonsense!" boomed Red Sky Man. "It won't take too long. What could be more important than a boy learning to provide for his family? How else will you two become warriors?"

Little Grey Bear Boy brightened at this idea. He, too, wanted to provide.

"Come with me," smiled Red Sky Man.

They began walking around the edge of the marsh. Little Grey Bear Boy still had a sinking feeling in his chest and a lump in his throat, but he had been taught to respect his elders, so follow he must.

Soon, the three found another pair of ducks swimming and diving for food.

"Okay," whispered Red Sky Man squatting down low. "This is what you must do…You there, Rabbit Boy, will aim your bow. Little Grey Bear Boy, you stand behind him and place your hands on his shoulders. I will stand by you and teach you the hunting chant, which will give him the true aim."

Little Grey Bear Boy did not like the idea of using the Grey-Eye magic for hunting, as it would not be fair to the ducks. Flying Rabbit Boy, on the other hand, was excited at the prospect of success, earned or otherwise. He notched an arrow to his bowstring and pulled back. His bow arm shook like it always did.

"All right," whispered Red Sky Man standing behind Little Grey Bear Boy. "Put your hands on his shoulders."

Little Grey Bear Boy did as instructed and Red Sky Man began to chant the ancient hunting chant. As he was chanting, Little Grey Bear Boy began to sense the vibration of the Grey-Eye magic. It felt a little different this time—there was a strange feeling of warmth behind his eyes as it took hold.

Flying Rabbit Boy's bow arm stopped shaking and straightened directly at the ducks. He loosed his arrow and it fired straight and true, guided by the Grey-Eye magic. The arrow stuck the hen first through the side of the neck then deflected directly into the front of the drake's throat. Both ducks killed with a single shot.

"Woo-ooo!" cheered Flying Rabbit Boy having finally succeeded where he had always failed. "Thank-you, Uncle, for your teaching!"

Flying Rabbit Boy dropped his bow and quiver of arrows and proceeded to take off his shirt, leggings, and moccasins. He ran out into the cold water, splashing about and cheering like a fool. He waded out to retrieve the ducks.

"You have done well," said Red Sky Man. "You know, there is much more I can teach you."

"Thank you, Uncle," said Little Grey Bear Boy. "I am grateful for your teaching, but I must heed my *moosum*, Painted Turtle Man, who has been helping me since before I can remember."

"*Tapwe*, I understand how you must feel about him. Perhaps you have learned all he can teach you. You don't need to decide anything right now, you are still a boy with plenty of time before you can start to walk man's road…All I ask is that you come to me when you are ready to earn a name and start to help your family. I know they could use another hunter…"

Little Grey Bear Boy wanted to agree with this reasonable request. For some reason his heart was pounding as Red Sky Man's eyes looked into him. A half-soaked Flying Rabbit Boy bounded back to them, a fat duck in each hand.

"Thank you, Grandmother Duck," he shouted up to the sky in front of them. "Cousin, get out your tobacco!"

Red Sky Man smiled. "Well, I will leave you boys to it. Think about what I said."

"Thank you again, Uncle," said Little Grey Bear Boy bowing his head respectfully.

Red Sky Man made his way back to the forest.

Flying Rabbit Boy was still smiling from ear to ear. Little Grey

Bear Boy rolled his eyes and removed a small pouch from his satchel.

"Brother and sister duck," he prayed. "We thank you for sacrificing yourselves so that our family can survive. We will honour your courage by ensuring every part of your body is used in a good way. Your meat will be eaten, your sinew will be spun into thread, your feathers will guide our arrows, and your bones will make whistles and charms. If there is even a scrap we are not able to make use of, we will see it returned to Mother Earth, so that the grasses, trees, and plants will nourish your relatives. All my relations, *ekosani*."

Little Grey Bear Boy put a clump of tobacco down at the edge of the marsh to honour the spirit of Grandmother Duck.

Flying Rabbit Boy was happier and more excited than Little Grey Bear Boy had seen him in a long while. Back at the village, they stopped by the Turtle lodge so he could do something he had been dreaming about.

Flying Rabbit Boy cleared his throat in as manly a manner as he could. "Ahem!"

Green Wing Woman, matriarch of the Turtle clan, came and opened the flaps. "Ohh, *tansi,* young warrior?" she said, observing the two fat ducks in Flying Rabbit Boy's hands. "May the Grandmother Turtle guide you in the ways of learning."

"May the Grandmother Bear guide you in the ways of healing," Flying Rabbit Boy answered appropriately. "I have come to seek your assistance. Mother Earth has given us her blessing this day, but I am afraid she has been too generous. Would you please accept one of these ducks? My family cannot make use of both and it would be wrong to let it go to waste."

With mock reluctance, Green Wing Woman accepted. "If it would help the Bear clan…"

"Thank you, *Nookum*," said Flying Rabbit Boy graciously. "I am in your debt."

"One day you will become a fine warrior." From behind her came the sound of laughing.

Flying Rabbit Boy could barely contain his smile. His cousin grabbed his arm and pulled him away. The boys bowed to the matriarch and went home, Flying Rabbit Boy with a new bounce in his step.

# NISTOMITANAW KĪKĀ-MITĀTAHTOSĀP

Though most of the clans had managed to replenish their food stores, the winter that year was long and difficult for the people of *Nisichawayasihk*. Life was especially hard for the Bear clan. Blue Elk Man and Brown Shield Man had again stayed behind when most of the other warriors had gone south for the great buffalo hunt in the fall. This year, the other warriors were not able to be quite as generous as they had been in previous years.

Again, the saving grace of the Bear clan was the assistance of Drifting Butterfly Woman, the young matriarch of the Crane clan, and her husband Many Fish. She continued to recruit White Willow Woman and Singing Doe to assist in the cleaning and smoking of the fish her husband caught.

Painted Turtle Man was having difficulties of his own. His sacred sight had somehow diminished, which many of the *Nehiyawak* attributed to his age. Whenever a warrior passed tobacco to Painted Turtle Man to be guided on the hunt or in some other endeavour, more often than not it would end in failure. One Deer clan warrior met with disaster. He was dragged back into the village on a makeshift travois pulled by Red Sky Man.

A crowd was gathering in the centre of the circle of lodges where Red Sky Man had pulled the travois. Despite the cold wind and blowing snow the villagers were curious to hear the details of what had happened. People gathered, trudging through hard snow and wrapped up in their buffalo robes. "I went to the place Painted Turtle Man's vision had guided me to," explained the warrior. "I found the bluff to the northeast where he had seen the moose in his vision. I positioned myself at the edge of the cliff as instructed, keeping downwind from the birch tree below, just as I had been told. As I waited, I began to get sleepy and I didn't notice a crow fly onto the tree I was under. The crow cawed loudly and startled me and I fell off the cliff and broke my leg. I called for help for some time before Red Sky Man found me."

"I do not think anyone should blame Painted Turtle Man," said Red Sky Man, though no one had thought to. "Although I did not see any moose sign, I am sure there was one on its way. It was an accident no one could have foreseen."

"What brought you out there?" Painted Turtle Man asked Red Sky Man.

"I was looking for spruce gum for a medicine I am making," answered Red Sky Man. "Anyway, it's a good thing I was there, or this warrior might have frozen to death."

The people of *Nisichawayasihk* murmured and offered prayers of thanks to *Kitchi Manitou* for preventing such a tragedy.

"A long way to go for spruce gum," said Painted Turtle Man, fixing his gaze on Red Sky Man.

"I needed a certain kind not found around here. You have probably never heard of it."

Painted Turtle Man nodded suspiciously, then noticed the sky was becoming cloudy. He looked back at Red Sky Man, smiled, and walked away.

"It is unfortunately the mind that is usually the first thing to suffer with age," Red Sky Man whispered to the man next to him.

Warriors who passed their tobacco to Red Sky Man that winter seemed to be blessed with unusual success. One young warrior of only fourteen summers had worn an elk tooth charm around his neck that Red Sky Man had blessed for him. When he went out hunting as directed, he managed to find and kill the largest elk anyone in the village had ever seen. The boy was immediately inducted into the Soaring Eagle Warrior Society for his success.

Eventually, not only warriors but anyone seeking help or healing stopped visiting the Bear medicine lodge. Slowly, even Painted Turtle Man's helpers began to abandon him.

"I am sorry, *Moosum*," apologized Soaring Spear Man, the last of his helpers. "I am grateful for your teachings. I must now go and learn what others might have to teach me."

"I understand," said Painted Turtle Man, mustering what little pride he had left. "Go forward and learn. Of all the teachings that will be presented to you by new teachers, take only what you need and leave the rest behind."

With that final lesson, Soaring Spear Man nodded and shook hands with Painted Turtle Man for the last time as his student.

One night, during a meagre evening meal at the Bear lodge, Walking Moon Woman spoke up. "My cousin. I have begun to miss the time we used to spend together. In this Bear lodge, I have only the young people to speak to. As I grow older, I wish to spend more time talking with my age mates. Younger people only ever concern themselves with the future. I wish to reminisce about the days that have passed, days which these ones were not around to see. You should come back into the Bear lodge so we can talk in the evening when I have my tea. You could also help to give me your advice on matters of importance to the family and the village."

"Your grandchildren are growing, my cousin," replied Painted Turtle Man. "The Bear lodge already seems too small for them. Also, I have many medicines that would take up too much space and cause you much grief. I am afraid I would just be a burden to you."

The truth was, having seen seventy-two summers, the old medicine carrier's body no longer had the strength to maintain a lodge by himself. Even with Little Grey Bear Boy and his cousin Flying Rabbit Boy trying their best to assist him, Painted Turtle Man did not have the help—or the muscle—he needed to continue.

"Nonsense," said Walking Moon Woman. "There is plenty of room. I will just have my daughters clean up some of their mess!"

"We would be honoured to have you back in the Bear lodge, Uncle," said White Willow Woman. "You could help to teach the children. Already they ask many questions and there is just not enough time in the day to finish our work and explain everything to them."

"*Tapwe*, you would be doing us a service," added Singing Doe.

"*Tapwe*," said Brown Shield Man, "and we would all be warmer this winter if we were to add the hides from the Bear medicine lodge to one home."

"I think we would all be more comfortable," nodded Blue Elk Man. It was a strange comment coming from the quiet warrior who had endured many hardships.

"It seems the whole clan is in agreement on this," observed Painted Turtle Man, looking from one adult to the next. "Who am I to argue with the Bear clan?"

Blue Elk Man and Brown Shield Man got to work the next day disassembling the Bear medicine lodge. White Willow Woman, Singing Doe, and the children helped pack up the medicines and possessions and moved them into the Bear lodge. The lodge poles were widened and once again Painted Turtle man was with the clan.

No sooner had the Bear medicine lodge gone down than a new Eagle medicine lodge went up. Red Sky Man, the new Eagle medicine keeper, had elevated himself quickly in the eyes of the people of *Nisichawayasihk*. This was not uncommon—the *Nehiyawak* often held newcomers in higher esteem than those who had grown up in their community.

On seeing this, Painted Turtle Man prayed. "*Kitchi Manitou*, is this your way of giving an old man a rest before calling me back on the long journey to the Spirit World? Show me how I can best be of service to the *Nehiyawak*."

He tried to focus on his one remaining task, the education of Little Grey Bear Boy and the other Bear clan children. "Your will be done, *Kitchi Manitou*..." he prayed whenever feelings of regret entered his heart.

The Bear clan struggled through the winter. They may have all grown a little thinner through the hard-faced moons of Old Man Winter, but they greeted a renewed Mother Earth in the spring together. Little Grey Bear Boy and his cousin joined Many Fish in learning how to use a net in the river to catch spawning fish. His own children being too young to learn the skills yet, Many Fish welcomed the opportunity to teach young men who were still earning their warrior names.

The river ice had broken and cleared, though the edge of the river bank still had snow and ice in the shaded areas. The water had not yet given up its winter chill and the two boys were careful not to fall in. To do the work they were doing it didn't take very long for their mukluks to get soaking wet with the cold water.

"You need to pull from the top of the net!" Many Fish laughed, as the boy's unpracticed hands struggled with the net. "Pull into the current!"

"But that makes it feel heavier," whined Flying Rabbit Boy.

"*Tapwe*, but doing things the harder way is usually the right way. When you pull with the current the net is lighter, so the fish can swim away from it. You need to catch them head on."

"Just pull!" growled Little Grey Bear Boy. The struggling boys managed to pull their net a ways up the river, getting it onto the land. Their cheering mothers and Drifting Butterfly Woman, matriarch of the Crane clan, greeted them and their full net.

"Thank you grandmothers and grandfathers of the water." Little Grey Bear Boy took out his pouch of tobacco and offered a pinch to the river. "You have blessed us with our fish brothers and sisters. We will no longer be hungry thanks to your generosity. Thank you, Mother Earth for your bounty."

"All my relations!" said the others when he had concluded.

"It has been a long winter," said Drifting Butterfly Woman to her friends, "and you two have become very skinny. I am starting to feel sorry for your husbands."

The women laughed at the playful jest. It was well known that the men of the *Nehiyawak* preferred their wives well-fed.

"*Tapwe*," laughed Singing Doe, "but these fish will change all that!"

Many Fish taught the boys how to scrape the bark off of a tamarack tree and cure it over a fire to make a carrying pole. Once gutted, they hung the fish through the gills on the firm poles, filling two. They carried the poles, one end on each shoulder, home.

With Flying Rabbit Boy in the front, Little Grey Bear Boy at the rear, and all the fish hanging between them, they looked like a large caterpillar. As usual, they stopped by the Turtle lodge to share their catch. They were greeted by Green Wing Woman, matriarch of the Turtle clan. Her granddaughters were quick to cast aside their sewing and quillwork to see what was happening.

"*Tansi,* Flying Rabbit Boy," called one of the girls. "What did you bring for me?"

"*Awas,*" said her sister. "He came here to see me, didn't you?"

"Well, I…" blushed Flying Rabbit Boy as the young Turtles laughed.

"*Awas,* you two, don't tease him," said the matriarch. "Go back inside and do your work."

"*Motch,* I don't think they…" he was too late. They went back into the lodge as ordered, whispering and giggling to one another.

"My boy," said Green Wing Woman to Little Grey Bear Boy, "you have certainly grown this winter."

"Thank you, *Nookum,*" he replied politely.

"You will soon earn a new name, it seems."

"Perhaps," answered Little Grey Bear Boy, his heart jumping at the thought. "I will leave such concerns for *Kitchi Manitou* to decide."

She smiled. "Humility is a fine quality in a young man. May the Grandmother Turtle guide you in the ways of learning."

"And may the Grandmother Bear guide you in the ways of healing," replied Little Grey Bear Boy.

When they returned to the Bear lodge, the cousins tied the tamarack pole across the lodge poles. Just as they were about to set up the smoking rack, they heard an announcement.

"People of *Nisichawayasihk,*" boomed the Crane clan warrior's voice, "come and greet the new visitors to our village!"

# NĪMITANAW

The Crane clan warrior announced the visitors in each of the four directions.

Near the centre of the circle of lodges stood two women, one in front of the other. The taller of the two looked to be about thirty summers. She stood with her hands on the shoulders of the younger woman, who appeared to be about thirteen summers. They wore strange clothes, made mostly of lightly coloured deer hide and quillwork forming diamond shapes. Their hair was braided with thin deer hide ribbons and mink fur hung from the ends.

The younger woman's head was bowed to show respect for the people of *Nisichawayasihk* and to indicate that the other woman would speak for her. The duty of greeting outsiders fell under the jurisdiction of the Eagle clan. "Welcome to *Nisichawayasihk*, the place where three rivers meet," began the Elder Eagle twin. "What brings you to our home?"

"I am called Yellow Moon Woman, from *Azaadiwi-ziibiing*, the place of the poplar tree river," she answered. "I am told that among the *Nehiyawak* of *Nisichawayasihk* walks a great medicine carrier who is blessed with the dreaming eyes and the secrets of the plant world. We have come to seek his teachings."

The Eagle clan members stood with the sun on their faces and chins up. One of the young warriors clapped Red Sky Man on the shoulder. The elder Eagle twin smirked and nodded at her younger sister.

"*Tapwe*," she said. "You are well informed. Our Eagle medicine carrier, Red Sky Man, is the one you seek."

"Forgive me, cousin," said Yellow Moon Woman. "The name I have heard spoken among the villages is Painted Turtle Man of the Bear clan."

The *Nehiyawak* muttered and whispered amongst themselves. Pilgrims from other villages seeking out Painted Turtle Man? This could be an embarrassing situation for *Nisichawayasihk*, partly because they did not hold Painted Turtle Man in as high esteem as the other villages apparently did, but especially because the Bear medicine lodge was no longer.

"We have been told that a great miracle took place here," continued Yellow Moon Woman. She looked at the blank faces around her, wondering what she had said wrong. "Last summer at the sacred sundance ceremony...."

"I think you may have been misinformed. The miracle came about by way of the Grey-Eye magic. It was the Eagle medicine carrier, Red Sky Man, who was overseeing that particular part of the ceremony." The twin allowed her voice to carry some of the annoyance she felt.

Walking Moon Woman stepped forward for the Bear clan, addressing the elder Eagle twin. "My sister. There are many ways in which the miracle could be interpreted. None of us can understand Creator's will. The interpretation you have shared is one of many. Here is another: it was under my cousin Painted Turtle Man's guidance that my grandson was blessed with the miracle, for the good of all the *Nehiyawak*."

No one among the *Nehiyawak* who witnessed the miracle claimed to understand its meaning, though everyone had an opinion about it. Although it had been Little Grey Bear Boy who produced the miracle, two eagles *had* appeared. Red Sky Man was the one who did the piercing and he was born of the eagle. Painted Turtle Man had taken Little Grey Bear Boy to the tree, but any sundance chief could have done that. The miraculous healing that had taken place was only done by Painted Turtle Man's hands and everyone knew that he and the boy shared an uncommon bond. Perhaps both the Bear and the Eagle where equally responsible? *Kitchi Manitou*'s will was never easily understood.

The Eagle twins and Walking Moon Woman looked into each other's eyes, neither one backing down. The tension between the two clans was palpable.

Drifting Butterfly Woman stepped forward for the Crane clan. "My apologies, cousin. I could not help but notice your beautiful dresses. They are unlike any I have seen before and I am not familiar with the place of the poplar tree river. Are you of the *Nehiyawak*?"

"I am sorry, cousin. We came from farther south than the *Nehiyawak* dwell. We call ourselves the *Anishinabe*, your neighbours to the south. My daughter and I hail from the Turtle clan and if this is the home of Painted Turtle Man of the Bear clan, we would ask to dwell among you for a time."

"Just what the Turtles need," whispered Red Sky Man to the younger Eagle twin, "more useless mouths to feed."

The younger Eagle twin giggled, stopping herself when the matriarch of the Deer clan began to speak.

"The *Anishinabe* people are welcome amongst the *Nehiyawak*. The great peace between our peoples is without beginning and without end."

The *Nehiyawak* nodded their agreement.

"How is it you speak our tongue so well?" asked Drifting Butterfly Woman.

"That is not my doing," explained Yellow Moon Woman. "It is because of my daughter, Water Lily Woman."

She presented her daughter to the people of *Nisichawayasihk*, pushing her forward slightly so she could be seen. The young woman raised her head to reveal shining grey eyes. The *Nehiyawak* vibrated as the ancient magic coursed through them.

"I wanted my daughter trained in the ways of the Grey-Eye magic," continued Yellow Moon Woman to the shocked crowd. "We wish for her to be taught by Painted Turtle Man of the Bear clan. Our village has not known the Grey-Eye magic for many generations and there was no one who could teach her. When we heard of the sundance miracle, we made our preparations and left our village as soon as the snows melted."

A wave of disbelief rippled through the *Nehiyawak*. It would seem *Nisichawayasihk* would again have two Grey-Eyes living in it.

Like everyone else, Little Grey Bear Boy stared at Water Lily Woman. Her eyes met his. He had been very young when Soaring Star Woman passed into the Spirit World—he had not remembered what grey eyes looked like. He had tried many times to see himself in the reflection of still water, but he could never quite tell what made his eyes so different from everyone else's. He could not imagine that his eyes could be anywhere near as beautiful as those of Water Lily Woman…

Green Wing Woman stepped forward for the Turtle clan, most of whom were staring at their new sisters.

"My daughter, my granddaughter," she addressed the newcomers. "The Turtle lodge would be truly blessed to welcome you into our family."

The people of *Nisichawayasihk* cheered as the two women embraced their clan mother and new sisters in turn.

Red Sky Man talked into the elder Eagle twin's ear. She nodded as he spoke. She then stepped forward for the Eagle clan.

"My sisters. I think we would be asking far too much of Painted Turtle Man to have him teach both of the Grey-Eyes. Perhaps one of them should be instructed by Red Sky Man…"

Little Grey Bear Boy snapped out of his dumb stare. He looked at his grandmother but she did not return his gaze. She held herself very still. Her face reddened as it dawned on her what Red Sky Man had done. Before she could gather her thoughts, Green Wing Woman again stepped forward for the Turtle clan.

"My sisters. My new daughter has come a very long way, guided by the Grandmother Turtle in search of learning. She came seeking the teachings of Painted Turtle Man and she should be able to receive them."

"My sisters, perhaps there is a solution to this problem," said Gliding Heron Woman, stepping forward for the Marten clan. "For many years, Little Grey Bear Boy has had the benefit of learning from

Painted Turtle Man. Perhaps he could spend some time learning what Red Sky Man has to teach, in order to allow our new daughter an opportunity to learn from Painted Turtle Man as she requests."

All of the clan matriarchs nodded in agreement—all but Walking Moon Woman. When the Circle of Clan Mothers faced a decision, all of the matriarchs had to agree or no action could be taken. Normally, this consensus served the greater harmony of the *Nehiyawak*. But, as happened occasionally, it could put those who were in the minority in a difficult position, as it did now with Walking Moon Woman.

All eyes in the village were on her as she stepped forward on behalf of the Bear clan.

"My sisters," she began, "this would seem a wise course of action, but it would be difficult for my grandson to be separated from the one he calls *Moosum*. It would make my heart sad to see my grandson unhappy, regardless of how wise the decision would be."

The *Nehiyawak* sighed sympathetically for Walking Moon Woman's predicament. A person's feelings were always held in the highest regard.

The elder Eagle twin again stepped forward. "*Motch*, my sister. It is not as though we are asking that the boy be separated from his *moosum*. He would simply spend some time with Red Sky Man during our Grandfather Sun's light. He would return to the Bear lodge to be with his family each evening before our Grandmother Moon appears."

The *Nehiyawak* looked back at Walking Moon Woman, hopeful for a resolution. She could not deny the wisdom of the Eagle matriarch's words, and could not resist further without seeming uncompromising or stubborn.

"It seems you have grown very wise, my sister," said Walking Moon Woman bitterly.

She spoke to the elder Eagle twin, but her eyes were fixed on Red Sky Man.

"I believe the Circle of Clan Mothers is now in agreement," said Drifting Butterfly Woman. It was her duty as matriarch of the Cranes to close the circle, though she was aware the decision was not ideal for the Bear clan.

"*Ekosi…*" she said after hearing no objection.

The people of *Nisichawayasihk* chatted excitedly about the decision and the benefits of having another Grey-Eye in the village where so many other villages did not have even one.

Painted Turtle Man felt as though a rock had been lodged in his chest and he glared at Red Sky Man. The Eagle medicine carrier was looking at Walking Moon Woman, a puzzled expression on his face. For a moment it appeared Red Sky Man had lost himself somewhere in the old woman's face. He recovered and turned to face Painted Turtle Man's scowl.

Red Sky Man sent over a smug upward tilt of the head to acknowledge his victory.

No one among the Bear clan was happy that Little Grey Bear Boy would now have to receive his education, at least by day, from Red Sky Man.

"I am not ungrateful for the opportunity," explained Little Grey Bear Boy when they had returned to the Bear lodge. "But, I don't see why I should have to spend time with Red Sky Man, *Nookum*."

"I am sorry, my boy," replied Walking Moon Woman. "The Circle of Clan Mothers has spoken."

"Why would you agree to such a thing?"

"The council's reasoning was sound. This way, you will have the benefit of two teachers."

"I agree with the boy," stated Painted Turtle Man. "He should be able to do as he chooses."

"Oh, is that how it should be?" asked Walking Moon Woman. "We should just let the children decide everything for themselves?"

"*Motch*. This situation is different."

"Don't worry. If any problem arises, I will use it to speak to the Circle of Clan Mothers again. We will just have to put our faith in *Kitchi Manitou* in this matter. If it is Creator's will, we will receive our reason soon enough. Perhaps, cousin, you should focus your attention on teaching the new Grey-Eye your plant medicine. This is what the Circle of Clan Mothers demands of you."

"*Tapwe*, I will give the girl the benefit of my knowledge. I guess I should be honoured the Circle of Clan Mothers can still find use for me..."

"I could help you, *Moosum*!" The family turned to look at Flying Rabbit Boy in surprise.

"And how would you help me?" asked Painted Turtle Man.

"I don't know. You have taught me many things. Maybe I could tell them to her for you…" The whole family kept staring, wondering when he would realize what they had realized.

Finally he did. "Well…did you see her?" he said defensively.

"*Awas*," interjected Singing Doe, "you must show respect to this young woman. She has been initiated into the moon lodge. You cannot tease her like one of the little girls."

"But she is almost the same age as me," reasoned Flying Rabbit Boy, "and she is a Turtle!"

"*Awas*!" exclaimed Singing Doe, "You have not earned your name yet. You should not even be thinking about women!" Singing Doe looked to her husband for help, but he only smiled his I'm-afraid-he-gets-it-from-me smile.

The family laughed and tried to carry on with their evening as usual. They finished their meal, said their prayers, and unrolled their buffalo hides for bed. Tomorrow, Little Grey Bear Boy would begin his instructions under Red Sky Man.

Although he did not care much for his new teacher, Little Grey Boy's mind was somewhere else. He drifted off to sleep thinking about the new grey-eyed girl who had come to the village. Even with his eyes closed, he could still see the intense grey colour, the half-moon shape, the long lashes and thin arched eyebrows…

Unknown to him, his younger cousin Flying Rabbit Boy went to sleep with much the same thoughts.

# NĪMITANAW PIYAKOSĀP

L ittle Grey Bear Boy dreamt he was walking through the village. Whomever he encountered would scream and run away. He tried to speak, to reassure them, but they only became more afraid and frantic. Even his own family feared him and ran. He did not understand why they were behaving this way, especially those he had known all his life.

He was at the lake, bending to see himself in the still water.

His eyelids had been painted red.

He awoke cold and shivering. Painted Turtle Man, who lay nearby, was awake. "What is the matter, my boy?" whispered the old man. "What have you seen?"

"It's nothing, *Moosum*," answered Little Grey Bear Boy. "I will go back to sleep…"

"Are you sure?" pressed the old man.

Little Grey Bear Boy sighed. "Why didn't you say more?"

"What do you mean?"

"When I told *Nookum* I didn't want to learn from Red Sky Man. You just went along with it. Why didn't you insist I stay?"

"Do you think I don't want to be your teacher?"

"Do you?"

"My boy," soothed Painted Turtle Man, raising himself up on his side. "We must all serve as directed by the Circle of Clan Mothers."

"But what about when they are wrong?"

"They are not wrong just because you disagree with their decision. Sometimes we must sacrifice for the good of the community."

"When I have mastered the Grey-Eye magic, I will not have to be the one to make such sacrifices."

"Be careful before you start down that road. Your gift is for the benefit of all the *Nehiyawak*, not just for yourself. Do you think *Kitchi Manitou* gave this to you to fulfill your own selfish desires?"

"*Tapwe, Moosum.* I am sorry I disturbed you." Little Grey Bear Boy straightened out his buffalo robe and settled back in to sleep.

"It was no disturbance, my boy. When you reach my age you do not sleep much anyway. *Ekosi.*" Painted Turtle Man rolled over and pulled his thin buffalo hide over his shoulders.

When Grandfather Sun rose Little Grey Bear Boy and his adopted grandfather went to make the morning prayers as they had every day for so many years. They smoked the peace pipe and offered thanks to Creator for their blessings. When the ceremony was finished, Little Grey Bear Boy cleaned the peace pipe and repacked the bundle of sacred items. They began the long walk back to the village in silence. Little Grey Bear Boy looked at his hands and waved them through the branches along the edge of the path. He concentrated hard on trying to make the branches move away before they touched his hand. Some of the leaves would twitch or stick upright but not in the manner he intended. Painted Turtle Man pretended not to notice.

When they reached the village, Painted Turtle Man turned to Little Grey Bear Boy.

"I will see you at home this evening."

"*Tapwe, Moosum.* I will come when I am able."

"Learn what you can," the old man said, "and if anything confuses you, I will try to help you make sense of it."

"*Tapwe.*"

Little Grey Bear Boy's legs felt heavy as he made his way to the Eagle medicine lodge. As he came near, Soaring Spear Man, now one of Red Sky Man's disciples, ducked inside. One by one, the young helpers exited the Eagle medicine lodge and nodded at Little Grey Bear Boy respectfully.

"He is waiting for you," said Soaring Spear Man, holding the door flap open. "Go on in."

"Thank you, my brother."

Little Grey Bear Boy entered the Eagle medicine lodge to find it full of strange medicines and charms. A dead bird of some kind hung from a cross pole set across the lodge near the top. There were many hunting tools and warrior's weapons, more than he had ever seen in one lodge. Perhaps the warriors of the village had brought them to be blessed. Red Sky Man waved him over to the far side of the lodge.

"*Tansi?* Grandson," he said.

Little Grey Bear Boy thought it was presumptuous for a man of forty or so summers to call him 'grandson.'

"Come sit down by the fire. There is much for you to learn."

"Thank you, Uncle."

Red Sky Man ignored the slight.

"Have you learned of the four elements of the medicine wheel?" he asked.

Little Grey Bear Boy was suspicious of the question. Was this a test of some sort?

"I have learned *of* them," Little Grey Bear Boy answered humbly, "but I am still learning *about* them."

"*Tapwe*, well said. The four elements of the medicine wheel are fire, water, earth, and wind. Today we will be learning about fire." He waved his hands through the flames one after the other, fluttering his fingers as he did so.

"All right..." said Little Grey Bear Boy, not sure if he was supposed to do the same.

"What are the seven colours of the fire?" asked Red Sky Man.

"The seven colours, Uncle?"

"You mean Painted Turtle Man never taught you the Seven Colours of Fire?"

"I am sure he was going to..." answered Little Grey Bear Boy confused. "Perhaps he felt I was not yet ready..."

"I hope you are ready now," continued Red Sky Man. "You'll be a man soon enough, won't you? I will help you to find the seven colours of the fire. Once you have learned them I will try to teach you how to bend the fire to your will."

"I was taught that the Fire Spirit gives us its blessing. And, that it cannot be controlled, only asked for its gifts."

"I see you have much to learn. Now look into the flames and tell me what colours you see."

Little Grey Bear Boy was not used to being scolded. He did as he was instructed, looking long and hard into the fire. Red Sky Man began tapping his hand against his thigh, then he cleared his throat.

"Uncle, I can see red, orange, yellow, and blue."

"Those are the ones anyone could see." Red Sky Man did not mask his disappointment. "Today you will tend the fire and see what colours are revealed. Often, certain colours can only be seen at certain times of day or night, or only when the fire is big or small. You will experiment with the fire and afterwards you will replace all of the wood you have used in your lessons."

"*Tapwe*, Uncle!" said Little Grey Bear Boy, lowering his eyes.

"Then I will leave you to it. I will come back later to see how you have done, *ekosi*."

Red Sky Man got up and left the Eagle medicine lodge. He muttered some instructions to Soaring Spear Man, who stood outside the lodge.

Little Grey Bear Boy stared into the fire. It was a hot summer day and the Eagle medicine lodge was sweltering. He let the fire burn down for a while, hoping it would be less hot with a smaller fire. Little Grey Bear Boy became thirsty and looked around the lodge for a water skin but couldn't find one. He waited for a time for Red Sky Man to come check up on him and then decided he should go find some water. He poked his head out of the Eagle medicine lodge.

"What are the seven colours of the fire?" Soaring Spear Man asked him.

"What?"

"What are the seven colours of the fire?" the helper repeated.

"I only know four," admitted Little Grey Bear Boy.

"Our teacher said you must remain in the Eagle medicine lodge until you have found all seven colours."

"I understand," said Little Grey Bear Boy. "It is very hot in there, and I am thirsty. Is there any water? I need to have a drink."

The two stared at each other for a time, then the helper spoke again. "You cannot leave the medicine lodge until you have found all seven colours."

"I see…" His grey eyes narrowed at Soaring Spear Man.

Little Grey Bear Boy went back into the lodge and again sat near the fire. He continued to stare into it, keeping it burning very low in an effort to keep the lodge cool, but without success. He took off his shirt and leggings. He was sweating now. If this was a test, he would prove himself to Red Sky Man. As he looked into the low fire, he began to notice the odd bit of green flame licking the coals. He now knew five of the seven colours of the fire.

He thought to himself for a moment, then decided to build up the fire again. He built it bigger and bigger, remembering he would have to replace the wood he used. Grandfather Sun made his journey across Father Sky and Little Grey Bear Boy felt as though he were in an all-day sweat lodge. He looked hard into the fire but could not find any new colours.

As Grandfather Sun began to set, Little Grey Bear Boy heard his mother's voice outside the Eagle medicine lodge.

"I do not care what you were told. I am his mother! I say it is time for him to come and eat with his family!"

"I am sorry, Auntie, I am only doing what I was told." Soaring Spear Man sounded frightened.

"*Tapwe*! Now you are being told differently by me!"

"What is the matter?" said Red Sky Man, suddenly.

"I am here for my son!" commanded White Willow Woman.

"Well, of course," chuckled Red Sky Man. "Our Grandfather Sun has begun to set. I would have thought he would have returned to you by now."

Little Grey Bear Boy emerged then from the lodge, fully clothed and exhausted. The evening wind bathed him in cool water. His hair was sweat soaked and he was covered in ash.

"I am sorry, Uncle. I only found five."

"Five!" exclaimed Red Sky Man with mock enthusiasm. "That is very impressive for your first day. Come back tomorrow and you will find the rest. Do not ask anyone for help. It is for you to learn on your own."

"*Tapwe,* Uncle. Thank you for your teachings."

"*Ekosi.*" Red Sky Man patted his pupil on the head like a loving father and smiled at White Willow Woman.

Little Grey Bear Boy brushed himself off and walked to his mother's side, trying to look strong. He may have been able to fool a lot of the *Nehiyawak* with this effort, but not his own mother. As they left, she scowled disapprovingly at the medicine carrier and his helper.

Red Sky Man only smiled.

# NĪMITANAW NĪSOSĀP

When Little Grey Bear Boy and his mother neared the Bear lodge, the boy ran ahead and inside. He grabbed the water skin out of Yellow Hawk Girl's hands and began to drink, letting the water splash across his cheeks and down his chin.

"Hey! I was using that!" she said.

"Show some respect for your sister," said Walking Moon Woman.

"I am sorry," said Little Grey Bear Boy between gulps, "but I am so thirsty. I have not had any water all day and it was very hot inside the Eagle medicine lodge."

"What have you been doing in there all day, my boy?" asked Painted Turtle Man.

"I have been tending the fire, trying to learn a teaching."

"And what teaching is that?"

Little Grey Bear Boy rolled his eyes. "I am not supposed to discuss it with anyone," he said. "I have to go back tomorrow."

"This seems a very strange teaching, that would deny a boy a drink of water," said Painted Turtle Man.

"I do not like this," said White Willow Woman. "He looks terrible."

"That's how he always looks," said Flying Rabbit Boy with a smirk.

Little Grey Bear Boy was too tired to laugh. "Is there anything to eat?" Little Grey Bear Boy asked. "I am starving!"

"You mean he did not feed you?" White Willow Woman gaped in disbelief.

"I think it was part of the teaching."

"You think?" asked Painted Turtle Man. "A teacher should inform his pupil if he is going to be required to fast."

"He seems to want me to learn things on my own."

"That is unusual," said Painted Turtle Man. "In my experience, a teacher teaches and a learner learns. Maybe I should go talk to this man."

"*Motch, Moosum*," pleaded Little Grey Bear Boy, "I can handle any test he wishes to give me. I am sure the teaching is coming. This is for my teacher to decide."

"Little Grey Bear!" shouted White Willow Woman.

"It's okay," said Painted Turtle Man. "He is obviously very tired. I don't care for Red Sky Man's methods or his teachings, but he is right. These decisions are no longer mine."

Little Grey Bear Boy was not very talkative that evening and he made his way to his bed roll right after finishing his wild rice and spit-fired rabbit. It didn't matter that the family tried to keep their usual chatter quiet—Little Grey Bear Boy fell into a deep sleep in a matter of minutes.

He dreamed again, the same as the night before: everyone in the village was afraid of him, but this time fire fell from the sky. In the midst of the fire storm, a silver-skinned woman wearing a white dress walked towards him. Her eyes glowed a bright grey and she spoke his name.

"Little Grey Bear Boy," Painted Turtle Man was shaking him awake.

"Is it time for the peace pipe?" he asked groggily.

The old man held a water skin to his adopted grandson's lips. "It is time for you to drink some water."

He drank gratefully. "Let me find my moccasins."

"There is no need. I have already smoked the peace pipe and said the prayers."

Little Grey Bear Boy looked up at his adopted grandfather, by whose side he had walked since he took his first steps. He had not missed going with the Bear medicine carrier to perform the sunrise ceremony since he was a child.

Painted Turtle Man read the boy's face. "I wanted to let you sleep," he said. "Do not be troubled. I offered prayers for the both of us."

"Thank you, *Moosum*," said Little Grey Bear Boy. "But I would rather have offered my own prayers."

"Save your strength. It is time for both of us to begin our tasks."

They left the Bear lodge and walked through the inner circle of the village. Painted Turtle Man walked towards the Turtle lodge while Little Grey Bear Boy headed for the Eagle medicine lodge, still holding his water skin.

As he followed the old man, he saw Water Lily Woman and her mother emerge from the Turtle lodge. They had been listening for his *moosum*'s footsteps. Little Grey Bear Boy looked at the three of them preparing to begin their teachings. Water Lily Woman smiled at Painted Turtle Man. A warm smile. A trusting smile.

Little Grey Bear Boy turned his back on them and continued on to the Eagle medicine lodge.

# NĪMITANAW NISTOSĀP

"Was that your grandson?" asked Water Lily Woman, as she and Painted Turtle Man walked toward the forest to begin their lesson.

"*Tapwe…*" he answered. "And at the same time, *motch*. I am Walking Moon Woman's cousin, but he has called me *moosum* since he was very small. His real grandfather died long before he was born."

Rising Hawk Man had been like a brother to the old medicine carrier. As a boy, Rising Hawk Man had taken him under his wing, teaching him how to hunt, trap, and fish. When it was time, Rising Hawk Man had become his sponsor for the Sundance ceremony. Of course, most of the *Nehiyawak* always believed Rising Hawk Man's only intention had been to catch Walking Moon Woman's eye, but that never mattered to Painted Turtle Man. They continued to be friends even after Walking Moon Woman chose him for her husband and moved him into the Bear lodge.

"I'm sorry to hear that," said Water Lily Woman, interrupting his thoughts. "But it is good he has someone like you in his life."

"I used to think so."

"Is everything okay?"

"He is growing up," Painted Turtle Man explained. "It's hard for us older people when they do that. They start to need us less and less. You will understand when you are my age."

"It seems like a difficult thing to understand. I hope I don't have to learn it for many years."

"*Tapwe.*"

They ventured deeper into the forest and the old man had trouble with fallen logs, even with Water Lily Woman's assistance. While she was unfamiliar with the territory, Painted Turtle Man knew every rock and tree around them. He had lived here most of his life, and as a boy it was here he took the first steps in becoming a man.

When Painted Turtle Man had become ready to walk the warrior road it seemed Rising Hawk Man had less and less time for him. With four small children to care for and another on the way, the young father couldn't run off to hunt whenever it suited him. Painted Turtle Man had become annoyed with his friend, desperate to prove himself and earn his warrior name. He had hoped to be inducted into the same warrior society so their friendship could become brotherhood. His last words to his old friend had been spoken in anger, as Painted Turtle Man questioned whether or not Rising Hawk Man thought him worthy of his warrior society. Had he only known those would be the last words he would ever speak to his best friend.

"I don't mean to burden you," said Painted Turtle Man. "Today is for you to learn about plant medicines, not for me to bother you with old people problems."

"It is no burden, *Moosum*. I am happy to learn anything you wish to teach."

"I'm glad you feel that way, my girl. Who knows how much time I have left to walk upon Mother Earth."

"Don't say such things, *Moosum*," she said, lowering her eyes. "I wish you many more winters to come. Besides, you accepted tobacco from my mother, so you must teach me everything you know before you journey on."

"I'll do what I can," smiled Painted Turtle Man. "A promise is a promise after all. Tell me, what is it you wish to learn first?"

"I want to learn how to treat injuries."

"Injuries?"

"*Tapwe*, to prevent the sickness that can come afterwards," Water Lily Woman eyes became glassy.

"I see," said Painted Turtle Man nodding. "I will teach you what I know. There are medicines that can be made into a tea to help with this, but the best way to prevent the sickness from coming is to scorch the wound with fire."

"With fire?"

"*Tapwe.*"

"How can fire help a wound?"

"A wound that is caressed with fire will stop bleeding and prevent the sickness."

"I never would have thought of that," said Water Lily Woman, helping the old man up a sudden incline in the terrain.

"Who would, without the teaching?" panted Painted Turtle Man, using his will to force his old legs to climb upwards.

"I am grateful we found you, *Moosum*. I am honoured you would share your wisdom with me."

"The honour is mine, my girl."

Painted Turtle Man's thoughts wandered as they entered the forest in search of healing medicines. The men who first treated Painted Turtle Man's wounds had no trouble finding fire the night the Red-Eye came to *Nisichawayasihk*. As they caressed his back with flame he cried out for his friend Rising Hawk Man. When he was told not to speak his friend's name, he knew it was too late.

"Now then," said Painted Turtle Man as they entered a clearing. "Today I will teach you how to make my red clover salve."

# NĪMITANAW NIYOSĀP

"You will not need that," Soaring Spear Man said to Little Grey Bear Boy, indicating the water skin with his lips.

Little Grey Bear Boy sighed and handed the water skin over before entering the Eagle medicine lodge. He found Red Sky Man sitting next to the fire. He took his place, as on the previous day, and stared into the fire, waiting for his teacher to speak.

"What are the seven colours of the fire?" asked Red Sky Man after a time.

Little Grey Bear Boy looked deep into the fire and considered the question carefully. "Uncle," the boy began. "I can see red, orange, yellow, blue and green."

"Is that all?"

"That is all I see."

"Very well," Red Sky Man said as he rose to his feet. "I will leave you to it. Remember, you have to replace all of the wood you use."

With that, he left Little Grey Bear Boy sitting by the fire.

This time, the boy wasted no time in removing his shirt and leggings in anticipation of the heat. He experimented with the fire, adding wood, moving it around, and staring hard here and there trying to make out different colours. He sang softly to the fire to help pass the time, thinking he might even coax the hidden colours into view.

Grandfather Sun crossed Father Sky and the boy was no closer to finding the seven colours than he had been the night before. As the light began to fade he built up the fire in an effort to make a good show of it when Red Sky Man returned. As the flame danced high and the sparks flew out the top of the lodge, Little Grey Bear Boy noticed something in the middle of the widest flames. He wasn't sure—his eyes had become sore with staring—but he thought he saw a flicker of white like the clouds.

"Could this be one of the seven colours of the fire?" he said, startling himself as he spoke. Little Grey Bear Boy went to the doorway and poked his head out of the flaps.

"What are the seven colours of the fire?" he asked Soaring Spear Man in a monotone voice.

"Red, orange, yellow, blue, green, white...and purple?"

Soaring Spear Man frowned.

"There you are, my boy!" called Painted Turtle Man, walking towards the Eagle medicine lodge. "Your mother wants you to come and eat."

Soaring Spear Man frowned again, but the memory of what had happened the day before, as well as the respect he felt for his former teacher, made him look down at Little Grey Bear Boy and nod. The tired and parched boy dressed quickly and left the lodge, joining his adopted grandfather on the walk to the Bear lodge.

"So what did you learn today," asked the old man, sipping from a water skin then handing it to the boy.

Little Grey Bear Boy took the water skin gratefully, drinking from it in gulps. "I don't think I understand this teaching."

"Well, what is it?" asked Painted Turtle Man as they crossed the centre of the circle of lodges. People were milling about and returning to their lodges for the evening meal.

"I am not supposed to discuss it with anyone," answered the boy as a pair of yapping puppies darted in front of them.

"I respect that you are paying close attention to your teacher, but sometimes the way to learn something is to ask others who might know. Do you think that is the case?"

"I can learn the teaching on my own." said Little Grey Bear Boy. "I'm not a child anymore, you know."

"Very well," conceded Painted Turtle Man. "I will be here if you need me."

////

Little Grey Bear Boy ate his meal and went straight to sleep. He dreamed again of the silvery-skinned woman in the white dress appearing out of the fire. She turned and began to walk away, turning into a white buffalo as she went.

Little Grey Bear Boy woke in a cold sweat. It was still night.

He had dreamed of the fabled White Buffalo Calf Woman, the one who had brought *Kitchi Manitou's* teachings to the *Nehiyawak* so long ago. The vision puzzled him. What did it mean? Did her appearance mean the *Nehiyawak* had lost their way?

Someone had placed a full water skin next to him as he slept. He opened it up and drank. Feeling refreshed and calmed he went back to sleep, unaware of the foggy old eyes of Painted Turtle Man watching over him.

In the morning, Painted Turtle Man woke him.

"Is it time?" the boy asked wiping the crust out of his eyes.

"*Tapwe*," said the old man, "it is time for you to go back to the Eagle medicine lodge."

"You mean you did the ceremony without me again?"

Painted Turtle Man smiled. "I am sorry. I woke up very early this morning. Father Sky was still black as Brother Raven's wings."

"That early, *Moosum?*"

"*Tapwe*, my boy, and when I came back just now I saw a very interesting looking bird. I could have used your sharp eyes with me. This bird looked to have black tips on his wings, but I could not be sure."

"I have never seen such a bird," said Little Grey Bear Boy.

"Nor have I," agreed Painted Turtle Man. "I am still trying to decipher the meaning of his message. Perhaps you will think of it today as you receive your teachings."

"But I did not see the bird for myself. How can I interpret a message I didn't receive?"

"Not every message we receive is for us to understand. Sometimes the message comes to us but is meant for another. That is why it is a good idea to talk about these visions with others."

Little Grey Bear Boy avoided the old man's gaze and took a long drink of water.

"I noticed your sleep was troubled. Is there anything you wish to discuss?"

"*Motch*…"

"You are a smart boy," said Painted Turtle Man, trying to conceal his disappointment. "Think about the bird this day and we can discuss it again later. We had better go and begin our day."

Little Grey Bear Boy made his way to the Eagle medicine lodge for the third day. He was shown into the lodge by Soaring Spear Man. Red Sky Man sat by the fire as usual.

"What are the seven colours of the fire?" he asked as Little Grey Bear Boy took his place.

"Uncle, I see red, orange, yellow, blue, green and white," answered Little Grey Bear Boy.

"Is that all?" said the Eagle medicine carrier.

"I am sorry, Uncle. That is all I have seen."

Red Sky Man got to his feet and began to leave.

"Can I ask you something?" Little Grey Bear Boy said quickly.

"What is it?"

"Last night, I had a dream."

"A vision?"

"*Tapwe*," he said. "The White Buffalo Calf Woman was in it."

"White Buffalo Calf Woman? You still believe in that stuff?"

"Uncle?"

"I thought you were grown up." Red Sky Man was laughing now. "I thought you were ready to walk man's road."

Little Grey Bear Boy blushed and looked down at the fire. Red Sky Man continued to the doorway. Before he left, he turned back to Little Grey Bear Boy. "You are running out of wood."

Little Grey Bear Boy's cheeks felt as though they were on fire. He took off his shirt and leggings for another sweltering day. To benefit from both a full fire and less heat, he kept the fire at a medium size. As he tried to focus on the task at hand, he could feel a burning sensation from behind his eyes.

By midday he began looking around the Eagle medicine lodge, hoping to find a forgotten water skin. He stared into the fire and sang songs, still only able to make out six colours. He began thinking about the bird Painted Turtle Man saw. What bird has black at the very tips of its wings? Little Grey Bear Boy's mind wandered and he began to picture the bird dancing in the flames of the fire. The tips of its wings were indeed black.

"Black," said Little Grey Bear Boy to himself.

At the very tip of the flames during the midday sun, he saw black. Counting on his fingers the colours he could see in the flames, again and again he came to seven. There was nothing more to do but to inform Soaring Spear Man and find Red Sky Man.

"What are the seven colours of the fire?" asked Soaring Spear Man.

"Brother, I see red, orange, yellow, blue, green, white and black," said Little Grey Bear Boy confidently.

Soaring Spear Man paused and frowned at Little Grey Bear Boy. "Uh... let me find R-Red Sky Man," he stammered.

"Can I go?" asked Little Grey Bear Boy.

"*M-motch*. I think you should wait until I have found Red Sky Man."

"Well hurry back when you have found him." For the first time in three days, Little Grey Bear Boy smiled.

Soaring Spear Man scurried off to the Eagle lodge and then went about the village searching for Red Sky Man. Little Grey Bear Boy held the door flaps open, trying to air out the lodge with the breeze that was blowing now and then. After a time, Soaring Spear Man returned.

"He must have gone out picking medicines," he said.

"Where does he normally go?" asked Little Grey Bear Boy.

"I am not sure," said Soaring Spear Man, scratching his head. "He never tells me where he is going."

"Would anyone else know where he went?"

"*Motch*."

"Can I go back to the Bear lodge?"

"I do not know…"

"Well what did Red Sky Man say to you?" Little Grey Bear Boy asked as politely as he could.

"He told me to ask you the seven colours of the fire if you came out," explained the exasperated helper. "But, he never said what to do if you got it right."

"So then I am right?"

"Uhm, I do not think I am supposed to say."

"How about this…since I used so much wood in my lessons, I will go and collect wood at the driftwood shore to the east."

"I know the place you mean."

"You can stay here, and when Red Sky Man returns, you can come and find me."

"I guess I can't keep you here for nothing," said Soaring Spear Man, hand on his chin.

"*Motch*," said Little Grey Bear Boy, "that would not help anyone. This way, we are both being useful."

Little Grey Bear Boy went back into the lodge to put on his shirt and leggings. "*Ekosi*," he nodded at the worried helper, trying not to smile too widely as he left.

Little Grey Bear Boy found Walking Moon Woman busy with her chores at the Bear lodge.

"*Tansi, Nookum.*"

"*Tansi*, my boy."

"Where is everyone?"

"Your father and uncle are out hunting and your mother and aunt are with Drifting Butterfly Woman," she answered.

"Where is Flying Rabbit Boy?"

"I think he went out hunting with his bow."

"Which way did he go?"

"He said he was going to go east."

"Well that is perfect!" exclaimed the boy. "I am heading that way to collect wood. Perhaps I will find him."

"You are going to collect wood?"

"*Tapwe, Nookum*, to replace the wood I used during my lessons at the Eagle medicine lodge."

"Don't the Eagles have enough young men to collect wood?" grumbled the Bear clan matriarch.

"I used it," he explained. "It is only right I replace it."

"What were you burning wood for?"

"I was learning a teaching."

"What teaching?"

"I am not supposed to discuss it with anyone besides Red Sky Man."

Walking Moon Woman was taken aback. "In what situation would someone tell you not to discuss something with your *nookum*?" she demanded.

"I am sorry, *Nookum*," said Little Grey Bear Boy, lowering his eyes, "I did not intend to upset you. I was only repeating what I was told. I am not even sure I have learned the teaching…"

"I do not like people keeping secrets in this lodge," she explained. "No good can come of it."

"*Tapwe, Nookum.*" Little Grey Bear Boy agreed. "But I must be respectful of my new teacher."

"Your 'teacher,'" she muttered. "All right. Go gather up your wood. No more secrets, understand?"

"*Tapwe!*"

He gave his grandmother a hug and a kiss and took a piece of dried meat she was pounding into pemmican. He gathered up some hide straps to tie the wood and left the Bear lodge hoping to find his cousin.

# NĪMITANAW NIYĀNOSĀP

L ittle Grey Bear Boy arrived at the sandy beach where the drift-wood was plentiful and began breaking up sections of the driest logs.

"*Tansi*? Son of the Bear clan."

Little Grey Bear Boy turned to see the grey-eyed Water Lily Woman. She was balancing a birch bark basket full of red clover on her hip, smiling. Her eyes appeared to shimmer in the sun.

"Oh, *t-tansi*. I'm sorry, I don't mean to disturb you," he said stumbling over his wood pile. "I was just collecting wood."

"You are not disturbing me," she said. "It is I who approached you. I was hoping I would run into you."

"Me? Why?"

"Well, isn't it obvious?" her eyebrows raised in the middle, as though the answer would have been apparent to even a child.

"Uh, I'm not sure…"

"I have never met another Grey-Eye before." Water Lily Woman stepped close and gazed into Little Grey Bear Boy's eyes. "I want to see what it looks like."

She was the same height as him, though with her hip balancing the basket, she wasn't standing up straight.

"My eyes?" he asked stepping back a little.

"*Tapwe*." she stepped closer again.

"I don't think mine look the same as yours."

"Why do you say that?"

"Well, I don't think my eyes are as beautiful."

"You think my eyes are beautiful?" she stepped back suddenly.

"Uh, that's not what I meant." He gave his head a shake.

"Then what did you mean?"

"Uh, I don't know…"

"Hmm…" She was enjoying his discomfort.

"How are your teachings with my *moosum* progressing?" He tilted his head towards the basket as they spoke.

"I'm not sure now."

"What do you mean?"

"Well, you have been learning from him for many years, right?"

"*Tapwe…*"

"It doesn't seem like you have learned very much, since you don't know what you mean when you speak."

Little Grey Bear Boy could think of nothing to say. He had wanted to make a good impression, but he didn't expect to meet her like this.

"I'm teasing you!" Water Lily Woman said, slapping his arm playfully.

Little Grey Bear Boy laughed politely. "Oh, haha."

"Do I make you nervous?"

"*Motch*, it's not that…" he explained. "I just don't usually talk to women."

"Why not?"

"I guess I'm trying to respect them…"

"So, you show your respect for women by never talking to them?"

"*Motch*! I respect them, so… I don't talk to them…"

Water Lily Woman laughed. "You're funny."

"I'm glad you think so," he said with relief.

"*Tapwe?*"

"*Motch*! I didn't mean it like that," he said, his relief disappearing. "I mean, I wouldn't want you to be offended. I was taught to be respectful of women. And you are a woman, so I respect you, I mean I respect you because you are a woman. Wait, I don't mean I wouldn't respect you if you weren't a woman. I just mean…."

"Why do you keep saying things you don't really mean?" She laughed again. Little Grey Bear Boy thought it was a sound like bird song.

He stammered and tried to think of an explanation.

"Wow, you are just too easy!"

They both laughed this time and she switched the basket of clover to her other hip. She caught him looking as she did so and smiled. He cleared his throat and looked away quickly.

"I'm not sure I should be talking to you alone."

"Why not?"

"Because you're a Grey-Eye."

"You aren't supposed to talk to other Grey-Eyes?"

"I guess no one ever explained," said Little Grey Bear Boy reaching down to gather his woodpile, "but if two Grey-Eyed people were to have a child, that child would become a Red-Eye."

"What's a Red-Eye?"

"A Red-Eye is someone who has magic like us but uses it for evil. The Red-Eyes once attacked our village and killed many of our people. Both of his parents were Grey-Eyes and that is how he became a Red-Eye."

"It's true, I've never heard that before, but, I think you might be assuming too much about us talking…."

"*Motch*, I didn't mean that!" Little Grey Bear Boy's face was now bright red. He bundled up his driftwood and began tying it together quickly.

"Again, you don't mean what you say," she teased.

"I just meant other people might think something like that would happen."

"So you are worried about what other people will think if you talk to me?"

"It doesn't sound very good when you say it like that." He pulled the rawhide tight and tied a knot. He stood up straight and brushed off his hands, indicating his work was done.

"Then how would you say it?" asked Water Lily Woman, stepping close.

"*Tansi*, cousin?" shouted Flying Rabbit Boy in an unnaturally deep voice. He made his way towards them along the shore. "Oh, I'm sorry. I didn't realize you weren't alone."

Little Grey Bear Boy wondered how this could be true when they stood so close together and apart from the trees.

"*Tansi?*" said Water Lily Woman.

"I don't believe we have been introduced. I am Flying Rabbit Boy of the Bear clan." He bowed.

"Pleased to meet you," she said, bending her knees formally. "I am Water Lily Woman of the Turtle clan. You two are cousins?"

"*Tapwe,*" smiled Flying Rabbit Boy, "but we are more like brothers. We are practically the same, him and I!" He hugged Little Grey Bear Boy around the shoulder as he spoke, nudging him. "Most people would say I am the better looking one," explained Flying Rabbit Boy.

"I don't think anyone says that," muttered Little Grey Bear Boy.

"You are funny," giggled Water Lily Woman.

"*Tapwe,*" said Flying Rabbit Boy. "Just one of my many fine qualities."

"What were you doing out here?" she asked.

"I was hunting. I'm earning my warrior name."

"And how is that going?"

"Well, not so good," Flying Rabbit Boy admitted. "You see, I was injured as a boy, saving my cousin here from one of the Red-Eye's warriors. I narrowly survived, and now I have a problem with my bow arm at the shoulder." He showed her his scars.

"Oh, you are so brave! What exactly is the problem with your shoulder?"

"I'm sure it is only temporary. But sometimes when I'm aiming, my bow arm shakes and I have a hard time striking my target. Though, recently I managed to kill two ducks with one shot, as I am sure you must have heard from your sisters…"

"*Motch,* I had not heard about that. I am sure my sisters are trying to keep you a secret," she said with a smile.

This thought perked Flying Rabbit Boy right up.

"I may be able to help you," offered Water Lily Woman.

"*Tapwe?*" said Flying Rabbit Boy.

"Really?" repeated Little Grey Bear Boy.

"*Tapwe*," she smiled. "As I was out picking red clover, I found something."

She drew a long black arrow out from the sleeve of her dress. "Someone must have lost it while out hunting."

"That is a very fine arrow," said Flying Rabbit Boy, reaching over and testing the firmness of the shaft with one hand. The feather fletching appeared to be perfect.

"It is," said Water Lily Woman. "But I will make it even better."

She held the arrow by the end with the stone tip pointing towards Father Sky, cleared her throat, and began to sing a chant. She placed her other hand upon the stone point. The boys felt a vibration in the air and the earth trembled slightly beneath their feet.

The arrow stood upon the palm of her hand. She ran her fingers down the length of the arrow until it was hovering in mid-air, supported only by the Grey-Eye magic. When abruptly she stopped chanting, the arrow fell. She caught it before it hit the ground. The two boys gaped at the young woman in complete disbelief and awe. She said nothing for a time—only breathed deeply. The buzzing in the air subsided and the earth stopped rumbling.

"I have imbued this arrow with the power of the Grey-Eye magic," she intoned. "When the time comes for you, Flying Rabbit Boy, to prove yourself a warrior, this arrow will not miss its target."

"Whoa," exclaimed Flying Rabbit Boy in wonder as he reached his hand out for the magic arrow.

"But!" she added, pulling the arrow back. "The magic will only work if your heart is true and your need is great. So do not use it until absolutely necessary."

"I don't know what to say," said Flying Rabbit Boy, accepting the magic arrow.

"This would be the first time that's ever happened to you," said Little Grey Bear Boy, arranging his stacks of driftwood loudly.

Flying Rabbit Boy marveled at the gift. "I am so honoured... Please, let me walk you back to the village. It's the least I can do." He reached his arms out to take her basket of clover, bowing his head low.

"The honour is mine, son of the Bear clan," Water Lily Woman said as she accepted his offer and handed him the basket.

Little Grey Bear Boy shouldered the firewood he had collected, carrying it awkwardly as the other two chatted easily. Flying Rabbit Boy regaled Water Lily Woman with tales of his modest achievements. She laughed at all of his jokes and encouraged him with questions.

Little Grey Bear Boy struggled to keep up with them under his heavy burden of driftwood. Grandfather Sun was beginning to set as they arrived in the village. At the Turtle lodge, she turned to the two young Bears.

"Thank you for seeing me safely home. I had a very fine day in the forest. Now remember what I said about that arrow."

"I will," promised Flying Rabbit Boy.

"In the meantime, I remember my sisters telling me you are a skilled fisherman."

"You have been correctly informed," bragged Flying Rabbit Boy as Little Grey Bear Boy rolled his eyes. "I would bring you some fish," explained Flying Rabbit Boy, "but it is difficult for me to pull a net up the river by myself. My cousin here is always at his lessons at the Eagle medicine lodge."

"I'm sure you will find a way," was all she said in reply.

"Oh yes, *tapwe*," stammered Flying Rabbit Boy. "I'm sure I will find a way."

"It was very nice to meet you, sons of the Bear clan." Water Lily Woman's grey eyes met Little Grey Bear Boy's once again. She smiled brightly at him and Little Grey Bear Boy felt himself freeze under the strange power of her gaze. Was this magic?

# NĪMITANAW NIKOTWĀSOSĀP

The boys dropped the wood at the Eagle medicine lodge before continuing on to the Bear lodge for the evening meal. To the astonishment of the adults, Flying Rabbit Boy talked on and on about one thing. "…and she comes from *Azaadiwi-ziibiing,* the place of the poplar tree river, which is south and east of here," he babbled. "Her people are very different from us, but in many ways we are the same…"

"What was she doing alone out in the forest?" asked White Willow Woman.

"I do not know, picking clover I think," answered Flying Rabbit Boy. "I was just returning from my hunt and I saw her talking to Little Grey Bear Boy."

Everyone stopped eating and looked at Little Grey Bear Boy. With the sinking feeling that he had just gotten his cousin into trouble, Flying Rabbit Boy finally stopped talking.

After a long pause, White Willow Woman spoke. "What were you talking about, you and Water Lily Woman?"

"Nothing," said Little Grey Bear Boy, his heart pounding under the intense scrutiny of his family. "I was collecting wood and she approached me. She said she wanted to look at my eyes. She had never seen another Grey-Eye before and she wanted to know what it looked like."

The women looked at each other. "You must understand," began Walking Moon Woman. "It is very important you avoid talking to this young woman. We know from the past that if two Grey-Eyes were to fall in love, their child would become a Red-Eye. Many people died when the Red-Eye and his warriors attacked our village, including my husband…"

"I was afraid something like this might happen," said White Willow Woman, wringing her hands.

"She is not interested in him," announced Flying Rabbit Boy. "After all, she gave *me* the arrow."

"She gave you an arrow?" asked Singing Doe.

"*Tapwe!*" said Flying Rabbit Boy proudly. "And she put the Grey-Eye magic into it. She said if my heart was true and my need great, this arrow would never miss its mark!" Flying Rabbit Boy drew the magic arrow out of the quiver next to him and showed it to the family. Yellow Hawk Girl tried to touch it but Flying Rabbit Boy pulled it out of her reach.

"I didn't know a Grey-Eye could do that," said Blue Elk Man, looking at his son.

"I didn't know either," responded Little Grey Bear Boy. "I still don't know how she did it."

"It might be a good idea to ask her," suggested Brown Shield Man.

"*Motch!*" commanded Walking Moon Woman. "He is not to talk to her."

"I don't think we need to be concerned about the Grey-Eyes," said Brown Shield Man proudly. "She has made her intentions towards my son quite clear with this gift." He took the arrow from his son's hands and examined it by the light of the fire.

"What do you mean?" asked Yellow Hawk Girl.

"Yeah, what are you talking about?" added Little Grey Bear Boy.

"Oh, my boys," chuckled Brown Shield Man, "you have much to learn about the ways of women."

Singing Doe scoffed at her husband but he continued all the same.

"You see, when a young woman gives such a gift to a handsome young man, she is showing everyone she admires him."

"*Tapwe?*" asked Flying Rabbit Boy, a huge grin on his face. "I never thought I would be chosen by a Grey-Eyed one."

"That is a great honour indeed!" beamed Brown Shield Man.

"Excuse me," said Singing Doe, "but he is only twelve summers. It will be some time before he earns a warrior name and he must be worthy of a woman before I will allow him to marry."

"It may not be so long," whined Flying Rabbit Boy. "Besides, it is wise for her to express her interest early."

Brown Shield Man laughed.

"It is true that such a match would be a great honour to the Bear clan," said Walking Moon Woman, silencing the others. "But what is most important is that her interest is diverted from Little Grey Bear Boy."

"*Tapwe!*" The others nodded.

Little Grey Bear Boy picked through his food. Suddenly, he felt very tired.

Painted Turtle Man turned to him. "My boy. I left something in the forest. Would you come with me to find it? I am afraid my old eyes will have trouble seeing it without more help from Grandfather Sun."

"Can't you get it tomorrow, *Moosum*? I've had a very long day."

"By then I will have forgotten where I left it."

"All right then," sighed Little Grey Bear Boy.

As the two left the Bear lodge, the family was still chattering about Water Lily Woman. Brown Shield Man was practically planning the wedding.

# NĪMITANAW TĪPAKOHPOSĀP

Painted Turtle Man led his adopted grandson a short way down the lakeshore. "How are you feeling?" he asked.

"I am well, *Moosum*," the boy replied. "Thank you for asking."

"That was a very polite answer," chuckled Painted Turtle Man. "Not the one I was looking for. You seem troubled lately and I am afraid I have not been able to spend as much time with you as I would like. We are here now, together, if there is anything you wish to discuss with me."

"Well, *Moosum*. I guess I have felt troubled. I do not understand the teachings of Red Sky Man and I feel confused after speaking with Water Lily Woman."

"Confused? In what way?"

Little Grey Bear Boy continued reluctantly. "I had a very strange feeling when I met her. It is hard to describe…"

"Just try your best. I will not judge you, I want only to help."

"I felt like there was something jumping around in my stomach," explained Little Grey Bear Boy, "and my heart was moving very fast. I felt hot in my cheeks…"

"*Tapwe*?"

"*Tapwe*, I feel that way whenever I see her and sometimes when I think about her."

"I see."

"What does it mean, *Moosum*?"

"It means you like her. And that is nothing to be ashamed of." Painted Turtle Man shielded his eyes from the setting sun. The waves lapped against the rocky shore in a constant and steady rhythm.

"But…But that would not be appropriate."

"My boy," smiled Painted Turtle Man. "Love is always appropriate."

"But she is a Grey-Eye. If she chose me for her husband, our children would be Red-Eyes."

"I am not so sure." Painted Turtle Man sat down on a moss-covered rock, pulling his left leg over his right. "It is true that when Soaring Star Woman and Grey Bear had a child, he became a Red-Eye. But that was only one situation and no one knows if it had ever happened before. True, he was a Grey-Eye when I knew him as a boy and he was not kind and gentle like you—he used to be mean to us younger boys, always finding ways to tease us or hurt us—but it is possible something else caused Dark Cloud Man to become a Red-Eye. By the time he became a Red-Eye, his eyes were no longer grey like yours."

"So I could still become a Red-Eye?"

"I do not think you could ever be a Red-Eye. What I am saying is that the Grey-Eye gift is so rare and precious that none of us understands it. Only *Kitchi Manitou* knows why this gift is bestowed on so few. Perhaps one day you will learn the secret. All you need to know for now is that you are beginning to walk man's road and you must start deciding matters for yourself."

Painted Turtle Man extended his arm towards Little Grey Bear Boy. He gently helped the old man to his feet.

"So what should I do about my…feelings towards Water Lily Woman?"

"It does seem her attentions are towards your cousin," said Painted Turtle Man. "Maybe you should step aside this time. There are many fine young women who would be proud to have you for a husband."

"What if I never feel this way about another?"

"I have lived a very long time and have seen many things. There is someone out there for everyone. Often, it is someone we have known all along, but did not have the eyes to see them."

"Is that how it was for you?"

"It was, something like that, yes," said the old man.

"Now where did you leave your things?" interrupted Little Grey Bear Boy.

"I have just remembered. I did take them with me. I am sorry I dragged you out here for nothing."

"I had a feeling you were going to say something like that," said Little Grey Bear Boy.

"I just thought you needed to get out of the lodge for a bit," said Painted Turtle Man. "I didn't think you wanted the others to know how you felt. Can you forgive me?"

"*Tapwe, Moosum.* I suppose I should be grateful."

"I suppose you should," the old man said with a smile.

The boy and his adopted grandfather made their way back to the village and returned to the Bear lodge. The rest of the family had begun preparing themselves to sleep. Little Grey Bear Boy unrolled his hide, said his prayers, and drifted off to sleep. His dreams that night were filled with a beautiful Grey-Eyed girl.

# NĪMITANAW AYINĀNĪWOSĀP

ittle Grey Bear Boy spent the next two days collecting wood to replace the wood he had used in the Eagle medicine lodge. Although it was hard work collecting, breaking, and bundling the wood, he enjoyed his time alone in the forest. Being kept in the Eagle medicine lodge for three days had made him feel trapped. Out in the great wide forest, with birds chirping and waves lapping the beach shore, he felt free and at peace. He could not help looking up once in a while, hoping to see Water Lily Woman approach.

He tried hard to shake these thoughts from his head. She was a Grey-Eye like him and pursuing his feelings for her would not be worth the risk. Besides, she had expressed her interest in Flying Rabbit Boy, and this seemed to make his cousin happy.

When he had replaced all the wood—and more for good measure—Red Sky Man sat him down in the Eagle medicine lodge.

"Now that you know the seven colours of the fire," Red Sky Man said, "I will teach you how to control it."

"How to control the fire?"

"*Tapwe*," snapped Red Sky Man. "Pay attention." The Eagle medicine carrier drew a buffalo horn rattle from his medicine bundle and cleared his throat loudly. "I am going to teach you the fire song. As you learn it, concentrate on the fire. Tell it what you want it to do for you."

"How can I do this?"

"Just pay attention!" he snapped again. "There is no reason for you to speak until I ask you to!"

Little Grey Bear Boy felt his cheeks warming. In all the time he had known him, Painted Turtle Man had never snapped at him in this way.

Red Sky Man began to shake his rattle and sing an ancient prayer song dedicated to the fire. The words were unfamiliar to Little Grey Bear Boy, as they were in the ancient language. As he began to pick up the song, he drew out his own turtle shell rattle and shook it to the beat. Once he felt he had the song, he started to concentrate on the fire itself. He began to feel a vibration in the air and a warm burning feeling behind his eyes—the same feeling he'd had when he helped Flying Rabbit Boy shoot the ducks.

As his mind began to wander, the flames began to dance out of the fire, coiling up through the fire, criss-crossing this way and that, like burning ribbons. Little Grey Bear Boy was in a trance and began to feel he was not in control of his actions.

His heart jumped and he snapped out of it, the flames disappearing in a flash. Red Sky Man jolted as well, as though he had been in a trance too.

"I did not tell you to stop," Red Sky Man said.

"I am sorry, Uncle," gasped Little Grey Bear Boy, shaken. "I was distracted…"

"You must concentrate!" he yelled.

The two stared at each other in silence. Little Grey Bear Boy bit his lip. There were many things he wanted to say to Red Sky Man, none of them respectful.

"That is enough for today," said Red Sky Man finally. "See to your chores. We will speak again after the sundance ceremony. *Ekosi.*"

"*Hiy, hiy,*" came the response through clenched teeth.

Little Grey Bear Boy gathered his bundle and rushed out of the Eagle medicine lodge, bumping into Soaring Spear Man and knocking him down with an unusual force. Some of the other Eagle helpers helped him back onto his feet. Little Grey Bear Boy could feel the vibration in the air and a burning behind his eyes. Trying to calm himself, he bowed in apology to the Eagle helpers, who all nodded back, a hint of fear in their silence.

# NĪMITANAW KĪKĀ-MITĀTAHTOSĀP

As the time of the sacred sundance ceremony drew near, Little Grey Bear Boy had many preparations to make under his sponsor, Many Fish. Although Flying Rabbit Boy had reached his twelfth summer, none of the older warriors had come with the offer of an eagle bone whistle. Many Fish had talked to Brown Shield Man about sponsoring him, but it was agreed that, since he was already sponsoring Little Grey Bear Boy, taking on another would be too much. In the end, it was Blue Elk Man who offered to sponsor him.

"Thank you, Uncle," said Flying Rabbit Boy, accepting the eagle bone whistle. "I am honoured…"

"I know you will make us all proud," responded Blue Elk Man.

Flying Rabbit Boy managed a brave smile but it was obvious he felt the *Nehiyawak* had neglected him.

The sundance ceremony was being held in a village to the northwest known as *Pukatawagan*, the big water fishing place. The *Nehiyawak* of *Nisichawayasihk* began their journey to the sundance ceremony on a bright morning just days before the summer solstice.

The sundance ceremony was mostly without incident, though once again many of the sundancers stayed close to Little Grey Bear Boy, hoping to witness some Grey-Eye magic. He ignored them and concentrated on his prayers, suffering himself for the good of the *Nehiyawak*. Normally, dancing and fasting would be all that was asked of a boy of thirteen summers, but the others expected some great act of magic.

Water Lily Woman had come with her mother to the sundance grounds. Against the protestations of Red Sky Man, she was accorded a place of honour as a Grey-Eye. She stood behind the drum and helped the singers. Some of the songs were familiar to her, others she had to learn quickly. When she sang the sacred songs, her voice carried farther than the voices of the men at the drum and the air around the sundance arbour vibrated. Many of the sundancers were blessed with visions.

Little Grey Bear Boy was at first annoyed by the apparent fickleness of the *Nehiyawak*, but in the end he enjoyed having the attention deflected from him. Plus, with everyone focused on Water Lily Woman, it was easy for him to do the same.

Little Grey Bear Boy had fulfilled his most serious obligation to *Kitchi Manitou* in his first year and did not have any reason to suffer himself more than the dancing and fasting would require. Red Sky Man approached him now and then throughout the ceremony to suggest he consider walking with the buffalo. The boy shook his head each time, getting nothing but a scowl from his new teacher in return.

On this issue, Little Grey Bear Boy's teachings were very clear. One only suffered himself in walking with the buffalo to fulfill an obligation to *Kitchi Manitou* for a special blessing. As this year had been uneventful in terms of sickness and injury in the Bear lodge, pride would be the only reason for Little Grey Bear Boy to pierce himself. *Kitchi Manitou* often rewarded show-offs at the sundance ceremony with a lesson in humility and he did not wish to be rewarded so.

When the sundance concluded on the fourth day and Flying Rabbit Boy had gone to the tree without incident, some of the sundancers who had completed their four-year commitment held a giveaway ceremony to mark the occasion. It was customary for the *Nehiyawak* to give away most if not all of their possessions on special occasions, both to help those less fortunate and to start a new beginning free of possessions.

The *Nehiyawak* were particularly generous with Water Lily Woman for her singing, and she and her mother struggled to pack all the items gifted to them for the walk back to *Nisichawayasihk*.

"Go and offer your assistance," Brown Shield Man suggested.

"*Tapwe!*" said Flying Rabbit Boy nervously. "Will you come with me, cousin?"

"Of course," smiled Little Grey Bear Boy. "But first, your chest… it's bleeding."

Little Grey Bear Boy helped wipe some of the blood from Flying Rabbit Boy's small wounds, then put a medicine salve on it to stanch the flow.

"Ok, you are ready," said Brown Shield Man, pushing his son in Water Lily Woman's direction.

Flying Rabbit Boy was nervous but did his best to muster his jovial charm.

"*Tansi*, Auntie," he said. "Can we offer you our assistance?" His voice cracked at the end, causing his face to turn red, which the polite women pretended not to notice.

"Thank you, sons of the Bear clan," answered Yellow Moon Woman. "I was hoping some young warrior would be brave enough to help. I suppose we will need to build a travois. The sundancers have certainly been generous."

"They were very grateful for the beautiful singing," said Flying Rabbit Boy, composing himself.

"Lily?" sang Yellow Moon Woman. "Aren't you going to say something? Did you not hear the compliment this young man just paid you?"

"*Tapwe*, mother," she said rolling her eyes jokingly. "*Ekosani*, Flying Rabbit Boy."

She looked at both boys. Little Grey Bear Boy squinted around the grounds, as though looking for materials to build a travois, pretending not to notice her piercing gaze.

When the travois was built and the two young men had harnessed themselves to it, the foursome headed for *Nisichawayasihk*. Each day, they stopped to rest and eat. Brown Shield Man, Painted Turtle Man, and Blue Elk Man remained nearby, but kept a polite distance. Blue Elk Man was getting bruised ribs from all the elbowing Brown Shield

Man was giving him whenever Water Lily Woman spoke to or walked near Flying Rabbit Boy.

When they arrived in the village, they were greeted at the Turtle lodge by the excited chatter of the Turtle clan girls, who marveled at the gifts as they were unloaded from the travois.

Straight away, Water Lily Woman began distributing the gifts among her new sisters—furs, hides, painted quills, sinew, necklaces, colourful feathers, shells, moccasins, and a deer hide hand drum. The happy commotion brought by the unpacking could be heard across the village. The younger of the Eagle twins happened to be passing by. Noticing the gifts, she did nothing but scowl. Water Lily Woman returned the scowl, her grey eyes bright with challenge. The younger Eagle Twin ignored her, and scurried into the Eagle lodge to gossip with her elder sister.

# NIYĀNANOMITANAW

With the help of Water Lily Woman and her mother, the fortunes of the Turtle clan continued to rise. The eligible young warriors of the village, including a few discreet Eagle warriors, visited the Turtle lodge to share their hunt and be seen by Water Lily Woman.

As the summer progressed, Flying Rabbit Boy grew more and more concerned with improving his standing among the *Nehiyawak*. That a warrior from another clan did not step up to sponsor him in the sundance ceremony continued to trouble him.

"I think it is because of my arm," said Flying Rabbit Boy to his cousin. As they were out checking their rabbit snares one day.

"You seem to blame your arm for everything," was the answer from Little Grey Bear Boy as he squatted down to untangle a failed snare and reset it. "It is not your fault they do not see your true value. It is the *Nehiyawak* who are mistaken in this instance. Many will regret not having brought you a whistle when you are a great warrior and hunter."

"You are just saying that because you are my cousin."

"I am saying it because it is the truth. Besides, my father was honoured to sponsor you into the sundance ceremony. Who do you think will feed him when he is an old man and I am out picking medicines?"

"I hope I do not have to get your father to sponsor me into a warrior society too…"

"Don't trouble yourself with that," said Little Grey Bear Boy standing up. "You have to be brave to get into the Dog Soldier Society."

Flying Rabbit Boy chased his cousin for the jab. Little Grey Bear Boy was laughing too hard to make a clean getaway. The two boys wrestled and laughed and forgot the concerns of older men for a short time.

"Seriously though," said Little Grey Bear Boy when they had tired themselves out. "Remember: the warrior society you join will be determined by the manner in which you earn your name."

"*Tapwe*! That is true."

Knowing his bow skill was diminished and remembering Water Lily Woman's interest in his fishing, Flying Rabbit Boy concentrated his efforts on developing his fishing skills. He came up with a solution to his dilemma of how to work the net while his cousin was training with Red Sky Man. He would drag one side of the net across the river and secure it to a tree, then swim across the river and pull the net upstream in an arc along the river bank. In this way he could do the work of two by himself. When not catching fish, he spent his time gutting and hanging them. The days of swimming and net-pulling were starting to show in his arms and shoulders.

"Perhaps you will earn *my* name!" said Many Fish one day, admiring his catch by the river bank.

As always he shared his catch with the Turtle lodge, which usually earned him a smile or a thank you from Water Lily Woman. The rest of his catch went to the Bear lodge, for Singing Doe, White Willow Woman, and Walking Moon Woman to smoke or dry for the winter.

"We are going to get sick of fish this winter," laughed Singing Doe with pride. "If you are going to keep catching them, you should see if anyone will trade for hides."

Flying Rabbit Boy kept his mother's suggestion in mind, and when the Trader's caravan came late that summer, he was ready for them. He had worked hard to catch and smoke a large store of fish and bartered for many things the Bear clan needed. Although he was not able to trade for buffalo robes, he did manage to acquire deer and elk hides, which his mother would make into fine shirts, dresses, and moccasins.

Little Grey Bear Boy was happy to see his cousin doing so well, especially since his own ability to acquire goods for the family was diminished now that he no longer spent time picking and mixing medicines with Painted Turtle Man. Most of his lessons under Red Sky Man focused on bringing out the Grey-Eye magic rather than learning how to live in harmony with all of creation. The medicine carrier had Little Grey Bear Boy try to use his magic to force ants out their hill, stop small birds mid-flight—even kill flies with his mind.

Red Sky Man took Little Grey Bear Boy out of the village one day a fair distance along the lakeshore.

"You are a difficult pupil," he said. "I will have to use stronger methods in order for you to progress."

Little Grey Bear Boy already considered Red Sky Man's methods aggressive, not to mention ineffective, but he kept this thought to himself.

"*Ekosi*! This will do," said Red Sky Man stopping and rubbing his hands together when they arrived at a secluded sand beach with a rocky outcropping jutting out from a small peninsula. "You will learn how to use the Grey-Eye magic to control the waters."

"Control? What do you mean?"

"If you spent as much time listening as you did asking foolish questions, you would already know the answers."

"Sorry, Uncle," muttered Little Grey Bear Boy, though he was not so sure if he was.

"I will try to teach you how to move the waters to your will."

"To what purpose will I move the waters?"

"Just do as I say and stop with the foolish questions!" Red Sky Man snapped. He took out his buffalo horn rattle and began the ancient water chant. Little Grey Bear Boy tried hard to listen and pick up the words. Like the fire song, the words were in the ancient language, and Red Sky Man said them quickly, as though the boy could understand fluently.

Little Grey Bear Boy wanted to ask him to slow down or to sound out the words so he could remember, but he knew only too well his teacher's disdain for questions. He began to chant the ancient water chant as best he could.

"*Motch, motch, MOTCH!*" shouted Red Sky Man. "You are saying the words wrong. Listen." He then began chanting louder and faster, making it even more difficult for Little Grey Bear Boy to understand. The boy responded to this teaching by muttering the chant louder and faster, but still wrong. The waters remained still, much to Red Sky Man's dismay.

"We will have to try a different method," fumed Red Sky Man.

"Maybe we should head back to the village," said Little Grey Bear Boy. "I think it is going to rain." He pointed up into the sky, which had clouded over.

"Nonsense," countered Red Sky Man. "I would know if it was going to rain."

"*Tapwe*, Uncle," mumbled Little Grey Bear Boy.

"This is what you must do. Take off your shirt and leggings and wade out into the water."

"What for?" The question escaped his lips before he thought to hold it back.

"Just do what you are told!" screamed Red Sky Man as the clouds rumbled.

Little Grey Bear Boy put down his satchel, took off his shirt, moccasins, and leggings and waded out into the water. It was surprisingly warm.

"Now," commanded Red Sky Man, "put your head under the water and use the chant in your mind. Do not come up for air. Just push the water away from your body. Perhaps when you start to lose your breath, you will discover your Grey-Eye magic."

"I am not sure this is wise."

"So now you think I'm stupid?" the medicine carrier growled.

"That is not what I meant, Uncle," said Little Grey Bear Boy, lowering his eyes. "I will give it a try…" Obediently, he dunked his head. He concentrated hard on the chant in his mind, but the wording continued to elude him. He held his breath for as long as he could but the water did not move. He finally popped his head up out of the water, gasping for air.

"Get your head back under," said Red Sky Man coldly.

"*Tapwe*, Uncle," the boy gasped.

Little Grey Bear Boy again dunked his head under the water and concentrated on the chant. He thought to move the water, but still did not know to what purpose. As he began to run out of air he started to feel nervous of what Red Sky Man would say. Eventually, his body needed more air and he was forced to pop up out of the water again.

Red Sky Man looked at the boy, his mouth set against him in disappointment. "Now what? My last pupil learned this skill on the first try."

"I am sorry, Uncle, I am trying. If you could just say the chant slower, I know I could get it right…"

"If you just concentrated on the chant, you would have the words."

"I am concentrating!" said Little Grey Bear Boy, louder than he meant to. "I will try again—my best."

"So far, your 'best' has not been good enough," snorted Red Sky Man.

Little Grey Bear Boy could feel his anger rising. It had always been easy to respect his elders as he had been taught—they had always been patient and kind with him. He took a deep breath and plunged his head back under the water. He did his best to think the water chant in his mind and focus all of his energy on moving the water. He thought he could feel some movement of the water but the familiar vibration of the Grey-Eye magic did not come. Nothing was happening for a time and he began to run out of air. He would have to muster some self-control to put up with Red Sky Man's anger.

He began to rise out of the water but something stopped him. Calloused hands and a heavy weight on his shoulders prevented him from breaking the surface. Red Sky Man was holding him down. Little Grey Bear Boy began to struggle, reaching full-blown panic when the last of the air in his lungs was released into the water.

An anger swelled inside him in a way he had never known before. He felt burning behind his eyes as the water around him began to vibrate. Then the water blasted away from his body in all directions. The force of the magic caused all of the birds in the trees and on the lake to fly off, chirping and squawking their surprise.

Little Grey Bear Boy stood up from the damp sand and shook Red Sky Man's hands off of his shoulders.

"There," smiled Red Sky Man. "All it took was a little encouragement."

"You tried to drown me!" choked Little Grey Bear Boy.

"Do not act like a baby. You did not drown."

"I would have!"

"But you didn't. This was a success. You should be grateful."

"A student should be able to trust his teacher…"

"Trust is not required for learning," said Red Sky Man. "Only obedience is required."

"I think I have had enough of your 'lessons' Red Sky Man," said Little Grey Bear Boy. "I am going home." He began to gather his clothes and his satchel and walk to the village.

"Don't be such a baby!" laughed Red Sky Man. "It worked, didn't it?"

Little Grey Bear Boy was furious and decided it would be better not to speak. As he walked away he could still hear Red Sky Man laughing at him. He glanced back to see an unusual sight: Red Sky Man walking out across the wet sand as the waters crashed down behind him.

# NIYĀNANOMITANAW PIYAKOSĀP

ittle Grey Bear Boy decided to take a longer way back to the village so he could clear his head and cool his anger.

Grandfather Sun was beginning to leave for the night, yet he did not want to go back to the Bear lodge and disrupt the harmony of his family. He found a large rock to sit upon and chase away his anger. He looked inside his satchel but could not find any sage. A good smudging would have been helpful. The first stars of the night sky began to appear on the horizon.

He thought about what had happened on the lakeshore, but was unsure about how to proceed. On the one hand he wanted to respect his elders and the decision of the Circle of Clan Mothers, but on the other hand he felt the Circle had made an error in entrusting his education to Red Sky Man. He did not want to make any decision without a pure heart.

As he was contemplating his problem, he felt a light tap on his left shoulder. He looked to his left but saw nothing that could have touched him. Then, feeling a warm nudge against the right side of his body, he looked over to see Water Lily Woman's bright grey eyes.

"*Tansi!*" she said playfully, sitting next to him on the rock.

"Oh, hello…" he said turning away, but it was too late—she had seen the look on his face.

"What's wrong?" she asked.

"Oh, nothing," he said, trying to look content.

"It must be something."

"I had a rough day, but I do not want to burden you with my troubles."

"It would be no burden," she pressed. "Maybe you just need someone to talk to."

"Maybe you are right…What brings you out here?"

"I came to see my father."

"Your father?" he asked looking around.

"Up there," she said pointing at Father Sky.

"I do not understand."

"I am waiting for the spirits to dance," she explained.

"Oh!" said Little Grey Bear Boy. "How do you know the spirits are going to dance tonight?"

"I have a sense of these things," she said. "I always know when my father is coming."

"How did he pass? That is, if you don't mind talking about it…"

"I don't mind," she answered. "I was very young when it happened. It was winter and he had killed a deer. He was a good hunter and provider for my mother and me."

"He sounds like he was a good man."

"He was." She was in a sort of dream state as she spoke, half remembering, half imagining. "His hands must have become numb from the cold because he cut himself while skinning the deer."

"Was it that bad?"

"Not at first. It healed over but then it began to swell and turn colour. He took a high fever and then he left us." She looked at her feet and tapped them one after the other against the rock.

"I am sorry," said Little Grey Bear Boy.

"Don't be," she said perking up and meeting his gaze. "That is what brought me to *Nisichawayasihk*."

"*Tapwe?*"

"*Tapwe*," she answered. "If we had known more of the secrets of the plant world, we might have been able to save him. When we learned there was a medicine carrier who knew those secrets and the Grey-Eye magic, we came as soon as we were able."

"Oh," said Little Grey Bear Boy. "That was wise. And how have your teachings been progressing?"

"Very well! I have learned so many new roots and plants and how to use them. Painted Turtle Man is a very good teacher."

"*Tapwe*," said Little Grey Bear Boy. "I miss spending time with him…"

"I am sorry I separated you from your *moosum*…"

"It wasn't your fault, I don't blame you."

Water Lily Woman looked into his eyes to be sure he meant what he said.

"I think it is important that others learn the secrets of the plant world," he assured her. "In fact, you came at a good time."

"Oh?"

"*Tapwe*. Painted Turtle Man had lost his medicine lodge as well as his proper place among the *Nehiyawak*. He was basically replaced by Red Sky Man as the village medicine carrier."

"How could that have happened? He is knowledgeable and an excellent teacher."

"I am not really sure, come to think of it," frowned Little Grey Bear Boy. "When Red Sky Man came to *Nisichawayasihk*, the *Nehiyawak* began to think he was better than Painted Turtle Man."

"Why would they do that?" she asked, "Why not have two medicine carriers?"

"I don't know," said Little Grey Bear Boy. "It seems the *Nehiyawak* always want to measure everyone against someone else."

"I know what you mean," laughed Water Lily Woman. "My sisters in the Turtle lodge are always talking about how well you use the Grey-Eye magic. They are always begging me to use it to help them with something."

"I didn't know that."

"*Tapwe*! It's true!"

"I don't know how to use the Grey-Eye magic. I don't know how I did the things I have done and I would not be able to do them again if someone asked me to."

"Are you just saying that to make me feel better?"

"*Motch*," said Little Grey Bear Boy. "I was jealous of how you were able to help Flying Rabbit Boy with his arrow."

"I didn't do anything to that arrow," she said. "Look!"

They looked up into the sky and saw the silvery green aurora beginning to flicker in the sky. The spirits of their ancestors were starting to dance.

"Do you want to meet my father?" asked Water Lily Woman.

"I would be honoured," he answered.

Water Lily Woman produced a small hand drum made of deer hide and got to her feet. She cleared her throat and began to beat the drum. Little Grey Bear Boy could feel the familiar vibration of the Grey-Eye magic as she sang. Her voice seemed to travel—it emanated from all directions. As the aurora flickered, a dancer emerged, a young man of about twenty-five summers. He danced with a thin hoop, which he would roll out in front of himself and spin it to return. He passed his body through the hoop in all directions as though it was as much a part of him as his arms and legs. Soon, more hoops appeared and he incorporated them into his dance, using them and his body to form different shapes and animals.

She finished her song but the hoop dancer continued. Water Lily Woman sat back down on the rock next to Little Grey Bear Boy.

"That is my father," she said through teary eyes.

"I am honoured to meet him," he whispered.

She leaned against him and he felt her warm breath on his neck and chest.

"Is there no one to dance for you?" she asked.

"*Motch*," he said softly, "I have not really known many who have passed on."

"Then you are lucky," she said as she placed her hand in his.

They watched the spirits dance together and Little Grey Bear Boy felt a flutter in his chest and warmth in his cheeks. His past troubles seemed very far behind him.

Eventually, the spirits stopped dancing and the aurora disbursed across the horizon. They sat together for a time, neither of them wishing to speak or move.

"We should return to the village…" he whispered.

"*Tapwe*…" she answered.

They stood up together and Little Grey Bear Boy started to pull away. Water Lily Woman squeezed his hand and looked into his eyes, pleading him not to let go. He smiled at her and nodded gently. They began to walk back to the village, hand in hand, and Little Grey Bear Boy felt as though he were floating on a cloud. He looked down at his feet and realized he was, in fact, drifting just above the ground in much the same way Soaring Star Woman had so many years ago.

As they neared the village, Water Lily Woman stopped and they landed gently upon the earth.

"I am glad we were able to spend this time together," she said looking up into his eyes. "But I talked to my Turtle sisters about what you said. They explained what the *Nehiyawak* think about what would happen if two Grey-Eyes fell in love…"

"I see."

"I want you to know I do not believe this taboo," she added quickly. "But I am concerned about what the others would do if they knew I liked you…"

"You like me?"

She gave no answer—only smiled at Little Grey Bear Boy. She had spoken what was in her heart before she had even realized it fully for herself. Water Lily Woman stepped closer to Little Grey Bear Boy until he could feel her body pressed up against his. His heart was pounding as their noses touched and he could feel her soft breath on his face. Their lips met. For a moment, everything around him evaporated and the only thing in his world was the woman in front of him. As their lips finally parted, the world around him re-materialized. The trees and moss had suddenly grown lusher and greener.

"Good night, Little Grey Bear Boy of the Bear clan," she said with a smile.

"Good night, Water Lily Woman…"

As she walked away, she turned back briefly and smiled. She entered the village and went quickly to the Turtle lodge. Little Grey Bear Boy was like a tree, rooted to the spot, still not sure that what had just happened was real. A mosquito landed on his neck and he let it taste his blood. At least now he knew he wasn't dreaming…

# NIYĀNANOMITANAW NĪSOSĀP

Little Grey Bear Boy entered the Bear lodge and stood in the doorway. Most of the family did not even look up from their evening meal.

"Where have you been?" asked White Willow Woman casually.

"I will no longer take instruction from Red Sky Man!" he said. This got their attention and they all turned.

"Has something happened?" asked Painted Turtle Man.

"What has happened, *Moosum*," answered Little Grey Bear Boy, "is that I have made a decision."

Painted Turtle Man let his raised eyebrows fall.

"The decision was never yours to make!" stated Walking Moon Woman, matriarch of the Bear clan. "I will decide what goes on in the Bear lodge!"

"*Nookum*," replied Little Grey Bear Boy. "I mean you no disrespect, but I know as well as everyone here this was never your decision either…"

Walking Moon Woman looked at Little Grey Bear Boy, astonished by his words. She wanted to get angry but she knew he was right. She relinquished. "I am sorry, my boy. I do not know how it ever came to pass that the Bear clan would lose control over its own destiny. I am so ashamed…"

The old woman sat back down where she was and began to cry. Singing Doe and White Willow Woman went to comfort her.

"What would you have us do?" asked Blue Elk Man.

"I had not thought about that..." admitted Little Grey Bear Boy.

"I have an idea," said Painted Turtle Man. "I have been thinking about this for quite some time. In fact, I was hoping something like this might happen."

"You were hoping my son would make my mother cry?" exclaimed White Willow Woman.

"*Motch*, my girl. I had hoped we would have reason to challenge the other clans meddling in our family's destiny."

"What is your plan?" asked Brown Shield Man.

"I think it is time my grandson began his vision quest."

The entire family was silent for a time.

"Your solution is to send my son away?" asked White Willow Woman.

"It would only be for four days!" assured Painted Turtle Man. "When one of the *Nehiyawak* has come to a crossroads in his or her life, then the time of the vision quest is at hand. He will walk the forest and commune with the spirits and with our animal brothers. He will ask *Kitchi Manitou* to give him a vision so he may make the right decision on which direction his life journey should take."

"How will we do this?" asked Blue Elk Man. "Red Sky Man will say it is for him to decide as Little Grey Bear Boy's teacher."

"It is time the Bear clan decides its own destiny," said Walking Moon Woman.

The next morning, White Willow Woman walked to the Crane lodge to inform Drifting Butterfly Woman that Little Grey Bear Boy would begin his vision quest. The Crane clan warriors spread the news throughout the village, as was their duty.

Later in the day, as the Bears were making their preparations, a Crane clan warrior came to the Bear lodge.

"*Tansi, Nookum*," the warrior said respectfully, addressing Walking Moon Woman. "The Circle of Clan Mothers will gather this night at the Eagle lodge."

"The Circle is to gather at the Eagle lodge?" repeated Walking Moon Woman.

"*Tapwe*, this is what I have been told." The Crane warrior bowed and left the Bear lodge.

"What does this mean, my mother?" asked Singing Doe.

"It means the Circle now meets in secret…"

"But that is not the way of the *Nehiyawak*," said White Willow Woman.

"*Motch*, my girl," answered Walking Moon Woman. "It is not…"

The Bear clan continued with their preparations. Anyone who saw them frowned or looked away. Painted Turtle Man continued about his work without a second thought to the gossiping *Nehiyawak*. The task at hand was to see his adopted grandson taking his first real steps towards becoming a man. Little Grey Bear Boy would walk the forest alone for four days and nights seeking a vision to guide him on his life's journey. Painted Turtle Man cared about nothing else than to see him readied for his quest—and to be there to help him interpret the vision.

"Have you got a tent?" he asked.

"*Motch*, I do not," answered Little Grey Bear Boy.

"What did you use at the sundance?"

"I borrowed one from my sponsor, Many Fish."

"Well, go and ask him if he will let you use it," instructed Painted Turtle Man.

"*Tapwe, Moosum.*"

Little Grey Bear Boy crossed the village and went to the Crane lodge. "Ahem!" he said outside the entrance way. One of the children came to the door and, seeing who it was, shouted: "It's the Grey-Eyed boy!"

"Little Grey Bear Boy!" said Many Fish, coming out. "What brings you here this fine day?"

"I came to ask you to loan me your tent."

"Are you going hunting?"

"*Motch*, Uncle. Painted Turtle Man says it is time for me to go on my vision quest."

"*Tapwe*," said Many Fish, touching his forehead. "I knew that…Of course you can use it. I am honoured you would come to me on such a special occasion as this."

"Thank you, Uncle. I am honoured you would help me, as you did with the sundance."

"Anytime, my boy. I know you will take good care of me when I am an old man." He winked.

Little Grey Bear Boy took the hides wrapped around four short poles. As he was returning to the Bear lodge with the tightly bundled tent, he heard a voice he had been dreading.

"What are you doing?" It was Red Sky Man.

"I am preparing for my vision quest…"

"Ha!" exclaimed Red Sky Man, cutting him off. "Don't bother, you won't be going anywhere." He walked away chuckling to himself.

Little Grey Bear Boy felt a burning sensation behind his eyes and a vibration in the air as he quickly returned to the Bear lodge. The grass beneath his feet turned yellow as he walked across it. He burst into the lodge. Everyone there could feel the power of his anger. The hides on the Bear lodge were strained as an unseen force pushed on them.

"What is the matter, my son?" asked White Willow Woman.

"I just saw Red Sky Man," explained Little Grey Bear Boy, trying to compose himself. "He told me not to prepare for my vision quest, that I would not be going anywhere."

"I can guess what topic you will be discussing at the Circle tonight," Painted Turtle Man said to his cousin. "Strange that the clan mothers inform Red Sky Man, when they have not yet informed you…"

"Yes, thanks for pointing that out," Walking Moon Woman said, frowning.

That evening, the Bear clan matriarch and her daughters made their way to the Eagle lodge. The three Bear clan women entered the lodge and found the other matriarchs already gathered, chatting among themselves. The chatter stopped as soon as the Bear clan appeared. Walking Moon Woman noted Red Sky Man sitting with the Eagle twins. Drifting Butterfly Woman stood just inside the door. It appeared she had just arrived.

"My sister," said the younger Eagle twin to Walking Moon Woman, nodding at her daughters. "This gathering is only for matriarchs."

"Will Red Sky Man be leaving us?" asked Drifting Butterfly Woman as she took her seat.

The younger Eagle twin scowled.

"Singing Doe and White Willow Woman can stay," said Talking Stone Woman, matriarch of the Deer clan. "It concerns them as well." The Bear clan women took their place in the Circle of Clan Mothers.

Drifting Butterfly Woman began the meeting. "My sisters. We have been called here to discuss recent events. It would seem there is disharmony in the village. On one side, the Bear clan wishes to send Little Grey Bear Boy on his vision quest. On the other, the Eagle clan has expressed concerns…"

"My sisters," interrupted Walking Moon Woman. "What 'concerns' can the Eagle clan possibly have for how I raise my grandson?" The matriarchs all nodded, with the exception of the Eagle twins.

"My sisters," said the elder Eagle twin. "It was previously agreed by this Circle that Little Grey Bear Boy would be taught by our Eagle medicine carrier. To our knowledge, this decision has not been rescinded. Should it not be the boy's teacher who decides when his pupil should seek a vision?"

Some of the matriarchs nodded while others looked down.

"My sisters," continued Walking Moon Woman. "It was agreed by this Circle that Little Grey Bear Boy would be taught by Red Sky Man during the day and by Painted Turtle Man by night. In the Circle's wisdom it was decided the boy could benefit most in learning from two teachers. My cousin has advised me that it is now time for the boy to begin his vision quest. Painted Turtle Man has known the boy since the very day he was born, as some of you might remember. I took many things into consideration before deciding this would be a good thing for my grandson…"

"My sister." It was the elder Eagle twin's turn to interrupt. "Should you have not also taken Red Sky Man's wisdom into consideration before making your decision?"

"I guess it never occurred to me to ask the advice of an outsider as to how I should raise my grandson!"

The clan matriarchs all looked down, ashamed of the implication that anyone should come between a mother and child. This was not the way of the *Nehiyawak* and they all knew it.

"But perhaps you are right about Red Sky Man. I would invite him to offer his wisdom…"

The matriarchs and the twins looked at each other in confusion, while Red Sky Man sat up straight.

"Thank you, my sister," he said, not missing a beat. "I do not feel the boy is ready to undertake the vision quest. He is only fourteen summers and still has much to learn. I believe his teachings are well behind what they should be at his age. Perhaps if he had the benefit of a teacher with previous experience with the Grey-Eye magic, he would have been ready."

The Eagle twins nodded proudly and searched the faces of the other matriarchs for approval.

"Thank you, Red Sky Man of the Eagle clan," said Walking Moon Woman. "I have taken your thoughts into consideration and have decided Little Grey Bear Boy will embark on his vision quest under the guidance of Painted Turtle Man."

Drifting Butterfly Woman was unable to stifle her laughter for a moment. Red Sky Man looked furious that he had been fooled by the Bear clan matriarch. The other matriarchs wondered why they had gathered in the first place.

"My sisters," announced Drifting Butterfly Woman when she had composed herself. "I for one do not believe there is anything more to discuss in this matter."

"My sisters!" exclaimed the elder Eagle twin. "I do not believe enough consideration has been given to this matter. If she could just be made to understand that…"

"My sister," said Talking Stone Woman, matriarch of the Deer clan. "A matriarch has spoken for her grandson. There is nothing left for any of us to discuss. Would the Eagles next tell me how to raise my family? I am glad Soaring Star Woman was not here to see what our Circle has become…"

The matriarchs looked up into the starry sky, remembering their great leader, now gone on to the Great Mystery. Soaring Star Woman had led them with wisdom and grace across many years. Somewhere along the path, they had forgotten her example and in so doing dishonoured her memory.

"My sisters," said Gliding Heron Woman of the Marten clan. "I am concerned about how we came to this. After we have all had time to clear our minds and hearts of anger and resentment, I will call for this Circle of Clan Mothers to reconsider who we would have speaking for us."

The younger Eagle twin gasped loudly and her whole body shook as she covered her mouth with her hand.

"My sisters," said the elder Eagle twin. "Perhaps it would be best if we…"

"*Tapwe!*" agreed Blue Lightning Woman of the Wolf clan. "That is a serious matter for another day. As far as this matter is concerned, I see no cause for further discussion."

"Thank you, my sisters," said Walking Moon Woman. "May the Grandmother Bear guide you in the ways of healing. *Ekosi.*" With that she stood up and left the Eagle lodge with her daughters. The Bear clan women returned to their lodge, heads held high.

# NIYĀNANOMITANAW NĪSTOSĀP

When the preparations were complete, the Bear clan gathered near the edge of the village to see Little Grey Bear Boy off. Singing Doe presented her nephew with a new pair of moccasins to mark the occasion. "I was making them for Flying Rabbit Boy," she explained. "It seems your need is greater."

He now had new moccasins, his medicine bundle, a blanket, and a tent. He also took Flying Rabbit Boy's bow and quiver of arrows, which he noticed was without the magic arrow.

"Be careful with my bow. I will need it to earn my name."

"Don't worry, cousin," answered Little Grey Bear Boy. "You'll get it back…"

"Make sure you pray," instructed Painted Turtle Man.

"*Tapwe!*" assured Little Grey Bear Boy. "Of course, *Moosum*."

"And remember too…"

"In what direction will you go?" called Red Sky Man stepping out from behind the Deer lodge, cutting him off.

"Why do you ask?" inquired Painted Turtle Man.

"Is it not customary for a warrior to inform others of his plans before leaving the village?" asked Red Sky Man. "I was always taught to let people know where I go so that if anything happens, they will know where to look for me. What if he needs help?"

"You are right," nodded Painted Turtle Man. "I am happy you are so concerned for my grandson. I will be instructing him to head east."

"East? Is that where your 'visions' have shown you?" The Eagle medicine carrier walked away laughing. Painted Turtle Man scowled at him as he left, then turned to his grandson.

"My boy," he whispered, "I will tell everyone you are headed east, and you will go that way at first...You know the place where you collect driftwood?"

"Yes, *Moosum*," answered Little Grey Bear Boy quietly.

"I will meet you there..."

"*Moosum*?"

"Trust me."

Little Grey Bear Boy caught a hint of desperation in the old man's eyes. "*Tapwe*," came his reply.

The family said their goodbyes, with Little Grey Bear Boy's mother reminding him to follow his teachings, his father warning him of the dangers of the forest, and his sister offering her prayers. Last, it was Walking Moon Woman's turn.

"Be careful," was all she said.

"Yes, *Nookum*. And thank you for everything."

"It is I who must thank you, for helping me remember who I am."

Little Grey Bear Boy nodded and hugged her, taking in the familiar scent of wild peppermint and cook fire smoke. This hug was different from those they had shared before. As a child he would lean into her embrace, enjoying the soft warmth and resting his head on her shoulder. This time she leaned into him and he felt the warmth of her cheek on his shoulder. For the first time, he realized he was now taller.

He left the village, heading east as instructed, and made his way to the beach where he had collected the driftwood for the Eagle medicine lodge. The heavier autumn winds made the waves crash upon the shore harder than in the summer moons. The leaves of the birch and poplar trees were starting to change from lush green to orange and yellow. Although this was a familiar place, it seemed different. A tingle went up his spine. Feeling like he did not wish to be seen, Little Grey Bear Boy crouched down low next to a large jack pine and scanned the trees and bushes for signs of movement. Soon, he heard footsteps shuffling near him. It was Painted Turtle Man, looking this way and that, his features strained.

"*Moosum!*" whispered Little Grey Bear Boy. "Over here!"

The old man walked right to the boy but still looked around for him. "Where are you?" He leaned against the jack pine and whispered, though he was standing right next to the boy.

"I am right here!" shouted the boy, frightening the old man. Little Grey Bear Boy looked down and saw his legs were missing. He had not noticed the buzzing in the air. He stood up and closed his eyes, trying to calm his beating heart. He cleared his mind. The vibration in the air subsided after a time he was again visible.

"That was a good trick," chuckled Painted Turtle Man, steadying himself on a firm branch.

"I am sorry, I did not even realize I had done it."

"That does not matter," said Painted Turtle Man. "What matters is that the magic works when necessary. Here, I brought you something." The old man handed the boy a heavy satchel.

"What is it, *Moosum?*"

"It is food, my boy."

"Food?"

"*Tapwe!* I know it is customary to fast on one's vision quest, but I want you to stay strong. I had a strange dream last night, and I fear something is about to happen."

"You had a vision?" Little Grey Bear Boy helped his adopted grandfather sit against the trunk of the tree.

"I think so, my boy, but I must go and see that it is true. I must go far to the southeast."

"I will go with you!"

"*Motch*, you travel a different path, but there is something you can do to help me."

"Anything, *Moosum*."

"I need you to turn me into a bird."

Little Grey Bear Boy was taken aback. He was surprised to be asked to use the Grey-Eye magic and worried he could not fulfill this request.

"*Moosum*…"

"I know it will be difficult and I should not ask such a thing, but it must be done."

"But *Moosum*, I do not know how," said Little Grey Bear Boy.

"Yes, you do! You once turned me into a stag. You also turned your cousin into a turtle when it was needed. Now I need you to turn me into a bird so I can travel fast and far."

"But how, *Moosum*?"

"I don't know. How do you think it will work?" Little Grey Bear Boy grabbed Painted Turtle Man's extended arm to help him up again. He brushed the dirt and fallen pine needles off the old man, playing for time. Little Grey Bear Boy was surprised by the question. With Red Sky Man, he tried to force the magic. The thought never occurred to him to think about how the Grey-Eye magic worked on its own.

"Well, the last time it happened the need was very great, *Moosum*."

"I tell you, my boy, this may truly be a matter of life and death."

The desperate look in the old man's eyes had returned. It was more than enough to convince Little Grey Bear Boy that he must do whatever he could to help.

"Okay, *Moosum*," he said, "I will try my best…"

"That is all anyone can ask," Painted Turtle Man said as he shifted from foot to foot and took some deep breaths to prepare himself.

Little Grey Bear Boy drew his turtle shell rattle out of his medicine bundle and began to shake it gently. He sang an Eagle song and concentrated hard on his purpose.

The Grey-Eye magic continued to elude him—there was no vibration in the air—and he was beginning to doubt himself. He closed his eyes and cleared his mind of all doubts and fears. He sang the song loud and passionately, beseeching the spirits of the ancestors for their blessing. He lost himself in the melody and began to feel warmth in his chest. Then—a vibration in the air. As he neared the end of the song and his voice became low, he was startled by the piercing cry of an eagle.

"Thank you, grandson!"

Little Grey Bear Boy opened his eyes and saw he was standing with a large golden eagle.

"*Moosum*?"

"You did it, I knew you could!" said the golden eagle. "Now I must go. You must journey north until midday and then head west. Continue west for another day and then go south. Travel south for a

276

day and then return to the village heading northeast. If it is the will of *Kitchi Manitou*, I will return to the village at the same time. I will be able to decipher my vision then and, if you have been blessed, I will try to help you understand your vision."

"What is the knowledge you are seeking, *Moosum?*"

"I have learned something terrible about someone in our village. But I cannot speak ill of another person until I have proof of the misdeeds. That is my teaching and I must stay true to my beliefs. I only hope my vision was wrong or that I will be able to address the problem before anyone is harmed." The eagle tried to walk on the large roots of the jack pine with much difficulty. He held up his great wings to steady himself, rustling up the dried pine needles and dust at the base of the tree.

"I am afraid, *Moosum*..."

"There is no shame in being afraid, my boy," explained the golden eagle. "There is only shame in allowing fear to prevent us from doing our duty."

The golden eagle stretched and began to flap its unsteady wings, testing. As the eagle grew steady, it jumped up and perched itself upon a large branch of the jack pine.

"Remember, my boy. You must make an offering of tobacco for any dream, vision, or animal you see on your vision quest. Listen to your heart and to the spirits of the ancestors for guidance."

"*Tapwe, Moosum*," said Little Grey Bear Boy. "Journey safely and return home!"

"And you also!" screeched the golden eagle. "May the grandmothers and grandfathers of the *Nehiyawak* guide and protect you on your vision quest!"

The golden eagle stretched out its wings and glided off the tree branch, rising higher and higher into the air to the southeast. Little Grey Bear Boy stood watching until it was no more than a speck on Father Sky.

When he was ready to begin his journey, Little Grey Bear Boy reached into his medicine pouch and pinched a wad of tobacco. He offered it to the four directions, then placed it at the base of the jack pine tree. He was ready.

# NIYĀNANOMITANAW NIYOSĀP

He started out north, as instructed, until midday, and then turned towards the west, travelling over rocks and moss, swamp and forest. He watched as Grandfather Sun passed across Father Sky, then began his descent. He had covered a lot of ground and found a suitable dry place to make camp for the night. He lit no fire, as he still had the feeling in his heart that someone was searching for him. He unrolled Many Fish's tent and ate some smoked fish from the satchel Painted Turtle Man had given him. He was alone in a strange land, far from any medicine-picking place or hunting grounds he knew.

Little Grey Bear Boy spent some time contemplating the next few days as Grandmother Moon shined her light upon him. He wondered what Painted Turtle Man was seeking. He thought about his family, his teachings with Red Sky Man, but most of all he thought about Water Lily Woman. The vision quest was a time and place for making decisions for the future. He smiled to himself, content in the realization that he would begin to determine his own destiny more and more. He would be guided in these decisions by signs from *Kitchi Manitou*. It was a comforting thought that eased him to sleep.

He awoke early the next morning and decided this was the day his quest would really begin. He continued west over rough terrain, progressing slowly. He paid close attention to the land, water, and sky, searching for any sign or vision the spirits might offer. He worked his way around creeks, lakes, and rivers as well as patches of muskeg, being careful not to sink into the wet, spongy moss.

Late in the afternoon he came upon a small clearing and witnessed what he thought must be his first sign. Two grey timber wolves were playing with a small pup in the meadow. The pup yelped and chased its mother and then its father, nipping at their ears. The small wolf family seemed to be playing without a care in the world. Without warning, the two large timber wolves straightened suddenly, their ears perked up. The pup crouched down and disappeared into the grass.

Little Grey Bear Boy crouched down low as the wolves scoured the countryside for danger. He did not want to disturb them and noted the wind was blowing slightly from the north. He took out another wad of tobacco and placed it on the ground in front of him. Backing out slowly and quietly, he decided this would be a good time to begin his journey south, keeping downwind from the wolves.

He continued south until nightfall, then found another suitable place to make camp. It was a small crevice in a steep cliff face. Years of wind and rain had brought sand and gravel to the ground. The lack of moss and grass would provide some relief from insects.

He felt he was on the right path, having been given a sign. To see one of the seven sacred animals was a blessing. He felt more at ease now and built his fire next to his tent. He warmed up some dried meat with a willow branch sharpened at one end. It was strange to eat without the sounds of laughter, but there was something else in his heart: a great feeling of independence and the swelling of pride that comes with being able to survive alone. He went to sleep under the starry sky thinking about what he had witnessed this day. He could not wait to discuss the sign with Painted Turtle Man.

# NIYĀNANOMITANAW NIYĀNOSĀP

The next day he continued south, coming after a time upon a large lake. He followed the rocky shoreline as well as he could. The lake was leading him further to the east than he wanted, but before midday the shores led him back south and west. As he approached the southernmost tip of the lake, he found himself on a high cliff overlooking the lake. Grandfather Sun was high in the sky as it was now mid-afternoon. Little Grey Bear Boy began to worry he had gone too far around the lake and perhaps he should have gone around the western shore instead.

It was then he heard the distant screech of a hawk. He looked up into the sky and towards the west. The hawk was flying over the lake. There was something in its talons but it was too far away for him to tell exactly what it was. Little Grey Bear Boy crouched down so as not to startle his animal brother and watched as the hawk glided over the water and came to its nest high up in a tree on the southern shore. He was able to tell by the ears that the hawk had caught a rabbit. Another hawk was there too, and had perched itself on the nest to be with its mate.

The two hawks began to eat the rabbit, tearing pieces of flesh and dropping them into the nest. Little Grey Bear Boy decided to go in for a closer look.

This was another sign from *Kitchi Manitou*, and Little Grey Bear

Boy stayed for a time to watch the hawk family enjoying their meal. He drew out his medicine pouch and took out another wad of tobacco to give thanks for this second sign.

It was now late in the afternoon and Little Grey Bear Boy decided he would try to make up some ground before settling in for the night. He continued south until the light began to fail and managed to find a decent spot for his camp next to a smaller lake. It was quite dark by the time his tent was up. He had pushed himself hard to stay on the path Painted Turtle Man suggested and now he was too tired for a fire. He ate some smoked fish and drank some fresh, cool water from the lake.

He was too exhausted to think about much that evening and decided to save his strength for the third day of his vision quest. He could not help but think about Water Lily Woman as he settled into his tent for the night. He was perplexed about what to do about his feelings for her. How could something so pure create something evil…

That night he had a strange dream. All of the women in his life were walking in a single file. Their gait was slow and steady and too uniform to be natural. He saw his grandmother, his auntie, his mother, Water Lily Woman, the Eagle twins, and all of the matriarchs of *Nisichawayasihk*. At the very end of the row he saw his sister. They were walking with their hands clasped in front of their bodies.

He began to see, in fact, that their hands were tied together and they were being dragged on a rope, one woman linked to another. On approaching them, he saw their eyes had no colour, no pupil—just whites. He tried to speak to them but they ignored him. It was as though their bodies were no more than an empty shell without a spirit inside of them.

He could hear strange voices—men arguing or grumbling about something. He awoke with a start, just past sunrise. He could still hear the voices of the men from his dream. Quietly, he squirmed out of his tent and lowered the poles. He dragged himself on his stomach towards the sound, which came from the lakeshore. What he saw made his heart shudder against the cool ground.

Two warriors wearing plain, unadorned clothing unlike the style of the *Nehiyawak* were walking. Five women walked slowly in a row between them, just like the women in his dream. Their hair was unbraided, loose, and scraggly. Their clothing ragged and dirty. Without quillwork, the leather looked bare and wrong. Their hands were tied in front of their bodies and linked to one another on a rope. The two men held each end of the rope.

"I do not see why they all need to be used for the ceremony…" said the first man. "We spend all this time and effort to capture them. What would be the harm in saving one or two for ourselves?"

"I am not disagreeing with you," grumbled the other man. "But who will be the one to ask Dark Cloud Man?"

"Not me, that is for certain. Maybe it should be you."

"*Motch*! I'm no fool…"

Dark Cloud Man? Little Grey Bear Boy's heart was pounding so hard he was worried they would hear it. He had to get a better look at what was going on. He crawled back to his campsite and picked up his medicine bundle and Flying Rabbit Boy's bow and arrows. He would have to leave his tent, bedroll, and food satchel. He moved carefully, as though on the hunt, to stay out of their line of sight.

They followed a path along the lakeshore. The women's gait was slow, steady, and unnaturally uniform, just like in the dream. Whenever they reached a place where some effort was needed to navigate the terrain, the men would push and pull them in whichever direction they wanted them to go. The women said nothing and went where they were forced.

Little Grey Bear Boy tried to get closer to see the women's faces. He needed to know if they were scared, injured, or sick. He knew in his heart something was not right about the scene before him.

At that moment, the two men began to turn in his direction. Little Grey Bear Boy looked down to see he was standing on a worn path. With nowhere to step off between the cliff and the lakeshore, he was trapped. He forced himself to think and feel just as he had when he disappeared in front of Painted Turtle Man. Taking his cousin's bow, he drew an arrow and aimed it at the lead man. He tried to find his breath.

As he was about to take the shot, he felt a vibration in the air. He looked down at his legs and saw they were no longer there.

"Maybe we could get one of the young ones to ask him," said one of the men.

"Those young ones would not know what to do with a woman, even if he let us!"

The men and their strange women came up the path, arriving at the exact spot where Little Grey Bear Boy had stood only moments ago.

As they came close, he could see their eyelids were painted red. Their expressions were vacant. Soulless.

He followed them most of the day until they arrived at an encampment. Several tents sat around a large, circular lodge. He had never seen this sort of lodge before, though the style resembled the big lodge of the Trader's people.

Little Grey Bear Boy watched as the men led the three women into the large circular building. Warriors were milling about the camp, shouting and cursing, pushing and slapping one another, all of them with their eyelids painted red. Little Grey Bear Boy drew as close to the camp as he dared.

A man emerged from the round lodge. "Gather around!" he ordered. "I have received our instructions from the Red-Eye."

"WE SERVE THE RED-EYE!" chanted the followers.

"Dark Cloud Man commands we attack in three days."

The men cheered and whooped.

"Will we be able to keep any of the women for ourselves?" asked one of the men.

"I did not ask him," snapped the leader.

"It might be a good thing..." offered one of the younger men, grinning.

"I am sure when we are successful, there will be plenty of women for all of us. Dark Cloud Man tells me the Turtle lodge is overflowing with pretty young women."

"YEEAAAYYY!" shouted the men.

Little Grey Bear Boy thought his heart was going to stop. It was his village they were talking about, he was sure of it. His vision quest was over. He had to get back at once and tell someone what he knew.

A crow landed on the top of the circular lodge and began cawing loudly. The leader looked up at it and nodded. "There is someone here!" he yelled. "Fan out and find him!"

It was time to run.

Little Grey Bear Boy moved to the south as fast as his feet could carry him. He would have to turn northeast to get back to *Nisichawayasihk*. He could hear men yelling behind him but also a barking and growling that did not sound like dogs, but something much worse. Something savage.

He continued south and had gone only a short distance when he ran right into a fast-flowing river. With the blood pounding in his head, he had not heard the rush of moving water. He waded in, looking for a shallow place to cross. The water pushed him hard along the current and everywhere he stepped seemed deeper and deeper.

Something came crashing out of the forest behind him. It was an abnormally large coyote, bigger than a bear. Its eyes were large and wild. Its tongue lolled, and foam dripped from its mouth. Soon three others joined it. They sniffed the ground this way and that, converging on the place where Little Grey Bear Boy had first entered the river. He had to get across. He dove hard into the water and swam as fast as he could. The river's current pushed him along. He went above and below the surface and down river, but was still far from the other side.

The four coyotes, alerted by the splashing, barked and howled along the river bank. They whimpered and yelped whenever they were bumped into the water. Soon, several of the Red-Eyed warriors joined them, firing arrows at Little Grey Bear Boy in the river.

"Find a place to cross!" screamed the leader. The men began to wade into the river in both directions, looking for a place to cross, just as he had. Little Grey Bear Boy swam harder and harder and eventually rode the current to the other side, downstream. He pulled himself out and staggered northeast, toward *Nisichawayasihk*, exhausted, soaking wet, and with a horrible cramp in his side.

Little Grey Bear Boy lumbered along as best he could. Hearing the howling of coyotes to the south, he realized they had found a way across the river. He picked up the pace, ignoring the pain in his side, but he was moving too slow. The barking and growling was getting closer. Soon, they were on his heels.

The bow was heavy. He drew an arrow with great effort. Is this where he would make his stand? Would the people learn of the attack only as they were being attacked? The coyotes reached him, but stopped short, looking at one another and then back at him. They bared their teeth and drooled. The fur on the back of their necks stood up straight. The largest of the four coyotes stepped towards Little Grey Bear Boy and spoke.

"You are a long way from home, Grey-Eye," it growled.

"Stay back!" shouted Little Grey Bear Boy, pointing his arrow at them.

"You do not command me, pretender. I serve Dark Cloud Man."

"WE SERVE THE RED-EYE!" shouted the others. The leader barked and leapt towards Little Grey Bear Boy. The boy loosed an arrow and it sank deep into the coyote's shoulder. The coyote yelped and fell over. When it got to its feet and pulled the arrow out with its teeth, Little Grey Bear Boy turned and ran. The other coyotes rushed to their leader, sniffing and licking at him.

As he ran, the boy drew his turtle shell rattle and tried to think of a song that would help him. The fire chant and the water chant were of no use—there was neither fire nor water nearby now. He looked at the dirt and rock beneath his feet as he was running and decided to sing a song dedicated to Mother Earth. Perhaps she could help him.

As the coyotes snapped at his back with their fangs, the earth beneath them rose up. Pillars of dirt and large rocks burst forth from the ground and blocked their path. One of the coyotes ran right into a large boulder and yelped. Another coyote was pitched high into the air and knocked over a tree as he came crashing down. Still, they continued their pursuit, dodging the pillars of earth and trying to gain on the boy.

Little Grey Bear Boy was running out of options. Exhausted, he knew eventually his body would betray him and he would be devoured by the beasts. He hurled himself forward with one last burst of energy, feeling his legs give out from under him.

"*Kitchi Manitou*, protect me!" he cried as he came crashing down. His body slid forward on the dirt, coming to rest in front of a slender pair of silver-skinned feet. The feet belonged to a beautiful woman wearing a long white dress. Her hair was as black as the night sky, her skin luminescent, like the moon. Her eyes were a bright grey—unlike anything he had ever seen before.

The air around him shook with a force he had never known. The coyotes in pursuit stopped abruptly. Her gaze was upon them. Little Grey Bear Boy could see her eyes beginning to glow with a light from within, like the Grandmother Moon. He covered his eyes and felt an intense heat as the four coyotes burst into flames and were destroyed.

Little Grey Bear Boy did not get up, but remained face down on the ground. He knew from his dreams that she was the White Buffalo Calf Woman of legend.

"Arise, son of the Bear clan," said the White Buffalo Calf Woman. Her voice resonated as though many women were speaking at the same time. "You have been chosen for a great purpose."

"*Nookum*," said Little Grey Bear Boy, getting to his feet but keeping his eyes down. "Whatever you would ask of me, I will do to the best of my ability."

"The *Nehiyawak* are turning away from my teachings. You will restore the balance."

"*Nookum*, I am not worthy of such a task."

"It is because you realize it that you have been chosen. I will make you worthy. You will learn the Seven Teachings of the Peace Pipe, and you will carry a peace pipe for the *Nehiyawak*."

"*Tapwe, Nookum…*"

"The *Nehiyawak* have lost the Teaching of the Buffalo. They do not respect one another because they no longer respect themselves."

"I do not understand, *Nookum*…" confessed Little Grey Bear Boy.

"Their hearts are full of jealousy. They wish to possess that which is needed by their brothers and sisters. They choose only their relations for tasks that would be better carried out by others."

"Is that so wrong?"

There was a white flash of light and Little Grey Bear Boy found himself standing beside White Buffalo Calf Woman in the Great Plains far to the south. A thundering herd of buffalo came directly towards them, shaking Mother Earth. Little Grey Bear Boy was afraid he would be trampled but she was unconcerned. The herd parted around them as Little Grey Bear Boy tried hard to keep his balance. Buffalo grazed as far as he could see in all directions. More buffalo than stars in the night sky. He could feel the love of Grandmother Buffalo filling his heart with her unending generosity to her human children.

"The Grandmother Buffalo teaches us that you cannot give what you do not have. One must first respect one's self before one can respect another. To covet the blessings of another is to disdain the blessings given to you by *Kitchi Manitou*. To deny the gifts and abilities of another for your own gain or for the benefit of your clan alone is an offence against the Grandmother Buffalo. What if she was to keep her gifts to herself or thought only of her own children? The *Nehiyawak* would starve without the sacrifice she makes of her own blood. The grandmothers of the Spirit World have never asked anything such as this of the human family."

"*Tapwe, Nookum*. I am beginning to learn. How can I make the *Nehiyawak* understand? I am just a boy and they will not listen to me…"

"You cannot bring the teachings back to the *Nehiyawak* simply by talking. You must lead the *Nehiyawak* by your own example. You must do as you say…"

"How will this show the *Nehiyawak* the way?"

"If you live the Teaching of the Buffalo, she will give you her blessings. The *Nehiyawak* will recognize that you are blessed and will seek to learn your ways. You will share this knowledge freely so they may also benefit. You must not lead them to believe you are favoured by *Kitchi Manitou* by virtue of your birth, but by the virtue of your efforts and choices. You will not take credit for these blessings. You will give the glory to the one who has blessed you, *Kitchi Manitou*."

"*Nookum?*" asked Little Grey Bear Boy. "I would be honoured to carry a pipe for the *Nehiyawak*. When will I take it up?"

"The peace pipe is already coming to you, son of the Bear clan. However, you must know this: when it comes to you, you will no longer wish to possess it."

"How can that be, *Nookum?*"

"That is the way of the pipe carrier!" Another flash of white light and they were again standing in the pine forest.

"Go now, son of the Bear clan. The people of *Nisichawayasihk* are in great danger."

"Thank you for your teachings, *Nookum*!" said Little Grey Bear Boy. "We are forever grateful for the blessing you have bestowed upon the *Nehiyawak*."

As White Buffalo Calf Woman walked away, Little Grey Bear Boy kept his head bowed and his eyes down. Finally, he could hold it in no longer. He looked up at her in time to see her transform into a white buffalo calf. The calf trotted away through the trees and rock, disappearing into the very air of the forest.

Little Grey Bear Boy remained still for a time, deep in prayer. When he had given abundant thanks, he offered the remainder of his tobacco.

# NIYĀNANOMITANAW NIKOTWĀSOSĀP

Little Grey Bear Boy was in a daze, not sure how to begin his mission. His stomach turned as he remembered that the people of *Nisichawayasihk* were in danger. There was no time to return to his camp. He must get to the village to rally the warriors to fight off the Red-Eye attack. Though still weary from the chase, he forced himself to continue to the northeast. He found blueberries in the moss as he travelled, picking them on the move and gulping them down as he continued on. In time, his strength returned. Now he knew why blueberries were the Grandmother Bear's favourite food. He started to be able to move faster and faster.

Grandfather Sun descended below Mother Earth and the stars of the night sky began to return. Little Grey Bear Boy saw the Mother Bear and her cub in the sky and used them to keep his bearings. He could not see his way in the dark and the branches of the forest clawed at his clothing and his skin. But nothing could stop him from his mission to get to *Nisichawayasihk*.

He did not understand why the Red-Eyes wished to attack his village, or what possible purpose they had for the women they captured, if not as wives and mothers. He decided he must do his duty to his clan and to the *Nehiyawak* and put his faith in *Kitchi Manitou*. His understanding of the reasons why mattered little.

He ran, jogged, and walked, pushing himself all through the night and into the morning. His throat hurt and his lips were cracked as the Grandfather Sun returned and shone down on him. It was about midday when Little Grey Bear Boy began to recognize rocks and trees and knew he was near *Nisichawayasihk*.

As he neared the village he slowed down. He could hear footsteps. His heart leapt at the thought that his journey and his task were near completion. All he had to do was alert the warrior societies and the men could mount a defence. The camp of Red-Eye warriors would easily be outnumbered by the warriors of *Nisichawayasihk,* but they may have been counting on their evil magic to even the odds.

"*TANSI! TANSI!*" shouted Little Grey Bear Boy through a parched throat.

The footsteps stopped and he continued in the direction he last heard them. Little Grey Bear Boy was desperate to tell someone, any-one, what was happening. The shape of a standing figure began to emerge through the trees and branches. It was Red Sky Man.

"You are back," said Red Sky Man. "Did you get lost? I thought you had gone east. You look terrible…"

"Uncle! I found a camp of the Red-Eye's men. They mean to attack the village."

Red Sky Man's eyes widened and his mouth dropped open. "Who have you told of this?" he asked.

"You are the first."

"That is fortunate," said Red Sky Man. "There is still time to save the village. You have done well." Red Sky Man patted Little Grey Bear Boy on the shoulder. Scanning the boy's eyes, he seemed to be look-ing there for something other than terror and fatigue. "Listen to me, Little Grey Bear Boy," he whispered. "Hurry to the Eagle medicine lodge and wait for me. Speak to no one. The Red-Eye may have spies in the village. If they learn that we know, they may attack sooner. We will need time to prepare the men and safeguard the women and children. I will quietly gather the warriors to prepare for battle. You have done well. You will earn your name for this!"

A sense of relief overtook Little Grey Bear Boy as he made his way to the village. Red Sky Man may not have been his first choice of whom to tell about the danger, but he was still one of the *Nehiyawak*.

Besides, it would take a person like a medicine carrier to rally the warriors. No one would believe a boy who still bore his childhood name.

Little Grey Bear Boy snuck through the village, carefully avoiding a young Wolf clan warrior on patrol. People walked around the village doing chores, blissfully unaware of the danger. He concentrated on not being seen and felt the vibration of the Grey-Eye magic making him invisible. He crept quietly into the Eagle medicine lodge without anyone noticing him.

None of Red Sky Man's helpers were in the lodge, which was fortunate. Little Grey Bear Boy was exhausted and thirsty. He found a water skin as well as pemmican in a leather pouch. After eating, drinking, and catching his breath, he contemplated all that had happened in the last few days.

His mind was occupied with the thought of being given a man's name and receiving a peace pipe. He puzzled over White Buffalo Calf Woman's meaning when she said he would not want the peace pipe when it came to him. How could someone not want such a great honour? It made little sense to him, but he chose to believe everything would become clear in time.

He listened closely to the sounds of the village outside the lodge. It all seemed very normal—people talked, laughed, and worked. He wondered if Red Sky Man was rallying the warriors and warning the people of *Nisichawayasihk*. He expected at any moment to hear people running, men shouting, and women calling for their children, but the everyday sounds continued uninterrupted.

A familiar voice echoed on the wind. "Can you hear me, Little Grey Bear Boy?"

"Who is it?" he whispered.

It came again, though it seemed to come from inside him this time. "Can you hear me, Little Grey Bear Boy?" Water Lily Woman? But, how?

"*Tapwe!*" the voice answered, reading his thoughts. "I am speaking to you now."

"Can you hear me?" he said inside his own mind.

"I can," she answered. "I need you to come to me. Something is very wrong."

"*Tapwe*! I have warned Red Sky Man and he is rallying the warriors. Everything is under control..."

"*Motch*, it is not. You must come to me. Things are not as they seem. I am at the place where you met my father..."

"But I was told to stay in the Eagle medicine lodge."

"You have been deceived. All hope of saving the people of *Nisichawayasihk* will soon be lost. You must come to me now."

In a flash, the sense of relief had been replaced with heaviness in his chest and panic. He had been instructed to do something by the one person in the village he did not trust. And now he was being asked to do something by the one person in the village he trusted completely. He chanced a look through the door flaps and could see some of Red Sky Man's helpers gathered in front. That he had indeed been deceived seemed more possible.

Little Grey Bear Boy drew out his knife and looked around. He remembered the night Flying Rabbit Boy had been attacked by the Red-Eye's helper and this gave him an idea. He went to the rear of the lodge. As quietly as possible he began to cut the hide to make an opening.

He paused for a moment, closed his eyes, and decided he did not want to be seen. When he felt the vibration, he opened his eyes: his legs were gone. He crept quietly into the forest and made his way to the rock where he had seen the aurora with Water Lily Woman. It seemed a little too easy to escape the village and he wondered where all the Wolf clan warriors were, not to mention the Eagle clan warriors who usually assisted them in guarding the village.

"Little Grey Bear Boy!" Water Lily Woman shouted as she became visible again. "I am so glad you came." Water Lily Woman ran into Little Grey Bear Boy's arms and embraced him. "I have been so afraid," she said.

"What has happened?"

"I saw him. I saw Red Sky Man. He was talking to two men who were not from the village. Their eyelids were painted red like the ones my sisters talk about. He told them he would give them a signal and that's when they should attack!"

"What?" Little Grey Bear Boy didn't want to believe what he was hearing. "But that would mean Red Sky Man is helping them."

"*Tapwe*!" Water Lily Woman continued. "Then he told one of them to head east to 'kill the boy.' I think he meant you!"

"It can't be."

"The one he sent east turned into a great coyote and I thought you would be dead by now. I have been hiding out here for two days. I am so worried about my mother!" She burst into tears. "Red Sky Man must be one of the Red-Eye's followers. He has fooled us all!" Water Lily Woman pulled Little Grey Bear Boy close.

Warmth rushed through him as he held her. For a moment, he wished they could stay like this forever and ignore all the troubles of the rest of the world. But then he remembered his sister, his cousin, his mother and father, his aunt and uncle, his grandmother, and of course his adopted grandfather. Everyone in the village was in danger and he and Water Lily Woman were the only ones who could help them.

It took all of his willpower to pull himself away from Water Lily Woman. She squeezed harder, then let him go.

"It will be okay," he said. "I will tell my father and he will rally the warriors. We will protect your mother and all the people of *Nisichawayasihk*."

"You do not understand," she said, trying to get the words out without crying. "The day you left, Red Sky Man told the village he had a vision. He sent all of the men south for the great buffalo hunt. There are only a few men left to guard the village."

Little Grey Bear Boy's eyes had always been soft and kind like his mother's. For the first time in his life his brows furrowed and the warmth in his eyes turned cold. Red Sky Man's treachery ran deeper than anything he had been exposed to or could imagine. Little Grey Bear Boy now bore the look of his father.

"Our people have been greatly deceived," he said.

"What will we do?"

"The only thing we can do," he said. "We must fight."

Grandfather Sun began to drop towards Mother Earth as evening settled and the two Grey-Eyes approached the village.

Little Grey Bear Boy entered the Bear lodge pulling Water Lily Woman by the hand behind him. Singing Doe and White Willow Woman looked up, smiling at first. Walking Moon Woman dropped a basket of freshly cooked wild rice when she turned and saw the two Grey-Eyes, hand-in-hand.

The Bear clan matriarch started. "What—"

"*Nookum*, you must listen to me. The Red-Eyes are about to attack the village. They are being helped by Red Sky Man, who I fear is one of them."

White Willow Woman gasped. "How can this be?"

"I don't know," answered Little Grey Bear Boy. "I came upon an encampment of the Red-Eye's warriors on my vision quest. They are only two days' journey to the southwest."

"And two days ago, I saw Red Sky Man speaking to two men who had painted their eyelids red," added Water Lily Woman.

Walking Moon Woman stared at the two Grey-Eyed children for a moment, trying to realize the danger her people faced. "We must act," she said. "Willow, go and find the children. Doe, go and tell Drifting Butterfly Woman to inform the *Nehiyawak*. I will go to the Turtle lodge and speak with Green Wing Woman. Carefully, now. We do not want Red Sky Man to know we are aware of his deception. We will rally the Circle of Clan Mothers and confront him. He is only one man right now. There are still enough warriors left in the village to deal with him."

"What should we do?" asked Little Grey Bear Boy.

"Stay here for the time being," commanded Walking Moon Woman. "Do not let yourselves be seen."

"*Tapwe, Nookum!*" said Little Grey Bear Boy obediently.

Through the door flaps, Little Grey Bear Boy and Water Lily Woman watched the three women make their way to the other lodges. They saw Red Sky Man returning to the Eagle medicine lodge with his helpers.

"He will know I escaped, then," said Little Grey Bear Boy.

"Then he will also know we are aware of the danger," said Water Lily Woman.

"*Tapwe.*"

"I wasn't done playing," Yellow Hawk Girl whined as her mother dragged her into the lodge.

"You are back," said Flying Rabbit Boy upon seeing his cousin. "Where is my bow?"

"Right here," said Little Grey Bear Boy, handing over the bow as promised.

"I am afraid you will need it this night, Flying Rabbit Boy," said Water Lily Woman.

"What is happening?" he asked, surprised to see her.

The two Grey-Eyes looked at each other. Little Grey Bear Boy nodded for her to tell the story, thinking it would be more believable coming from her.

Flying Rabbit Boy's face turned red as he realized what she was telling him. He touched the scars on his shoulder. "They will find I am a boy no longer..." he growled.

"My cousin," said Little Grey Bear Boy, "this will be the night we earn our names. Together." The two boys clasped arms and locked onto each other's eyes.

Outside, people were yelling and arguing.

"It is time!" announced Singing Doe, poking her head into the lodge.

The young people looked at each other, drawing courage from their mutual determination. Flying Rabbit Boy grasped his bow and shouldered his quiver. He went to his bed roll and drew the magic arrow from its hiding place. Little Grey Bear Boy took out his turtleshell rattle. They walked out of the Bear Lodge to find all of the remaining people of *Nisichawayasihk* gathered in the middle of the village.

"What is the meaning of this?" shouted Red Sky Man. The Eagle twins stood on either side of him.

"My sisters!" boomed Walking Moon Woman to the Eagle twins. "Our people have been deceived by Red Sky Man. He is conspiring with the Red-Eyes to attack our village and may in fact be a follower. I accuse him and demand justice!"

The *Nehiyawak* gasped and the few remaining warriors eyed Red Sky Man suspiciously.

"My sister!" countered the elder Eagle Twin. Her voice was shrill. "On what grounds do you make such an accusation?"

"Little Grey Bear Boy found their camp two days from here," explained Walking Moon Woman confidently. "And Water Lily Woman saw Red Sky Man talking to two of the Red-Eye's warriors not far from where we stand now."

"*Tapwe*? Is this true?" It was Drifting Butterfly Woman, matriarch of the Crane clan.

"*Tapwe!*" shouted the two Grey-Eyes confidently.

"How can you say such a thing?" shouted Red Sky Man. "I have only ever served the people of *Nisichawayasihk*! I do not deserve to be shamed in such a way by two children."

Many of the people of *Nisichawayasihk* looked back at the Bear clan. The *Nehiyawak* would rather have believed the two young people were making mischief than to believe they were in great peril.

"My sisters," said the elder Eagle twin. "Many of us have heard of the bad heart Little Grey Bear Boy holds towards the Eagle medicine carrier. Red Sky Man is a strict teacher, but that is no reason for a boy to make such an allegation without proof!"

An eagle in the sky above screeched suddenly. The *Nehiyawak* watched as it circled low toward them. Those with eagle bone whistles around their necks sounded them in honour of the omen.

The eagle circled lower and lower, its great wings blocking out the remaining light of the setting sun for a time. To their amazement, the eagle landed in the middle of their circle, its gold feathers glinting in the setting sun.

"Perhaps I can help," the golden eagle said in a familiar voice. The people jumped back, some stumbling, as the eagle turned into Painted Turtle Man.

"What is this evil magic?" demanded Red Sky Man.

"Interesting question," answered Painted Turtle Man. "Especially coming from you, Dark Cloud Man."

The people of *Nisichawayasihk* fell silent as the pieces of truth gathered into one.

"What did you call me? Where do you—"

"I have come from *Bonibonibee*, the place where the water rises and dips. My grandson was kind enough to turn me into an eagle so I could make the long journey. That is the place where you said you came from, is it not?"

"Well, I am not…" mumbled Red Sky Man, looking around.

"I was amazed by what I saw there," continued Painted Turtle Man. "Not just the fact that the water of the lake goes up and down throughout the day, but by the scars covering Mother Earth. I have not seen scars like that since Dark Cloud Man called down fire from the sky when he and his Red-Eye warriors attacked our village so many years ago. I was only a young boy, but every man remembers the day he earned his name."

"You senile old fool." Red Sky Man laughed. "How can you expect the *Nehiyawak* to believe such a story? I am half your age! You are a bigger liar than your grandson." Red Sky Man continued to laugh, joined by some of his helpers. The rest of the *Nehiyawak* hung their heads, clearly ashamed of being fooled by the Bear clan's wild story.

"I thought the same thing." Painted Turtle Man was laughing now too. "But then I met an old woman there. She was 'touched by the Spirits' and was tending to her chores amongst the remains of her fallen villagers. She seemed to have been piling food next to them for years, as though she expected them to roll over and eat. I spoke with her and she told me an interesting tale. She said a medicine carrier had come to the village to teach their young Grey-Eye. His teachings were cruel but effective. After a time, the young boy's eyes changed to dark brown and soon he knew only evil in his heart. The new medicine carrier had somehow taken control of the entire village, stripping the Circle of Clan Mothers of their power. When the matriarchs finally gathered some warriors to oppose this so-called medicine carrier, he called down a rain of fire and destroyed the village."

"This still does not explain how Red Sky Man could be Dark Cloud Man," said Talking Stone Woman.

"*Tapwe*," said Painted Turtle Man. "But then she told me everyone in the village had started to grow older at an unnatural pace. I had noticed that my grandson began to gain in years when he started learning from Red Sky Man. At first I thought he was just beginning his manhood growth earlier than other boys. Then I recently noticed my former helper, Soaring Spear Man, too had gained years on his face after having served Red Sky Man for a time."

All of the people of *Nisichawayasihk* looked at the eldest helper, who did seem old beyond his years.

"It seems when Dark Cloud Man is close to someone, he draws out their life energy. I remember when we captured the Red-Eye warrior—Flying Rabbit's Boy's attacker—he had a young face with old eyes." Painted turtle Man ran his fingers across the crow's feet at the edges of his own face.

Brown Shield Man shouted: "*Tapwe*! I took that man's life. I will remember his face until the day I die. It seemed he had the face of a boy with the eyes of an old man."

Others nodded in agreement. Even the Eagle twins were now looking at each other's faces, realizing the years that had been added in the short time Red Sky Man had been with them. The *Nehiyawak*, including the Eagle twins, began to shuffle away from Red Sky Man.

Red Sky Man smiled and shook his head as he walked towards the middle of the village where the small centre fire was burning. "It would seem you are still just a nosey child, Brown Bear Boy!" said Red Sky Man.

"There are only a few of us left in this village who would remember Painted Turtle Man's childhood name," shouted Walking Moon Woman.

"So you remember his name, but you forget your own cousin?" Red Sky Man shouted back. "I once loved you and you rejected me for that fool, Rising Hawk Man. Can you remember the day I killed him?" The sky grew dark suddenly as heavy clouds rolled in at an unnatural speed. Red Sky Man was laughing a low growling laugh as he walked about the centre of the village. The people were scattering away from him as he came near. The few remaining warriors, including Brown Shield Man, had brandished their weapons.

"Fools! You are too late!" His eyes glowed red. At a wave of his hand, the centre fire exploded into the sky, creating a pillar of fire. "I have returned to claim that which is rightfully mine!"

Mothers scurried off with their children, screaming. "I will have dominion over *Nisichawayasihk* and control the destinies of all who live there. I am Dark Cloud Man, of the Eagle clan, son of Soaring Star Woman. I am the leader of this village by right of birth. No one will deny me that which is rightfully mine."

A hard rain began to fall and the sky crackled with thunder and lightning. An eerie howl of coyotes came from the southwest.

"They are coming!" shouted Little Grey Bear Boy.

Brown Shield Man took his spear and hurled it at Dark Cloud Man. With the Red-Eye magic, Dark Cloud Man had created a shield of fire around himself that deflected the spear.

"We must do something!" screamed Water Lily Woman as the people of *Nisichawayasihk* ran about, tripping over one another.

"The children—get them away," yelled Little Grey Bear Boy. He began to run towards Dark Cloud Man, shaking his turtleshell rattle. Other warriors began shooting arrows and hurling spears and war axes, but none could penetrate the fire shield. Dark Cloud Man's laugh echoed through the darkened sky.

Little Grey Bear Boy began to speak the ancient water chant. The raindrops began to swirl around his body. As he got closer and closer to Dark Cloud Man, he raised his arms and clapped in the direction of the fire shield. A great stream of water shot at Dark Cloud Man, who gasped and tried to strengthen the Red-Eye magic. He groaned loudly as the water began to weaken it. Finally, it overtook the shield, knocking him backwards.

"Ugh," grunted Dark Cloud Man, rising to his feet. "So you were listening to my teachings after all."

Brown Shield Man and Many Fish appeared at Little Grey Bear Boy's side, weapons raised.

"You have betrayed the people of *Nisichawayasihk*," said Little Grey Bear Boy. "You will face the justice of the Circle of Clan Mothers for your misdeeds. I hope they are merciful…"

"*AWAS!*" Dark Cloud Man drew his buffalo horn rattle. "I don't take orders from women. They are only slaves to me and my warriors." His eyes glowed red. Three giant coyotes leaped out of the forest behind him, snarling and yapping. The yelling of the Red-Eye warriors could be heard behind the coyotes, approaching fast. Little Grey Bear Boy looked at his uncles, who were trying not to show their fear of the magic. He closed his eyes and shook his rattle, singing the Wolf song under his breath.

A strong vibration of the Grey-Eye magic took hold around him and he heard a deep snarling and growling on either side of him. As he opened his eyes, he saw he was now flanked not by men, but by two great wolves. Brown Shield Man howled. Many Fish joined in and the two beasts leapt at the coyotes. As they grappled, more coyotes came out of the forest while Red-Eye warrior-men ran out firing arrows and hurling spears.

Little Grey Bear Boy saw Dark Cloud Man heading back to the village, Red-Eye warriors protecting him on either side.

"Get the women," he ordered, pointing his buffalo horn rattle at the Turtle lodge.

Little Grey Bear Boy ran after him, speaking the water chant again as the raindrops gathered in a great spiraling torrent. Dark Cloud Man noticed him just as he pushed the water with all of his force. Dark Cloud Man waved his hand, deflecting the water by speaking the same chant. The stream turned on Little Grey Bear Boy and the waters hit him hard, sending him flying into the Wolf lodge and knocking the lodge over.

Little Grey Bear Boy was dazed. All he could hear was the ringing laughter of Dark Cloud Man over the screams of women and children. He looked up to see Red-Eye warriors dragging women by the hair and clubbing old men who were trying to defend their grand-daughters.

"Are you all right?" Flying Rabbit Boy was by his side.

Before he could answer, a girl of no more than thirteen summers screamed as a Red-Eye warrior dragged her out of the Turtle lodge. Flying Rabbit Boy notched an arrow and aimed it at the Red-Eye warrior. His arm began to shake and he loosed the arrow too soon, missing the Red-Eye warrior's face, but narrowly.

The man looked over at the two. His eyes were wide and unfocused as he raised his club and ran at them. Flying Rabbit Boy fumbled for another arrow while the Red-Eye warrior gained on them. Little Grey Bear Boy shook his rattle and sang the Mother Earth song, and a great pillar of earth shot up from under the Red-Eye's feet, hurling him high up into the air.

"Tell everyone to make for the sundance grounds."

"*Hiy, hiy!*" answered Flying Rabbit Boy, running off.

Little Grey Bear Boy got to his feet and saw the great coyotes running about the village, mauling whoever was near, mostly men and boys. He could make out embers in what used to be the firepit of the Wolf lodge. He shook his turtleshell rattle and sang the fire chant, sending flames at the Red-Eye warriors and coyotes. The attackers were rolling around in flames, but neither earth nor water would extinguish them. The smell of burning fur and flesh was filling the air.

Beside him, not far off, Painted Turtle Man fought with two Red-Eye warriors. They attacked with knife and spear while he defended with an Eagle staff. Out of instinct, Little Grey Bear Boy ran towards the old man, but by the time he was close enough to help, the old medicine carrier had bested his two younger foes with superior skill and technique.

"*Moosum.* Are you all right?"

"Do not worry about me. I am not afraid to die today. You must help the defenceless ones with all you have."

"*Tapwe, Moosum!*"

"Find Water Lily Woman. The Grey-Eye magic might be stronger if you stay together!" Without another word, Painted Turtle Man ran over to the Marten lodge to assist the old matriarch, who had been knocked over by a Red-Eyed coyote and was bleeding from her cheek.

Little Grey Bear Boy ran back to the Bear lodge. All the hides had been torn off the poles. Water Lily Woman was using them as a floating shield to keep the Red-Eye warriors back. Five of them were pushing hard against her magic and cutting up the hides with their knives.

Little Grey Bear Boy shook his turtleshell rattle and sang the Mother Earth song as he ran towards the Red-Eyes. The earth moved around him, rumbling up into two great balls of dirt and rock that gouged the ground. With a wave of his arms, he sent the great mounds of earth rolling towards the men. The wet dirt and mud rolled over the warriors, hurling them into the forest, knocking over all the trees in their path.

"Get to the sundance grounds," Little Grey Bear Boy shouted. "Come with me, Water Lily!" She took his hand and they ran back towards the centre of the village.

"Stand and fight!" screamed Dark Cloud Man as Red-Eye warriors began running away. Still many rallied around him. Little Grey Bear Boy saw his cousin fighting with a Red-Eye warrior. He ran over to help and saw it was Yellow Hawk Girl they were fighting over.

"Get away from my sister," yelled Little Grey Bear Boy as he slammed his body against the Red-Eye warrior, knocking him back. The man got back up to his feet and picked up a spear sticking out of the ground nearby. He smiled and thrust the spear at the young people defending the little girl. He was joined by two of his fellow warriors, both brandishing spears of their own.

"You will not harm my children," came a deep voice that startled even Little Grey Bear Boy. He looked behind him to see the tall muscular figure of Blue Elk Man.

"Father!"

"Get behind me!"

"I can help you, father!"

"Do so with your magic!" replied Blue Elk Man as he unraveled his rope and brandished his stake.

The three Red-Eyes had formed a line, each trying not to be the one in front. Blue Elk Man walked towards them and drove his wooden stake deep into the earth.

"I am Blue Elk Man of the Marten clan," he announced to his enemies. "I am a warrior of the Dog Soldier Society. I will stand my ground even if it should cost me my life."

The Red-Eye warriors all looked at each other. They knew this meant he was not allowed to kill. They came forward with their weapons, confident now. Little Grey Bear Boy began to shake his rattle but could not find a song to sing. He was too worried about his father to put the right words together. He began to panic as the three warriors set upon his father.

Blue Elk Man was a skilled and determined warrior with no fear in his heart. He easily bested the first man, breaking his jaw with a swipe of his spear. The second man dove at Blue Elk Man with a knife, stabbing wildly. Blue Elk Man side-stepped the sloppy attack and tripped the Red-Eye with his rope, flipping him over. He then plunged his spear right through the Red-Eye warrior's thigh.

The third Red-Eye warrior was not as brave or foolish and he stayed out of reach. He called for re-enforcements and soon other Red-Eye warriors and two great coyotes joined him. The Red-Eye army was forming up to attack Blue Elk Man. The attackers wore the clothing of different nations. It seemed the only thing they had in common was the red paint streaming down their faces in the hard rain.

For some reason their appearance made Little Grey Bear Boy think of the Windigo-con song from the sundance. He shook his turtle shell rattle and began to sing. Water Lily Woman joined in, creating a strong vibration as the double power of the Grey-Eye magic took hold.

As they chanted, Blue Elk Man transformed into a great Windigo. He looked like a grizzly bear or sasquatch, but with great elk antlers sticking out of his head. He had four great and powerful arms and his roar shook Mother Earth. The coyotes snarled and leaped at him. The Red-Eye men fired arrows and threw spears. Blue Elk Man the Windigo swatted the coyotes out of the air with his great long arms and deflected arrows and spears with his mighty antlers.

Two great wolves, one of which was missing a leg, attacked the Red-Eye army from the rear. The Windigo beast threw the coyotes and men off, and the wolves attacked. Those who were able began to flee.

A weak scream arose from the edge of the village. Little Grey Bear Boy grabbed Water Lily Woman by the hand and pulled her away from the battle.

"What about your father and uncles?"

"They are fine by themselves," he answered. "We must find Dark Cloud Man and end this."

They found old Walking Moon Woman yelling at Dark Cloud Man outside the Bear lodge. "*Awas*! Leave them alone. They are your relations." She pulled on his shoulder as he threw a girl to his warriors.

"Now they are my slaves," he replied, shrugging off her hold. "You will forever regret not choosing me when you had the chance." He pushed her hard with both hands, sending her sprawling to the wet ground.

"I only regret not allowing my husband to kill you when we were young," she said through clenched teeth.

From out of the Bear lodge two Red-Eye warriors were dragging White Willow Woman and Yellow Hawk Girl away. Flying Rabbit Boy and Singing Doe tried, in vain, to stop them. The Red-Eyes pushed them off with little effort.

"You will stop this!" said Little Grey Bear Boy.

"What?" scoffed Dark Cloud Man. "Are you still alive?"

"You cannot kill me so easily."

"Are you so sure of that? My army has taken the village. I am the master now."

"Your so-called army is defeated! My father and uncles are finishing what is left of them now."

Dark Cloud Man looked up at the village and for the first time noticed the warrior bodies strewn about.

"This cannot be. Cowards. You have betrayed your master!" His eyes glowed red and a great rumble came from the sky. "Very well. If I am not to rule here, no one shall."

"Don't do this!" Walking Moon Woman ran towards him just as

he raised his hands, a strange and horrible chant on his tongue. She grabbed him, trying to pull his hands down out of the air.

Dark Cloud Man slapped her hard, knocking her back onto the ground.

"*Nookum!*" Little Grey Bear Boy ran to the old woman's aid.

Walking Moon Woman got up onto her knees as a ball of fire broke through the cloudy sky. A hole had been punched through the clouds, making visible the stars of the night sky. The fireball came down to the earth and Dark Cloud Man pointed one of his arms at Walking Moon Woman. The fireball swerved and struck her directly, exploding the earth beneath her and knocking Little Grey Bear Boy backwards. Of the Bear clan matriarch, nothing was left.

"**N**ookum!" Little Grey Bear Boy screamed.

Dark Cloud Man continued to chant, his eyes glowing red and tears of blood oozing from the sides. The Red-Eyed magic continued bringing fireballs down in a rain of fire upon *Nisichawayasihk*. The remaining villagers ran about in a panic, screaming and crashing into each other. There was nowhere to run and nowhere to hide from this curse. Fire ignited the trees in the forest and the remaining lodges.

Little Grey Bear Boy summoned the waters about him again, though it had stopped raining and there was less to be had. He raised his hands in the air and clapped them at the Red-Eye. The stream of water, small but powerful, fired at Dark Cloud Man, but was repelled by the shimmering dome of energy that surrounded him.

Water Lily Woman spoke a chant and raised the rock and boulders from the broken ground and hurled them at him. The rocks bounced off the dome. Flying Rabbit Boy fired an arrow at the Red-Eye, which shattered upon the dome as well.

"It is no use," said Little Grey Bear Boy. "We need to break his concentration."

A fireball came hurtling towards them and they dove in different directions, the earth exploding where they had stood.

The fireball had struck nearest Little Grey Bear Boy. Dazed, he looked up to see the Eagle lodge tear in half as a fireball hit. The younger Eagle twin sat in a shower of smoke and debris. "Where is my sister?!" she screamed, panicked. "She was hiding right next to me. Where is my sister?"

Little Grey Bear Boy tried to regain his senses and speak clearly. "Auntie! The lodge is falling…"

The Eagle lodge, or what was left of it, began to tip over towards the woman. Little Grey Bear Boy got to his shaky feet and limped towards her, but he came crashing down. His leg was bleeding and there a shard of stone protruded from a deep wound. He watched helplessly as the lodge continued to tip, the broken ends of the support poles sharp as spears.

She saw the danger too late. As a scream rose in her throat, a grey-haired figure knocked her over, throwing his body on top of hers, the broken poles stabbing deep into his back.

"*MOTCH!*" screamed Little Grey Bear Boy, as he dragged himself towards the impaled body of his adopted grandfather.

The younger Eagle twin dragged herself out from underneath Painted Turtle Man, gasping. The old man coughed blood as one of his punctured lungs tried to breathe.

"*Moosum!*" she cried. "Why? After everything…"

"My girl," choked Painted Turtle Man. "I never cared about anything you said or did to me. You are a woman of the people of *Nisichawayasihk*. I have always loved you as though you were my own daughter. You need to live and help the *Nehiyawak* rebuild their lives after all of this has passed."

Little Grey Bear Boy dragged himself next to the old man, trying to keep the shard in his leg pointed upwards, while the younger Eagle twin wept.

"*Moosum.*"

"My boy. It is time for me to go. My beloved wants me by her side once more. You must take up my bundle and carry my peace pipe for the *Nehiyawak*. Will you do this?"

"I don't want your peace pipe!" sobbed Little Grey Bear Boy. "I want you to stay with me."

"I know, my boy," answered the dying man. "I want that too, but it is not meant to be. I will watch over you from the Spirit World. I will tell *Kitchi Manitou* about the man you have become…" Painted Turtle Man, medicine carrier of the Bear clan for the people of *Nisichawayasihk*, drew his last breath upon Mother Earth and his spirit left to join the Great Mystery beyond.

The rain of fire continued all around and Little Grey Bear Boy could hear Dark Cloud Man's maniacal laughter. Water Lily Woman came running to his side. "*Moosum!*" she cried when she saw the old man.

"He has left us," said Little Grey Bear Boy.

"What will we do?"

"I don't know," said Little Grey Bear Boy looking up into the sky. Through the holes in the clouds he saw a green flicker of light. "We have only one chance. The Spirits are dancing. We must ask your father to help us."

"I do not feel him this night," cried Water Lily Woman.

"Someone is dancing for me," replied Little Grey Bear Boy. "I can feel it." He looked down at his hand to see he was still clutching his turtle shell rattle. He began to shake it and sing the Dancing Spirits song. Water Lily Woman wept as she sang. The lone Eagle twin looked up at the sky and watched the clouds part to reveal the aurora in all its quiet magic. She knew the song they were singing and added her voice to it. From their hiding spots behind rocks and trees, the surviving people of *Nisichawayasihk* added their voices and sang in harmony.

The flickering lights in the sky began to take shape. Soaring Star Woman appeared, beside her a man none of the others recognized. Little Grey Bear Boy knew this was his great ancestor, Grey Bear, the last Grey-Eyed Bear before him.

"My son!" echoed the voice of Soaring Star Woman from the sky. "You have shamed and disgraced the Eagle clan. What have you done to the *Nehiyawak?*"

"Mother!" cried Dark Cloud Man. "It is you who shamed Grandmother Eagle. We are destined to rule the *Nehiyawak*, not to be their slaves. I have taken back what is rightfully ours."

Now Grey Bear spoke. "Nothing is given that is not earned by our own efforts. You deserve nothing by virtue of your birth. You were brought into this world naked and alone. It was the *Nehiyawak* who took care of you and kept you alive when you were helpless. Is this how you now repay their kindness?"

"I will not serve the *Nehiyawak*!" screamed Dark Cloud Man. "It is they who must serve me."

"Then you do not serve Grandmother Eagle," roared Soaring Star Woman's spirit. "We Eagles do not command the *Nehiyawak*. We put ourselves in front of the others to protect them. We bear the blows and the hard words of our enemies to keep the *Nehiyawak* in harmony with those around them. That is the duty of the Eagle clan and it is no greater than the duty of any other. If you cannot live your life in service to the *Nehiyawak*, then you are no son of mine!"

The red faded from Dark Cloud Man's eyes as his mother's words wounded the remaining piece of humanity in his heart. The glowing energy dome around him faded.

The remaining lodges were broken, fallen, or in flames. What was once a circular village was now a flaming ruin. Sections of earth had been torn out and smoking craters where fireballs had struck pock-marked the ground. The dead bodies of friend and foe were strewn about in lifeless heaps. Children cried over dead parents and the survivors dragged the injured towards the cover of the forest.

From the opposite side of the remains of the village, Flying Rabbit Boy saw his opportunity. He drew the magic arrow from his quiver and notched it to his bow.

"My need is great and my heart is true…" he whispered as he aimed at Dark Cloud Man. The arrow flew high and far the length of the village. The arrow began to drop and Flying Rabbit Boy feared it would not make the distance.

"AAAAAAAHHHHH!" screamed Dark Cloud Man as the arrow plunged deep into his thigh.

////

The two Red-Eye warriors who had been standing with Dark Cloud Man looked back and saw Flying Rabbit Boy. They raised their weapons and charged after him, screaming wildly. With the instincts of a great hunter, Flying Rabbit Boy drew one arrow after another, firing them deep and true into the hearts of the attacking warriors. He notched another arrow and was ready to fire at anyone who threatened the people of *Nisichawayasihk*, but the last of the Red-Eye warriors were running or limping away. Dark Cloud Man pulled the arrow out of his thigh and broke it in half. He raised his hands in the air but could not make the Red-Eye magic work.

"You fools. You are too late to stop me. My servants are everywhere. I will have dominion over all the people of Turtle Island and there is nothing you can do!"

He spat on the ground and jumped up, turning into a crow and cawing loudly at the *Nehiyawak* as he flew away.

No one cheered or celebrated the end of the battle. What was there to celebrate? The land was destroyed, the lodges were burning, and the bodies of friend and foe covered the ground in pieces and lifeless heaps.

"We have to leave this place," said Blue Elk Man, now returned to human form, as he pulled an arrow out of his shoulder.

"Where will we go, father?"

"I don't know, Little Grey Bear Boy. Mother Earth is beginning to flood. The rain of fire has upset the three rivers and the ground is drowning."

Little Grey Bear Boy looked down at his feet and for the first time noticed the streams of water snaking across the ground, filling the great holes left by the Red-Eye's curse.

"We sent the *Nehiyawak* up to the sundance grounds," said Water Lily Woman.

"That is higher ground," said Blue Elk Man. "It will have to do for now. Gather the injured and get them there. Find any who are capable and have them return to help the survivors."

"*Hiy, hiy!*" said the two Grey-Eyes obediently. Their eyes met for a moment and Little Grey Bear Boy felt like he wanted to smile at Water Lily Woman, but he could not find the joy in his heart. He nodded instead and limped off to help the injured.

"Use the lodge poles to make a travois!" Little Grey Bear Boy yelled at some boys. "Take everything you can carry to the sundance grounds!"

"*Tapwe*, Uncle!" they yelled.

Little Grey Bear Boy was shocked to be called 'uncle' by boys not much younger than himself. He cleared his heart of pride and whispered his thanks to *Kitchi Manitou* for this blessing.

He went about the shattered village, barely able to remember where he was amidst the ruins. A familiar voice cried out from behind a great furrow of earth and clay.

Little Grey Bear Boy stopped as though held by deep roots at the sight of Brown Shield Man's broken body. There were arrows, spearheads, and jagged coyote-teeth tears all over his bloody body. Flying Rabbit Boy knelt over him.

"My boy. I am so proud of you. You have given me great honour this day. You will make a fine husband for…"

"Please, Father!" Flying Rabbit Boy held Brown Shield Man in his arms. "Stay with me…" But Brown Shield Man of the Wolf clan, husband of Singing Doe, had begun the journey into the Great Mystery.

Little Grey Bear Boy fell to his knees at the sight of his broken clan.

"Somebody help me!"

Little Grey Bear Boy and Flying Rabbit Boy looked over to see Water Lily Woman trying to lift the lodge poles off the Marten lodge.

"The matriarch is still alive!" she called.

Little Grey Bear Boy got up and wiped the tears from his eyes. He dragged himself over, cradling his injured leg, to what was left of the Marten Lodge. Gliding Heron Woman lay on her stomach, her feet sticking out at odd angles, legs pinned by what was left of the Marten lodge. She was moaning in agony.

Flying Rabbit Boy sat on the ground nearby. "They have killed my father!" he choked.

"I am sorry," said Little Grey Bear Boy.

"Be sorry for the Red-Eyes," sputtered Flying Rabbit Boy. "They will know my vengeance in time."

Flying Rabbit Boy got to his feet and came to help the Grey-Eyes lift the lodge poles off the matriarch. They managed to lift it enough for Water Lily Woman to drag the matriarch out.

"My legs!" cried Gliding Heron Woman.

"They are broken, *Nookum*," said Water Lily Woman. "You boys make a travois, I will tend her wounds."

The two boys used the poles and rope to make a travois to transport the old matriarch. When they finished, they looked across the ruins of the village and saw Blue Elk Man tying off Many Fish's right leg, which was just a stump from the knee down.

"Let us get her to the sundance grounds," said Little Grey Bear Boy but Water Lily Woman stopped him.

"You are in no condition to begin a journey. I will tend to your leg first." She gathered some hides from the ruins of the Marten lodge and cut them into strips. She folded a length into a bandage and put the long strip into her mouth.

"This will hurt!" she said as she pulled the shard of rock out of Little Grey Bear Boy's leg.

"Agghhh!" he screamed as Flying Rabbit Boy caught him as he fell over.

"You are going to be okay," said Water Lily Woman with a shaky voice. She wrapped up the wound and tied it off.

"Thank you ..." said Little Grey Bear Boy. He wanted to say so much more to her but could not find the words.

"You boys take her, now. She may be the only elder matriarch left in the village..." Little Grey Bear Boy and Flying Rabbit Boy looked at each other in surprise; they now realized the importance of their task. Without a word, they began dragging the travois with the old woman on it out of their destroyed village.

They looked about for Red-Eye warriors who may have lingered behind. The Grandfather Sun was beginning to climb Father Sky.

"Our *nookum*?" Flying Rabbit Boy asked.

"He killed her."

Flying Rabbit Boy tripped but regained his balance quickly.

"Ohhh!" the delirious old woman moaned as the travois jumped. The boys said no more to each other and continued to the sundance grounds.

When they arrived, one of Blue Elk Man's sisters came to help the matriarch. The people of *Nisichawayasihk* were sitting and lying about, cold and dazed. Children were crying and women were tending to the wounded or wailing for those who had passed on.

"My boy!" called White Willow Woman as she ran over and hugged him. "Thank *Kitchi Manitou* you are alive!"

"My brother!" said Yellow Hawk Girl as she joined them. "You saved me."

"I thought you might have been captured before you made it here" said Little Grey Bear Boy.

"We managed to outrun the Red-Eye's warriors in the dark."

"I am afraid many others were not as fortunate," said Flying Rabbit Boy.

"Drifting Butterfly Woman is coming," said White Willow Woman. "You must tell her what you know."

"What is happening?" asked Drifting Butterfly Woman with wide eyes.

"The Red-Eyes have left," said Little Grey Bear Boy. "But *Nisichawayasihk* will soon be no more. The rain of fire has upset the three rivers and the earth is flooding. We will not be able to go back."

"I see," said Drifting Butterfly Woman bravely. "Do you have any news of my husband?"

"He is alive," said Flying Rabbit Boy, "but he…" Little Grey Bear Boy glanced quickly at his cousin and they both looked down.

"What is wrong?" Drifting Butterfly Woman asked.

"My love!" called a man's voice from the forest. Drifting Butterfly Woman looked up to see Blue Elk Man half-carrying Many Fish. He smiled and waved at her as he hobbled on one leg toward her. She ran to him, soon joined by their children, who were all crying for his lost leg.

"Father. Should we return for the others?"

"There is no need, my boy," answered Blue Elk Man. "These are all that remain of the people of *Nisichawayasihk*."

There were not many left of the once proud village—children mostly. How could these few be all the people of *Nisichawayasihk*?

# NIYĀNANOMITANAW KĪKĀ-MITĀTAHTOSĀP

"Who will speak for the Bear clan?" called Drifting Butterfly Woman.

Singing Doe, White Willow Woman, the three children, and Blue Elk Man were now all that remained of the Bear clan. The two women's eyes met and neither was sure how to proceed without the elders.

"Singing Doe speaks for the Bear clan," answered White Willow Woman.

"Very well. Please join us, Singing Doe. There are important matters to discuss." The six women now representing their clans gathered around the travois on which rested the elder matriarch of the Marten clan. The women surveyed the situation reluctantly. Of the original village of more than one hundred, only around forty survived.

"I am told nothing remains of *Nisichawayasihk*," began Drifting Butterfly Woman, "and even if something did remain, the danger would be too great to stay."

"What will we do?" asked the younger Eagle twin.

"We must find a new place to live," said Singing Doe, now matriarch of the Bear clan.

"But where is there such a place?" Yellow Moon Woman, new matriarch of the Turtle clan, asked.

"There is a place..." muttered Gliding Heron Woman from the

travois. "We called it *O'pipon-na-piwin*, the wintering place. Whenever there was a drought or bad hunting in the fall, we would go there. It was discovered by one of the hunters after Dark Cloud Man had left us the first time. He would not know that place…"

"Do you remember how to get there, *Nookum*?" asked Drifting Butterfly Woman.

"We must go north and east."

The women of the new Circle of Clan Mothers looked at one another but said nothing. There was nowhere else to go, and this plan was better than no plan at all.

"It is decided then," announced Drifting Butterfly Woman. "*Ekosi.*"

Word spread to the remaining villagers and they gathered their meager possessions to begin the long journey. Drifting Butterfly Woman asked around about how much food had been saved from the village. It was not much.

"We do not have much food," Singing Doe informed the remaining Bears. "But we are more fortunate than others…"

Flying Rabbit Boy looked down at his bow and counted the arrows in his quiver. The responsibility of being a man swelled in his chest and he knew what he had to do.

"I will be back," he said, giving his mother a kiss before running off into the forest.

The others helped gather children and attend to the wounded. It was midday by the time the people were ready to embark on their journey.

As Little Grey Bear Boy helped his father shoulder the travois carrying Many Fish, he saw his cousin return. Flying Rabbit Boy had his bow slung across his back. He carried three rabbits.

"It seems you have learned to use your bow," said Singing Doe.

"It is as though I cannot miss!" he whispered to Little Grey Bear Boy, raising his bow. The boys mustered a brief smile but the moment faded.

"Go and give them to Drifting Butterfly Woman," said Singing Doe. "She is gathering all the food for sharing."

"*Tapwe*, my mother," answered Flying Rabbit Boy. As he marched over to where Drifting Butterfly Woman was dividing up the remaining food, Water Lily Woman joined him.

"What have you got there?" she asked as playfully as she could muster. "Are those all for me?"

"Grandmother Rabbit has blessed us. But I have been blessed by you."

"Me?"

"The magic arrow. Ever since I shot Dark Cloud Man with it, I have not been able to miss."

"I am afraid you misunderstood," said Water Lily Woman. "I did nothing to that arrow."

"*Awas*! Don't be so modest." Flying Rabbit Boy laughed at the game.

"I'm sorry," she said. "I thought your cousin would tell you I was only playing. I do not know of any magic that can make an arrow hit its mark."

"But then how…"

"All I did was tell you to go fishing. I told you to catch fish because I knew it would give you the muscles to steady your injured arm. It seems you lacked only the confidence to hit your targets. The skill was always yours."

"So, you lied to me?"

Water Lily Woman looked up quickly, alarmed, but saw Flying Rabbit Boy was only teasing. She gave him a peck on the cheek before running off.

"I love you," he whispered as she left.

# NIKOTWĀSIKOMITANAW

The journey to the northeast was long and difficult. Before they left, those who were able returned to *Nisichawayasihk* to collect their remaining possessions. They found the ground flooded to below the knee. The bodies of those killed in battle floated along with broken lodge poles and other debris. They were forced to leave the dead where they lay, there being no time for proper burials. The three rivers would be doing the job for them. Little Grey Bear Boy went to the ruins of the Bear lodge and found Painted Turtle Man's medicine bundle.

Flying Rabbit Boy was given a special assignment by the Circle of Clan Mothers, a great honour for the boy. He was to stay behind and wait for the warriors who had gone on the Great Buffalo Hunt to the south.

"Words will not be needed to explain what has happened," Drifting Butterfly Woman told him. "The warriors will see for themselves."

Gliding Heron Woman instructed the *Nehiyawak* to tie pine boughs to the bottom logs of their travois in order to hide their trail. She fell in and out of consciousness throughout the journey and the other matriarchs had to wake her from time to time to guide them. On a few occasions, it took the women a very long time to wake her. It seemed her injuries were more serious than two broken legs.

The *Nehiyawak* travelled for many days as the leaves of autumn began to fall and frost began to greet them at sunrise. Six of the injured villagers died of their injuries on the journey and were buried under piles of rocks in secret graves. The women quietly sang the mourning song all the way to *O'pipon na-piwin*.

On the eighth day of the journey, the sound of many feet running through the forest could be heard. The remaining warriors prepared to defend what was left of the people of *Nisichawayasihk*. It was Flying Rabbit Boy, accompanied by nine of the warriors who had returned from the Great Buffalo Hunt. "We found no buffalo," reported Sharp Stone Man. "We were ambushed by Red-Eye Warriors and fourteen men were killed. It seems we have all been set up from the beginning by Dark Cloud Man, the Red-Eye."

"The winter will be especially hard without the blessings of Grandmother Buffalo," said Drifting Butterfly Woman. "And with so few hunters…"

"We will find a way, Auntie," said Flying Rabbit Boy.

The remaining warriors returned, some to their mothers, wives, and children; others, to no one at all, only sad tidings. The *Nehiyawak* seemed destitute, not only in material things but in their hearts as well.

Little Grey Bear Boy tried hard to keep up their spirits, a difficult task considering the circumstances. In the evenings, by the camp fire's light, he told the stories Painted Turtle Man used to tell. With his Turtle Shell Rattle, he made the flames dance in the air to the delight of the children. Water Lily Woman helped by singing the children off to sleep with her melodic voice.

By day, Flying Rabbit Boy scouted the path ahead and reported back to the Circle of Clan Mothers. He always seemed to return from his scouting duties with a rabbit or a ptarmigan to eat. One day he came back empty handed. He waited for someone to comment on his lack of success this time. That was when he reported having taken a full-grown bull moose.

This was the best news the *Nehiyawak* had received since they fled *Nisichawayasihk*. Already, they had gone through most of the food they had salvaged and many had gone to bed hungry these last few days. The entire camp turned in the direction of the slain moose, following Flying Rabbit Boy. Normally shy, Singing Doe, matriarch of the Bear clan, walked with her head a little higher, as all of the *Nehiyawak* praised her son's skill with the bow.

When they arrived at the place where the bull moose lay, they made camp. The women went to work immediately, skinning and butchering the carcass, and ensuring every family received their fair share. As they did so, the men seemed to gather together suddenly. One of them drew out a large elk hide drum and struck it four times.

"People of *Nisichawayasihk*!" announced the remaining Crane clan warrior. "Take notice on this day! Show your respect as the White Wolf Warrior Society inducts its newest member." Those *Nehiyawak* who were able, rose to their feet.

"I wonder who they are taking?" whispered Flying Rabbit Boy.

"Who do you think?" answered Little Grey Bear Boy.

"The White Wolf Warrior Society calls Flying Rabbit Boy of the Bear clan," announced the senior warrior. "Come forward!"

Flying Rabbit Boy gripped his bow and walked forward with his back straight and his chest out, but his watery eyes revealed his nervousness. Blue Elk Man followed behind him.

"Who presents this child?" asked the senior warrior.

"My brothers," answered Blue Elk Man. "I am sent to speak for your brother, Many Fish of the Deer clan, White Wolf Warrior, wounded in battle."

"Speak!" barked the senior warrior.

"This boy is a boy no longer," announced Blue Elk Man. "He has provided meat so the *Nehiyawak* can eat. He has also proven himself a warrior by defending the *Nehiyawak* in battle. He has killed two of the Red-Eye warriors and severely wounded the Red-Eye himself. He has no more need of a boy's name. We demand you give him a man's name as well as his father's place in your brotherhood."

The warriors whooped and shrieked and sounded their drums loudly.

"*Tapwe*! Your words speak the truth. But first he must be rid of childish things. Let any who are in need come forward and claim them."

The *Nehiyawak* looked around at each other. Although a giveaway was necessary, no one wanted to take from the boy the few possessions he still had. Flying Rabbit Boy looked down and realized all he had left was his trusty bow. After an awkward amount of time had passed, a young boy approached. Flying Rabbit Boy thought of the day he had been given the bow in the same manner.

"This bow helped me become a warrior," he said sadly. "I hope it will do the same for you one day." The wide-eyed boy accepted the very bow that had injured the Red-Eye. It was already a thing of legend.

"You came into this world naked and alone," preached the senior warrior, "and you will leave our Mother Earth in the same way. Speak now the oath of the White Wolf Warrior Society, that we may accept you as our brother."

Flying Rabbit Boy spoke the words he had heard his father say so many times before.

"I hereby pledge to protect the *Nehiyawak* with my life and to walk humbly upon Mother Earth. I will hold myself no greater and no lesser than any of *Kitchi Manitou*'s creations. I will strive for equality in all my deeds and with all my words in accordance with the laws of the White Wolf Warrior Society. This I swear in Creator's light, and before all the *Nehiyawak* gathered here today, before you my brothers of the White Wolf Warrior Society, from this day forward, until Creator calls me home."

The warriors cheered and the *Nehiyawak* joined in the long howl of the White Wolf Warrior Society.

"We have heard the words spoken!" announced the senior warrior. "With the *Nehiyawak* gathered here today we accept his vow. He will be called Flying Rabbit Boy no longer. From this day forward all shall know him as Flying Arrow Man of the Bear clan, warrior of the White Wolf Warrior Society."

The *Nehiyawak* cheered again and a warrior presented Flying Arrow Man with the White Wolf Robe. Blue Elk Man came forward and presented him with a new bow.

"This is a man's bow," said Blue Elk Man. "You will need it to feed the *Nehiyawak*."

"I will do my best, Uncle."

"That is all anyone can ask of us," answered Blue Elk Man. "Your father was like a brother to me. I would be honoured to hunt with you as once I hunted with him."

"The honour would be mine, Uncle!" replied Flying Arrow Man.

There was no time for much celebration and the feast was a little subdued—they had to store as much of the moose meat as they could for winter. Nonetheless, this was the happiest day of Flying Arrow Man's life.

"I'm proud of you, cousin!" said Little Grey Bear Boy.

"I'm sorry I was named before you."

"I'm not jealous. To think like that would only create a rift between us. You deserved to be named before me because you had to work harder to earn that honour. You accomplished more than me and without the assistance of the Grey-Eye magic."

"I think you are right," teased Flying Arrow Man. "I suppose you will have to call me 'Uncle' now."

"*Awas!*" said Little Grey Bear Boy, giving his cousin a push. "Don't count on it!"

The people continued their journey to *O'pipon-na-piwin*, the wintering place, with a renewed determination. Little Grey Bear Boy helped his father from time to time in dragging the injured Many Fish on the travois. The Eagle warriors were also dragging a travois which appeared to have a bound figure tied to it. The younger Eagle twin walked beside the travois, one hand on it at all times. She noticed Little Grey Bear Boy and Many Fish looking at her and nodded to them politely. They nodded back after a moment, not used to having an Eagle Twin observe the common niceties.

"I guess they must have found her sister's body," whispered Many Fish from the travois.

"I am surprised they were able," answered Little Grey Bear Boy. "I didn't think there would be anything left of her…"

Finally, as the days of autumn ended and the cold winds of the north started blowing, the *Nehiyawak* came upon a very large lake.

"This is the lake," moaned Gliding Heron Woman. "I remember this place, we are not far. A rocky arm reaches into the water followed by a sandy beach. After the beach there is a high cliff face. That is *O'pipon-na-piwin*…"

The *Nehiyawak* followed the shore of the great lake as instructed and after three days they came upon the place the old matriarch had described.

"*Nookum*," asked Drifting Butterfly Woman. "Is this the wintering place?"

The old woman didn't answer.

Drifting Butterfly Woman touched her face. "She has left us."

The women took up the mourning song and wailed in tribute to the fallen matriarch. She had rationed her life force perfectly.

The *Nehiyawak* got to work immediately, erecting makeshift lodges. There were hides and poles enough for only two lodges, so the Bears and the Cranes shared one and the Martens and the Deer another. The Eagle, Wolf, and Turtle clans were too large to share a single lodge with anyone and did their best to make do. The Eagles again seemed to be the most comfortable, as their warriors had managed to salvage more from *Nisichawayasihk* than the others.

The lodges went up quickly and a new centre fire pit was dug out. The *Nehiyawak* worked quickly and were resettled after only two days. On the third day an Eagle warrior came to the shared lodge of the Bears and Cranes.

"Auntie," said Sharp Stone Man to Drifting Butterfly Woman. "My mother wishes for the *Nehiyawak* to gather."

"It shall be so," said Drifting Butterfly Woman, as was the duty of the Crane clan.

"I suppose some things will never change," said White Willow Woman.

"We will have to be nice for now," counseled Drifting Butterfly Woman. "Few will survive the winter without the Eagle clan warriors to provide meat."

"My son will keep us fed."

"And my husband!" added White Willow Woman.

"I am afraid I am not so fortunate…" lamented Drifting Butterfly Woman.

"We have not forgotten how you cared for us in our time of need," said Singing Doe. "And we will now repay the kindness you once showed us, my sister."

The women got to their feet and left the lodge together. Flying Arrow Man and Little Grey Bear Boy helped Many Fish out of the lodge so he could see what was happening.

The entire Eagle clan had gathered in front of their lodge. They had laid out many items on a great elk hide in front of them. Nearby was the body they had dragged back from *Nisichawayasihk*. It seemed they wanted to have an elaborate funeral.

"People of *O'pipon-na-piwin*!" announced the lone Eagle twin. "Today we pay honour to a great leader of the *Nehiyawak*!"

Singing Doe looked at Drifting Butterfly Woman.

"The Eagle clan believes this man deserves to be buried in the proper way among the *Nehiyawak*," she continued.

"Man?" whispered Little Grey Bear Boy.

"I don't understand…" said Flying Arrow Man.

Two of the Eagle warriors came forward and drew back the blanket that had covered the body. It was Painted Turtle Man. The survivors gasped at the sight of the Bear clan medicine carrier, the one so many had called '*moosum.*'

"This great man has served the *Nehiyawak* since long before any of us were born," she said. "It is in his honour that the Eagle clan would give away all of our earthly possessions to whomever is in need."

The people of the *O'pipon-na-piwin* murmured their approval.

"Furthermore," added the Eagle matriarch, "I would humble myself before the *Nehiyawak*. I have acted shamefully and am no longer capable of leading the Circle of Clan Mothers. I must walk with humility and follow the lead of those better suited to serve the people. I would support the leadership of my sister Drifting Butterfly Woman, of the Crane clan, if all of my sisters are in agreement."

The remaining matriarchs nodded in agreement and Singing Doe smiled at Drifting Butterfly Woman. "You are the youngest woman ever to be named leader of the Circle of Clan Mothers," she said.

"I only wish it were under better circumstances," Drifting Butterfly Woman replied.

"We are in agreement," announced the lone Eagle twin. "I have only one more mistake I need to correct. Last year, a young woman of the Turtle clan presented herself to the Eagle lodge. In my foolishness

I turned her away, much to my son's dismay. He loves her. I would offer my son, Sharp Stone Man, to her, if she would still have him."

The eldest of the Turtle girls stepped forward and walked over to the Eagle lodge. She stood in front of Sharp Stone Man and reached out her hand. He took her hand and let her lead him back to the Turtle lodge. The *Nehiyawak* cheered this union and the balance it would bring to the new village.

"Let all who are in need come forward and claim what they can use," said the lone Eagle Twin.

With that, the Eagle clan became the poorest family in *O'pipon-na-piwin*. The *Nehiyawak* milled about, receiving their gifts and paying homage to the great medicine carrier of the Bear clan. Painted Turtle Man was given an honourable burial in a place upon the cliff next to Gliding Heron Woman. This place would become the burial site for the people of *O'pipon-na-piwin*.

"It is a new beginning," said Water Lily Woman.

"*Tapwe*," agreed Little Grey Bear Boy.

"What will we do?" asked Flying Arrow Man.

"We will do what we can," answered Little Grey Bear Boy. "My *moosum* once told me that life is not about what happens to us, it is about how we handle the things that happen. We will face whatever the future holds, together as *Nehiyawak*, because we must."


EKOSI

# ACKNOWLEDGEMENTS

There are so many people I wish to thank, without whom this book would not be possible. First and foremost I must thank my beautiful wife Angie for putting up with this obsession for so long. I hope that the joy these words bring to the people will make up for the many nights I was home, but not home. Next, to my sister Angela, who taught me to read and write when the teachers had dismissed my intelligence because of the colour of my skin. Thirty years later, you again pushed me to rise above what was expected of me and to complete the first draft in only a few short months. To Beverley Rach at Fernwood/Roseway for discovering my work amongst the slush pile of undoubtedly better written pieces and seeing what it could become. To my editor, Sandra McIntyre, for taking a lump of coal and turning it into a diamond. To Edith Friesen for encouragement and inspiration and for welcoming me into the world of authors. It would have been a very lonely place to walk into if I'd had to walk it alone like so many others. To Niigaanwewidam James Sinclair for giving me a reality check early on. Your candour saved me from a lot of disappointment and heartbreak when I learned what to expect from publishing.

To the Elders who took the time to give me the teachings: Jules and Margaret Lavallee, Rodger and Caroline McDougall, David Blacksmith, Colin Mousseau, Myra Laramee, Calvin Pompana,

Wilfred Ambigosis, Roger Armite, Art Shofley, Wes and Anne Charter, Gerald Morgan, Wilfred Buck, Carl Stone, Marcel French, Allen Sutherland, Bill Crompton, Horace Halcrow, Mervin Garrick, Martin Nicholas, Phillip Gatensby and many others whose names I never learned but whose teachings stayed with me long after our paths diverged.

To my family and friends who read early versions, bits and pieces and encouraged me to do this: Ryan and Thera Gorrie, Karl and Patricia Schwab, Remi and Marcia Landes, Kathleen Mazur, Phaedra Jenner, Joanne Henry, Delaphine Bighetty, Ron Phillips, Keely Phillips, Grant Stone, Bill and Fay Richards, Angie Renee Bonner, my nieces Alexis, Savannah and Samiya Busch, my nephews Jerome Busch Jr and Fred Kosmolak, Cynthia Robinson, Dwayne Bird, Karl Barker, Brad Cockerill, Reg Bergmann, Linda Thaler, Tammy Lynne Elder, Lora Kay, Shawn Reynolds, Malcolm McColl, Julian McKay, Marilee Bittner-Fawcett and all my friends on the "Grey Eyes, a Native Novel" Facebook Group.

To those Indigenous authors who came before me and broke the trail for a new generation to follow.

And last but not least, to the students of the Aboriginal Centre of Winnipeg's Adult Ed class of 2012 who read the unedited manuscript as I was writing it and provided feedback by way of their assignments and quizzes: Robert Colomb, Gabriel Merasty Jr, Alexis Thomas, Kristin Sinclair, Betty Maud, Brandi Hanslip, Brittney Phillips, Cheryl Shappee, Courtney Bird, Effie Ross, Kenneth Bradburn, Kristin Monkman, Norma Prince, Terrance Prince, Sharla Bluebird, Stephanie Head, Blackwolf Hart and any other students whose names I didn't get. Reading your comments, analysis and critiques helped shape the work. I hope that seeing my journey and helping me along the way will inspire you to succeed in whatever endeavour you choose. *Ekosani*.

Consider donating this copy of *Grey-Eyes* to Eagle Touch the Clouds, a non-profit initiative to build a Native American literature section in public libraries in Canada and the USA.

In Canada, send to:
Eagle Touch the Clouds
PO Box 32045 London PO
Westbank, BC, V4T 3G2

In the USA, send to:
Eagle Touch the Clouds
PO Box 111259
Tacoma, WA 98411-1259

www.eagletouchtheclouds.com

GREY EYES
Frank Christopher Busch

F rank Christopher Busch is a member of the *Nisichawayasihk* Cree Nation in northern Manitoba. Educated at the University of Manitoba, his articles on First Nations social and economic topics have been published in such Canadian newspapers as the *Vancouver Sun,* the *Winnipeg Free Press,* and the *National Post.* Frank honed his writing skills while working at a law firm during the Indian Residential School Settlement Agreement, where he interviewed hundreds of survivors and wrote their stories for their claim against the Government of Canada. He wrote *Grey Eyes,* a novel, in response to the message he received over and over from residential school survivors: "I just want my culture back."

Visit www.greyeyesnovel.com for more information.